ELAINE FOX

Man at Work

AVON BOOKS
An Imprint of HarperCollins*Publishers*

This is a work of fiction. Names, characters, places, and incidents are products of the author's imagination or are used fictitiously and are not to be construed as real. Any resemblance to actual events, locales, organizations, or persons, living or dead, is entirely coincidental.

AVON BOOKS
An Imprint of Harper Collins*Publishers*
10 East 53rd Street
New York, New York 10022-5299

ISBN: 0-380-81784-5
www.avonromance.com

First Avon Books paperback printing: July 2002

Printed in the U.S.A.

10 9 8 7 6 5 4 3 2 1

For Greg,

who proves that lawyers can make great heroes

1

Thursday, October 3
WORD-A-DAY!

FOLLY: n., a foolish deed,
perhaps an imprudent involvement
with a member of the opposite sex

They pinched her toes, slid slightly on her heel, were perilously high and would make her calves feel like bowling pins by the end of the day, but Marcy had to have them.

They were the perfect shoes for her newest red power suit, which she just happened to have on.

Dressing for success is no joke, she could hear her boss saying. He of the three-hundred-dollar tie and Egyptian cotton shirts. He had actually held a seminar on the topic for all the new junior associates the year she'd joined the firm.

You've got to spend money to make money, her friend Trish had said on too many shopping trips to mention. Easy for her to say. Trish had been born with money.

But over the last couple of years, Marcy had realized they were both right. At least as far as being a Washington, D.C., lawyer in the firm of Downey Finley & Salem—Downey Fin, to most—was concerned.

Gotta play to win, Marcy thought gamely, handing over her gold American Express card to the salesman.

"Don't bother putting them back in the box," she said. "I'm going to wear them."

They'd have to be her stakeout shoes, she thought with a private grimace. She'd forgotten her sneakers and she had a very important meeting right after lunch—a meeting to be attended by several senior partners, making the power suit and perfect shoes imperative.

So she'd be wearing the new shoes to her lunch hour "stakeout" at the Planners Building & Design construction site—or rather, at the restaurant across the street—to surreptitiously investigate the details of a case she was working on. It was her first solo case, a personal-injury lawsuit by a former subcontractor against Planners Building & Design.

Not that she was working on it strictly alone. Her boss, the renowned Win Downey of Downey Fin, was overseeing everything she did and supervising the case. But for the most part, it was hers to conquer.

She held up one foot as she leaned against the counter, listening to her credit card come through approved on the machine, and studied her latest purchase. Never in her wildest childhood dreams would she have imagined spending three hundred and eighty-two dollars on a pair of shoes.

Dressing for success is no joke, she thought again. Damn right it wasn't.

She signed the credit slip and took up the bag containing the box with her old shoes in it.

"You enjoy those now," the salesman said. His thick

graying eyebrows were raised over a face that smiled with a million laugh lines. She hoped he was working on commission.

"I will. Thank you very much." She gave him a bright smile and strode from the store in her brand-new, stiletto-heeled stakeout shoes.

"Hey! Hey *you!* Cut it out!" Marcy glared across D Street at the unkempt, beer-bellied man leveling another kick at a puppy. The whimpering creature cowered against the chain-link fence. Mud coated the dog, the man's steel-toed work boots, the gravel parking lot of the construction site, and the street across which she marched with all the rage a five-foot-four-inch woman could project. "I'm talking to *you,* lowlife."

She crossed the muddy gravel impervious to what it was doing to the hem of her camelhair coat and the brand-new stakeout shoes.

"Hey, buddy." She grabbed the man by one arm to get his attention. "I'm talking to *you.*" She was too angry to feel fear for this bully, this grubby, stupid excuse for a person, though some part of her warned that fear might be the healthiest emotion.

The man—quite large, now that she was close, and smelling strongly of sweat and smoke—turned to glare at her with flat, red-rimmed, milk-chocolate eyes. "What the f—"

"I said, *cut it out,*" Marcy said through gritted teeth. She couldn't stand men like this. Men with the attitude that anything smaller and weaker than they were deserved whatever they felt like dishing out. "Are you aware that what you're doing is called animal cruelty and is punishable by a twenty-five-hundred-dollar fine and up to two years in prison?"

Marcy had no idea if this was correct—the type of law she practiced was corporate, insurance, personal injury, not criminal cases involving ill-bred miscreants—but *he* didn't know that.

He laughed once. "You expect me to believe you're a cop?" He spat a wad of something dark to the ground by her feet. She noticed a brown fleck on the toe of her shoe. If they hadn't been so expensive she'd have thought about throwing them away when she got home.

"Yeah, or something." She bent down to grasp the little dog's collar, but the band was so tight she could barely get her fingers inside it.

The puppy cowered against the fence, looking at her with brown, fear-filled eyes, but making no move to bite or fight back. Its black ears lay tight against its head and the black, white-tipped tail curled around its scrawny haunches with the tender impotence of a child's security blanket.

"It's okay," she crooned, pulling the puppy gently toward her by the scruff.

But Rambo had other plans for her. She felt his burly grip on her upper arm as she was yanked upright. He turned her to face him, so close she had to hold her breath against the foul smell of his.

"That's my goddamn dog, bitch, and if you don't take your goddamn hands off it I'm gonna break your goddamn neck into a buncha goddamn tiny pieces."

She leveled a cool glare at him, revealing none of the fright that was beginning to blossom in her breast, and said the first thing that popped into her head. "That's very good. Excellent vocabulary. Now can you make *goddamn* into a verb?"

Honest to God, for a second she thought he was going to hit her. His grip tightened so that she could almost picture the bruises he would leave and his opposite shoulder drew back as if to wind up, when suddenly he spun around so quickly she was dragged sideways by his hold before stumbling out of his grasp.

"You graduating from dogs to women now, Chuck?" a new male voice asked. This one was deeper, calmer, and free of that construction-worker accent they all seemed to put on with their hardhats.

So she was understandably confused when she regained her balance and straightened to see a tall, broad construction worker with dark brown hair that was badly in need of a cut and torn jeans that were badly in need of a needle, hauling her nemesis nearly off his feet by the collar of his down vest.

"What the hell you doin', Harley? Get the hell offa me."

The dark-haired man—*Harley?* she repeated to herself with inexplicable disappointment—let Chuck bat his hand away, but there was no illusion that he was backing down. He merely stepped forward and looked down on the shorter—fatter—man and asked in that deep voice, "You going to leave her alone or not?"

Chuck shrugged his vest back into shape and took a step back, belligerent but clearly not interested in fighting the new guy. "She's trying to take my goddamn"—here he glared at her—"dog. Not that it's any business of yours. Why'ren't you on the job, anyway?"

The dark-haired man tilted his head. "I heard yelling.

Female yelling. Thought someone might be in trouble."

He passed his gaze over to Marcy and she felt her pulse trip. He had stunning eyes. Light, light gray, piercing as sunlight and steeped in intelligence. Maybe he was the architect, she thought brightly, before he turned back to the other man.

"Nobody here you need to worry about, Harley. If you know what's good for you, you'll get back to work." Chuck pushed the back of his hand across his nose and sniffed loudly. "I don't know what the hell kind of bee flew up your butt this morning anyway. Shoving your nose into everyone's business but your own, carping about them railings, or that scaffolding, or the damn OSHA regulations. Who the hell's superintendent around here anyway? *Me*, that's who. Why'nt you just get back to your own damn job while you still got one?"

OSHA? Marcy thought. If this guy was complaining about the Occupational Safety and Health Administration's regulations, then her case could be even more solid than she'd thought. She took the opportunity of the man's diatribe to coax the little dog away from the fence and gather it up in her arms. She wasn't going anywhere without this puppy, she told herself. If she left it here it'd just get kicked again. And who knew? possibly killed. No, this little guy was one she could save. She tilted the dog briefly on its back, looked, and amended mentally, *little gal.*

The brute turned suddenly back to her and grabbed the dog from her arms before she could protest. "Now Max and me'll just be getting back to our coffee."

"Wait just a minute," Marcy commanded.

In the moment it took for the man to realize her order did not need to be heeded, he'd stopped and she tried to snatch the puppy from him again. But he yanked it back and held the dog at his side by the scruff of its neck.

Marcy winced at the strangled look on the dog's face.

"Now you listen here and you listen good," the superintendent said, stepping close and grabbing her by the lapel.

This time, however, before he could get another word out he was spun away from her once again and sent to the ground with one efficient, well-placed punch. The puppy scrambled toward the trailer at the edge of the parking lot.

Marcy stared up at the dark-haired man, who stood over his victim with a calm, hard expression. "I told you to leave her alone," he said in that low voice.

Like Clint Eastwood, she thought, only not as hokey.

He turned to her and she closed her gaping mouth.

"You might want to get going now," he said mildly.

She raised her brows. "Right. Sure. Thanks." She glanced around for the dog but didn't see it. Chuck climbed to his feet, brushing futilely at his mud-covered clothes.

"That's it, Harley," he growled. "You're *fired*, you hear me? Fired. I don't wanna ever see your ugly face again. You set foot on this property again and I'll have you fucking *shot*, you hear me? You know I ain't lyin'. *Jesus.* Sticking up for chicks and dogs like some kinda . . ."

As the man ranted on, Marcy started backing away, thinking perhaps it would be best to come back later for the dog, maybe with a police escort. She glanced around the lot and saw a chain-link dog run next to the trailer.

He probably kept it in there at night, she thought. She could come back later and get it. That little padlock would be a cinch to get past. Despite her law-abiding bent, she knew a thing or two about vandalism. The neighborhood she'd been raised in had encouraged it.

The dark-haired man turned his back on the superintendent's tirade and walked toward her.

"Let's get moving," he said. His voice was quiet, with no urgency. It was pitched more as if he were in a library and didn't want his words to carry. She found it ridiculously sexy.

She turned and they both started down the street on foot, trailed by the superintendent's vitriol.

"You think that's gonna get you some, Harl?" the vile man called after them. "Huh? You think she's gonna give you a look at that hot, rich-girl body now you stuck up for her? Well I wouldn't count on it, jackass. That bitch thinks she's too good for you, and some damn dog ain't gonna make you look any better. She prob'ly more worried *you* gonna pee all over her prissy clean rugs than any dog . . ."

They reached the corner of the block and Marcy turned to the man with a cautious expression. He'd just lost his *job* because of her. What on earth could she say to mitigate that? What if he was angry?

But when she looked up at him he was smiling. Not a big moronic grin, just a small, interested smile.

"You got your nice coat all dirty," he said, shifting those startling eyes from her coat to her face.

She glanced down at her mud-streaked coat, then back at him, amazed he wasn't mad or at least upset.

"I'm so terribly sorry," she said. "About your job, that is. Thank you so much for trying to help me but I feel just awful that he fired you because of it."

He shrugged and gazed at her assessingly. "It's just a job. I'll find another one. You come to this part a town lookin' for trouble or you just happen to get lucky and find it?" He moved one hand to encompass the decaying, trash-strewn street, the empty storefronts and the car nearest them that was gray with rust and resting on cinderblocks.

She smiled and scratched absently at one of the splatters of mud on her sleeve. "I was having coffee in that diner." She indicated the one place up the street with life in it, across from the construction site. "Then I saw that man kicking the dog. And it's just a puppy, for goodness' sake. It's not like it could fight back, or do anything even to warrant such brutality, so I had to do something. I just had to." She swallowed hard. "But I'm very sorry my concern got you into trouble. I'm sure it was folly for me to get involved in the first place, but how could I have just watched him kicking the little thing without doing something?"

The man's face registered something like surprise, and then amusement. One eyebrow rose and he said, "'Folly'?" with a mocking smile. "Where you from, sugar?"

Marcy felt her blood stall with disappointment. *Sugar*. Oh, how she hated that. *Sugar, darlin', dear, honey*. She hated all of those names, endearments meant to charm that only belittled.

All the guys from her old neighborhood were like

this, and she wasn't having any. No pretty boy with dirt under his fingernails was going to charm her. Not again. She knew what she wanted and it wasn't someone like this. Been there, done that.

It was a shame about him, though, she thought. He was awfully good-looking, but she wasn't going to go all mushy over a pair of nice eyes in a face that said "*sugar.*"

"I don't think where I'm from is important. But I thank you for your help, and I'd like to help you." She reached into her purse for her pen and paper. She had a client who owned Donneville Construction Company, one of the biggest in D.C., and she was sure she could get this man a job. But before she could even get the pen from her purse he was turning away.

"No thanks, doll," he said. "I don't need a check that's just gonna clear your conscience and cloud mine. Charity's not my thing, so I'll just be on my way."

Marcy glared at his retreating back. She should let him walk away, she knew, but she couldn't stand his condescension. "I wasn't *going* to write a check, smart guy," she called after him. He turned back to her, his expression openly skeptical. "I was going to help you get another job. But since you're such an all-fired macho big shot, I'm sure you'll do fine on your own."

"'Macho big shot'?" he repeated, that same ironic look on his face. "That the best you can do, sugar?"

"*Oh!*" she growled and spun on her heel. Infuriating, insufferable—*vainglorious!* she thought triumphantly (she'd been unable to use yesterday's word from her word-a-day calendar until this guy came along)—man.

Before she got too far, however, she stopped and turned back. "Hey!" she called.

She watched his steps slow before he turned, involuntarily noting his athletic physique.

He didn't say anything, just looked at her with his head cocked.

"Does that guy live in that trailer?" she asked, gesturing back toward the construction site. "The superintendent."

He paused as his lips formed another mocking smile. "Sure. Didn't you see his swimming pool out back?"

She took a deep breath and counted to five. "I'll take that as a no."

"Take what you want."

She smiled, making an effort to make it smug, as she stalked away. Good. He'd proven himself too ill-mannered to feel bad about. Plus she'd used her word for the day, she told herself, trying to calm down. That guy had done her a favor. She'd even used yesterday's. Though she only used it to herself, she might be able to employ it again later, when she told Trish about what had happened.

She liked improving her vocabulary, though the calendar she had this year was ridiculously tough. Most of the words were too bizarre for use. Today's—*folly*—had been the easiest by far.

She walked briskly back to her car. Now she'd have to get her brand-new shoes polished. She looked at her watch. She had about forty-five minutes before the meeting. Maybe the shoe-shine guy in Union Station could clean them up. He was such a nice man, and she enjoyed talking to him.

Except when he asked about her love life. Not that she minded his asking, just the fact that she always had to admit that her love life consisted of exactly one date in the last year. Whenever she told him that, he just shook his head and murmured, "What a shame, what a shame."

With which she had to agree. She had to start getting out more, she told herself. When you start going gaga over shaggy guys in torn jeans it's definitely time to start dating again.

And she was sure he was out there, her perfect man. Every pot has a lid, as her mother said. Or every lid to a pot. Something like that.

But when she found him, that perfect man, he would never, *ever*, call her anything but her name. Or maybe "darling." She frowned. No, just her name. Marcy. She frowned again, wondering for the zillionth time in her life why in the world she couldn't have been named after her aunt Arabella.

Truman Fleming turned off his headlights and parked about ten storefronts away from the diner in which the spunky brunette had said she'd had coffee that morning. The street was deserted and nearly dark, as two of the three streetlamps on the block had either been busted or burned out. It was a downtrodden street, the building under construction just the beginning of an urban renewal project for that part of town.

Ordinarily he would have liked cruising this seedy part of town in the middle of the night. With his tattered work clothes and his banged-up truck he might look as if he belonged here, as if he were meeting someone for some nefarious purpose.

But tonight it just made him think about the girl, the doll from this morning, the dog defender, and how out of place *she'd* looked. Because she *was* a doll. Perfect skin, thick, dark, shiny hair that fell just past her shoulders, brown eyes rimmed with plush black lashes. He pictured her standing there in her mud-stained pricey shoes with Chuck's grimy hand on her tailored coat and felt a contraction deep in his gut.

Why hadn't she just stayed in her K Street office—he'd bet money she worked somewhere along that money-laden corridor—and left this part of town alone? Why did she have to come here with that ramrod spine and those gusty dark eyes and butt heads with Chuck Lang, of all people? Lang was a two-hundred-and-fifty-pound keg of trouble just waiting to explode. Yet she'd stood up to him on behalf of a skinny little dog most people wouldn't have even noticed.

She'd impressed him, and that annoyed him. He didn't want to be impressed by a fancy girl like that.

He shook his head and got out of the truck. It didn't matter. She was gone now and he didn't even know her name. Probably something like Muffy. Or Honoria. Something either cute and dopey, or rich and pretentious like the world she came from, the world she belonged in. The world he wanted nothing to do with.

He shut the door of the truck as quickly as he could and walked down the street, hands in his pockets, shoes scuffing the ground.

Just as he'd known it would be, as it had been every morning when he'd arrived at work, the dog was locked in the run next to the trailer. It whined and pressed itself up against the chain link in an effort to get to him, licking the metal links in supplication. He scratched its soft black fur through the fence.

On the latch was a padlock, a flimsy one. One good strike from a rock and that thing would pop right open.

At least that's what he'd thought. Twenty minutes and four generously scraped knuckles later the lock remained in place. The dog, on the other hand, was on the opposite side of the pen, eyeing him with an expression that said he'd turned out to be far more incompetent than even this little depressed dog had feared.

Damn, Truman thought, walking around the pen, mentally measuring the stupid thing. About four feet by two and a half. He could pull the truck up and slide the whole works into the back, maybe. Then, when he got home, he could somehow snip the links of the fence and get the dog out that way. But it was a pretty big pen when one looked at it with the idea of picking it up. Why couldn't it have been one of those fence things without a bottom? Why couldn't the damn dog have just been tied to a backhoe?

He sighed. There was nothing to do but try. One thing was certain, though. That damn lock wasn't going anywhere. At least not with his limited resources here in the dark. He made a mental note to pick one up for his toolbox. Who knew they were so secure?

Truman walked down the street and pulled his truck around to back into the gravel drive, lights off. He stopped the engine and listened for a minute, but the car he'd heard was apparently on another block and the sound disappeared.

His mother would just love to hear he'd been nabbed for stealing. She'd probably have him committed to a hospital for the criminally insane. She already questioned his mental health whenever they happened to talk.

He opened the tailgate of the truck, then turned and grabbed the kennel by the fence, pulling backward with more weight than he would have thought necessary. It rocked heavily over the gravel as the dog danced nervously from one side to the other.

After an absurd amount of effort he got the thing close to the truck and tried to lift one end up onto the tailgate. But as soon as he did the dog let out a little yelp and scrambled toward him, its nails scratching furiously against the metal bottom. A rivulet of sweat dripped from Truman's temple.

He took off his denim jacket and threw it in the cab. After another ten minutes or so of trying to heft the kennel toward the truck bed with the dog running back and forth, he stopped and took a breather.

His shirt was damp from exertion and the dog was terrified. In addition, the gravel around the scene had been scraped away so mud caked everything in sight, from Truman's boots to his shins to the back of the kennel to the dog.

He stood panting against the back of the truck, glaring at the wiry little dog in the ridiculously strong kennel. The front of the thing was propped against his thigh, and his arms were cramping with the effort of holding it there, when he heard the low hum of a well-tuned engine. He craned his neck around. No lights shone on the street but he could hear a car approaching. Tire tread on pavement. After a minute he saw a silver Lexus pull up in front of the diner. A second later a small, slim form emerged from the car and approached the gravel drive where he was parked.

It was her. He could tell from the way she walked, with purpose and grace. Muffy.

A second later, as she quietly rounded the front of his truck and caught him standing there with half the kennel practically in his lap, his guess was confirmed.

She stopped when she saw him and crossed her arms over her chest, looking at him. After a second she tilted her head and asked conversationally, "Whatcha doin'?"

He cursed himself for being caught in such an awkward position. Not stealing the dog; he didn't care about that. The dog needed stealing, they'd established that much this morning. No, he was angry for being caught pinned to the back of his truck by an unwieldy kennel that—it was suddenly obvious—would not be going into the truck bed through any of his efforts.

"I thought I'd take this dog to the SPCA," he answered, more calmly than he felt. He wished he could have stood straighter. He wished he weren't so sweaty. He wished the damn dog would quit wiggling against the side of the kennel in an effort to get to the girl because the metal bottom was cutting into his thighs.

"You can't take her to the pound." She moved her hands to her hips. Slim hips clad in jeans that fit, well, perfectly. Her thick shiny hair was pulled back tonight, but that only made her dark eyes more alluring.

He cleared his throat and tried to look casual. "Why not?"

"Because they'll euthanize her."

He smirked. "So, you might say it would be *folly* for me to take it to the pound. Is that right?"

Folly, he thought with a mental smile. Who used words like that anymore?

He couldn't tell in the dark, but he sensed Muffy's expression was irked.

"At best," she said dryly, "it would be folly. Mostly I was thinking it would be stupid to go through this much trouble just to take a dog to its death."

He shifted under the weight of the kennel. "Maybe someone will adopt it. But in any case, it won't be getting kicked anymore." The kennel was beginning to cut off the circulation in his legs. "So you going to help me or what?"

She took a moment to answer. A long moment, it seemed to Truman, but that might have been because he was picturing his toes turning black from lack of blood.

"Okay," she said finally.

"Good, take the back and help me—"

"But is there a reason you're taking the kennel too or are you just being greedy?"

"There's a reason," he said, more sharply than he'd have liked. But damn it, he was in pain. And he didn't want to look like a fool in front of this woman. "Maybe you didn't notice the padlock on the gate. Makes it difficult to open."

She tilted her head to look at the kennel's front gate. "You call that a lock?"

Before he could answer she was motioning with her hand for him to put the kennel down.

"Come on," she said. "Slide that thing back and let me take a look. There's an easier way to do this."

Picturing the many times he'd clobbered the lock

with rocks, he shoved the kennel back, immediately regaining sensation in his legs. He leaned back against the tailgate and tried to ignore the feeling of pins and needles from his thighs to his toes.

"Good luck," he said. "It's a pretty tough . . . lock." His words slowed as she took what looked like a metal toothpick from the back pocket of her jeans.

She knelt down before the kennel, taking a moment to scratch the dog behind one ear, then took the lock in one hand and pushed the pin into it with the other. In a matter of seconds, with a twist of the wrist one way then the other, the lock popped open. She took a minute to look at its battered face, then tossed it to him and pulled a piece of rope from her jacket pocket. With a smile she held it up to show him, then opened the kennel, tied the rope to the dog, and let it out of the pen.

Truman didn't want to look at his watch, but he was pretty sure no more than two minutes had elapsed. He was also pretty sure he'd been struggling with the stupid kennel close to half an hour.

He exhaled slowly, looking from the tongue-lolling smile of the puppy to the smirk that so help him God actually looked cute on the girl.

"Spend a lot of time trying to break into Daddy's liquor cabinet, did you?" he asked finally.

"Something like that." She pushed a stray lock of hair back into her ponytail. "But don't feel too bad. I wouldn't have been able to drag that kennel all the way over here to the truck."

"Thank you for not dwelling on the fact you wouldn't have needed to." He stood and flipped the tailgate of the truck shut behind him. "So what're you going to do with it, now that you've got it?" He gestured toward the dog, whose tail swooped an arc in the gravel where it sat.

Her brows drew together and she looked down at the mutt. Truman took the opportunity to study the curve of neck her ponytail revealed.

"I don't know, exactly. My building doesn't allow pets."

The words hung in the air a moment before she looked back up at him, a tentative smile on her lips.

"I don't suppose you considered anything other than the pound?"

He shrugged. "Nope. But I'm sure someone will want it."

"She can't go to the pound. They've got hundreds of dogs and there's no guarantee someone will adopt her. Can't you take her?"

She looked so pretty asking, with her hands clasped around the dog's rope and her eyes imploring, that Truman had a moment of insanity and started to nod.

"Yeah. I guess. *For a while,*" he amended. "I can keep it till you find a home for it."

She exhaled with a smile and he felt good, having been able to offer some bit of relief.

"But . . ." she paused. "Do you have a yard?"

He laughed once, and shook his head. "Not much acreage to be had where I live, sugar."

Her eyebrows drew together. "Have you ever owned a dog before? Do you know what to feed one? You do realize, don't you, that you'll have to go home every night to let her out? You can't just let her sit inside while you go drink beer and—"

"Hey, slow down, honey," he said, holding his hands

out and enjoying her obvious ire at his language. Typical rich girl, he thought. Couldn't solve the problem herself but was more than willing to tell someone else how to do it. "I said I'd keep the damn thing *for a while*. That's all. I'm not an idiot. I'm not going to let it starve."

"Yes, but she needs to be let out, too, you know. She can't just—"

"If you're so worried about it, take it yourself." He turned away and started to walk toward the driver's side door.

"No, no!" She followed him around the side of the truck. The dog scurried beside her and jumped up on his leg when they neared. "I'm sorry. I just want to be sure she doesn't end up in the same situation she's in here."

He started to protest but she interrupted.

"Not that I think you'd abuse her or anything like that. You did, after all, come here to save her just like I did. I just need to be sure—"

"I'll take care of it fine. But here." He opened the truck door and reached in for the knobby, tooth-dented pencil he kept in a rubber band on the visor. He plucked an old receipt from the floor of the cab and wrote down his address. "Here's where I live. For when you find a taker." He handed it to her.

She handed him the dog's rope and looked at the paper. He saw her expression as she noted the address was in Southeast, the poorest, most crime-ridden part of D.C.

"Why don't you give me your phone number too?" She started to hand the paper back.

He shook his head. "Don't have one."

She looked at him in surprise. "You don't have a phone?"

He laughed cynically. "I was saving up." He pushed the pencil back into the visor.

"All right." She started to turn away, then stopped. "What's your name, anyway?"

He gazed at her, at her trim leather coat and her perfectly cut jeans. She even wore some kind of expensive little ankle boots and her ears shone with gold.

"Folks around here call me Harley," he said. "Harley Fleming. 'Cause I used to ride my bike to work."

One of her eyebrows rose. "You can afford a Harley but you can't afford a phone?"

"For your information, I had to sell it. For this." He patted the steering wheel of the truck. "Besides, I'm not making any judgments about your designer jeans."

"They're Levi's. Nobody wears designer jeans anymore. Come on, what's your real name?" she persisted. "I can't call you Harley."

"Why not?"

"Because it's stupid. Now please tell me. What is it? Tom? Dick? Harry?"

He exhaled. "Tru. Short for Truman."

Her brows rose. "Like the president?"

He got into the truck. "A lot like that, yeah."

Why did he always have so much trouble getting people to call him by a nickname? All his life he'd wanted a nickname. So he could say he was called something—anything—other than *Truman*. But they never seemed to stick. So he was always Truman. Or, with occasional good fortune, Tru.

"Well, okay, *Truman*," she said, writing it down on the

receipt he'd given her, "I'll be in touch. Take good care of her." She bent to tickle the puppy behind the ears.

He arched a brow in her direction.

"And here's my card," she said, standing and pulling one out of her jacket pocket. "In case you need to get hold of me for any reason."

He took the thick, embossed card and fingered it. Holding it up to the light he read out loud, "Marcy Pag—lin—ow—ski? Paglinowski?" He lowered his hand. "And you didn't like *my* name?"

"Yeah, well, at least I didn't name myself after my car."

He started his engine and she stepped back.

"Don't forget her," she called over the noise, pointing to the dog sitting at his feet.

"You are a worrier," he said. "Now get along, Lexus, before the police get here and arrest you for breaking and entering."

"Very cute. I'll be in touch." She backed toward her car. "Don't do anything with her."

He frowned. "Like what? You accusing me of something deviant or just neglect?"

"I mean don't take her to the pound or give her to some irresponsible drug-dealing buddy or anything."

"I don't have any irresponsible drug-dealing buddies," he said, thinking of his empty, ugly little room in the working-class neighborhood in Southeast. He'd been there nearly seven months and made nary a friend. It was as if the locals sensed he didn't belong there.

"All right," she said skeptically. "Well, I'll be in touch, like I said."

"You do that, sugar," he said, flashing her a grin. "I'll be waiting for you."

She walked back to her car and started it up, a soft, well-oiled sound barely audible over the mechanical exertions of his truck. He looked down at the puppy, smiling up at him with that enormously long tongue still hanging out the side of its mouth. He reached over to the passenger seat and pulled a box with a couple of stale doughnuts onto his lap.

"You know what?" he said, frowning, to the dog. He handed it half a powdered doughnut and took a bite out of the other half. "I think I'm gonna call you 'Folly.' "

2

Monday, October 7
WORD-A-DAY!

APROPOS: adj., appropriate,
most often, something suitable
whether one likes it or not

Marcy stared at her computer but didn't see the letters on the screen. All she saw was Truman Fleming handing that dog a piece of his doughnut.

She could think of nothing else he could have done that would have set her mind more at ease. Granted, the fact that he'd shown up and tried to steal the dog had said something good about him, but still. How was she to know he'd treat the puppy well? Maybe he'd just shut her away and ignore her. Or give her to someone on the street, thinking at least she wouldn't be getting kicked by that awful man.

But when he picked up that doughnut, then stopped and gave a piece of it to the dog . . . well, it said a lot about him, that's all. And it made her feel a lot better about not being able to take the dog herself.

"Marcy," a voice boomed from her doorway.

She jumped and glanced up to see Winston Downey, the senior partner who oversaw her cases, standing in the doorway. The fact that he was her supervisor didn't make her half as nervous as the fact that Winston Downey was a large part of the reason she'd gone to law school. He'd come to speak at her college during her junior year and she'd thought him brilliant. So she'd written to him and found him not only intelligent but kind. He'd given her advice and encouragement on going to law school, and when she'd graduated he'd invited her for an interview. The rest, as they said, was history.

She really wanted to impress Winston Downey.

"I was looking at your notes on the Burton case," he said, leaning casually against the doorframe, his graying hair perfectly coifed. "They're going to claim an insulating act of negligence, you know."

Marcy saved the file she was in and leaned back in her chair. As usual, her palms began to sweat immediately. "You're talking about the painting contractor."

Win, a name so apt he'd been accused of changing it, nodded, his arms crossed over his chest.

Despite working under his direction, the case of *Burton v. Planners Building & Design* was Marcy's alone and she was determined not to fail. If she impressed him with this one she'd be on her way. And the law firm's name of Downey Finley & Salem, she'd joked to herself more than once, definitely needed some punching up with a little Paglinowski.

"They can try," she said, relieved that she'd already researched this point. "But even if there *was* negligence on the part of the painters, it wasn't superseding. They have zero evidence that a sub removed a brace from that scaffolding. They don't even have any evidence that a brace was removed at all. It's all just speculation."

"And the corresponding case—"

"*Petty versus Charles Brothers Construction,*" she responded, riffling through the papers on her desk. "I've got the Westlaw abstract right here . . ."

"That's all right, Marcy," Win said, and she looked up to see an approving smile on his face. It felt like daybreak after a long hard night. "Sounds like you're on the right track."

He started to turn.

"By the way," she added, "I went by the site a few days ago and they *still* haven't got any railings on the open-sided floors. I was thinking I'd go back tomorrow with a camera."

Win turned back with a laugh, confirming her hunch that he'd get a kick out of her investigation. "You're kidding. Still? These guys are even dumber than we thought. Why don't you get our man . . . what's his name? The investigator. Get him to take some pictures."

She smiled. "Actually, there's no need to incur the extra expense." Someone handed Win a piece of paper and he looked down at it. She waited a second, then continued, hoping to regain his attention. "I sat in a diner across from the site last Thursday and no one paid any attention to me. I'll just get the firm's Nikon and take a few shots through the window at lunch tomorrow."

"You'll need a corroborating witness," he said, his eyes still on the paper in his hand.

"Yes, I think I can get a guy."

She willed herself not to blush. For some reason the thought of Truman Fleming invariably brought heat to her cheeks. Not that she thought about him often . . . just every couple of hours since last Thursday.

Part of that, however, was because of the case. In a brainstorm late yesterday afternoon she'd remembered the obnoxious superintendent's words just before he'd fired Truman. Something to the effect that he'd been asking a lot of questions that weren't his business: about the railings, the scaffolding, and the OSHA regulations. Three things that were intimately related to her case.

Win's eyes were on her again. "A guy . . ." he prompted. "Who'll testify to the accuracy of the pictures?"

She cleared her throat and sat up straighter. "Yes, that, and I also believe he might testify to ongoing and perhaps previous safety violations at the site."

Now why had she said that? She had no idea if Truman Fleming would tell her anything at all and now, if he wouldn't, she'd look bad. For all she knew he'd crawled back to Chuck and gotten his job back. If that were the case there was little chance he'd get on the stand at all. Not many people wanted to testify against their employer.

Still, she had a feeling he would. After all, he'd stolen the superintendent's dog solely to save it.

"A fact witness from the site *would* be fortuitous," Win said, gazing down the hall. "Stan!" he called to a passing attorney, then stopped himself. He glanced back at Marcy and said, "I just wanted to check in since we didn't have the meeting today. We'll talk more about this in next Monday's meeting. You're on the right track, though. Keep going."

Marcy breathed a sigh of relief as he left. She was on the right track. He approved of all she was doing. And maybe, just maybe, since he'd had nothing to add, he thought she was doing as good a job as could be done.

She hoped so. Because she was doing as good a job as she could do.

Tru barely heard the knock over the sound of the television, but Folly did, and ran yapping to the door. He'd had the TV loud to hear the game as he warmed his dinner—a can of Dinty Moore beef stew and the last two Brown 'n' Serve rolls—but it had been a waste of time. The Redskins were losing. Again.

It didn't take much to lure Folly from begging at his side, Tru noted, moving toward the door. He wasn't much of a cook, it was true, but tonight's gourmet repast was straight out of a can. He'd have thought that alone—as opposed to the slop he created himself—would recommend it.

Well, it didn't take much to distract him from the meal either, he thought, laying the bowl of stew on the little table by his chair. Dinner was the most depressing time of day for him. It always made him think of home, which made him feel shallow and uninspired.

He hit the volume on the TV as he passed it and grabbed the dog by its new red collar before opening the door.

There stood Marcy Paglinowski. In the brown-gray

atmosphere of the bare-bulbed hall, she looked like a porcelain figure in a Dumpster.

Pretty, he thought. *Pretty, pretty, pretty.* High color stained her cheeks, and her lips, with just a hint of some natural-colored lipstick, smiled tightly.

"Lexus!" he said, and smiled. This was going to enhance dinner a thousandfold.

Folly squirmed in his grip and he let her go, whereupon she immediately jumped up on Marcy's coat. Marcy held a brown paper grocery bag in one arm that Folly seemed unusually interested in.

"Hello," she said.

Truman thought she was talking to him, but as she bent to pet the squirming black dog at the same time, she might have been talking to Folly.

Which was when it hit him. She'd probably found a taker for the dog. Disappointment speared him. He should be glad, he told himself quickly. He couldn't keep the thing. Once he found work she'd be stuck inside all day. Still, he'd liked the puppy's company.

"Come on in," Tru said, stepping back from the door and extending an arm into the living room.

Seeing it now through her eyes, however, he wished he'd just stepped out into the hall and asked her what she wanted. For one thing, he knew perfectly well the hole in the couch—new, thanks to Folly—would look a lot bigger through a rich girl's eyes. And the lack of rugs, pictures, tables, or even one decorative item made the place look more depressing than it actually was.

She straightened and stepped just inside the door. Folly bounced at her side like a pogo stick.

"I'm sorry to bother you. I'd have called, but . . ." She shrugged and made a sympathetic face that said *well, you know as well as anyone you don't have a phone.*

"No problem." He cast his gaze around the room once more. He hadn't even noticed those dirty dishes on the floor next to the sagging armchair before. How long had they been there?

"Wanna sit down?" He motioned her toward the couch.

She paused, looking doubtful, then stepped into the room. Avoiding the cushion that was belching foam like an overstuffed washer, she placed the bag on the floor and perched on the far side of the couch, close to the arm. He sat diagonally in the sagging armchair, hoping his leg blocked her view of the dishes.

She looked slowly around the room, her expression unreadable, before directing her gaze to his face. "So, how are you doing, Truman?"

Why did she sound like a doctor getting ready to take his temperature?

"I'm fine. Just fine." Folly sat next to him and he laid a hand on her side, scratching. This was good, he thought. Marcy would never see the dishes behind the dog, and the rest of the place, while sparsely furnished, was reasonably clean. "I was just, uh, cooking my dinner. But it can wait."

She glanced at the TV and made a disgusted sound. "I see they're getting killed *again*."

Truman looked at her in surprise. "Don't tell me you're a football fan." He laughed.

"As a matter of fact, I am. Why is that funny?"

"Well, this year it's funny if they have any fans at all, but you . . . well, I just wouldn't'a taken you for a football-watching . . ." He hesitated, searching for the right word. ". . . chick."

She closed her eyes briefly. The *chick* got her, as he knew it would. Just like *sugar* and *doll* had the other day. He didn't do it to annoy her. Well, not *just* to annoy her. He mostly did it to remind himself that she was exactly the kind of woman he had to stay away from. For some reason that was hard to remember, especially when he got caught up in wondering things like how she got her hair so shiny.

"Listen, Truman," she said. She was looking at him now, those dark eyes so direct they made him want to squirm. "I need to ask you a few questions about that construction job you were working. The one on D Street?"

He raised a brow. "So you're not here about the dog?"

She looked confused. "The dog? Oh! No, sorry. I've been asking around but no takers yet." She shook her head, then glanced at his hand against the dog's side and smiled slightly. "She looks pretty happy here, though."

He folded his arms across his chest, inside of which a disturbing commotion had ensued when she smiled that little sultry smile.

"She's all right. For now."

Her expression suddenly brightened. "Oh, and I brought her some food. Just so, you know, you don't get stuck with the feeding bill on top of everything else."

She reached into the grocery bag and pulled out an eight-pound bag of some generic-brand food.

"Oh, uh, thanks," Truman said. "I just bought a bag

myself." He motioned toward the kitchen, where against the hall wall leaned a forty-pound bag of premium Eukanuba.

Marcy looked from the bag to the bowl of stew at his side and gave him an ironic look. "You realize the dog is eating better than you are."

Truman flushed, wishing he'd left the canned stew in the kitchen, and asked, "You said you needed to ask me some questions?"

She got right back to business. "Yes. I don't know if you looked at the business card I gave you, but I'm an attorney."

An attorney, he repeated to himself. One more reason to keep away from her.

"Yeah, I saw that." It didn't take much for him to look unimpressed. He'd in fact been disappointed when he'd seen it on her card. "Downey Fabric and Softener, or something, right?"

"Downey, Finley and Salem," she corrected, leaning forward to put her elbows on her knees.

Too late, he realized he should have asked to take her coat. Of course, where he would have taken it was a mystery.

"We're working on a case," she continued. "Which is why I was in that part of town last Thursday. We represent a man who was injured on the site, and I'd like to know if I could ask you some questions about conditions on the job."

If he'd been a cartoon, Tru knew a light bulb would be glowing over his head right now. "Bob Burton? Guy who fell off the scaffolding a few months back?"

She nodded once. "Were you working on the site at that time?"

"Yeah. How's he doing?"

"I'm afraid he has a broken back, among other things."

"No shit." Tru was surprised. He'd heard Burton's injuries weren't bad. But then, come to think of it, Chuck Lang was the one who'd told him. "He paralyzed?"

"No, thankfully. But he's going to spend the better part of a year in bed at the very least."

"Huh." Tru leaned back in the chair. So she was here for information. To help Bob Burton, who was an ass but didn't deserve to spend a year of his life laid up with a broken back. "So what do you want from me?"

She leveled those midnight eyes at him and he had to hand it to her, she was tough to read. "You were aware, were you not," she said, "that there were serious OSHA noncompliance issues at the site?"

He narrowed his eyes. "That sounds an awful lot like an accusation to me."

She sat back and held up her hands. "No, no. I'm sorry if I gave that impression. It's just, I remembered something your superintendent said. Before he fired you he complained that you'd been poking your nose into business that wasn't yours, as he put it. Business about scaffolding, for example."

Truman's mind worked fast. He knew what sort of information she wanted, and he probably had some that would help her. But the last thing he wanted to do right now was go into a courtroom and testify for Bob Burton. Or anybody. He'd had enough of courtrooms for a while.

"Trying to remember?" Her tone was wry. As if she knew what he was thinking.

"Look, I can tell you a few things that weren't right. Things that shoulda been done but weren't. But I'm not going to court or anything. I can't testify."

She sighed. "I know it's intimidating to think about going to court. But trust me, it's not like it is on TV. Most of it's just . . . well, boring, really. But let's not go that far yet. For all we know this case'll never get to court."

"Oh, it'll get to court," Tru muttered. With his luck it would.

She shook her head. "No, not necessarily. It could well settle out of court."

"Settle, huh." He looked at her. She was hungry for this case. He could see it in her eyes.

"Yes, that means the company could offer some kind of settlement. Like money," she explained, misunderstanding him. "To Mr. Burton, so that we don't go to trial. They already rejected the idea of a settlement once, which is why we filed suit. Now we're trying to get as much evidence for our case as possible because there's still a chance they could change their minds and settle if we come up with something really damaging as we go through discovery."

She was so patient, just like a schoolteacher, he thought, amused.

"Discovery?" he asked, folding his hands in his lap, elbows on the arms of the chair. "What's that?"

She leaned forward again, warming to her subject. "That's a pretrial procedure. Each party obtains evidence, documents, and, yes, some testimony, that the other party may use at trial. The more information that comes out, or rather, the more information damaging to their case that comes out, the more likely it is that it'll never go to trial. And Planners Building and Design will settle."

She was enjoying this, it was obvious. Being the expert, the one with all the education. She probably hadn't been out of school very long and so didn't get to be a know-it-all as a junior associate at Downey Fabric and Softener, he thought.

"I get it." He scratched his stomach uncouthly. "So old Bob's gonna get a windfall, huh? Some big chunka change to retire on?"

She frowned. "That's not how we look at it. He's earning that money right now, with every day he spends in bed, every pain pill he has to take, every surgical procedure he may have to undergo. And usually, Mr. Fleming, clients in cases such as these would give back any money they receive in order to be healthy again."

"Sure, sure." He waved a hand. "And every crook in jail is innocent. I know the drill. Why don't you just hire some expert to say what Planners was doing wrong?"

"We will. But we also need someone who was there, who can say what the situation was around the time of Mr. Burton's accident."

He scoffed. "Hell, there were plenty of guys around. Why me?"

She smiled again, that small one that made her eyes go sleepy. "Because you're the one who was concerned about what was happening."

"I wasn't the only one—"

"And you're the one who lost his job saving a puppy from abuse."

He looked at the ground and shook his head. "I

knew that was gonna come back and bite me in the ass somehow."

"Look, why don't you think about it? We can get together in a few days to talk about the site a little bit and see where we are. Would that be all right?"

Tru looked at her speculatively for a moment longer than he believed was comfortable for her.

"I may not need to call you at all," she added, "but I'd like to get a really clear picture of the kinds of things that were going on there around the time of the accident. I've already noted that there weren't and still aren't guardrails on the open-sided floors. That's the biggest one right there. I'm going to take some pictures tomorrow. But were there any other safety violations you can think of around the time of the accident?"

Truman scoffed. "Only a few dozen."

"Great, maybe you could make a list. If you feel like it, that is." She smiled warmly.

Then something she'd said struck him. He leaned forward. "You're going to take pictures tomorrow? Are you *nuts?* You think Lang's going to let you stand there and gather evidence after you stole his dog?"

"First of all, he doesn't know it was me who stole his dog."

"Who else would it be?"

She shot a pointed look toward the hand that still scratched Folly's side.

"Second," she continued, "he won't know I'm gathering evidence. He doesn't even know I'm a lawyer, let alone whom I work for or whom I'm representing."

"Yeah, but he's damn sure gonna know you're not a tourist taking pictures of the scenery. He's not gonna care what your motives are, he's just gonna mind you being anywhere in the vicinity."

"And third," she said with exaggerated patience, "I'll be in the diner across the street, taking pictures through the window. He'll probably never even see me."

Tru gave her a hard look. "I don't know. I don't like it."

And he didn't. He hated the thought of her in Lang's clutches, as she'd been on Thursday. He couldn't bear to think what might have happened if he hadn't shown up when he did. He didn't believe for a second that Lang was above some rash act of violence.

"It's not for you to like or dislike." She stood and pushed her purse up onto her shoulder. Folly jumped up at the same time and squirmed toward her. She bent to pet the dog, then held out her hand to Truman. "But thank you so much for talking to me, Truman. Maybe we can get together later in the week?"

Tru took her hand, its softness renewing his trepidation about her photo shoot tomorrow. "I told you, I'm not testifying. I'll try to help you but I'm not going to court. I can't."

The dog leapt on her coat, its tongue flapping in and out as it tried to lick her somewhere, anywhere.

"Of course you can. It's easy. Trust me." Her smile was calm, her determination unruffled.

"Folly, *no*." Truman grabbed the dog's collar and pushed her to the ground. "I mean it." His eyes rose to Marcy's. "I won't—"

"You named her 'Folly'?" Marcy looked at him with such a delighted expression it made his heart nearly skid to a halt, not to mention his words. "What a wonderful name!" She bent to pet the dog good-bye but smiled back up at him. "Though let's hope it's not too apropos, huh?"

"Oh, it's getting more and more apropos all the time," he said dourly, wondering again as he looked down at Marcy how in the world she got her hair so shiny.

3

Tuesday, October 8
WORD-A-DAY!

INELUCTABLE: adj., unavoidable; in some cases, the irresistible lure of another's company

It didn't strike Marcy until the next day, as she was packing up the Nikon to go to the diner, that Truman had said *I can't* when they'd been talking about testifying.

Can't? she thought, straightening from stuffing as many lenses as would fit into the padded camera bag. *Can't* as in *I can't set foot in court or I'll be arrested? Can't* as in *I'm someone with a record? Can't* as in *my parole officer won't let me?*

She had automatically assumed that *can't* meant "won't" or "don't want to," but now it seemed quite possible that there might be something wrong with Truman Fleming.

For the purposes of the case, that was.

She had to admit, he didn't exactly seem the type to be nervous about testifying. Being intimidated by a courtroom was something she ran into all too often, but that's not what Truman Fleming was saying, she was suddenly sure.

Damn, she thought, plunking heavily into her desk chair. He was a fugitive. Or an ex-con. Or some kind of petty, two-bit vandal whose face was known all too well by the courts.

She was more than familiar with the type. Growing up in a bad neighborhood with two trouble-making brothers had taught her a lifetime's worth of lessons about the variety of ways a young man can get into trouble and ruin his future. She might even have joined them in their legally-challenged pursuits had she not been taken under the wing of a concerned history teacher in eighth grade.

Marcy picked up a pen and bit the end of it, feeling far more devastated than the circumstances warranted.

"Hey!" Trish Hamilton stopped in Marcy's doorway. "What did the bartender say to the horse?"

Marcy pulled the pen from her mouth and smiled. "What?"

Trish, another junior associate and her best friend in the firm, flipped her long, gorgeous, blond hair behind her and said, "Why the long face?"

Marcy groaned, then laughed.

"So?" Trish asked.

"Oh, it's nothing, really. I just figured out that what I thought was going to be a really great fact witness might not be suitable."

"For the Burton case?"

Marcy nodded. "I mean, I'm sure I can find someone else who'll testify to the conditions at the site, but this guy . . ." She shook her head. "This guy was going to be so good."

Trish entered her office and leaned her hands on the back of one of the client chairs. "What's wrong with him?"

Marcy sat forward, elbows on her desk, her chin in her hands. "I'm not sure, but I suspect he might have a record."

Trish grimaced. "Well, maybe you could use him anyway, depending."

"Yeah, depending." Marcy spun her chair to look at the dry-erase board on the wall behind her. It was full of facts pertaining to the case and had *Fleming* printed boldly under *fact witness.* "The thing is, I *know* this guy would come across well. He's really credible. And heck, with a haircut and a shave he'd be pretty handsome."

Trish laughed. "Hope you got his number."

Marcy spun the chair back. "No phone. The guy's pretty hard up, unfortunately."

"That *is* unfortunate. Why are all the good-looking ones poor?"

They laughed together.

Trish, Marcy knew, had grown up with lots of money. Not only did it show in the way she dressed, it showed in the way she moved, and spoke, and colored her hair. She was polish personified, and Marcy would have given anything to come across with as much class as Trish did.

Trish would never think twice about a guy like Truman Fleming. One look at the pile of dirty dishes by that ratty old chair and she'd be heading for the hills. Which is just what Marcy should be doing.

But then Trish, being the smart one, probably wouldn't be attracted to the man in the first place. As a responsible lawyer Trish would take him as the great potential witness he was and that would be it. And Truman *would* make a great witness. It wouldn't even take much to clean up his language; he wasn't completely rough. Marcy would just need to get rid of the *sugars* and *gonnas* and have him tone down the swear words. He'd be good on the stand, she was sure of it.

"Anyway, I've got to go," Marcy said, rising and zipping the camera bag. "Guess there's no sense crying over spilt milk. If he can't testify, he can't. I'll just have to find someone else."

"You'll find someone." Trish turned and headed for the door. "Let me know how it works out."

"Sure," Marcy said. But first, she was going to ask Truman straight out why he couldn't testify. That way she could spend at least one more conversation looking into those lovely gray eyes and lamenting the fact that they belonged to a man who used the word *chick*.

"Hey, Trish?" she called, shouldering the bag and her purse and heading for the door.

Trish stopped in the hall and turned.

"What do you think of guys who use the word *chick*?"

"I think they're juvenile chauvinistic assholes," she said without missing a beat. "Why?"

Marcy shook her head and waved the subject away with one hand. "No reason. That's what I thought too."

The street was not as quiet as it had been when she'd come for the dog, but for a city street it had a distinctly deserted feel, considering it was the middle of a workday. The drizzly, overcast weather didn't help matters much either. Marcy parked at the corner and walked briskly toward the diner, passing spray-painted windows and boarded-up shops that were no doubt havens of illicit activity.

She'd meant to change into jeans for the assignment so she wouldn't look so out of place, but she had another meeting after lunch and there was no telling if there'd be time to change back. Better to look out of place here than there, she'd decided. But as she walked past two bums engaged in an argument in the doorway of an empty storefront she thought otherwise.

She reached the entrance to the diner and ducked in without looking back. Taking a seat by the front window, she scanned the street and construction site to see if anyone was around to notice. All she saw were construction workers busy at work on the open-sided structure.

Her eyes dropped to the trailer where evil Chuck had been the Day of the Dog. She didn't see him or anyone else in the gravel lot. Beside the trailer, however, the kennel stood battered and open, strangely lopsided, as if someone had taken a sledgehammer to it. Or a steel-toed boot.

The lone waitress in the diner sauntered around the counter and came to Marcy's table.

"Get you something, hon?" she asked. Her black curls were held in a hair net and her pink dress was covered by an apron. If it hadn't been for the digital watch she wore she might have sprung straight from the 1950s.

"Coffee. Tuna salad on rye. And fries, if you've got them." Marcy slid the menu back between the ketchup and the napkin holder.

"We got 'em. Anything else?"

"That'll do it." Marcy looked at her watch. One thirty. "Oh, ma'am?"

The waitress turned.

"Do those construction workers ever come in here for lunch?" Marcy gestured toward the project outside.

"The ones that do, they been and gone. Most of 'em's only here in the morning, anyway. For coffee and Danish, you know. Then more coffee. And *more* coffee." She laughed, her face lighting up, and turned back to the counter. For a second Marcy was amazed. *Imagine having a smile that transformed like that,* she thought.

Unbidden, she remembered Truman Fleming's smile the night she'd shown up at his apartment. *Lexus!* She couldn't help feeling pleased at the memory. His had been a transforming smile too, with deep dimples on either side of his face and eyes that crinkled warmly. A smile that had truly enlivened his whole face.

She shook her head again and unzipped the camera bag. It would be *such* a shame if he couldn't testify. He was just so appealing. As a witness.

She lifted the Nikon from the bag and pulled out the low-light 135mm lens. The thing was enormous, wide and heavy, but with the lack of sunlight and the fact that she was shooting from indoors she thought she'd need it. She'd have to be fast, though. She'd just take a few quick shots, have lunch, study the scene, take a few more, and go. Hopefully if anyone happened to look her way, and happened to be able to see in, they'd just see a woman eating lunch.

The sound of the shutter seemed abnormally loud in the diner. Two other booths were occupied, and one old man sat drooping over what looked like a bowl of soup at the counter, but still the place felt empty. Like the street, it was afflicted with an aura of desertion, whether people were there or not.

Marcy put the camera on the bench beside her when she saw the waitress returning with her sandwich.

"You an investigator or somethin'?" the waitress asked, setting the plate down and giving the camera a long, wary look.

Marcy shook her head. "A writer. I'm doing a story on construction projects, thought I'd take a few shots to go with it."

"Seem like you'd get a better shot if you was outside." She placed a hand on her hip and looked out the dirty front window.

"Yes, you're probably right. I'll do that when I'm finished eating." Marcy took a bite of the sandwich and thought about leaving.

"Hmph. Thought maybe you was one a them investigators, taking pictures of a deadbeat dad or somethin'."

Marcy laughed and picked up the ketchup. "Nope. Nothing that interesting."

"I always thought that'd be fun. You know, checkin' up on people who's cheating on their wives and such. Takin' pictures."

"I don't know. Might be dangerous, I'd think." She pounded the bottom of the bottle until a blob of ketchup shot out.

"Hm, maybe."

A second later a large man in a dark suit entered the diner.

"Uh-oh," the waitress said under her breath. "Here comes trouble."

She turned away from the table and strolled back behind the counter without looking at the man again.

Marcy put the ketchup away and discreetly studied the man as he stood inside the door, squinting at the guy slumped over the counter. He was looking for someone, apparently.

He was an odd-looking man, with a neck like a watermelon that made his head look the size of a pea. His dark hair was slicked straight back and the coat of his blue, three-piece, pinstriped suit was buttoned over an impressively large girth. One hand fingered the button at his middle, and Marcy noted a large ring with some kind of red stone in it.

He looked like a Hollywood gangster.

She picked up her sandwich and took another bite, a bite that stuck in her throat as the man's eyes found her and he started toward her table.

She forced herself to chew, taking a swallow of water to get the bite down.

To her horror, he sat down directly across from her.

Even sitting, he towered over her. He seemed to block all the light too, because the booth, despite being perpendicular to the window, darkened with his presence.

Her palms began to sweat.

His eyes were black and sharklike. They bored into her without blinking.

"That your camera?" His voice was low and tinged with a Jersey accent.

Her eyes flicked to the Nikon on the seat beside her. She shrugged. "Sure."

He let the silence linger a minute. Letting her cook in her own sweat a moment more. *A good tactic,* she thought. One that was working.

"What're you doin' with it?" He folded his hands on the table between them. A demure move for so large a man.

"Taking pictures. What's it to you?" She forced herself to pick up a fry, dip it into the pool of ketchup on her plate and eat it. She'd learned years ago, on the streets of her old neighborhood, that the most effective way of dealing with a thug was to get tough—no matter how tender you might feel inside.

"You takin' pictures a that?" He indicated the project across the street.

She sighed, as if bored by the man. "Again, what's it to you? I'm just sitting here eating lunch, minding my own business. What are *you* doing?"

His face flushed slightly at that and she could feel a rivulet of perspiration run between her breasts. She hadn't taken off her jacket to eat, which was good, she thought now. Her Mace was in its pocket.

"I'm here to protect the interests a my employer." He shrugged uncomfortably in his suitcoat, jutting his chin forward in a quick motion as if the collar were too tight for his muscularity.

"Yeah, so? Who's your employer?"

She knew perfectly well what he was going to say and she was already mentally packing her bag to go. She could shove the camera into the case without zipping it, grab her purse and slide out. No, she had to pay for her meal, which meant she had to get out her wallet, then put it back, put the camera away, and slide out. That was all going to take too long.

He cocked his head toward the window. "*That's* my employer. And he don't like nobody takin' pictures of his place without his permission."

She ate another fry and took a long moment to study him while chewing it. "Actually, I don't need his permission. Whattya think of that?"

The man flushed again. "*He* says you do."

She ate another fry. Her stomach was a knot. It felt like all the fries were piling up in her esophagus. "The law says I don't."

At that the man stood up, his bulk pushing both the table in front of him and the bench seat behind him askew with a loud screeching sound. Marcy found herself nearly pinned in her seat by the dislodged table. Every fry in her throat wanted to come back up.

"Lemme tell you somethin', lady. Around here *he*"—he jerked a thumb toward the window—"is the law. And Guido"—he punched a sausage-thick finger into his own chest—"is his deputy. I listen to him, and you listen to me. Get it?"

Marcy's mouth went instantly dry. She looked up at him, her eyes riveted to his tiny head. In fact that was probably his nickname. *Tiny*.

"Sure," she said.

"Now gimme the camera."

She looked over to where the camera would be, but the table was so crooked now she'd have to work her hand down between her body and the seat to get to it.

"I can't," she said. "Besides, it's not mine."

He narrowed his already narrow eyes. "Uh-huh. I begin to see. You're doin' somebody else's dirty work."

"Look," she said, and issued a little apologetic laugh. "I'm just a writer, doing a story on construction sites. I picked yours at random. I won't use it, okay? I promise."

"Gimme the camera," he repeated, this time with one meaty paw outstretched.

She tried to look rueful. "Listen, I would, if it were mine. But I can't becau—"

At this he leaned over and she thought for a second he was going to grab her by the throat. Instead he placed his fist on her plate, flattening what was left of her fries.

"Because it belongs to the paper and they'll charge me for it," she squeaked quickly.

Dimly, in the back of her mind, she'd heard the bells on the diner's door jingle as Guido had leaned over. Still, she was surprised when a body stopped next to their table. From the corner of her eye she saw the torso of a man, but she dared not take her gaze from Guido's in case he went for her camera, or her throat.

"Hey, Arthur," a low voice said.

Arthur?

Guido straightened slowly and Marcy took her first breath in what seemed like twenty minutes. They both turned to the man beside the table.

Marcy couldn't stop the smile that burst upon her face at the sight of Truman Fleming. He wore jeans and a black shirt under a jean jacket that made him look broad-shouldered and rough, every bit capable of calling off Guido, even if he wasn't nearly so . . . *girthsome* as the thug.

"What're you doing here? I thought you was fired," Guido said, brushing flattened french fries off his knuckles. The tone of his voice was caught between belligerence and timidity. It was an odd combination.

Marcy took the opportunity of his distraction to snake her hand down her side and into her pocket. She gripped the little silo of Mace tightly.

"The real question is, what're *you* doing here, Arthur? Something tells me you're doin' somethin' bad. You ain't doing nothing bad, are you, Art?"

Guido flushed again, only this time a deeper red. His beady eyes darted to Marcy, then back to Truman.

"Come on, Harl," he said in a stage whisper, almost as an aside. "I ain't doin' nothing. I just gotta job here, okay?"

"Then you won't mind if I join you, will you?" Truman pushed the table back to its original position and started to take the seat beside Marcy. When he looked down he saw the camera and his gaze sat heavily on her for a moment. *I told you so,* it seemed to say, and she felt herself flush just like Guido. Uh, Arthur.

"Harley," Arthur whined, sounding like a kid not getting what he wants.

"Not now, Arthur. I think you've done enough for today. How 'bout if the lady and I leave, that make you happy?" Truman glanced at Marcy. She made an acquiescent face and began packing up the camera.

"Yeah, just leave, okay? And leave quick, he's watchin' me."

"That's *your* problem, Art," Truman said, but he helped her move more quickly by picking up the camera bag.

She slid out of the booth and they started for the

door. Just before they reached it, however, she stopped and Truman nearly collided with her back.

"I haven't paid!" she whispered to him, pawing at her purse.

"Forget it," Truman growled.

"No, I had a whole lunch. I've got to pay for it." She stepped toward the counter, still foraging for her wallet.

Truman leaned over, slapped a twenty on the counter, and nodded once toward the waitress. "Now come on," he said, taking Marcy by the elbow. "Let's go before they send someone really scary."

Truman walked fast down the sidewalk, his grip hard on her elbow. Marcy practically had to trot to keep up. Her purse kept sliding down her arm and the camera bag bumped uncomfortably against her backside. All the while a feathery drizzle dampened her hair and wet her face.

"Wait a minute," she said breathlessly when they were half a block away. She yanked her elbow from his grasp and pushed her purse back up onto her shoulder. As she pulled the camera bag to her other shoulder she looked up at him. Her savior. Again.

"I guess I owe you another thank-you. This is the second time you've saved me from an overbearing thug." He seemed to get more handsome every time she saw him, but maybe that was just because she was getting used to the hair that was a little too long and the face that should have been shaved today and wasn't.

"I'd've thought you'd stop going back to the place all the thugs hang out after the first time."

"I've got a job to do." She shrugged, then eyed him

speculatively. "You didn't seem very afraid of him. Do you know him? Is his name really Guido, or Arthur?"

"Honey, his name is whatever Chuck Lang tells him it is. And believe me, you don't want to mess with Chuck Lang."

Marcy frowned and looked back down the street toward the site. "Chuck Lang is the superintendent?"

"That's right. Now let's get going."

At that moment Arthur emerged from the diner.

"Listen," she said, pulling the camera bag around front and unzipping it, "if you don't want to mess with Lang, I understand. But I've got . . ." She pulled the camera from her bag and put the viewfinder to her eye. ". . . a job to do and that man—"

Truman grabbed her arm. "Are you *crazy*? What are you *doing*?"

She fired off a couple of quick shots then started to stuff the camera back into the bag when she heard shouting. She looked up to see Arthur lumbering toward her.

"Jesus," she muttered, her pulse accelerating with his every step. She turned quickly.

"Where's your car?" he asked.

"Right there, at the end of the block."

They crossed the road quickly and Marcy punched the button on her key. The satisfying sound of doors unlocking met their ears just as Arthur's voice carried to them on the breeze.

"I know who you are, *Miss Paggalousy*."

Marcy's blood ran cold and she stopped, the door handle in her hand.

"And I want that camera," Arthur yelled, poking a finger down at her through the air.

He was getting closer, and Truman looked at her over the roof of the car.

"Give him the film." His eyes were hard as diamonds.

"*What?*" She looked at him incredulously. "Are *you* crazy?"

"Just give him the film," Truman said, walking quickly around the front of the car toward her.

Arthur's labored breathing was audible now. "I can *find* you, Miss Paggalousy."

Truman grabbed the camera from her, popped open the back and pulled the roll out, exposing every shot she'd taken that day.

"*Hey!*" She made a grab for the camera. "Truman, what the—why are you—"

He pulled the last of the film out and handed the camera to her. Then, heading back around the front of the car he threw the film canister down the street toward Arthur.

"There you go, Arthur. Go back and tell him to leave the chick alone."

Arthur hove to a heavy halt in front of the film canister, the negatives hanging out like a long dark tongue. Bending over and placing his hands on his knees, he breathed like a man who'd just caught a cannonball in the gut.

Truman turned and growled at her, "Get in the car."

Marcy flung the door open and flopped into the car, tossing her purse and the camera bag onto the backseat.

Truman got in the other side and slammed the door shut.

"Get going," he said.

"I hope you realize—"

"You can berate me later. Just, right now, *get going.*"

She started up the engine, fury making her heart hammer. She'd been home free. She had the pictures and was leaving. Now she'd have to come back. What the hell was he thinking?

"Go back that way," he instructed, directing her away from the construction site.

She threw the car into gear and pulled a three-point turn in the middle of the road.

"Turn right down here, then right again on Third."

She glanced over at him. They were heading back toward the site.

She pulled onto Third Street.

"Slow down and park right behind that van." He pointed to a primer-gray van on the right side of the road. "Now give me the camera."

She looked at him dumbly. "What?"

He turned his gaze to her face and her heart did a somersault. No doubt the result of all the adrenaline of the last fifteen minutes, she thought.

"You do have another roll of film, don't you?"

She looked back as he reached for the camera bag. "Of course."

He opened the car door and got out, then bent back down to look in at her. "I'll be back in two minutes. Keep the car running and be ready to bolt, got it?"

"Are you taking more pictures for me?" she asked, amazed.

"Yeah. I'll be right back." He started to close the door.

"Wait wait wait!" she called, leaning as far across the passenger seat as she could. He bent back down to look at her with exaggerated patience. "I need shots of the scaffold—"

"I know what you need." He slammed the door and walked off down the street, looking much more at home in the environment than she did.

She had the brief thought that he might be absconding with the camera—after all, there was still the possibility that he was an ex-con—but shrugged it off. She knew where he lived, for one thing. For another, she was pretty sure he'd shown up at that diner today solely to check on her.

The thought sent a spiral of pleasure through her. He was going to help her, she thought. He was going to help her with this case.

She could get him to testify. Even if he did have a record, it would be irrelevant to his knowledge of the worksite. And he'd tell her all about what was going on at the site. Why else would he be taking pictures for her now? He *would* know what she needed, even better than she did.

She took an uneven breath, momentarily thrilled by the idea of all the things she needed that Tru Fleming could take care of.

But those things were beside the point, she told herself firmly. He would help her with *the case*, not . . . uh . . . personal issues.

Still, she smiled and crossed her arms over her stomach, where an entire flock of butterflies had for some reason set up camp. Even if he just worked with her she'd get to see him. It was inevitable.

4

Thursday, October 10

WORD-A-DAY!

SOTERIOLOGY: n., the theology of salvation; or the many ways in which one can save and be saved

Truman was a fool. No doubt about it. He was getting himself into a tight spot, and for what? A pretty girl. Anything done solely for the sake of a pretty girl was inherently foolish.

Marcy had dropped him off at his truck after the photo incident and taken off like a shot, her sleek silver Lexus hissing away on the rain-wet street like some sort of vehicle from another planet.

A meeting, she'd said. And she was late. *Busy woman, very important,* he thought resignedly. *Thankyouverymuch and seeya.*

This was exactly the problem with girls like her. They chased the almighty dollar like it was the Holy Grail and believed that everyone around them should behave the same way.

Had she known what Truman was doing—running from that very dollar as if it were the plague—she would no doubt be even more horrified by him than she already was.

He exhaled heavily and glanced down Pennsylvania Avenue. He was definitely a fool.

Behind him, Grandview Construction was erecting a twelve-story office building on the site of the old Bilgemore Tavern, a pub reputed to have hosted numerous politically significant conversations in the early to mid-nineteenth century. Grandview's concession to this historical importance was to erect a plaque inside the cold gray marble vault they were calling a lobby.

In addition to this insult to Pennsylvania Avenue, the American people, and history in general, they were not looking for carpenters with Truman's limited work experience. He could be a laborer, the foreman had said. For seven dollars an hour.

Truman sat in the driver's seat of his truck with the door open and his feet on the running board. A clean autumn breeze blew from the south and the sun warmed him enough to keep him from wanting to return to his apartment. He'd spent yesterday and most of today looking for work, with no luck, but he wasn't worried. He knew he'd find a job eventually. He just didn't happen to have two nickels to rub together at the moment, so finding one today would have helped, at least as far as lunch was concerned. As it was, he didn't dare spend his cash on a burger lest he not be able to buy gas to look for work.

It didn't help that after the photo incident with Marcy he was out a badly needed twenty bucks. Not only that, but Chuck Lang could easily have seen him that day, standing under the dubious protection of the thrift shop's torn awning, taking pictures of the construction site. That King Kong of cameras Marcy had was not exactly inconspicuous. Even if Lang hadn't seen him, he'd bet one of the dozens of other men on that building had and had immediately sent word to the superintendent. After all, nobody liked his work scrutinized, and there were enough shady personalities employed by Planners Building and Design to be paranoid that the camera was there specifically to nail them for one thing or another.

Still, better him than Marcy, because they knew who she was, too, and coming to get him was better than going after her. He could tell by the look in her eye as he'd ripped the film from her camera that she had every intention of going back for more pictures. Better to nip that right in the bud, he'd told himself.

But now here he was, twenty dollars poorer and the object of Chuck Lang's wrath. Again.

What he ought to do, he thought, was go talk to Arthur, try to find out exactly what the threat was against Marcy. If they knew who she was, they probably knew what she was there for, so they wanted her to drop the suit. But why wouldn't they be going after Burton in that case? Maybe they were doing that too, but it was a heck of a lot harder to go after a man who never left his bedroom.

He shook his head again. What the hell was he getting involved for? He wasn't a cop. He didn't even play one on TV. Did he really think he'd be able to burst onto the scene like DeNiro and threaten them all with tough talk and a mean face to leave the girl alone? And then they'd do it?

No. He heaved another sigh. There *was* something he

could do, though. Something that would ultimately get Chuck Lang and his minions off everyone's back. He didn't want to do it, but now it seemed like he had to.

Damn it.

Tru turned back to the steering wheel and pulled the tooth-marked pencil from the rubber band on the visor. After rustling up some paper—a miraculously clean napkin from Burger King—he set about making a list. A list that would almost certainly get him in trouble and had the potential to expose him completely.

Why was it that the right thing to do for someone else was always the wrong thing to do for yourself?

Not that he was doing this for Bob Burton. No, what motivated him more than anything, he was ashamed to admit even to himself, was that he was doing this to see Marcy again. Marcy, with her designer wardrobe, luxury car, spa-pampered skin, and six-figure paycheck.

He was a fool.

Ten minutes into his list making, Truman heard the low hum of a car slowing in the lane next to where he was parked. From the corner of his eye he noticed a dark sedan creeping up alongside his truck. He lifted his eyes to see the tinted window of a black Mercedes descend, like an inverted stage curtain, to reveal the grinning face of his old friend Palmer Roe.

"By God, I thought it was you!" One of Palmer's hands was draped across the leather steering wheel and the other turned down the volume on his Alpine stereo system. He leaned across the glove-leather interior to see out more clearly. "Truman Fleming, as I live and breathe.

Where the hell have you been? I haven't seen you since last Christmas, when you did me the favor of lightening my wallet of several heavy bills with that stupid elf bet."

Truman grimaced at the memory of the scene. Christmas shopping at Georgetown Park. Truman was reaching the critical point in his disgust with his way of life and had made a bet with Palmer mostly to see if the two of them were as reckless and dissolute as Truman was starting to believe. A thousand dollars on whether or not the reindeer in front of the mall Santa's sleigh was male or female, and which elf they'd trust to make the decision for them.

Truman had said male, not caring either way. Palmer, female, with a fervent, "Look at those eyelashes!"

The elf had said, "Who gives a shit?" then sided with Truman just to get them out of the way.

Palmer had paid him in cash on the spot and Truman had stuffed the entire wad into the bucket of a startled Salvation Army Santa on Wisconsin Avenue.

"I guess you could say I've taken a little vacation," Truman told him now.

"Well, it obviously hasn't done you any good. You look like hell. Get in the car. Let me take you to lunch."

Truman glanced down at the Burger King napkin in his lap. He was about done. And he *was* famished. Should he consider this cheating? he wondered. Lunch with Palmer would be a far cry from Burger King or the cheap canned food he could afford at home. At the same time, however, he felt an overwhelming urge to talk. Not about anything in particular, just to someone who *knew* him, someone with whom he did not have to pretend to be somebody else.

"Come on, Tru. Don't tell me you have to be somewhere. You look like you just came from the landfill." Palmer's brow furrowed. "Is there a landfill in D.C.?"

Tru chuckled. "You're not asking in terms of lunch options, I hope."

"Get in," Palmer said again, with a grin. Truman heard the *thunk* of the electric locks opening. "I'll take you to Old Ebbitt's."

Truman sighed. He was a flawed man, he thought, tempted by a steak and martini lunch and unable to resist.

"So give me a hint, Tru. You just dropped off the face of the earth," Palmer said, sliding onto a stool at the bar. Chin up, he shot the cuffs of his dark blue suit and straightened his yellow tie in the mirror behind the bar. "What happened to you?"

Inside, the Old Ebbitt Grill was cool and rich. Dark wood contrasted elegantly with glittering bar bottles and flickering gas lighting. The bartender wore a white apron and polished the already gleaming wood with a soft, thick cloth.

Truman had to smile at the familiar sights. It felt good to be here, he thought. But it felt even better knowing that not only was he probably the only man in here without a tie on, he was the only man in here without a *two-hundred-dollar* tie on. It didn't matter, though. Palmer looked—and was—rich enough for the both of them.

"I know." Truman picked up the bar menu. "I've been taking a break."

"A break?" Palmer motioned for the bartender. "Martini, dry, two olives. Truman?"

"Budweiser."

Palmer made a face, then motioned the bartender on his way with an expression that said, *there's no accounting for taste.*

"I heard you quit your job," Palmer said. "Not that that was such a tragedy. I suspected you'd finally figured out you could work anywhere you wanted. But when you didn't turn up in any of the regular circles I decided some action was required."

Truman laughed. "What did you do?"

Palmer cocked a brow over mocking eyes. "Me? Nothing. *I* haven't taken leave of my senses, after all. I just said action was *required.* I didn't actually provide any."

Truman nodded, smiling, as the bartender delivered his beer. "I counted on as much."

The two ordered and the bartender disappeared toward the kitchen. It was late afternoon and they were the only two patrons at the bar.

"But then the mystery quite overcame me." Palmer cocked his head and looked Truman up and down, taking in the ratty jeans and flannel shirt.

"Did it?" Tru asked, not looking at him.

Palmer, Tru could see in the mirror, turned his gaze to his glass. "I confess it did. I actually spoke with your mother. Twice, in fact. But she wouldn't say anything beyond the comment that you'd lost your mind. Knowing your mother, I imagined you must have taken an extended vacation in Mexico or perhaps the Midwest."

Truman swigged his beer.

Palmer swirled his martini and glanced back over at him. "You're not going to tell me, are you?"

"I'd rather not."

"Then let me guess." Palmer took a healthy draught of his martini and turned to face Truman, one elbow on the bar. His face, so often contorted with mirth or sarcasm or both, betrayed a telling seriousness.

Truman smiled slightly. "Guess away."

"You've pitched it all to live frugally."

Truman glanced up at him, startled, but Palmer ignored his look.

"You've taken up with a sultry Puerto Rican waitress," he continued, his voice low and dramatic, "from some yet-to-be-trendy ethnic restaurant and are living in her cold-water flat over an Asian grocery store in Arlington. At night you listen to salsa music and dance voluptuously until the neighbors pound on the ceiling with a mop handle, at which point you go into her dimly lit, lingerie-strewn bedroom and make mad, passionate love."

Truman stared at him, amused and aghast. The vision was ridiculous, clearly, and yet Truman feared it was close to the one he'd had upon quitting his job and devising his plan.

"Tell me I'm on the mark or I'll be devastated," Palmer said. Then he added more seriously, "I know you were pretty fed up with things as they were."

Truman gazed into his beer. "Dead on," he said, smiling wryly.

"If it's any consolation," he said, too casually, "Melinda's father went belly-up last spring. She actually had to get a job."

Truman glanced back up at Palmer. "This had nothing to do with Melinda." He paused, then smiled, as if that short fling could have had anything to do with a life decision of any sort. If she'd had that kind of influence, it would only have been because she represented so many women he'd known. "Though I do think a little gainful employment will do her good. When I talked about quitting to find some real meaning in life, she thought, I meant I wanted to prepare for the Ashworths' regatta."

"Don't sell the girl short now, Tru," Palmer said with a mock offended air. "We all know there's nothing like a little competition on the high seas to teach valuable life lessons."

"It's not exactly the America's Cup." Truman turned to look fully at his friend. "What about you, Palmer? Doesn't all the . . . I don't know . . . *superficiality* get to you sometimes?"

Palmer shrugged and took a sip of his martini. "I'm the shallow sort, really."

"I'm serious. Surely women like Melinda, and *Sharon*"—he paused, emphasizing a girl Palmer had thrown over the previous year after she'd sold her family's champion miniature poodle to buy a mink jacket with hat and boots to match—"get to you after a while, don't they? With all their manipulations and not-so-subtle aspirations."

Palmer looked thoughtful. "Yes, I guess they do tire me, though I understand them too well to judge them harshly. I am the same animal, basically, you know."

"You're not—"

"I'm not like you, Tru," he said, looking him squarely in the eye. For the second time in the space of an hour Palmer's perpetually grinning face was sober. "I may see the problems you talk about and privately agree with your assessments of the crowd, but I'm not a reformer. I'm a product of and willing participant in the system."

"But you tire of the power- and money-hungry just like I did. I know you do."

Palmer shrugged. "I guess I'm not willing to believe that everyone in our social strata is shallow by default. There are some . . ." He paused, a smile creeping back to his lips.

Truman smirked. "Who is she?"

Palmer flashed him a look. "She's a hard-working girl, though I won't pretend she's anything like your Puerto Rican waitress."

Truman laughed.

"She's from Connecticut. Went to Radcliffe. But she seems to have a balanced head on her shoulders." He shrugged again, then laughed it off. "Time will tell." He polished off his martini and looked around for the bartender to signal for another. "Where'd the bum get to now?"

"Well, I hope you're right," Truman said. "About the girl. Me, I want one who doesn't care if I'm a prince or a pauper."

"Good luck convincing one you're the latter." Palmer spotted the waiter across the room, approaching with their orders, and signaled him for another martini anyway.

Truman pictured the look on Marcy's face as she'd stepped into his apartment the other night.

"I think I've got that part figured out," Truman said, salivating guiltily at the sight of his steak. "Now I just have to convince myself."

* * *

When Marcy had left Truman last Tuesday, she'd kept him in her rearview mirror so long she'd nearly rammed into a parked car. Embarrassed, she'd floored the gas pedal on South Capitol Street in order to disappear from view, not to mention make it to her meeting on time—a meeting in which she'd had a hard time thinking about anything but Truman Fleming.

Even today, it was difficult to concentrate on the meeting at hand when scenes from the diner kept passing through her mind. How happy she'd been to look up and see that it was him threatening that Guido person. She pictured him striding purposefully off to take those pictures for her. *Nice athletic physique,* she thought again. Probably due to all that manual labor. And he had a nice way of carrying that physique around, a kind of manly grace. Yes, there was something fascinating about him, she thought. Something unusually, suspiciously fascinating.

She shook the thoughts from her head and tried to focus on the contract in front of her. One of the senior partners was briefing them on the case but it was no use. She couldn't keep her mind on it. Besides, it appeared simple; there was no copyright infringement so there was no suit. She wondered why the meeting continued on for so long in the face of such obvious evidence. No doubt the senior partner thought he was teaching her and the other junior associates something by going on about all the various and futile arguments the plaintiff might make. Which was ridiculous. The judge would throw it out on summary judgment, she'd bet any amount of money.

Her thoughts strayed back to Truman. Far less clear than the copyright case was why Truman would have shown up at that diner to help her. The only plausible reason was to make sure she was all right. Or was she just flattering herself? Going back to the job site after getting fired was pretty unlikely, and showing up by accident would be an astounding coincidence. Plus, he'd known she would be there, so he must have been there for her, right?

It was sweet. Chauvinistic—he obviously didn't think she could take care of herself—but sweet.

At last the meeting ended. Marcy packed up her overstuffed briefcase and took the long elevator ride to the garage and her car. The drive to southeast was congested, as usual, giving her plenty of time to think about how close the homeless shelter where she periodically volunteered was to Truman's apartment.

What was his story? Maybe he'd never graduated from high school. Maybe he'd been a hell-raiser like so many boys and had dropped out. But still, a lot of people overcame troubled childhoods. Why would Truman, who seemed so intelligent, get stuck doing something that paid so poorly he had to live in a slum?

She was dying to ask him all of this, but something told her he wouldn't be very forthcoming. Besides, it would be beyond insulting to ask him why he hadn't made anything of himself.

In any case, he must be making halfway decent money. Most of the guys she'd dated in high school had worked construction at one time or another and could make a fortune in the span of a single summer. Skilled construction workers were valuable commodities, she thought, unwilling to dwell on the fact that Truman Fleming of the lovely physique and intelligent eyes might not be skilled. So maybe he had a plan to get out of Southeast.

She pulled up right in front of the soup kitchen and walked through the brisk evening air to the stairs, then into the front hall. The place looked and smelled like the old school it was, with its linoleum floors and the odor of pine cleaner, but wafting in from the old cafeteria were the delicious scents of Italian cooking. Marcy smiled to herself. Calvin Deeds was here.

"Marcy P.!" The tall, white-haired, craggy-faced man greeted her with open arms when she rounded the corner toward the kitchen. His face creased even more with his broad smile. He must have been coming from the restroom because he was emerging from the residential part of the building.

"Calvin, how *are* you?" She smiled warmly back at him and reciprocated his tight, comforting bear hug.

"It's been too long. Much, much too long. You're not letting that place steal your soul now, are you? Remember they start by stealing your life." He smiled with the words but Marcy knew he meant them. One thing about Calvin, he always had his eye on the big picture: the meaning of life. Part of that, she knew, was because his wife was battling cancer. It helps you remember what life is all about, Calvin always said. His ability to make lemonade out of the lemons life had dealt him never ceased to amaze Marcy.

"I don't think they've got either yet." Marcy stepped back and hefted her purse higher on her shoulder. "But they've certainly stolen my time."

"Life *is* time, my girl." He put an arm around her

shoulders and walked her back toward the kitchen. "Hopefully you'll never learn that the hard way."

When they reached the kitchen, Marcy dropped her bag on the floor in the corner and turned to Calvin. "How is Penelope?"

At the expression that clouded his face Marcy could have kicked herself for the question. Dread curled her fingers.

"Passed out of her misery six months ago, God rest her soul." He turned away and took up an apron hanging from a hook by the door.

"Six months! Calvin, I—I didn't know. I'm so sorry." She pressed her palms to her cheeks, hot with shame, and dropped them when he turned to her with a rueful smile.

"How could you know?" he asked. "I wasn't exactly sending out announcements. And you're probably too young to be reading the obituaries. I have to admit, though, it was something of a relief. For her, certainly, but also a little for me."

"I understand. It had to be awful watching her go through that. I just wish I'd realized how long it's been since I've seen you. I wish I'd been here for you. I'm so sorry." She put her hand on his as he began to tie the apron behind his back, squeezed, and took the strings from him.

He cleared his throat and spoke with a gruff kind of bravado. "There was nothing anyone could do. It was something I had to muddle through on my own. I'm only just now starting to realize it's true."

She finished tying the apron and he moved toward the counter.

She shook her head in admiration. "And yet here you are, helping people. Calvin, you're incredible."

His brows rose, and he looked down at the counter. "I'm not just helping them, I'm sorry to say. This place is having to help me, too, these days." He picked up a pile of zucchini and took it over to the sink. "In fact, in many ways it's been my salvation."

"Sure, work can be a great distraction. It's good to keep busy. But not many people would salve their wounds by helping others." She plucked another apron off the wall and moved to the cutting board next to him.

"Don't make me out to be some sort of saint, Marcy. You know I do this for me. Always have." He turned on the water and started scrubbing the vegetables. "Now more than ever."

She took up the first few clean zucchini and a knife. "Yeah, yeah, I know. You can't resist an appreciative audience for your cooking." She could tell by the way his ears were turning red he was embarrassed to be going on about his problems. "It's all about recognition with you, isn't it? Fame and fortune. So what are we doing here? Slicing? Dicing? Julienning?"

"Slice them, please, m'dear. I think we'll start with a minestrone tonight."

She smiled, knowing the food would be better quality than most people ever ate, let alone those patronizing a soup kitchen. After all, Calvin Deeds's restaurant was one of the best Italian eateries in the city.

"So how are things at Bella Luna?" she asked, cutting a zucchini lengthwise before turning the pieces to slice a row of half moons.

Calvin was silent so long Marcy turned to look at him. His mouth was turned down and his throat worked as if he were holding back tears.

"Calvin, what is it?" She dropped her knife and turned to take his arms in her hands.

He turned toward her but didn't look up. "Marcy, things have been bad, since Pen fell ill. It went on for so long. You know me, I don't like to talk about bad things, but, well, I've had kind of a rough time of it. The medical bills, you know . . . they've been quite . . . astounding."

"But—she was insured, surely?"

He shrugged and turned back to the sink. "Not adequately, apparently. Listen, honey," he said, regaining his composure, "I don't want to burden you with all this bad news. Let's talk about you, all right? Any young men in your life these days?"

Marcy put her hands on her hips. "Calvin, it's not a burden. Now, I know you don't like to dwell on things, so just tell me what's happened and then we'll be done with it."

He shook his head and she gazed with pity on a knot in the back of his white hair. He'd always been fastidious about his appearance. Never a hair out of place. Yet here he was close to tears with his hair messed up, and now that she was more a tuned to his situation, she noticed the wrinkled shirt.

"I lost the restaurant, Marcy. I had to sell it, to pay the bills. And . . . well, I may as well tell you everything, since you'll find out eventually anyway. I had to sell the house, too. I'm living here now."

"Here?" Marcy gasped. How in the world had she

missed all this? At the very least she thought she'd have heard about the restaurant changing hands. She must have been working too much.

"It's not so bad. They've been quite kind. And since I do the cooking, I get my own room."

"But surely you could stay with someone," she protested. "You could stay with *me*." She began mentally rearranging furniture to accommodate him. A month or two on the couch wouldn't kill her.

He smiled down at her. "That's sweet, honey. Sure, I have friends I could've imposed on, but I guess I didn't want to deal with all the pity. Here, I'm just another anonymous soul. *And* I can do some good."

He plopped more clean zucchini on the cutting board next to her and gave her a stern look. "Marcy P., I don't think those squash are going to cut themselves."

Clearly, he didn't want to discuss his diminished circumstances. But it galled her to think all this had happened to him and she'd had no idea. She might have been able to help him. Maybe she could fight his insurance company, get more coverage. But you couldn't just come right out and tell someone that maybe they'd had their life ruined needlessly. Wasn't that akin to telling someone they might not have had such bad luck if they'd been smarter?

Marcy pressed her lips together and turned back to the cutting board.

"Calvin, I just want to say, and I'll only say this once because I don't want to make you uncomfortable, that if you want me to look over the policy to make sure the insurance company did all they should for you, I'd be happy to do it. Or if there's anything at all you'd like me to do, it would make me feel a lot better to be able to do it for you."

"Well, now I am embarrassed," he said, and she couldn't believe it but she thought she heard him chuckle. "I had a lawyer look it all over, hon, and they did what they should. I'm sorry, I should have thought of you. Now it's just time for me to get back on my feet. And I will, don't you worry."

"I know you will, Calvin." She continued slicing the vegetables in front of her. "I'm glad you talked to someone. And I don't doubt for a minute that you'll be back in *Washingtonian*'s list of top one hundred restaurants in no time."

He sprayed water over a pile of tomatoes. "Thank you for that vote of confidence. In the meantime, I'm going to regale tonight's clientele with my famous marinara sauce. Where is that gentleman who always shows up here with the Mad Dog twenty-twenty? Perhaps he'd spare a little of that fine wine for the sauce."

The last thing Marcy felt like doing was dressing up and going to a benefit ball, but Trish had asked her weeks ago and at the time it had seemed like a good idea. Plus she'd already bought a killer dress, exactly the kind the ever-stylish Trish had advised for their mission.

It was silly, though, Marcy felt now, after seeing Calvin the night before, to be spending one of the only nights she wasn't working late in an overdecorated ballroom with a bunch of strangers. Then again, Calvin would no doubt approve of the reason she was going. He worried about her single and frequently dateless state.

Benefits, Trish had told Marcy, were the intelligent

woman's alternative to bars when it came to meeting men. At bars you met worker bees, guys who dressed like men but would always be just guys, and tired, older fellows for whom the term *ambition* had lost all meaning. These last were the worst, Trish contended, because they were so hopelessly sad, inspiring some women to try and fix them.

At benefits, on the other hand, you met the real upper crust of Washington society. The *suitable* men. The classy ones with the coveted "three *Ps*": pedigree, property, and philanthropy. (The last was important because in most cases it showed they were not stingy.)

In other words, Marcy translated to herself, *money and the balls to show it off.*

There was nothing like walking into a roomful of men in tuxedos, Trish said, knowing that every last one of them not only owned their tuxedo but most likely had at least another one in the closet at home.

A man with a tuxedo, Marcy was informed, was a man with taste.

Marcy stood in front of her full-length cheval mirror—an antique she'd splurged on just the week before—and turned this way and that to examine the dress she'd put on. It was black and full length, but the fact that the silk clung to her like a second skin and the spaghetti straps holding it up looked nearly too fragile for the job kept the gown from being at all conservative. And one should never dress conservatively at these things, Trish said. Wound once around her neck was a black tulle scarf that draped the length of the gown on either side.

Marcy wasn't sure about the scarf, but without it she

felt as naked as she'd ever want to be in a room full of people so she left it on.

The only jewelry she wore were diamond drop earrings (a present to herself after her last, stunningly large raise) and a costume diamond bracelet. Just enough to keep her from looking plain, but not so much as to appear to be overcompensating for a lack of real jewels.

She stopped twirling for the mirror and put her hands on her hips, sighing. It wasn't so much that she regretted agreeing to go to this thing. She just hadn't planned on being this tired when the event finally rolled around. She wondered how long she'd have to stay. Fortunately she was meeting Trish there, so she wouldn't be tied to her stamina. Trish always wanted to stay long after Marcy had worn out, though Marcy probably would want to stay too if she dripped eligible men the way Trish did.

She picked up her tiny black handbag and tried to stuff her hairbrush into it. As she'd feared, the handle was too long. She had just rummaged a smaller one from the bathroom cabinet when someone knocked on the door.

She paused. Had she missed the intercom? Usually Javier, the doorman, announced any arrivals, but she'd heard nothing. *It must be Trish,* she thought. No doubt Trish forgot they were supposed to meet at the benefit. Since Javier knew her he probably just let her come up.

She stuffed the small brush into the handbag and opened the door.

When Marcy appeared at the door, Truman felt his heart thud once, *hard*, against his ribcage and then it seemed to stop. His mouth went instantly dry.

She looked incredible. Like some beautiful, young

Italian widow in a classic movie, with her hair pulled back and her eyes dark and mysterious. And that perfect smooth gorgeous skin, from her cheeks to her cleavage. *So much* perfect smooth gorgeous skin. He couldn't help imagining himself flicking those tiny straps off her shoulders, first one, then the other, and peeling that black silk down to reveal . . .

"Truman," she finally spoke. She looked and sounded as surprised as he felt. One hand rose to her throat while the other held a little black purse.

He peeled his tongue off the roof of his mouth and spoke. "Marcy. Sorry, I guess I—I've caught you at a bad time."

Though he couldn't say it was a bad time for him, now that he'd seen her in that dress. He wondered what her skin would feel like, what she would do if he laid his hand on her bare shoulder, there near her collarbone, and ran his palm down her arm.

A long scarf of something sheer wound around her neck and dropped to the floor, giving her the look of a delicate bird that had just escaped capture.

She glanced briefly down at her dress and moved the hand from her throat out to the side in a helpless gesture. "Actually, yes. I'm just going out." Her brow furrowed and she made a move as if to look down the hall. "How did you get up here? Did Javier let you in?"

"Ah . . . he looked busy. Someone had let a stray cat in, so I decided not to trouble him." Tru smiled slightly, proud of the diversion.

She looked at him warily. "I see. How did you find out where I live?"

"Phone book. Listen, I did what you asked, I made up a list. But we can talk about this later. You've obviously got to be, uh, go someplace." He started to turn.

She reached out and nearly grabbed his arm, but stopped before she touched him.

"Wait, a list? Of what?"

He shrugged. "Just a few safety violations and stuff. Things I could think of that might help Burton's case against Planners."

He stuck a hand in his pocket, felt the folded up Burger King napkin, and imagined taking the pins from that demure little net she had her hair pulled back in.

Her eyes lit up; he again sensed the hunger she had to win this case. "Gosh, I wish you'd come by earlier, but . . . well, can I see it? the list?"

Tru couldn't help but look her up and down again. Indeed, he could barely keep from reaching out and touching the fabric of that dress, fabric that seemed to have been melted onto her body, right down to where it flared gracefully at the bottom and draped to the floor.

He glanced down the library-silent hallway toward the elevators. "Someone picking you up?"

She shook her head. "No, I'm meeting them there."

He scoffed. "Some date. Dress like that demands a limo and some champagne at the very least, I'd think."

Her cheeks grew pink. "It's a girlfriend I'm meeting. Listen, I have a few minutes. Why don't you come in for a second?"

He smiled to himself. A girlfriend. Not a date. She was dressed to kill and it wasn't a date. There couldn't be a man in her life.

He seemed to think it over, cocking his head and looking past her into the apartment. White rug, white furniture, one of those tall decorative vases full of some improbably colored and uselessly decorative sticks next to the couch. "I don't know. I wasn't all that thorough writing things down, you know. Thought I'd explain them to you when I got here. But . . . well, maybe we should do it another time."

She looked at him in exasperation. "I was hoping to hear from you all week, and now, the one time I have plans, you decide to show up? How long do you think it's going to take?"

"Depends on how much you understand and how much detail you need." The one time she had plans? No doubt she was climbing that legal ladder fast, working hundred-hour weeks and dropping friends like flies.

She placed a hand on her hip and he noted the fake diamond bracelet. "All right. When can you do it?"

He shrugged again. "I don't know. I was free tonight."

Hell, he was free every night, but she didn't need to know that.

"I can come by your place after the benefit, if you think you'll be up. It's down near the Capitol so I'd be relatively close to your place."

"Later tonight?" His mind spun, imagining Marcy in his apartment in that dress late tonight.

"Or—"

"No, later tonight's fine," he said quickly. "I'll be up. I'm kind of a night owl. And yeah, the next few days're real tight for me."

She raised a brow at that but didn't comment. "Fine. I don't think I'll be late. This thing . . ." She flung a hand down at her dress to indicate the event she was attending. "I don't have to stay long."

"Those formal things break up pretty early, do they?"

"For me they do. If I'm later than, what, eleven, should I not stop?"

He paused to consider. "I'm up till midnight, usually."

"Okay, before midnight, then."

"Midnight," he repeated, glancing over her midnight-black dress again. It was enough to make breathing difficult, that dress, he thought, trying not to gape. "Okay, see you later."

"Okay," she said. But she didn't close the door. She waited for him to turn toward the elevators, and even then he didn't hear the click of the hasp until he was several doors down.

5

Friday, October 11
WORD-A-DAY!

PERICLITATE: v., to imperil; as in willfully exposing oneself to a forbidden desire

"*Tonight?*" Trish stared at her, mouth agape in, of course, a classy way. "You're going to his place tonight? Are you crazy?"

Trish's voice bounced loudly off the marbled walls of the ladies' room in the Phoenix Park Hotel.

"What do you mean?" Marcy looked for a dry spot on the sink counter on which to put her purse, then pulled out her compact and tried to disguise her guilty blush by dusting her face profusely. Unfortunately, there wasn't enough powder in the MAC case to hide it. She leaned in toward the mirror. "It's close by here and if I get the information tonight—and it's as good as I think it'll be—then I can start drafting a settlement first thing in the morning."

"But Marcy, his place is in Southeast. And it's after dark. And you're dressed . . ." She moved a hand up and down, Carol Merrill–fashion, to indicate Marcy's dress.

"I know, but his street isn't that bad." She thought briefly of that morning's word for the day. Was she periclitating herself? "He's on the first floor. I'll just dart right in. Besides, I'd like to see the dog."

Trish made a face. "The dog's going to ruin that dress, if nothing else. Why don't you just wait and talk to him tomorrow? Schedule a lunch."

Marcy flipped the compact shut. "For one thing, I don't think this guy *does* lunch. For another, he said this was the night he was free this week. And I just really don't want to wait for this information. If Planners doesn't intend to settle then I want to know that and get going on the suit."

It was true, she told herself. She really did want to get a move on the case. Besides, she was right here, just a few blocks from his neighborhood. What was the big deal? So she was dressed up.

She smiled to herself, remembering the look on Truman's face when she answered the door in this dress. Okay, so she wasn't immune to the kind of flattery his expression bestowed. And she was aware of the fact that *his* flattery was particularly gratifying, but that didn't mean anything. She could enjoy his appreciation the same way she enjoyed countless harmless flirtations over the years. It was fun, that was all.

"Okay, so you're going to his place, dressed to the nines, to get mauled by the dog and what else?" Trish looked in the mirror and patted a lock of her hair, where not a curl had drooped and not a strand was out of place.

"He's got information on safety violations at the building site. Plus, I got the pictures developed that he took for me on Tuesday and I need to ask him about some of them. He got a bunch of the faulty scaffolding but he took a few more and I'm not sure what they're supposed to show."

Trish shook her head. "I don't know . . . I still think I should go with you."

"There's really no need, Trish." Marcy pushed her compact back into her purse, unwilling to analyze the strong gut reaction she had against Trish coming with her. "Besides, you're having a good time here. Who's that guy you keep dancing with?"

Trish flipped a hand away nonchalantly. "That's just Palmer Roe. I met him a couple months ago and he's nice enough, but way too much of a playboy for me."

"*He* certainly seems interested. And you know what they say, there's no man more loyal than a reformed rake."

"I don't know anyone who says that. Besides, *reformed* seems like the key word there. If you watch," Trish said sourly, "he'll *seem* interested in anyone he happens to be talking to."

"That's too bad. He looked like a shoo-in for the three *Ps*." Marcy sent her friend a teasing grin.

Trish laughed. "Oh he's got them, all right. In spades. But that's not enough. Fidelity should start with a *p*."

"You just want everything, don't you?" Marcy joked.

"You know it. And you should too, Marcy." Trish turned to her with an earnest expression. "No compromises, now. Don't forget that when you're over there in Southeast getting, uh, *briefed* on safety violations." She gave Marcy a knowing look.

Marcy was sure her blush was now rendering the powder on her face useless. "What on earth does that mean?"

"I mean," she said seriously, "that I sense trouble with this guy. Romantic trouble."

Marcy scoffed. "You couldn't be more wrong."

"Couldn't I? You said he was handsome . . ."

"No, I said he *could be* handsome, if he cut his hair and shaved. And at the time I was only thinking in terms of his appealing to a jury."

"Right. Those blue-collar working men you'll be hoping to get are so traditionally sympathetic to handsome men."

Marcy gave her a dry look. "As it turns out, we're not going to have a jury. Win thought it best to opt for a bench trial and opposing counsel agreed."

Trish continued to give her a skeptical look. "Are you honestly saying you're not attracted to this guy?"

"Trish," Marcy said, putting a mental foot down for both herself and her friend, "I am *not* going over there for any romantic reasons. Even if I did feel the slightest desire for this guy, which I *don't*, you know he could well become a witness for the case. And you *know* how bad getting involved with a witness would be. So believe me, I'm not going to be tempted to do anything foolish."

Trish cocked her head. "Uh-huh."

Zipping her bag shut, Marcy gave her friend a patient look. "I'm not. For one thing he's too . . . I don't know, rough or something, for me."

Trish's brows rose and she smirked. "Rough? He's too rough? How would you know that?"

"I did not mean that in a sexual way and you know it."

Trish laughed.

"He's just rough around the edges, you know?" Marcy continued, heading for the door. "He probably wouldn't go to a symphony performance if you paid him, for example. And the ballet I'm sure would only provoke a bunch of bad men-in-tights jokes. We'd just have completely different tastes."

"Not to mention worlds." Trish followed her out the door.

"Yeah, well . . ." Marcy's blush was manageable this time. Still, she kept walking, her heels clicking on the marble floor. When she reached the front door she handed her coat check ticket to the attendant and turned to her friend. "Listen, don't worry about me, I'll be fine. Have a good time tonight, okay? If you're working tomorrow, stop by my office. I want to hear all about it."

"You know I will. But *be careful.* And I don't just mean getting there. Remember there's as much danger inside that apartment as there is outside. Maybe more."

Marcy laughed. "You're relentless."

"No, I'm intuitive."

"Then you're overreacting."

Trish smiled and looked skeptical. "I certainly hope so."

Trish was right.

Marcy pulled up in front of Truman's building and turned off her headlights. This *wasn't* safe.

In her rearview mirror Marcy watched a couple of shadowy figures emerge from an alley, merge into one silhouette, then part, one of them returning to the alley. The other ambled off down the street, slinking quickly around the corner.

She picked up her little black purse and thought about how slow she'd be if she had to run in these shoes and this dress. The spike heels might inflict some damage, but let's face it, she thought, she'd never get that close. Everyone here was armed.

She glanced at Truman's building, at the glowing light in his apartment, and marveled at how far it seemed from the sidewalk to the front door.

She was losing her edge, she thought. She hadn't even remembered to pack her Macc. She briefly considered going home and explaining to Truman later. But she was here now and it seemed silly to flee because of a few yards of vulnerable territory.

One more glance in the rearview mirror told her there was no one out in the open. No doubt every darkened corner harbored a pair of eyes to watch her, but there was nothing she could do about that. She was sure she could make it from her car to the door before even the alley shadow could get to her.

She opened the car door.

At the same time, the door to Truman's apartment building opened and a figure emerged, silhouetted by the hallway bulb behind it.

Half in, half out of the car, Marcy decided that maybe this really wasn't worth it. The person coming out the door was probably harmless but represented one threat more than she was able to talk herself out of. The settlement draft could wait another day, or even week, if it meant meeting in a reasonable place at a reasonable hour in reasonable clothes, couldn't it? The figure moved quickly toward her and just as she was dipping back into the car, the light from the block's one unbroken streetlamp illuminated Truman Fleming.

"Marcy?" he called softly in the dark.

For a fleeting moment she imagined him coming toward her in the dark of an English cottage garden for all those romantic reasons Trish was so afraid of. He would call to her just like that, his voice soft and urgent on the autumn air. She envisioned it all like a stolen moment in a Victorian woman's diary . . . forbidden love.

Her stomach flipped once.

She straightened out of the car. "Yeah." Her coarse American voice burst the bubble of her reverie. She punched the button on her key to lock the car and slammed her door shut.

"I was watching for you," he said as she rounded the front of her car. "I thought you might be nervous, you know, in this neighborhood."

She held the skirt of her gown up slightly with one hand as she stepped over the curb and, natural as could be, he reached for her other hand to assist her. She paused, startled, and looked at her hand in his. A pretty courtly gesture for a construction worker, she thought, moving forward again.

"Let's go in." He led her up the walk a few paces, letting go of her hand as they neared the entrance to the building. As she started to move ahead of him, he, seeming to think twice, preceded her through the door.

They entered his apartment and the first thing she noticed was that the hole in the couch had been mended. Not in any attractive way—a sheet folded around the cushion and secured with duct tape to contain the foam—but still, it helped the look of the room considerably.

Marcy clutched her wrap around her shoulders and stopped just inside the door. The rest of the place was cleaner, too. No dirty dishes, no shoes on the floor, the TV was off and pushed into a corner. Not that the place had looked that bad last time. Just typical guy mess. But what had struck her, later, as she'd been thinking about it, was the lack of anything of a personal nature. No pictures, no knick-knacks of any kind, no radio, no magazines or newspapers, not even any tools. It was as if he'd landed there with just the clothes on his back.

"Come on in," he said, edging around her into the living room.

In the light she could see that he wore an unwrinkled shirt and his hair was brushed. He didn't look at her, so she had an ample moment to realize anew that she'd lied outright to Trish. This guy *was* handsome, haircut and shave be damned.

He glanced up at her as she stepped further into the room and she looked away. Which is when she noticed there was no sign of the dog. Marcy felt a sudden fear. Had she run away? Had he gotten rid of her? If he'd taken her to the pound without telling her she'd kill him.

She glared at him. "Where's Folly?"

He motioned toward the back of the apartment. "She's in the bedroom. I knew you'd be all dressed up and her manners ar—ain't what they should be yet, so I put her away."

"I'd like to see her," Marcy insisted, awash with worry that he no longer had the pup and was afraid to tell her.

Truman's gaze dipped slowly to her dress, then jerked back up. "You sure?"

"Of course." She looked around for the bedroom door. She hadn't even realized there was a bedroom. Since the kitchen was the only other visible room she'd assumed the place was an efficiency.

"Okay. Be right back." He headed back through the kitchen.

She watched him go, noting the way his hair fell into thick burnished layers in back. He'd once had a decent cut, it looked like.

A second later the frantic scratching of nails on the floor sounded before Folly apparently gained her footing and came charging into the room.

Marcy bent down and caught the puppy as she bounded toward her, smiling and petting and scratching the dog as she wound around her, tail flapping against her dress, the wall, the furniture.

"Well, at least the fur's black," Truman said. "It'll match your dress."

"She's grown so much!" Marcy held her chin up as Folly tried to lick her on the mouth. The pup was so exuberant she had to laugh. "What a handful! I'd say some obedience classes are in your future, missy." She scratched vigorously behind the dog's ears. Folly appeared to grin.

After a minute, Marcy looked up to see Truman watching her, on his lips a slight smile.

Marcy rose and Folly leaned up against her, begging for more. "So, where shall we do this? Have you got a kitchen table?"

"I thought we could do it out here." He gestured toward the couch. "It's more, uh, comfortable, believe it or not. I've got a pad and pencil, if you need it."

"Great, thanks." Marcy gathered up her skirt and pulled her wrap up her arms from where it had slid down her shoulders.

"Do you want me to take that? Your shawl?"

She imagined letting him take it, imagined sitting there on the sofa naked from the cleavage up. "That's all right. I'll hang on to it. I'm a little chilly."

He frowned. "I'd turn up the heat but, you know, it's . . . I don't have any control. I'm usually hot here, myself, but I guess I usually wear more than . . ." His gaze dropped to the low bodice of the dress and his hand went palm up. ". . . that."

Marcy pulled the shawl closer around her. She should have changed before she came, she thought. What an idiot. It wouldn't have been that hard, she could have stuffed some jeans and a T-shirt into a bag and changed at the hotel. But noooo. She had to see that enticed look on Truman's face again and now she was paying for it. She felt like a tease.

She cleared her throat. "You said you had paper?"

"Oh, yeah, right." He turned and headed back to the kitchen. "Do you want something to drink? I don't have much."

She heard a refrigerator door open.

"Just water would be good," she called. If he tried to offer her wine she'd turn it down. She didn't want him getting any kind of wrong idea.

"No problem. That's about all I've got anyway. Unless you like Budweiser."

That was *not* disappointment she felt, she told herself. Besides, if he'd actually bought wine it probably would have come in a box. Which, she admonished herself, would only further illuminate the vast differences in their chosen paths.

"No thanks," she said firmly.

"I'll just put Folly back in the bedroom, too," he said from the kitchen. "I'll be right in. Come on, Folly." He whistled a short, distinctive signal.

Folly leapt up from Marcy's side and trotted into the kitchen.

Marcy started to protest, but stopped. They'd get more done if she wasn't distracted by the puppy. And she had a sudden sense she should try to get this done quickly.

After a second Marcy noticed in the corner of the room, beside where the TV had been stowed, a short corner shelf upon which three books lay. They were leather bound and incongruously handsome in the dimly lit apartment. She was about to get up and investigate when Truman reappeared with a glass of water, a yellow legal pad, and a Bic pen.

They got down to business quickly, Marcy taking copious notes on all that he'd come up with. Initially, she'd been dismayed to discover his list had been written on a napkin, but as it turned out that didn't cheapen his information. If anything, it was more than she'd hoped for.

Dozens of OSHA violations, a safety supervisor who worked a crew of men rather than supervising the site, the possibility (rumor had it, according to Truman) that someone had fallen from the first floor for the exact same reason the month before, and—the pièce de résistance—Truman seemed fairly certain the subcontractor who employed Burton had *specifically asked* for railings on that third floor and had met with a hostile attitude—from Lang, of course.

Marcy's heart skipped with glee at the strength the case was gaining. She asked Truman question after question, her mind racing with all the Planners-damaging points she was accruing, when she thought she saw Truman hiding a yawn.

"I'm sorry." She put the pen down on the coffee table and pulled the yellow sheets on which she'd written back over the top of the pad. "I've kept you way too long. What time is it, anyway?"

He pushed his arm out as if to reveal a watch under his sleeve but there was nothing there.

He grinned sheepishly. "Must have left it by the bed. Let me check."

He got up and went back toward the kitchen. Marcy rose too, her limbs stiff from sitting so long, and let the shawl drop to the couch. He was right, it was warm in here. She grabbed her empty water glass and headed for the kitchen, more curious about the rest of the apartment than she was thirsty.

Even though she heard the rustle of her silk dress as she moved through the dingy apartment she had an odd sense of déjà vu, and it wasn't comfortable. She'd grown up in an apartment like this one, only it had been crammed full of the detritus of five people. But the peeling paint, the scratched, creaking floors, the crookedly hung doors, and the smell of other families' dinners were all dreadfully familiar.

Truman's kitchen was tiny, but very clean. She moved to the faucet, sensing there would be no bottled water in the fridge, and filled the glass, looking around herself as the water ran.

A box of corn flakes stood next to a small bag of sugar on the counter. A roll of white paper towels, no holder, lay next to the sink. A bar of soap and some generic dish detergent were next to the faucet. There, on the sill of a dirt-shrouded window, stood a paper cup rooting an offshoot from a spider plant.

She felt drawn to this last, and walked over to the plant to touch its tender green leaves. The cup was full of water and a few roots had emerged from the cutting.

So there were two touches of humanity in the place, she thought. The books in the living room and this tiny nurturing attempt at plant life. For some reason it touched her.

Truman emerged from the bedroom. He looked startled to see her in the kitchen but recovered quickly and leaned one hip against the counter. She took a sip of water.

"So you think you got what you need?" he asked.

She looked up into his eyes and saw again that look of admiration that had so gratified her earlier in the evening. She looked down into her glass, remembered she'd left her wrap in the living room and felt all too aware of the short space between them, not to mention the fact that she could not leave the small kitchen without him moving to let her by.

"Yes, it's excellent information. Thank you so much." She met his gaze again. "On behalf of Mr. Burton, thank you. This will help him immeasurably."

He crossed his arms over his chest and cocked his head. "I wasn't particularly trying to help Burton."

She swallowed. "Well, for whatever reason, you did the right thing. You'll help stop Planners from continuing any unsafe practices."

He smiled. "Oh, I doubt that."

She warmed under that smile, noting the way it crinkled his clear gray eyes and caused those deep dimples to appear. She found herself smiling back. Too late, she realized the moment had lengthened as he held her gaze, and she wasn't sure what to do. She felt as if he'd gotten hold of her glance and would not let it go. She cast about for something to say but there was not one thought in her head.

He shifted. She thought he was going to leave the kitchen and end this uncomfortable moment, but instead he moved toward her. One hand reached out and touched her arm.

Marcy felt as if she were underwater. As if any move she made would be slow and ineffectual, so she held still, in a state of suspended animation until whatever he would do next.

His fingers closed around her arm and he gently pulled her toward him. She moved slightly, enthralled as much with what he was doing as her body's electrified response to it.

His right hand took her other arm and the heat from his skin on hers made her flush. She parted her lips, suddenly in need of more air.

His palms ran up her arms and rested on her shoulders. His left hand fingered the strap of her gown, then let it go. Somewhere in her mind she thought she should stop this, but it was so late, and so dark, and this night and this apartment and this man seemed so far away from her present life that she had the odd sense that it wouldn't make any difference.

Then his hand moved to cup her cheek, and suddenly he was kissing her.

She felt the shock of his lips on hers and her body reacted of its own accord. Her lips opened, inviting him in, and his arm snaked around her back. She put her hands up to maintain her balance and they found his chest. Her fingers curled involuntarily into the flannel material of his shirt.

His tongue invaded her mouth. She bent her head back, which pressed her body up against his, and his hand pushed into her hair, loosening the chignon.

Marcy's heart galloped and every nerve ending reached out, grasping at the contact, longing to be touched. His right hand slid up her back as their mouths fused and melded, his fingers touched the bare skin between her shoulder blades, and she shuddered with pleasure.

Then the shriek of a car alarm pierced the night.

Marcy pushed back so fast Truman's hand got caught in her hair and pulled the chignon netting loose, spilling her hair onto her shoulders.

He pulled his hand back, the net caught on a finger.

"We can't do this," she gasped, pressing her palms down her sides as if to straighten the jumbled mess of nerves beneath her skin.

"Why not?" His eyes were probing, his voice low.

She couldn't look at him, could not believe what she'd just allowed to happen.

She swallowed. Her heart raced and her skin tingled with such desire even her shock could not squelch it. If she were drunk or anonymous, she thought, she'd throw herself right back into his arms. She'd never felt anything so powerful as the draw to be touched by him.

"You're a *witness.*" The final word hissed out between her mortified lips.

"I haven't agreed to that." He was still so close she could hear him breathing after the low-spoken words.

"Well, I haven't agreed to *this.*" She looked up then, to find him gazing down on her, his eyes shimmering with desire.

What was she doing?

"I think you have," he said then.

His hand moved as if to touch her again and she took a quick step back. He held out the net that had secured her hair. She snatched it back and folded both hands around it.

"I can subpoena you." She forced herself to hold his gaze. "After everything you've told me tonight, I can force you to testify."

He looked at her and the expression in his eyes was oddly kind. "But you won't."

"How do you know? Why won't I?"

"Because your case doesn't need a hostile fact witness."

She swallowed hard. He was right. Apparently they both knew that if she did subpoena him he could go in there and do what every other hostile witness would do who didn't mind perjuring himself. He'd just say he didn't know anything.

Then something occurred to her. "Wait a minute. How do you even know what a hostile fact witness is?"

He shrugged nonchalantly. "I watch a lot of TV. You know, *The Practice*."

He reached his hand out again, let his fingers touch the skin of her arm.

She took a deep breath. "Please don't do this. I can't do this."

"Are you married?" he asked.

She looked up at him and knew her expression was surprised. "No. But . . . I have a boyfriend."

He gave her a skeptical look.

She threw her hands out to the side. "All right, I don't have a boyfriend, but I cannot get involved with you. I need you for this case, for one thing. You know I won't compel you to testify but you've helped me so far. Surely you intended to continue by testifying."

He studied her intently for a moment, his jaw working as if he were trying to come to a decision. "If you can't find anyone else and you decide your case really needs my testimony, then I'll do it. But only if you do all you can to do without it first."

She nodded. "Sure, yeah, okay." They looked at each other for a long moment and, God help her, she wanted nothing more than to kiss him again. "Will you let me go now?"

His brows drew together. "I never stopped you." His voice was gentle and she knew, as she'd known all along, that he wouldn't and hadn't stopped her from leaving.

She looked pointedly at the narrow space between his body and the door anyway.

He followed her gaze, then took a quick step back, gesturing for her to leave the kitchen, if that's what she wanted.

She took a deep breath and moved quickly past him, into the living room.

Here the sound of the car alarm was much louder and the obvious finally struck her.

She spun around to look at him coming from the kitchen behind her. "That's *my* car alarm."

6

Monday, October 14
WORD-A-DAY!

PERENDINATE: v., to defer day by day;
the way one might put off, say,
deciding about a man until the next time
one sees him, or perhaps the time after that...

"Hello, you have reached the Paglinowski residence. I can't take your call right now, but please leave a message and I'll call you back as soon as I can. Thank you."

Beep.

"Uh, Marcy, hi. It's Tru. Fleming. Listen, I want to apologize for Friday night. I'm really sorry about what happened. It was completely my fault. Not the window. The, uh, you know, [throat clearing] the kiss. Though I'm sorry about your car window, too. I just want you to know that it won't happen again, believe me, I know that. It *can't* happen again, so don't worry about that. The kiss, that is. Hell, anything could happen to your car. [uncomfortable laugh] Um, so, I guess that's all I wanted to say. To apologize. I just want you to know I really mean it. Oh, and I hope you got your window fixed. It's supposed to rain tomorrow. Okay then, ah . . . Bye."

* * *

"So, you're the new guy?" A short, bulky man with curly brown hair and an Irish look to his features strode over to Truman. Around them the simultaneous sounds of a jackhammer, a crane, and a nail gun cluttered the air.

"Tru Fleming." Truman held out his hand and the shorter man took it in a stout, thick-fingered grip.

"True?" The man turned his head slightly and looked at him askance. "What kinda name's that?"

Truman made an effort not to sigh. "Short for Truman, but that sounds a little . . ." He searched for the proper adjective for this man. *High-falutin* was too southern. *Snobby*, too condescending. *Blue-blooded*, too literary.

"A little stiff in the shorts," the man supplied, with a laugh and a smile that brought out the leprechaun in his face and eyes.

Truman laughed. "Exactly."

"My name's Donnie. Donnie Molloy."

"Good to meet you, Donnie."

"Likewise. Okay, you and me gonna be workin' the north end. You got any objection to workin' up high?"

"Nope."

"Good." Donnie nodded his head once, then cocked an eyebrow in Tru's direction. "I like to sort out the nervous Nellies right off the bat. We don't need no dainty boys around here, I'll tell ya."

Their footfalls crunched in the gravel outside the project as Truman followed Donnie around the building. Truman was happy to have gotten work here for a number of reasons, not the least of which was that it would probably be more interesting than the Planners project.

They were constructing an office building behind the façades of several row houses. The façades were real, the last vestiges of the old homes that had been torn down, and would camouflage the higher rising office building behind to keep it architecturally compatible with the neighborhood.

And it was going up in the area of D.C. called Foggy Bottom, which was considerably closer to K Street and the office of a certain lady lawyer.

Of course, the fact that it was also near a bunch of other K Street lawyers had its drawbacks, but it wasn't as if he'd be going to the Prime Rib for lunch and running into them.

The biggest reason he wanted to work here, however, was because he'd gotten a tip from a guy on the D Street site that another fired Planners employee had found work here—the guy who, it was rumored, had fallen from the first floor only weeks before Bob Burton's accident.

The very guy who, as it happened, Truman was talking to now.

"So, Billy tells me you was at Planners 'fore this, over there on D. That right?" Donnie glanced back at him but didn't stop walking.

"Sad but true," Truman said, following Donnie into the dank interior of the unfinished building. The smell of sawdust and wet cement hit him like a rag to the face.

"'Sad but true,' ain't that the truth." Donnie chuckled, stopped before a freight elevator, and jerked the lever back. Heavy machinery screeched and churned;

clinking metal and grinding gears echoed around them. "I hate them Planners bastards."

Tru glanced around the first level as they waited for the elevator. "You know Chuck Lang?"

Donnie scowled and cast Truman a sidelong glance. "Hate *that* bastard most of all."

"Join the club. Are you the guy who worked over there?"

"Yeah, but I ain't the only one. We got five or six here bailed from Planners."

"Is that right?"

"Yeah, don't nobody like workin' for them." Donnie turned to him, legs splayed and arms crossed over his chest, his expression outraged. "Lang *fired* me just for askin' about worker's comp. You believe that shit?"

The elevator shuddered to a halt in front of them. Donnie dropped his pose and heaved open the metal gates.

"They can't do that," Truman said as they clambered onto the metal floor grate.

Donnie scoffed and shut the gates. They jerked upward. "Well, I'll be damned if they didn't. Told me to get my tools and get the hell out. If I was there longer'n it took to do that they said they'd blackball me all over town."

"No, I mean, it's illegal for them to do that. You could sue."

"Sue?" Donnie commenced laughing long and hard, the sound bouncing off the metal and making it ring. "Where you from, anyway? Like I can afford to pay some cutthroat lawyer. Talk about rat bastards. I wouldn't trust no lawyer anyway, I'll tell ya."

Tru thought about Marcy, pictured her in that black silk dress, and imagined Donnie turning her down. *Bet he'd trust that lawyer,* Truman thought. Though she'd probably have a thing or two to say about the man's, uh, colorful language. Elite girls always played puritan around working class people.

"So what were you asking about worker's comp for? You hurt or something?" Workers milled around the floors they rumbled past, some drinking coffee, some fastening on toolbelts, some gathering materials.

Donnie pulled his dungarees up with one hand, puffing out his chest at the same time. The fingers of his right hand grasped the metal grate of the elevator as they shuddered up the side of the building, floor by floor.

"I'll tell ya. I damn near broke my neck on that project."

Bingo, Tru thought.

"Took a header off the building while I was doin' some welding," the man continued. "Lucky I was only one floor up. Lucky too the damn blowtorch shut off 'fore it hit me in the stomach. I's so covered in shavings and shit I'da smoked up like one a them snake things on Fourth of July."

Tru paused at the odd visual that produced, then asked, " 'Took a header'? You mean you actually fell off the building?"

Donnie looked at him as if he needed lessons in the English language. "That's what I'm tellin' ya. Landed on some sandbags, so nothing broke. I was plenty sore, though. And my golf game wasn't the same for weeks.

Thought maybe I oughta let some doc check me out. That's why I was askin' about worker's comp. I was wonderin' if it would cover just a checkup after, you know, a fall like that."

"They didn't have any railings up?"

Donnie scoffed again as the elevator ground to halt. "Hell no. They didn't have no railings on any floor on that place. Here, though, they got railings all over the goddamn place. Safety lines too. Donneville's a sight better company to work for than Planners, I'll tell ya that."

The man was a goldmine, Truman thought. Marcy would love him for this. "When did all that happen? The fall, I mean. And you getting fired."

"'Bout eight months ago now. Happened February second and next day they fired me. Bastards." He opened the gates and spat onto the concrete of the ninth floor.

February second, Truman calculated, as they exited the elevator. About six weeks before Bob Burton's accident.

". . . supposed to rain tomorrow. Okay then, ah . . . bye."

Marcy pushed the repeat button and listened to the message again. The first time around she'd smiled at his window clarifications but now, at the end of the message, she frowned.

He meant it. He didn't want to kiss her again.

She supposed she should be relieved, but she couldn't be that dishonest with herself. The whole weekend she'd felt bad about the kiss, but it had rocked her in a way she'd never felt before. She found it difficult to be relieved that he apparently did not feel the same way.

He was right, of course. If he hadn't said it, she'd have had to leave him a similar message, no matter what she felt about it. If he'd had a phone. And an answering machine. So he'd saved her the trouble of having to say it face-to-face.

She sighed and pushed *repeat* again, listening to the timbre of his voice this time more than the words. That deep voice was so soothing. Lulling, one might even say. She could almost imagine him saying something completely different, something sleepy and intimate, tender.

She pictured his hand holding the phone . . . Where had he been when he made the call? she wondered. It didn't sound like a pay phone, there was no background noise. She sat down on the straight-backed chair next to the machine, an elegant Queen Anne that more often held her purse than her person, and looked at the machine.

She'd spent the entire weekend analyzing why she'd succumbed *so easily* to his kiss, despite all her protestations and resolutions that her attraction to him was objective, but could come up with no good reason other than temporary insanity. Worse than trying to figure herself out, however, was imagining what Win Downey would say if he knew of this turn of events. She cringed every time she thought about it.

Unprofessional conduct. Jeopardizing the case. Selfish disregard for the client. Schlock lawyering . . . The phrases passed through her head with unrelenting energy throughout the day. She also imagined him exploding into an uncharacteristic tirade about the irresponsibility of what she'd done and how she didn't deserve the chance he was giving her to handle this case.

Of course she didn't tell him. She'd *never* tell him. Nor would she tell any other living soul, though that hadn't been easy today.

Trish, who unlike Marcy hadn't worked on Saturday, had stopped by her office first thing.

"*So?*" Trish had plunked herself in the chair across the desk from Marcy's with an expectant look. "How'd it go Friday night?"

Marcy marshaled her features into a positive expression and said, "It went *great*. I got everything I needed and more."

Trish cocked an eyebrow. "*Everything* you needed?"

Marcy forced a chuckle and ignored her own blush. "You have a filthy mind, Patricia Hamilton. I got all the *information* I needed. Excellent information, as a matter of fact."

Trish's expression cleared, somewhat reluctantly, it seemed. "Great. And he told you what all those pictures were for?"

Marcy closed her eyes. *Oh damn. The pictures.*

"You forgot to ask about the pictures, didn't you?" Trish smiled slyly. "Mind if I ask what distracted you?"

This time there was no controlling the blush. Marcy stood up and slapped a palm on the dry erase board behind her, in what she hoped was apparent frustration, turning away from Trish. "*Damn*. I *knew* I forgot something."

"Well, you'll just talk to him about them next time. Has he agreed to testify?"

Marcy picked up the dry-erase marker and wrote *pictures* slowly and carefully next to Truman's name on the board, buying time for her face to cool off, before turning back.

"If I can't find anybody else, he said he would testify. But he gave me tons of useful stuff. Stuff I can look for and get in discovery."

"So he's not wanted for anything? Not an ex-con? Not a fugitive."

Marcy laughed, then realized she hadn't asked him *why* he wouldn't testify. She guessed the question was just one more casualty of the evening, like her objectivity. "No, of course not," she said unevenly.

"And he didn't even *try* anything?" Trish persisted.

Marcy affected a chastising expression and sat back down.

Trish held her hands up. "I'm just asking. I'm also wondering what in the world's wrong with him. Lord, girl, you looked fan*tas*tic in that dress. Any guy worth his salt would've been all over you."

Then Truman was worth his salt, all right, Marcy thought.

"Do you think he's gay?" Trish looked genuinely curious.

Marcy sputtered a laugh. "No. No, I don't think he's gay." She tried to imagine anyone looking at Truman and thinking he was anything but one hundred percent, heterosexually masculine. "Though I appreciate the thought that anyone who doesn't jump me must be gay."

Trish smiled. "Well, honey, you are one hot chick."

"And what about Palmer?" Marcy counter-assaulted. "You're something of a hot chick yourself, you know."

Trish threw out a noncommittal hand. "Palmer Schmalmer. He's a jerk."

Marcy sat forward, her elbows on the desk. "Methinks the lady protesteth too much. Or something like that."

Trish scowled. "He flirted around all night, then went home with some blonde bimbo in a tube top."

"A *tube top?*" Marcy laughed. Guffawed, really, but she toned it down quickly to a mere laugh. She'd been working to get that uncouth laugh out of her lexicon of sounds for years now.

"Oh, you know, one of those sequined, two-piece, strapless dress things but it looked for all the world like a tube top to me. The man has no taste whatsoever."

"You think he should have gone home with a different blonde, then?" Marcy picked a pencil up between two fingers and tapped it absently on the blotter. She tried not to dwell on the idea of contacting Truman about the pictures, but her mind kept straying back to it.

"I think he shouldn't spread himself quite so thin." Trish's expression was arch. "Besides, I see what you're doing. You're trying to distract me from your close encounter with the construction worker. Do I sense some evasion going on? And why would that be?"

But at that point Marcy had distracted her with the facts Truman had given her, and the details of the case that was beginning to develop quite nicely.

Now, staring at her answering machine, Marcy felt confused. Just hearing his voice sent chills up her spine. Those good, stomach-quivering chills that simultaneously produce pleasure and pain. Those chills, however, were exactly the reason she should avoid him. She wanted to get in touch with him about the pictures, but common sense said if she couldn't keep her hands off him she should find another witness.

But she *could* keep her hands off him, she told herself. This was ridiculous, treating the situation as if she had no will, no control, no power to change things. So there was some mutual attraction and it had gotten out of hand. Surely they could get past that, couldn't they? Certainly Truman seemed to think so.

She stopped breathing for a second and put a hand to her throat. She pushed the repeat button and listened to the message once more.

Was the reason "it *can't* happen again" because he wasn't going to see her anymore? Wasn't going to help her?

Why did she end up spending so much time analyzing the word *can't* when it came from Truman Fleming?

She exhaled slowly. Maybe it was best if he decided not to help her. She'd already spent too much time agonizing over what Win Downey would say if the truth were ever to come out that she had . . . uh . . . *consorted* with a witness. So how could she still consider using him as a witness?

If she *didn't* use him as a witness, there'd be no reason not to . . . consort with—or even date—him, would there?

At this her stomach flipped over—and not in a good way.

She couldn't *date* Truman Fleming. He was a construction worker. He lived in a slum. He drove a barely running pickup truck, now that he wasn't snarling around on a *Harley*. He was everything she'd worked her whole life to avoid, or, more accurately, to escape from.

She covered her face with one hand, picturing another guy on a motorcycle. A younger guy. A boy named John Calabresi, who was the bad boy of Georges Heights, the dismal little neighborhood east of Washington in which she'd grown up. She had wanted John Calabresi with a passion, but he'd wanted—and subsequently impregnated—Marcy's best friend, Karen Lipnicki. That's when Marcy learned what became of girls who succumbed to their desire for bad boys.

Even at the tender young age of fourteen Marcy had known that she wanted out of Georges Heights and the miserable life that went on there. Girls routinely got pregnant in high school, married their ne'er-do-well boyfriends, and lived hard, angry lives of dissatisfaction.

That's what had happened to her mother. Her father, devoid of ambition just like Truman, spent Marcy's early years going to various construction jobs. Then, after getting fired from all of those, for reasons ranging from drunkenness to absenteeism, he'd spent the next fifteen years lying on the couch with a beer, while Marcy's mother worked two, sometimes three, jobs.

That was *not* what would happen to Marcy. She was going to find a guy with some integrity, some determination, and a career he wouldn't give up for life on the couch with a beer.

She'd sworn off John Calabresi then and she'd swear off Tru Fleming now.

So, she concluded with no small amount of determination, as long as she was swearing off Truman Fleming there was no reason she couldn't have him for a witness.

* * *

Truman knocked on the door of Marcy's apartment, then rubbed his hands together. Damp palms, he noted. That would be impressive.

He hadn't heard from her since he'd left his message the day before, but then, why would she respond? And how? He knew full well that if he hadn't told her it would never happen again she'd have told him the same thing. As far as he was concerned, the best defense was a good offense.

Nothing seemed to be happening behind the door so he knocked louder. He'd slipped past the doorman again—noting this time with some concern how easy it was—because he preferred to see Marcy's unplanned reaction to him. But now he thought the doorman might have saved him a long trip up that impossibly slow elevator.

He knocked a third time and at long last there was some rustling behind the door. He glanced at his watch: eight thirty P.M. Could he have caught her with a date? Maybe they'd been . . . busy, or something.

Footsteps approached. Marcy opened the door.

She was still in a suit but her hair was mussed in back. Her eyes looked puffy, as if she'd been sleeping.

"Uh, hi." Truman's mind went momentarily blank at the sight of her. She probably looked just as pretty in the morning . . .

He ran a hand through his hair, though he'd just combed it, and tried to glance discreetly behind her to see if anyone else was there. "Sorry to disturb you. Have you got a minute?"

Her brows drew together and she blinked several times quickly. "What have you got against the doorman?"

"Nothing. I just don't like to put anyone out. After all, *I* know I'm not a burglar."

"I think they're more worried about solicitors." She stepped back from the door and motioned him in.

"That explains why he's not very hard to get by. I'd keep that in mind if I were you. The place could be teeming with unsavory characters."

"Clearly." She looked at him wryly. "I've already decided to start using the peephole." She led him into the living room. "How's Folly?"

He followed her into the apartment. The air smelled like fresh-cut flowers, though he saw none as he looked around. He noted the way the drapes matched the furniture, which matched the carpet, which matched the walls. All were white. Including the decorative sticks in the vase.

"She's great. I got her a bone so she won't chew on the furniture." He turned back to her.

"A bone?" Marcy looked at him with concern. "They'll splinter, you know, and can—"

"Relax. It was a fake bone. She's fine."

They stood awkwardly a moment until Marcy said, "I got your message."

"I figured you did."

She looked at him frankly. He liked the way she did that.

"And I agree with it completely," she said.

In her dark purple suit, with her dark hair sticking

up in back and her eyes puffy from sleep, she just didn't go with the apartment. In fact, his whole image of her didn't go with the apartment. She had so much more life and personality. The apartment was . . . sterile. Like a hotel room. Designed to be tolerated by many people and loved by none.

He wondered about that. Was there nothing she loved. Or was there a reason she didn't want to show it?

He cleared his throat. "I figured you would."

"I was hoping, however, that it didn't mean you were no longer going to help me. I have a few questions about the pictures you took, for one thing."

He spread his arms out to the sides. "I'm here, aren't I?"

Her lips curved. "You certainly are. And with very little warning. I'm tempted to get you a phone just to make things easier on myself."

So there it was, he thought. Slipped onto the table just that easily. The I've-got-money-and-you-don't gauntlet. The let-me-fix-you attitude. Let me fix you and then maybe I'll let you kiss me without panicking.

He crossed his arms over his chest. "I don't need your help."

She shook her head and ran a hand over her hair, discovering the tangle in back. "I know. I know. I'm sorry—"

"Fact is I like not having a phone."

One hand fooled with the knot. "I'm sure you do. I didn't mean—"

"And I like not being beholden to anyone."

"I kn—"

"And I don't think—"

"Oh for pity's sake," she interrupted, digging her fingers into her hair in frustration. "Lighten up, Fleming. It was a *joke*."

He paused. "Sure, I know you think it was, sugar. But the fact is you got to be careful what you say to people. How you joke."

She abandoned the knot and this time it was she who crossed her arms over her chest, her expression darkening. "You call me *sugar* and you're trying to tell me how to talk to people?"

He shrugged. "I'm just trying to help you. I don't think you have any idea how someone like you comes across to someone like me."

She laughed once, disbelieving, and shook her head. "I know a lot more about *someone like you* than you know about *someone like me*, let me tell you, Truman Fleming. And if there's one thing I hate it's someone trying to tell me how to act."

"I'm not telling you how to act. I just wanna help you see how the real world is, sweetheart." He arched a brow and looked pointedly around the room. "It might help you relate a little better to . . ." He wanted to say "the world" but he amended it at the last minute. "Your client. Not to mention the jury, which I'm sure you'll be hoping to stock with salt-of-the-earth types like myself."

"Give me a break. First of all, it's going to be a bench trial, not a jury trial. And second of all, my eyes are open, Fleming. So while they are and we're on the subject, let me just help *you* out a little. You might want to reconsider the disparaging uses of *sugar* and *honey* and *sweetheart* because you apparently have no idea how you're coming across to someone like me. Someone, that is to say, female."

He smiled slightly, letting his gaze return from the room to rest on her lovely flushed face. "I know exactly how I'm coming across to you."

The unspoken *sugar* hung in the air for so long he might as well have said it.

"Wait here," she said then, abruptly, and walked around him to disappear down the hallway.

Tru stood motionless in the room for a moment. Was she calling security? Unleashing a pit bull? Getting a gun?

Finally, he let his eyes wander from the hallway to examine the room while she was gone. Even the throw cushions on the couch were white. He was glad to see, however, a pair of dark purple pumps askew on the floor by the loveseat. A token bit of clutter, but it made him feel better.

He strolled toward the window when his attention was caught by an abstract painting hanging over the couch. It was huge, white with beige blotches, and, well, he didn't pretend to know a whole lot about modern art, but it was pretty damn ugly. In fact, the longer he looked at it the uglier it became, until he was so incensed by it he wondered how much she paid for it, and determined that paying for it at all would amount to an unqualified crime. He'd bet it was titled *Anger* or *Fraud* so the artist could claim to be rewarded by the average person's response to it.

He turned his back on the thing and headed toward the dining area, just off the living area and attached to a small galley kitchen to the left. The table was glass with wood—blond, of course—trim. The chairs were white leather and chrome. In the middle of the table were two white candles that had never been lit.

From there he moved to the kitchen, which was scrupulously clean. Nothing on the counters, nothing on top of the refrigerator, no magnets on the front, nothing in the sink. He bet the cabinets were sparsely stocked as well, and the refrigerator full of take-out boxes. On a whim, he opened it up and was surprised to see a bowl full of fresh salad and several bags of vegetables along with a family-size tub of yogurt. On the top shelf were two boxes of granola, a carton of skim milk, and a jug of orange juice. She was a healthy little thing.

He left the kitchen and walked back out into the living room. Blond wood bookshelves held legal tomes and textbooks, with a few novels thrown in. Thrillers, it looked like. Old ones.

He heard her enter the room behind him and turned. She'd changed clothes and now wore a pair of jeans and a pink shirt that looked like silk. Her hair was brushed and her face had a freshly scrubbed look to it.

"I didn't have a chance to change when I got home." She stopped by the couches and looked at him by the shelves. "Anything you'd like to borrow . . ." She waved a hand as if to say *go right ahead.*

"Just seeing what you had. Not much light reading here." He walked slowly toward the couch.

"Yeah, well, I don't have much time for light reading these days. Listen, I have these pictures you took." She sat down on the couch and pulled the pictures from their envelope. "Most of them I think I know what you were documenting, but there are a few . . ."

Truman sat next to her, not too close, and leaned toward the pictures she laid out on the table. Her stomach growled.

He looked at her. "You eat dinner?"

She laid one hand on her stomach and studied the pictures. "No, I just got home. Well, a little while ago. I took a quick nap."

"Come on." He stood up and held out a hand.

She looked at it as if not quite sure what it was for, and did not get up.

"Come on," he repeated impatiently. "I know just the place. It's not far from here and they've got the best half-smokes you've ever tasted in your life. Come on. My treat." He smiled.

She looked disconcerted and glanced back at the pictures.

"Bring 'em with you," he said. "We'll go over them at the restaurant. I haven't eaten either."

"Half-smokes?" Slowly, she gathered the pictures together and stood up, not taking his offered hand.

"Yeah, you know, big hot dogs?"

She rolled her eyes. "I know what a half-smoke is. It's just that those're not exactly health food."

He shook his head, with an exaggerated sigh. He was so tired of thin women getting all worked up about junk food.

"Honey—" he began. She glared at him and both his hands shot up in surrender. "Sorry. *Marcy*. You don't look like you've got anything to worry about, health-wise. Besides, they're the best half-smokes in town."

"I don't know," she said skeptically. "I've had some pretty good half-smokes."

He tilted his head and grinned, delighted. "*No*. You?"

His mood lifted even more as she picked up her purse.

"But we're going dutch treat." Her voice was firm.

"Even better." He stepped back to let her go before him. "And you can drive."

7

Tuesday, October 15
WORD-A-DAY!

BAY: n., a position from which one is unable to retreat: a position one might inadvertently have gotten oneself into because of a pretty face

They walked down the hall in silence, their footsteps soft as snowfall on the thick burgundy carpet. Truman pushed the down elevator button and stood back. The two of them looked at each other in the cloudy brass doors.

Marcy tilted her head back to look at the numbers lighting up one by one over the elevator, and Truman furtively looked at her.

Her thick dark hair tumbled around her shoulders, making him think of the night he'd touched its softness, the night he'd touched *her*. Her arms were crossed over her chest and he imagined loosening them, then loosening her jacket, her blouse, the button of her jeans . . .

The elevator dinged and Truman nearly jumped out of his skin.

Marcy shot him a puzzled glance.

The doors opened to reveal a white-haired couple

dressed in evening wear and a middle-aged man in a blue windbreaker.

Marcy stepped onto the elevator and pressed the already lit *L.* Truman felt the white-haired man's eyes on him as he followed her. With obvious disapproval, the man took in Truman's leather bomber jacket, worn jeans and scuffed-up workboots, then shifted himself and his wife closer to the back of the elevator. Away from the Bad Element, Tru knew. As if the man should be making judgments about what *anyone* wore; he had on a *cravat,* for pity's sake.

There commenced a bit of whispering between the older couple, out of which Truman thought he deciphered, "heard there was a plumbing problem" and "isn't there a freight elevator?"

The car crept slowly downward, stopping at the tenth floor for apparently no reason, then resuming its painfully slow journey. Nine . . . eight . . .

The whispering behind him continued. Truman felt his ire rising.

"So, honey, where should we go for dinner tonight?" he finally asked in a boisterous voice. He moved closer to Marcy and toyed with the idea of putting an arm around her shoulders, but that would probably be going too far.

Marcy turned as if to see whom he was talking to, then gave him a look that inquired none too subtly if he'd lost his mind.

Truman turned to the older couple with a jocular smile. "You two look like you're going out. Where you going? Someplace you'd recommend?"

The woman looked alarmed to be addressed so directly and took a sidestep closer to her husband. The two of them were practically pressed into the corner.

"We're going to a private party," the man intoned with a sniff, looking down his nose at Truman. He drew the word *private* out so long Truman thought he might have gotten lost in it.

"A private party, huh? I never get invited to those. All the parties I go to are public."

Everyone was quiet as the doors opened on the fifth floor. "Going up?" a lady with a walker asked.

"Down," the man behind Truman intoned, with heavy irony.

The doors closed. Truman silently seethed. What gave people like Mr. Cravat the right to be so superior? Money? He wanted to turn around and scoff in the man's face. People like him were the precise reason Truman had gotten as far away from wealth as possible.

He eyed Marcy next to him, with her gold earrings and Saks Fifth Avenue jacket. Well, maybe not as far as *possible.*

"I know, dear," the woman behind him said, in response to some frenzied whispering by Mr. Cravat. "I suppose we could mention something to the management. Perhaps the freight elevator is inadequately marked."

"Perhaps he can't *read*," the man stage-whispered back.

Truman looked to Marcy again, hoping to catch a sympathetic look back, but she kept her attention on the lighted numbers over the doors.

"Well, we've never seen workmen on here before," the wife continued.

Did they think Truman was deaf?

"I suppose we could go to the Watergate," Truman said to her, in a musing tone of voice, "but the *people* there are so awful."

He leaned against the side wall and glanced at Mr. Cravat and his wife. The guy next to them in the windbreaker studied the contents of his pockets, which seemed to consist mostly of a napkin, coins, and some lint.

"*Truman.*" Marcy's voice was low. She finally shot him a look, one not quite as commiserating as he'd hoped. "I thought you knew where we were going."

"Yeah, I do. Smokey Joe's. Good place. Nice people. I think you'll like it."

"Truman?" the old man murmured. His wife whispered something to him in return and they both looked at Truman with renewed expressions of curiosity.

Tru turned away, suddenly mortified. Did he *know* these people?

"Smokey Joe's is good," the windbreaker man volunteered. "I like the pulled pork barbecue."

"Pulled pork barbycue!" Tru thundered, in an exaggerated southern accent. "Now *that* sounds good, don't it, Miss P.?"

Marcy's mouth dropped open and she looked at him as if he'd suddenly whipped out a banjo and started playing Dixie.

"But us," Truman motioned to himself and Marcy, "me'n her, we're goin' for the half-smokes. Nothin' like a big ole hotdog when you're really hungry."

The elevator dinged and sank gently to a stop at the lobby. Truman felt it like a release from purgatory. Almost before the doors were open he'd taken Marcy's arm and steered her out of the car and across the lobby of the building.

"What in God's name was that all about? Are you insane?" She jerked her arm from his hand.

Truman steered her past the front doors and discreetly watched the older couple exit the building. He stopped her by one of the gold-trimmed sofas in the lobby, one armrest overshadowed by a robust ficus tree.

Once he was sure the people were gone, he closed his eyes and leaned on the back of the sofa.

"What on earth is the matter with you?"

He opened his eyes to see Marcy glaring at him. "Sorry, I was just trying to liven things up a little. You know that's about the slowest elevator on God's green earth you've got there."

She shook her head and cast her gaze to the ceiling. "Why me?" She looked back at him. "You acted like a schizophrenic. What was with all that redneck *barbycue* crap?"

"Nothing. I just—well, those people were snobs, didn't you think? They needed a little shaking up."

She started walking toward the back of the lobby. "So what? So they're snobs. Who are you? God's official shaker-upper?"

Truman followed her, considering the question. "You think He's got one of those? Because that would explain a *lot*."

She reached a door marked GARAGE and leaned back to push through it, giving him a sarcastic look while she was at it. "It certainly would."

Truman's boots echoed hollowly in the parking

garage as they walked down the second aisle. He did a little two-step to liven up the rhythm, but stopped at Marcy's quelling glance.

"Are you always so serious, Miss Paglinowski?" Tru asked, trying to relinquish his ire. This was what he got for hanging around a rich girl—he had to suffer the judgment of a pompous cravat wearer in an elevator. He should have known better. Hell, he *did* know better. He just . . . he couldn't stop seeing her, for some reason.

They reached her car and Marcy rounded the trunk to the driver's side. Truman waited on the passenger side for the quiet *shunk* of the automatic locks opening.

They got in and slammed the doors. The sound bounced off the walls of the garage, but was muted inside the car.

Marcy put the key in the ignition and turned to look at him without starting the car. "I don't know what to make of you. And yes, I guess I am always serious around unpredictable people."

"Guess I'll have to try to be more predictable, then. See if I can't make you smile once in a while."

"I would appreciate that." She looked back out the windshield, one hand gripping the steering wheel, and she started the car.

The guy was crazy. That was the problem. Not just unpredictable. *Certifiable.* He'd probably spent time at Bellevue, or Chestnut Lodge, or some other asylum for the hopelessly insane, and that was the reason he couldn't testify.

Marcy pulled the car up in front of a narrow restaurant with a foggy window on which the words SMOKEY JOE'S TAVERN had been stenciled several hard decades ago. They were on U Street, northwest, an area that was seeing some renewal but hadn't completely turned the corner yet. Marcy wasn't worried, though. This neighborhood was gentler than the one she grew up in, and was practically upscale, embassy-strewn Kalorama compared to the street that housed Truman's building.

"Is it open?" She peered across Truman, through the passenger side window, to the door. Lights were on inside but no people were visible.

"Darlin', it's always open." Truman pushed open his door and climbed out.

Marcy frowned, then followed suit. The joint lived up to its name immediately, she noted as she pushed into the foggy room. A group of men in plaid flannel coats and baseball caps belched clouds of smoke into the air from a table just inside the door. In front of them were plates piled high with partially denuded spare ribs. Cave dwellers huddled around the kill.

Several tables stood empty of people but stacked with dirty dishes. She moved through the room toward two clean tables in the back and picked the least crummy one.

A bar ran along the back wall behind her over which several patrons hung their heads, beers in front of them and cigarettes in their hands, looking like Snoopy doing his vulture imitation. Everyone in the room seemed to be smoking.

"Trust me, the food's good," Truman said as he took the seat across from her.

A waitress arrived with a wet rag and two menus. "What can I get y'all t'drink?" she asked, running the rag swiftly around the table in front of them, scattering crumbs to the chairs, the floor and their laps.

"You a beer drinker?" Truman asked Marcy.

"Yes, but—"

"Miller okay?"

She opened her mouth to say she had to work the next morning, but Truman obviously wasn't interested in that part of her reply.

"A pitcher," he nodded at the waitress.

"Comin' up." She took one last swipe at the table with the rag and swept off.

"I hope you're thirsty," Marcy said, brushing crumbs off her jacket.

"I am." He laid his menu on the table and punched a finger at it. "This is what you want, right here. With the works."

Marcy picked up her menu, looked at his selection and said, "Fine," and put the menu back down on the table.

He looked up at her. "Oh, now don't do that. I hate women who say 'fine.'"

"You hate women who say 'fine'?" she repeated, leaning back in her chair.

"Yeah, that passive-aggressive 'fine' that means anything but. I thought you were above that, Miss Marcy." He leaned back in his chair too and looked at her with what appeared to be genuine disappointment.

She pressed her lips together to keep from smiling. "Well, now you *are* getting predictable. I meant 'fine' in that your choice is fine with me. Fine, great, looks good, I'll eat it. You do a lot of judging books by their covers, don't you?"

"No I don't."

"Sure you do." She leaned forward and placed her elbows on the table. "Take that couple in the elevator, for example. You didn't like them because they looked affluent, isn't that right?"

"No, that's not right. They didn't like *me* because I *didn't* look affluent. That's when I didn't like them."

She smiled then. "Don't you think you might have been reading a little bit into their expressions?"

"It wasn't their expressions, it was what they said. Didn't you hear them? They thought someone dressed like me should be using the freight elevator."

"Oh come on." She scoffed. "I'm dressed like you."

He laughed. "Yeah, right."

"I am. We've both got jeans on, I'm also wearing a leather coat—"

"Suede," he corrected. "There's a difference. And you look nicer. You exude rich girl, right class."

Her smile broadened. "There you go judging me by my cover."

"I'm not judging you, just identifying you. But others judge you that way, I've seen it."

"Have you?"

"Yeah. And what's more, that's what you want to exude. But that's all right, I happen to like your cover."

His head was bent downward, toward the menu, but his eyes were looking back up at her. It was a very seductive look, Marcy found. She swallowed hard.

"You're saying you like the 'rich girl, right class' cover?"

He sobered a moment, seeming to study the menu despite their having already decided what to order. "That's not exactly what I said."

"Sure it is. You like it despite the fact that you have no idea if my 'cover' is representative of the real me."

One side of his mouth lifted. "I have a pretty good idea."

She laughed and looked off toward the bar. This was really funny. She wondered how far to string him along before clueing him in to the truth. Or maybe she'd never clue him in, it was too much fun seeing him so smug while being so completely wrong.

The waitress returned and Truman ordered for them both while Marcy looked on in amusement.

"So where are you from, Truman?" she asked impulsively.

He glanced up at her. "From here. Washington."

Her brows rose. "Really? Right in D.C.? Or from the area, Maryland or Virginia."

"In D.C." He inclined his head, looking at her warily. "Why do you want to know?"

She laughed and leaned forward, elbows on the table. "Don't worry, I'm not going to do a background check or anything. I'm just curious. I find you . . . interesting."

He dropped the menu and leaned back in his chair. "I find you interesting too, Miss Paglinowski."

His look sent an illicit shiver down her spine. "I also like that you pronounce my name correctly."

He grinned. "When it comes to you, I want to make

sure I get everything right. So, where are *you* from?"

"No, no," she shook her head, still half smiling. "We're not done with you yet. Have you got any siblings?"

"Only child." He crossed his arms over his chest, a bit of body language Marcy found revealing.

"Happy family? Dysfunctional? Good childhood? Bad?"

He shrugged with one shoulder. "Happy, good, I guess."

She cocked her head. "Interesting . . . Are your parents still in the area?"

He paused, his eyes narrowed and his lips curved with amusement. "Am I going to get to play this game with you?" he asked. "Because I feel like I'm giving up a lot of chips without any chance of winning something back."

The waitress arrived with the beer and plunked two mugs on the table. A splat of beer sloshed over the side of the pitcher. "Right back with your smokes," she said.

"Oh, you'll win something back," Marcy said, thinking of ways she could sidestep the truth of her own background as neatly as he was his.

His gray eyes warmed, and the slight smile on his lips suddenly seemed intimate. "I like the sound of that," he said.

Marcy blushed, realizing how he'd taken her words, and quickly leaned forward to pick up the pitcher. She poured one mug for him, then one for herself, automatically tilting the glass while she poured.

"Don't get your hopes up too high, Fleming." She put the pitcher down and raised her mug. "To not judging books by their covers."

He nodded, his eyes fairly glowing as they rested on her, and raised his glass. They touched mugs and Marcy took a long, cool draw off the beer. It tasted heavenly.

"So tell me, since I'm not allowed to guess by your appearance, why you won't testify for my client." Marcy leaned forward onto her elbows, her arms crossed in front of her on the table. "I'm not trying to pressure you, I just want to know."

Truman sighed and leaned back, letting one hand turn his mug in the wet circle at its base.

"Of course I realize you don't owe me an explanation," Marcy added, feeling some compassion for him as she looked at his downcast eyes. "It's just that my imagination has been working overtime trying to figure out why you won't, and so far I've had you both in jail and in a mental institution."

His lashes rose and he laughed, exposing those deep dimples. He looked so openly amused Marcy was relieved. So she hadn't hit any nails directly on the head, anyway.

"I don't have a great reason, except that I don't like courtrooms. I've . . . had some experience in them, let's put it that way. But no, I've never been in jail." He looked back down at his mug.

Marcy's brows rose, which he caught when he glanced back up.

He chuckled. "Nor have I been in a mental institution. Though I've a few relatives who'd like to see me in one right now. But that's beside the point."

She expelled a breath and took another sip of beer.

"Join the club. My relatives don't understand me at all. My mother's always saying she doesn't know where I came from."

Truman laughed. "That's funny, my mother says *I* don't know where I came from. So what don't your folks approve of about you?"

She shrugged and made a circle in the sloshed beer with her finger. "Oh, you know, the whole lawyer thing."

He smirked. "Went for your J.D. when you should have been going for your M.R.S.?"

She sighed. "Something like that."

"The social debutante goes public defender?"

"I never did criminal law."

"And more power to you. Go where the deep pockets are."

She bristled. "Downey, Finley and Salem does a lot of pro bono work. We also represent individuals over corporations more than the other way around, *and* the companies we do represent are socially and environmentally responsible."

Truman laughed and held up his hands. "Okay, okay. You're a bunch of saints."

Marcy felt herself blush and took another sip of beer. "I guess I'm just a little tired of the 'evil lawyer' assumption."

"Yeah, me too." He heard his own words and added quickly, "You know, living in this town you hear an awful lot of lawyer jokes. I'm kind of tired of them myself."

"How about a judge joke, then?" she asked, embarrassed at her touchiness and wanting to make light of it. "What's the difference between God and a federal judge?"

He shook his head.

"God doesn't think He's a federal judge."

Truman laughed. "I hadn't heard that one."

The waitress arrived with their food and they set to work on the half-smokes for a minute. After her first bite Truman looked at her inquiringly.

"So?"

She smiled around the mouthful. "It's good." She nodded, then swallowed. "It's really good."

They concentrated on the food for a few minutes, then Marcy put hers down, pulled a napkin from the dispenser by the wall and wiped her fingers.

"So, your whole objection to testifying is that you just don't like courtrooms?"

He gave her a wary look over his half-smoke, chewed, then answered. "Pretty much."

"What if I—"

"No."

"But I can—"

"Marcy, let's just eat first, then we can discuss the case, all right? I had kind of a rough day." He picked up the pitcher of beer. "Here, have another drink."

He filled up her mug, put the pitcher down and she picked it back up. "If you had such a rough day, then maybe you should have another drink." She filled up his mug.

He reached for the mug and held it aloft. "To new friends," he said, looking at her with what she thought was irony in his eyes.

She picked up her beer. "All right."

They touched mugs again and Truman smiled.

For a second, Marcy tried to resist, tried to remember that she was here to convince him to become a witness, not a new friend, but she couldn't hold out. She smiled back and, with that, they fell back into easy conversation.

An hour and a half later they left the restaurant, and Marcy unlocked the car with her remote.

"Listen, the reason I stopped by tonight," Truman said as they walked toward the car, "is to tell you that I met the guy who fell off the Planners project six weeks before Burton's accident."

Marcy stopped walking and looked up at him. "What?"

"Remember I told you there was a rumor someone else had fallen, same as Burton?"

She nodded, quickly determining the dramatic effect this would have on her case.

"Well, I met him. I'd been given a tip about a place to find a job, where other people who'd left Planners had gone, and right off the bat I met this guy. He's a good guy, credible, but had no idea someone else had fallen, not to mention the fact that he himself might have a suit. I told him you might get in touch with him."

Marcy stared at him. Not only had he come up with a fabulous witness, one that would, if admissible, deeply affect a judge considering whether or not Planners knew of the danger of their negligence, but he'd also given her the opportunity to bring a new case of her own into the firm. A chance to make a little rain. A chance to impress Win Downey.

Her heart pounded with excitement and her face flushed. "Truman, do you realize what you've just done for me?"

He shrugged and looked away.

"I'm serious. This is huge!" On impulse, with the excitement of a win coursing through her veins, she took him by the arm and stood on tiptoe to kiss him on the cheek.

But the touch of his skin on her lips seemed to ignite something within her. It was electric, touching Truman. She stepped back and looked away, embarrassed. Given half an instant more she would have kissed him again, only this time on the lips.

"How can I ever thank you?" she asked, moving quickly around the car to the driver's side door.

He paused at his side and looked at her over the roof of the car. To Marcy he seemed utterly unaware of the electricity between them.

"You can keep me out of the courtroom," he said.

She nodded slowly. Then paused. "But you could have a case of your own, you know. You were fired for asking about safety regulations, right?"

He started to smile and they both got in the car. "No, I believe I was fired for decking the superintendent."

She grimaced, appalled that she'd momentarily forgotten the events of that day—amazing what she could forget when she touched Truman Fleming—and put her key in the ignition.

"Well, you're still important to this case. For one thing . . ." She pulled her purse from the well of the passenger side, where she'd tossed it when she'd sat down, and dug through it for the pictures. "I need to know what a few of these photos are documenting."

This time, at least, she wasn't going to forget what her mission was.

Truman took the envelope from her hands and pulled out the pictures. Marcy tried to concentrate on the photos and not the hands that held them. The first few she understood. When he got to the middle of the pile she stopped him.

"That one. What's that?" She pointed to the picture in his left hand, brushing his thumb as she did so. Ridiculously, her heart accelerated at the contact. She was more aware than she wanted to be of how close they sat, how when she leaned over to look at the picture, her shoulder was intimately close to his.

"That's the area the contractor was talking about when he asked Lang to install the guardrails. That's where his guys were working that day." Truman laughed cynically. "I remember Lang was so hostile, saying something like 'Yeah, OSHA, my ass. I'll put guardrails up when—'" He stopped suddenly, and cleared his throat.

Marcy looked over at him. When she did, he turned his head to look at her. Their faces were inches apart.

"When what?" she asked quietly.

His lips were right there. She'd barely have to move at all to graze them with hers.

He inhaled slowly. "'When monkeys fly out my ass.'"

She blinked, then laughed slightly. "Lang said that?"

He nodded. Something in his eyes looked resigned. And tortured.

She held his gaze. "You heard him, didn't you? You were right there."

He nodded again.

Boy. She had him at bay, she thought, remembering that morning's word for the day. Sometimes that calendar was downright prophetic.

"*You're* the evidence that the subcontractor requested the required guardrails and the defendant refused," she said. "Planners not only *knew* of the violation but they *refused* to fix it. Truman, you have to testify."

Tru's lips pressed together and a muscle jumped in his jaw but he did not relinquish her gaze.

Marcy's pulse accelerated. She told herself it was because her case had just gained an incredibly strong witness, not because Truman Fleming's pale gray eyes were looking at her so deeply it seemed they'd caught something in her soul.

She swallowed, her breathing suddenly shallow.

She should move away, look away, end this moment, she thought, but every nerve reached out for the man who sat next to her in the car.

"Marcy," he said quietly. It was almost a question.

She sat frozen, wanting so badly to touch him she couldn't breathe. But she couldn't. Shouldn't. She had to control herself. It was important, she recalled in a vague way.

The moment lingered and Marcy's nerves crawled with the desire to lean forward the scant inches it would take to kiss him. The heated look in his eyes told her that's what he wanted. That, and more.

She thought she'd shake her head, tell him no. Instead she shifted forward so slightly she wasn't sure if she'd actually moved.

But she must have, because then Truman's mouth was on hers. Barely. Gently. The kiss was so feathery, yet so intimate, Marcy sighed against his lips. He pulled back a fraction, his eyes delving into hers.

There was something in them that she recognized. For one crazed moment, Marcy had the incredible feeling that she knew Truman as well as she knew herself. And he knew her. That *here* was the man she'd been hoping to find, the one who might understand her and love her anyway.

This time she closed the gap between them and their lips came together again. But there was nothing gentle about this kiss. Marcy's hands reached for his shoulders as he caught her waist and pulled her to him. Their bodies connected across the center console of the car. The parking brake dug into her thigh but even that bit of reality couldn't squelch the desire—no, the *knowledge* that this was right, that she and Truman belonged to this moment, to this determined exploration of each other.

Their tongues entwined and their breath mingled frantically. Truman's beard stubble scratched her cheek and his hands squeezed her waist as Marcy leaned into him. She felt the strength of his long fingers at her ribs and longed for them to touch her skin. But she could only get so close. Out of frustration, she reached down and released the parking brake. The car, still in park, rocked slightly forward.

They barely noticed.

Leaning across the seat, held close to Truman's chest, Marcy's shirt came loose from her jeans and as Truman's hands moved downward his fingers touched skin at the small of her back.

Marcy inhaled sharply and held his face with her hands, kissing him deeply. Vaguely, in the back of her mind, she thought she should stop this before it went too far, but she couldn't. Not yet. She just wanted that contact, that feeling of Truman's hands on her bare flesh.

His fingers slipped under her shirt and she pressed herself against him. He lost no time in moving that hand around her ribcage to her breast and she gasped as his thumb found the peak of her breast through her bra.

In one quick move, Truman readjusted their bodies so that Marcy was practically in his lap, reclined against his arm, and he was leaning over kissing her, her arms around his neck. Their mouths engaged in this soul-stirring kiss as Truman's hand lightly explored the sensitive skin along the line of her bra. Marcy trembled, nearly arching beneath his touch, wanting him to move the stupid undergarment out of the way and touch her, take her, hold her with nothing between them.

But that would be too far, wouldn't it? some persistently rational part of her brain queried. Stop it at the kiss, she thought desperately. Do not go any further. Stop it now and it would just be a kiss . . . they'd gotten past a kiss before . . .

But then he was pushing her shirt up, over her breasts, and the cool air felt like another caress, arousing new sensations, provoking a desire that was already nearly out of her control. His fingers moved her bra and found her nipple. She moaned, leaning her head back against the car door. The windows were completely fogged, she noticed, glad of the fact that she couldn't see the dim lights of Smokey Joe's so Smokey Joe's couldn't see her.

But the momentary thought made her pause. This couldn't happen. It was ridiculous, making out in a car on a city street, when—

Truman's head bent forward and he took her breast in his mouth.

Marcy's thoughts flew out the window.

She plunged her fingers into his hair and closed her eyes. It was heaven, nirvana, a release she hadn't felt in months, *years*. Her body was possessed not by her, but by some inner creature that thrived on passion and had been starved for too long. A creature that could not now be controlled.

And besides, this was *Truman*. The guy with the stunning eyes, the gorgeous, capable hands, the body that arrested her attention by just walking down the street. Truman, whose smile transformed his face, whose knowing glance could send a shiver down her spine in the middle of a diner. Truman, who saved her, and who could, she knew in her heart, be trusted with anything . . .

Truman's hand trailed down her belly, making her skin quiver as he titillated every nerve. His fingers neared the waistband of her jeans and she shuddered.

This was no good—or too good. He was not right for her. If she backed off now it was just a kiss—and a little groping. Okay, his tongue was doing amazing—she gasped as his lips pulled lightly on her nipple—*incredible* things to her breast, but that was still . . . it wasn't below the . . .

He unbuttoned her jeans.

She flushed—a shot of heat straight down through her center.

His fingers prodded gently under her jeans, pushing beneath her panties, causing the zipper to descend with his hand.

She grabbed his wrist. She should stop this, before . . .

But, *oh God,* she wanted him to touch her *there.* She couldn't stop him, not before, not until . . .

She held tight to his wrist but did not pull his hand away. He parted her legs with a short downward push and then his fingers slid into that area so suffused with heat and desire Marcy could not stop herself from pushing her hips up into his hand, and pushing his hand into her heat.

She gulped a lungful of air and he moved his lips back to hers. She kissed him hungrily as his fingers toyed with her, making her arch and move and cling to him as if she were drowning and he was her only salvation.

"Let's go to your apartment," Truman said quietly against her lips.

She might have said no. She might have used the interruption to bring them both down to earth. It was a golden opportunity to come to her senses.

Except that the instant after he said the words, he leaned upward and oh-so-gently kissed her on the forehead. When he pulled back, his fingers slowing but still doing miraculous things, she saw that the look in his eyes was one she'd longed to see her whole life. The look of a man who *saw her*, the real her, without any of the background noise of her past, her future, her career, her life . . .

She rose slowly, composed herself as quickly and cursorily as she could, and drove to her apartment.

The elevator doors closed them in and Truman, wanting to do anything to keep her from changing her mind, turned to take her in his arms.

At the same moment Marcy turned too, and they

clutched each other as if, instead of ascending toward her apartment, the cable had been cut and they were hurtling to the ground.

Truman's lips found hers again and her fingers plunged into his hair. They kissed as if they were inhaling the elixir of life from each other's lungs. As if the time they had to be parted from the car to the elevator had been too much to bear.

Truman's muscles quaked with the effort not to crush her to him. She was like no one he'd ever held before, the emotion in his chest something far beyond the usual wave of lust he felt for a woman. No, this feeling was something else. This was a desire like survival, an instinct so powerful he had no choice but to obey it.

The doors opened and they made their way down a hallway so silent Truman thought the thundering of his heart might awaken every neighbor on the floor.

Marcy dug into her purse for her keys, then unlocked the deadbolt with a hand that Truman saw trembling.

Would she change her mind now? he wondered. Something in him sank at the thought that she might.

But she pushed the door open and held it as he followed her in. She didn't turn on a light, but took his hand and led him down the hallway toward her bedroom.

Carefully coordinated pictures passed him on the hallway walls, but as he rounded the doorjamb into her bedroom he saw that *here* was where the real Marcy lived. Unlike the stark, white impersonality of the rest of the apartment, this room was crammed with mismatched furniture, frothy curtains, overgrown plants, framed snapshots and knick-knacks that would have clashed gloriously with the studied tone of the living room.

Marcy moved away from him to turn on a dim light, a small Tiffany-style lamp on a bedside table littered with books. In the moment they stood apart, Truman's heightened senses noted that these were not the law books and aging thrillers that resided on the living-room shelves. These had colorful covers and titles in curling script. These were novels that the passionate Marcy read.

The Marcy who went to sleep every night in the wide, canopied bed that sent Truman's pulse shooting into the unhealthy range.

He held his breath as she walked silently back to him across the carpet of the bedroom.

Never in his wildest dreams did he think they'd get to this point.

Okay, maybe in his *wildest* dreams . . .

He looked into her eyes, into the dark, sultry depths that concealed so much and yet communicated so eloquently. She wanted him, he thought, with something like awe. She looked at him so intently, so ardently, that he knew there was no chance she'd change her mind.

She was, he thought, incredibly beautiful.

He took her upper arms in his hands when she got close and made her pause. She looked up at him questioningly. He wanted to say something to her, something perfect that would reveal the astonishing emotions rocketing around in his chest at this moment, but no words came.

Instead he leaned down, his hands cradling her face, and kissed her again, a long, deep, lingering kiss that he hoped might convey some of what he was feeling, not just the physical desire.

But Marcy's hands moved to the button of his jeans and he . . . well, hell, who was he to argue?

His hands moved down her arms, his thumbs grazing her breasts, then down the curve of her waist to pull the pink shirt from her jeans once again. He snaked his hands under the material to her skin, his palms touching her, just as she released the zipper of his jeans, and they both inhaled sharply with pleasure.

Truman walked her backward to the bed and sat her down, pulling her shirt up over her head. He loved the way her hair fluttered messily as the shirt came off. Her cheeks were flushed and her eyes were dark and alive. He thought he'd never seen anything so seductive.

She pushed his jeans down his legs and he stepped out of them, then eased her back down on the bed. Stripping off his shirt, he watched as she unbuttoned her own jeans and pushed them off. Then they were both casting their clothing off as if they couldn't do it fast enough.

They came together, naked, at last, and Truman knew he had never felt so incredible in his life. She was unbelievably soft, and yet so strong when her arms moved around his shoulders and pulled him close that he was sure, like himself, no questions lingered in her mind as to whether this was right or wrong, smart or stupid, sensible or dangerous.

He dipped his head to her neck and tasted the skin below her ear. He felt her shudder as she tilted her head back and he moved his lips lower. His hands cupped her breasts and he moved his mouth to one peak, taking the nipple into his mouth and working the tip with his tongue. He thought he heard her gasp, and then her hands were in his hair, holding him close, her pelvis pushing upward.

He moved his hands down her sides and trailed one

hand across her hip. She jumped lightly when he touched her inner thigh, but she pressed upward again as he moved his fingers back to the heat at the apex of her thighs.

She was more than ready for him, just as she had been in the car. He pushed his fingers gently inside of her, then moved them out and across the point he knew she longed for him to touch again. She made a low sound deep in her throat and he continued.

"Truman," she breathed.

Truman moved back up her body and kissed her with a fierceness she returned so emphatically a thrill streaked down his spine. He was rock hard, and started to guide himself toward her when he felt her hand move between them to grasp his manhood in a light, sure grip.

He inhaled sharply.

She guided him toward her and he pushed upward, sliding so swiftly inside of her he was afraid he would hurt her.

But she arched upward, saying, "Don't stop. Oh God, don't ever stop."

Which is when Truman let go of all control.

He pushed into her, some inner will demanding the act be fulfilling, their bodies connected, their movements conjoined.

At the same time Marcy clung to him, making sounds of pleasure beneath him. She was lithe and potent, her body finding his rhythm and accelerating his arousal with every thrust. She seemed to anticipate his moves as her hips drove against his. She was like a woman from a dream, sent to stimulate him in ways he'd never known. The two of them moved as if they were one organism. One beating heart.

Their sweat mingled, their breaths came and went in synch, their hands sought each other and held tight, until Truman came with such intensity that he cried out.

The next moment Marcy arched upward and called his name, shuddering with release.

In the morning, Marcy awoke, heavy with a delicious sort of languor, and gazed about the room. She needed to hold on to the feeling as long as she could because it would not last, she knew. Self-recrimination would come. But for now she clung to the feeling that last night was good and right. Clung to it as if she'd never feel it again.

Which was possible, because Truman was gone.

8

Tuesday, October 22

WORD-A-DAY!

GENEALOGY: n., study of one's descent from a person or family; connections which are quite often inexplicable or impossible to account for

Marcy stabbed her key in the lock, twisted the knob, and kicked the door open. Dropping her briefcase, purse, and three plastic grocery bags, she lunged for the phone, catching it just as the machine started to pick up.

She blew a breathless "hello" into the receiver as the machine labored to reset itself.

"Marcy? That you? Do I have the right number? I dialed two-oh-two—"

"It's me, Mom." She closed her eyes and put a hand to her forehead, pushing the hair from her eyes. She had *not* been hoping it was Truman. She had just thought it *might* be him. Not the same thing as hope at all. But, all right if it *was* hope, it would be hope that he had called with a reason—a really excellent reason—why he hadn't called before this.

"It don't sound like you. Everything all right?"

"Everything's fine, Mom. I just walked in the door."

She bent to pick up her grocery bags and tucked the cordless phone between her ear and shoulder.

"What? Just now? It's near nine o'clock. You out on a date, I hope? Working in a place like that you oughta be meeting a lotta rich young men."

"I was working. And I'd never date someone I work with." An image of Tru Fleming on the witness stand flashed through her mind. *What a mistake*, she thought for the thousandth time, caving in to her desires like that.

It just hadn't *felt* like a mistake.

"So you're still not dating anyone? Marcy, I told you when you went to that school, that *law school*"—she said it the way she'd say *Leavenworth Prison*—"that you was throwing away the best years a your life. Such a pretty girl, everyone says, and there you go spending all your time in that office. Mark my words, one day you're gonna wake up and be thirty and not know what hit you."

Marcy could practically mouth the words along with her mother. She heard this tirade nearly every time the woman called.

"I haven't woken up to that day yet," Marcy said, heaving the grocery bags onto the glass dining room table. One of the candles on the table fell out of its holder. She bent to push it back in. She really ought to melt a little of each into the base to hold them there, she thought. "And for your information, just the other day someone told me I was one hot chick. So I guess I don't have to worry too much yet, Mom."

She thought of the way Truman had looked at her as she'd taken off her clothes, and blushed hotly despite the fact that she was alone.

"Well, looking young ain't the same as being young, missy." Marcy heard water running in the background as her mother spoke. "Your face ain't the only part turning thirty. You want kids, you better start looking around and fast."

"What on earth would I want with kids?" Marcy unloaded a bag of onions into the bottom drawer of the refrigerator. "I'd just spend my life calling them up and harassing them over the phone, probably."

"There's worse ways to spend your life."

Marcy smiled. Her mother turned off the water and Marcy thought she heard dishes clinking. "You certainly seem to enjoy it. How's Darren?"

Darren, Marcy's youngest brother, had just gotten out of juvey—the juvenile detention center—a month ago on his eighteenth birthday. He'd started robbing houses at the ripe old age of thirteen and been caught red-handed when he was fifteen. By that time he'd burgled so many he was lucky he only got juvey, in Marcy's opinion.

"He's all right," her mother said. "They set him up with a job, them social workers. He likes it all right."

"Good."

"Mitchell's living with that girl now, you know, that redhead." Water sloshed in the background. She was obviously washing dishes.

Marcy shoved a milk carton and two bottles of water into her refrigerator. Like mother, like daughter, she thought. Chatting on the phone was a waste of time if you weren't doing something else at the same time.

"Which redhead? Mitch only goes out with redheads." Her older brother was a notorious runaround. While he only dated redheads, he'd cheat on them with just about anyone.

"The real one."

Marcy laughed. "*That* narrows it down considerably. Good, I guess. Glad he's settling down."

"Yeah, ever since they fired him down at the laundry he's been happy as a clam. She works at the bottling plant, you know."

Marcy rolled her eyes. Like father, like son. "What did he get fired for this time? No, you know what? Never mind. I don't even want to know. So what's up with you, Mom, anything? How's Dad?"

"Don't talk to me about that no-good louse. He ain't been home since Saturday. Someone told me they seen him at the track nearly every day this week. I told him not to come home if he lost any more money, so I guess he lost more money."

"Well, at least he's listening to you these days."

Her mother laughed. Marcy smiled to hear it.

"That's my girl," her mother said. "Looking on the bright side. Listen, hon, Uncle Bruce is having a birthday party for Aunt Phyllis. I thought you might wanna show for it. Aunt Phyl's turning sixty this year. You know she's older than your Uncle Bruce by a few years."

"Is she really? Uncle Bruce looks like he's got ten years on her."

"Oh, she worries him to death, always nagging him about this or that. Giving him gray hair, she is. She oughta be glad she's got him. Leastways he comes home at night, and don't leave his paycheck with the horses."

"Maybe all that nagging's what's keeping him on the

straight and narrow." Marcy sat down on one of the leather-and-chrome chairs and lit one of the candles in the middle of the table. Holding it sideways, she let the wax drip into the candle holder.

"If it is, he's the strangest man in America. Nagging don't work at all on your daddy. Any case, I think you should bring a date, honey, just to show Aunt Phyllis you ain't one a them lesions."

A burst of laughter shot from Marcy, jostling the hand holding the candle. She scratched at the quickly cooling dollop of wax on the glass table. "Lesbians, Mom. Aunt Phyl doesn't think I'm a lesbian."

"I don't know . . ." She drew the words out ominously. "Last time I was over there, I guess it was day before yesterday, she looked *very suspicious* when I told her I didn't know if you was dating anyone right now. Very suspicious."

"Oh, *Mother*." She picked at the wax with a fingernail, then crumbled it onto a paper towel in front of her. Truman hadn't called her since she'd slept with him. Chances were *he* wouldn't be her date to any family functions in the near future. Not that she wanted him to be. They both knew it was wrong. That's why he'd left before she woke up. And that's why he hadn't called. She had known that's how it would be when she'd dragged him into her bedroom. Hadn't she?

"Well, you know how she was after she found out about Celia."

"Just because her daughter turned out to be gay doesn't mean everyone who doesn't happen to be dating is. Besides, who cares what Aunt Phyl thinks?"

"Well, I do, because I gotta listen to her talk. But the

party's Saturday, so you set about finding yourself someone to bring. They think they're gonna be cooking out but I heard it's gonna rain."

Marcy sighed and pushed the candle into the stick. "What time?"

"Six. And bring a salad. You know, potato, macaroni, something like that. But if you get it at Giant make sure you put it in your own bowl. You know how Aunt Phyl hates store-bought food."

"Sure, Mom." She lit the other candle.

"Promise me you won't forget to bring a date. I'm sicka standing up for you kids. Think of your poor old mother. What with Darren and everything I want something I can be proud of."

"Can't you be proud of what I do, Mom? I mean, I know it's not childbearing, but . . ."

"I'm not talking about childbearing!" she protested over the clanking of what sounded like a pot and some silverware. "You know I'm proud of what you do."

Marcy felt disproportionately pleased by this statement. Her mother's praise was rare when it came to her career.

"But you know," her mother added, and Marcy sighed. "A lot of men get scared off by career women, 'specially ones with a big high-powered job like yours. No, seeing my girl with a nice boy would suit me just fine."

"I'll see, Mom." She dripped wax into the other candle holder.

Someone knocked on her door. Marcy's heart leapt. Only one person she knew arrived at her door unannounced.

"Mom, listen, I've gotta go. Someone's at the door." She blew out the second candle and stuck it back in the holder, her heart racing.

"All right, but don't forget Saturday! Bring a date! And a salad!"

"Bye . . ."

Marcy pushed the phone's off button. If only a date were as easy to get as a salad, she thought, and started for the door. Passing by the powder room, she paused, and with only a slight second thought ducked in to check herself in the mirror.

Now remember, she told herself, don't let him seduce you back into bed, not even if he has a really *good* excuse for not calling. Even if it's dramatic, unarguable, and hopefully, believeable.

She pinched her cheeks and wiped a finger under each eye to get rid of mascara smudges, then moved to the door, smoothing her hands down her skirt.

The knocking sounded again. Heavy, insistent. She had the thought that something might be wrong and opened the door wide.

Her heart hit her stomach on the way to her feet.

Standing in the dimly lit burgundy hallway was Guido. *Or rather, Arthur*, she told herself. Thinking of him as Arthur made him much less intimidating.

"Uh, Miss Paggalousy," he said in his thug accent. He gave a shallow bow. "I don't know if you remember me, we met in the diner down on D Street. Guido. Guido Crumpton."

Her brows shot up. Guido *Crumpton?* A guy with a neck like a watermelon and a head like a pea and she might not remember him?

She swallowed and looked at him warily. "Sure. Yeah, I remember you, Guido. Something I can do for you?"

Where the hell was Javier, anyway? It had been annoying enough when Truman slipped by him, but *this* was a serious security breach.

Guido moved forward, heedless of the fact that Marcy had closed the door to the width of her body. As he continued toward her she had no choice but to back up or hold her ground and see if he had a weapon to brandish.

She backed up.

He wore a black suit this time, with those wide, chalk-type pinstripes, and his cologne was so strong it nearly knocked her over. He stood in her foyer—an area designated by a square of parquet flooring instead of walls—and trailed his beady black eyes around her apartment. Unfortunately, it was all too obvious she was alone.

"I'm just, uh, checking in with you, Miss Paggalousy—"

"Paglinowski." She tried to affect a cool air.

"Yeah, Miss P., that all right? So yeah, I'm just checking in with you. Just wanna make sure you ain't been getting into any trouble or nothing."

She inhaled slowly and shook her head. "I'm not looking for any trouble, Mr. Crumpton."

"Please." He held one hand up and graced her with a greasy smile. "Guido."

She smiled tentatively. "Guido, then. I've never been looking for trouble. I've just been doing my job."

He laid a hand on his chest and made as if to bow again, but stopped short. "Just as I am, Miss P. Doing my job."

She narrowed her eyes. "Which is . . . ?"

He stepped further into the apartment, reaching the white carpet and looking down the hallway. He turned back with a smile. "Making sure you ain't getting into no trouble. Like I said."

"Oh, sure. Well, no, I'm not. Getting into any trouble." One of her hands still rested on the knob of the open door. No one passed by in the hall. Of course. No one ever passed by in the hall. She often felt as if she lived in the building all by herself. Guido could be revving up a chainsaw and no one would emerge.

After taking a few more steps into the room and looking into the dining area Guido finally turned back to her and jutted his chin out. "You got a boyfriend, Miss P.?"

She had the brief thought he could be moonlighting for her mother. "Yes, in fact, I do. I do have a boyfriend. In fact, he's coming over tonight. I don't know what's keeping him. He's bringing Chinese. Food. You know." For a second she envisioned Truman showing up with an army of Chinese soldiers. Then, remembering she was upset with Truman, she asked more bluntly and bravely than she'd intended, "What is it you want, anyway?"

To her surprise, Guido appeared to blush. Or maybe flush with rage. "Just what I told you. Checkin' in. Makin' sure everything's okay. Everything's okay, right?"

She nodded.

"Then I guess I'll just be going now. Since your boyfriend's coming and all." He came toward her, his bulk swaying slightly with his duck-footed walk.

She watched him nervously.

He passed close by her, then stopped in the doorway. "You have a nice night, Miss P."

She nodded vaguely.

"All right?" he insisted, jutting his chin toward her.

"Yeah, okay. Sure."

He put his hands in his jacket pockets. *Now,* Marcy thought, *now's the time he's going to pull out his weapon.* But he just left his hands in his pockets and sauntered down the hallway.

Marcy closed the door behind him, shot the bolt, attached the chain and leaned back against the door, exhaling hard. What in God's name was *that* all about? Was this guy dangerous or what? His visit had turned out pretty innocuous, she told herself. *Just makin' sure everything's okay.* Then why was her heart thundering so wildly? And why were her palms sweating?

She waited a few minutes, regulated her breathing, then grabbed the phone and called the front desk.

"Javier? Did a big man in a black suit just leave the building?"

"Big man? Black suit?"

She rolled her eyes. What did he *do* down there? "Yes. Uh, dark, slicked-back hair. *Lots* of cologne."

"Ah!" Javier laughed his strangely high-pitched laugh. "Big *smelly* man! *Sí,* he just left."

"Thank you." She exhaled and hung up the phone. Then she grabbed her jacket and purse.

She had to talk to Truman. The hell with being mad at him. She could deal with that later. Right now, only Truman would know what sort of threat this guy was.

The knock on the door, followed by Folly's tongue all over his face, woke Truman from a nap. He'd been dreaming about Marcy, one of a series of disturbing dreams he'd had about her this week, which was why he was having to take a nap on a Tuesday evening. In all of them, she was telling him that sleeping together had been a mistake—that she'd only done it because she'd never slept with a construction worker before. Try as he might to tell himself that these were just dreams, he couldn't shake the idea that he'd tapped into the truth. Which was one reason he hadn't contacted her. If she came to him, he'd been thinking, then maybe he could trust that the emotion he'd seen in her eyes last week was real. Then, maybe, just maybe, he'd believe the princess could fall for the pauper.

Folly licked him in the face then dashed for the door, coming back to lick him in the face again and run back to the door, her nails sliding and scratching on the wood floor. Truman wiped his face with one hand.

The dog was just calming down when the knocking commenced again and Truman rolled off the couch trying vainly to straighten his hair while shaking the grogginess from his head. It had to be her. Nobody else visited him. Nobody else knew where he was.

He stretched and stepped quickly across the living room to open the front door.

He nearly slammed it shut again, out of disbelief mixed with a healthy dose of disappointment. But he didn't. He wouldn't do that. He couldn't.

Not to his own mother.

She stood, regal and silver-haired, clothed in navy blue Chanel and clouded in Joy perfume. She was flanked by her chauffeur, Kenneth, who held two brown paper grocery bags, out of which everything from celery to bread protruded.

"Truman." Her voice held a familiar note of disapproval, which she always managed to tinge with surprise so he could feel he'd disappointed her in some new and unexpected way. "You look awful." She turned to her chauffeur. "He looks awful, doesn't he, Kenneth?"

Kenneth gave Truman a sympathetic look and said, "Yes, ma'am."

Folly sniffed at his mother's hem, then turned to Kenneth and jumped up, sniffing the bottom of a grocery bag.

"Folly, *no*." Truman leaned forward and grabbed the dog's collar, hauling her back into the apartment.

His mother cast a jaundiced eye on the animal.

"What the devil is that?"

"It's a dog, Mother. Hang on, let me get her out of the way." He and Folly tripped and stumbled to the bedroom—Folly doing her best to return to the door and Truman doing his best to prevent her—and shut her in. She whined, scratching pitifully at the door, and Truman rolled his eyes. *Women*.

He returned to find his mother still standing at the door, like a newspaper subscription collector.

She glared at him as he came back into view. "What on earth is the matter with you? Why do you persist in living this wretched life?"

These were not questions and he was not expected to answer, he knew.

"Kenneth," she continued, "take the bags to the kitchen. If there is one." She peered around Truman as if an army of rats might jump her if she stepped into the room.

"You're looking well, Mother," he said, leaning forward to kiss her on the cheek. "This is a surprise."

She looked at him skeptically but allowed the kiss. "I imagine it is. I had Reginald looking for you for weeks and now I understand why he had such a time of it. Nobody would look in this place except as a last resort."

Reginald was his mother's butler. She'd hired him a few years ago after the death of Truman's father, saying she needed a man around the house, and Reginald fit the bill perfectly. He was a jack-of-all trades while maintaining the highest standards of decorum, this last being the most important skill in his repertoire, according to Mrs. Fleming.

Behind the door across the hall a shouting match in Spanish erupted. The voices rose quickly, a man and a woman, and then a baby began to cry. Truman's mother looked over her shoulder in distaste.

"Care to come in?" he asked mildly.

She stepped over the threshold, her shoes dipping into the apartment as slowly as a timid swimmer's feet.

She looked around the room slowly. Truman didn't need to watch her to know what she felt, so he simply stood there, trying to wake up.

After a moment Kenneth emerged from the kitchen and went wordlessly out the front door.

"Honestly, Truman. What are you doing?" His mother turned to him with an expression of profound sadness. "Couldn't you have looked for the meaning of life on a trip through Europe, or South America? Even the Australian outback? Why does it take *this*?" She fanned a hand out, palm up, and displayed the room for him.

"Because I'm not looking for the meaning of life, Mother." He sighed and walked toward the couch, but he didn't sit down. He couldn't, much as he wanted to show the distance he had found between them. Remaining standing until a lady was seated had been ingrained in him since birth by this very lady.

"Then what *are* you looking for? If it's anything other than cockroaches there has to be a better place than this." She shook her head.

Kenneth came through the door with three more bags of groceries and disappeared into the kitchen. They were quiet for the few minutes it took him to deposit them and come back through the living room. He slipped back out the door.

Truman wondered if the limo was sitting out there open between trips, and if so, how many bags of groceries disappeared every time Kenneth came back into the apartment.

"Mother, I told you when I left what I was doing."

"No, you didn't. You said you didn't know what you were doing. And now I see how completely true that was."

"Actually, I said I didn't know what I was looking for. Not specifically. But I told you I wanted a different experience, a new perspective."

"Heavens, Truman, you could have gotten that any number of ways without resorting to this. And now where are you? Have you learned anything? Is your career any further along? Has your life"—she cast a majestically skeptical look around the room—"*improved* at all from this venture?"

Truman sighed. "My life has broadened. So yes, in that sense it has improved."

"Broadened," she scoffed.

"Mother, I've spent my entire life meeting the same kinds of people, going to the same kinds of parties, having the same conversations year in and year out. Don't you understand why I might want to do something different?"

"Of course I do!" She strode into the room, affronted, and cast a wary eye at the couch before deciding to sit down on the sagging armchair.

Truman sat opposite her on the couch, forward in the seat with his arms on his knees. At least she seemed to be listening to him this time. When he'd first told her of his plan to ditch everything and see how "the other half lived," as she put it, she'd gone off on a tirade that had brooked no interruption. She was against the idea and had no desire to understand anything about it.

Now she held up a bejeweled hand and wagged a coral red–tipped finger at him. "I lived in Italy and Greece for several years, traveled all over Europe, I've been to India and Egypt and Kenya and Japan. Lebanon, even! Oh, you should have *seen* Beirut. It breaks my heart what they've done to it."

Tru smiled gently. "I know, Mother."

Her hawk-gray eyes were back on him in a flash. "No, you don't, or you wouldn't be living in this hovel. My point is that to truly get perspective you should see how other *peoples* live, experience other cultures—"

"But what about *our* 'peoples,' Mother? This country is teeming with lives we'll never understand, never even see. Hell, you probably don't even know how your chauffeur lives. And yet people like Dad were running the country and making laws affecting these people."

"Your father was an excellent senator, God rest his soul. He took into consideration every single one of his constituents when he voted on bills. By God, some campaign years I thought he tried to personally meet and shake hands with every single one of his constituents."

Truman raised a brow. "Shaking hands with someone doesn't show you how they live."

Kenneth came back through the room with another armload of groceries. Against his will, Truman's stomach growled.

His mother glared at Truman and waited for Kenneth to pass through before continuing. "Truman, no matter what you say, I will never think living here is good for you. Your career should be skyrocketing right now, and what are you doing? Working in some filthy low-paying profession. Did you know that Palmer Roe just bought his *third* vacation home?"

Truman laughed. "Where's this one? On the tenth fairway at Augusta?"

Palmer couldn't have had a more apt name. Or rather, more apt initials. His middle name was Aaron, and "PAR" Roe was well known for spending more time on the golf course than in the office.

"You've become quite the snob, haven't you?" his mother accused.

Truman could only issue a breathless, incredulous laugh.

"Don't you think those people you work with now

would give their eyeteeth to have what you have?" she continued. "Wouldn't they drop their shovels in a second, and take your desk for even a fraction of the salary you used to make?"

He shook his head. "It doesn't matter. I don't care what they would do in my place. I'm doing something for myself. For my *own* edification."

But she didn't want to hear it. She waived a hand, erasing everything he'd had to say. "A man your age should be looking for a suitable woman and settling down. People your age should have children, for goodness' sake! Who are you going to meet in a place like this?"

Tru thought of Marcy and smiled slightly. "Oh, you'd be surprised."

His mother snorted delicately. "I'd be horrified, more likely. This place is probably teeming with gold diggers. It would have to be!"

"She can't be a gold digger if she doesn't know I've got any gold, Mother. Unlike the women I used to meet." He thought about Laura, a woman he'd been temporarily fooled by several years back. She had said all the right things, had all the right opinions, but when Truman had started looking to join the Peace Corps, and had suggested they enlist together, she'd dropped him like a hot potato. Shortly thereafter, she'd gotten married to Christopher Hildreth Higgins IV, and the last Truman had heard of her she was president of the Kalorama Garden Club, spearheading an effort to put window boxes on the "ugly, rundown houses in Southeast." She called the program "Petunias for the Poor" and apparently ousted from the group a woman who suggested they replace petunias with potatoes in the hope of feeding a few of the poor.

Truman's mother leaned forward and looked at him with renewed awareness, her manicured hands clutching the arms of the chair like a couple of gold-encrusted talons. "Are you saying you've met someone? Are you . . ." She looked around the apartment as if he might have stashed someone somewhere. ". . . *dating* someone around here?"

He thought of Marcy, how eminently *suitable* she would be to his mother. How eminently *un*suitable she was for him, for the person he wanted to be.

"What if I were, Mother? What if I were dating the Hispanic single mother upstairs? Would you accept that? What if I were in love with her? What would you think of that?"

The color rose so high in his mother's cheeks Truman was worried he might be compromising her health.

"And *are* you dating this Hispanic single mother upstairs?" She seemed to be holding her breath, but the lapels of her suit jacket trembled.

He sighed. "No, Mother. I was just—"

"No. Of course you aren't." She sat back in her chair, her color returning to normal. "And do you know why?"

He just looked at her, fatigued by the whole conversation.

"Because you and she have nothing in common, that's why. You'd have nothing to talk about. And you wouldn't understand each other at all. This is why people marry within their own circles. Shared backgrounds, shared histories, shared experiences and values."

"Shared billing in the Washington Social Register."

"There is nothing wrong with the Social Register, Truman Foster Fleming. Who taught you to be so superior?"

Kenneth came back from the kitchen and went out the front door again.

"How much stuff did you buy?" Truman asked, walking to the front window and peering through the dusty venetian blinds. Outside, a small knot of children had gathered to watch the limo and the uniformed man hauling a seemingly endless stream of groceries out of it.

"Just enough to get you through a week or two."

Truman watched Kenneth pluck three more bags from the car and come back toward the apartment. "Maybe we should help him. How much more has he got?"

His mother rose and walked toward the kitchen. A moment later Kenneth came back through the door.

"How many more have you got, Kenneth?" Truman asked.

"This is it, sir. I'm afraid I haven't put much away, just the frozen things. I wasn't sure where you would want things."

"Don't bother putting any of it away, Kenneth," Truman's mother said, re-emerging from the kitchen. "We've got to get going and Truman needs the practice. He's obviously eaten nothing but take-out since he moved."

Truman smiled cynically. As if he could afford take-out.

"Truman, darling, I hate for things to be so contentious

between us." She came toward him and laid a hand on his cheek. "But you really must come to your senses soon. You're my only son. I want to see you settled and happy."

"I am happy." He kissed her cheek.

"Don't be ridiculous." She kissed him back and turned to Kenneth. "No one could be happy here, could they, Kenneth?"

"No, ma'am."

Truman held his hand out to the chauffeur. "Good to see you, Kenneth. I hope you won't mind keeping my whereabouts to yourself, at least for now."

They shook hands. "Of course, sir."

"And Mother, please tell Reginald the same thing. I just want to be left alone for a while."

His mother laughed and headed for the door. "Heavens, Truman, do you think I want anyone to know you're *here*?"

9

Tuesday, October 22
WORD-A-DAY!

BONUS WORD
PECKSNIFF: n., a contemptible, often hypocritical, individual; very like one who claims to be pursuing one end while actually pursuing another more advantageous to him or herself

Marcy drove thoughtfully along the city streets, sure of her route, but questioning her motives.

She wasn't *that* afraid of Guido, she had to admit. If she was, she'd have immediately filed for a temporary restraining order against the guy. No, when it came to Guido she mostly had the feeling she might learn something from the thug. If he was keeping tabs on her, then she would, in a way, be keeping tabs on Planners. His actions could be an interesting gauge of how strong her case was.

They weren't scared yet, she knew, based on the benign nature of their goon's little visit, but they would be once they got wind of her evidence. If Guido's behavior escalated, then she'd know she was hitting a nerve, and she'd think more seriously about a restraining order.

So why was she driving to Tru Fleming's house at nine-thirty on a Tuesday night? To give him a piece of her mind about not calling her? No, she thought firmly, she was not that petty. She was going to treat this as casually as he did.

And she was going to make sure it *never* happened again.

So. The reason she was going to Truman Fleming's house at nine-thirty on a Tuesday night was to ask him how much of a threat Guido really was, of course. Truman had known the man when they'd met in the diner. And Truman had known how to call him off. So maybe Truman was the man Marcy needed to have around to make sure everyone played fair. Fight thug with thug.

Not that Truman was a *thug*, exactly. But he was big, strong, and seemed able to speak goon, when he wanted to.

She pulled up in front of his apartment, across the street from Truman's truck. At the end of the street a long shiny black car turned the corner with excessive caution, disappearing behind a decaying block of rowhouses. No doubt a pimpmobile, she thought. It had that sleek limo look, and who else but a pimp would have a limo in this neighborhood?

Across the street a group of kids stood watching the car drive away. All eyes turned to her, however, when she got out of her car and pushed the doorlock and alarm buttons, causing the lights to flash and the alarm to give a little *whoop* of confirmation.

"Down, boy. Stay," she said to the backseat, as if a large Doberman were crouched inside.

She strode up the cracked cement walkway and pulled open the door to the building. The smell of Mexican food wafted out of the apartment across from Truman's. It was all she needed to realize she hadn't eaten dinner, again.

He answered the door immediately upon her knock, on his face a wary expression that immediately turned to surprise, then something else. Guilt, it looked like, which was exactly what he should be feeling.

"Expecting someone else?" she asked, shifting her purse higher up on her shoulder.

His hair was slightly wet and pushed back from his face, as if he'd just splashed himself with water and run his hands through his hair. With its length away from his face his great eyes and high cheekbones stood out even more.

"No." He shook his head, then dipped it once to the side. One lock of hair from that long-ago cut grazed his eyebrow. "Well, sort of. I thought you might be someone else, but you're not. Which is good." He stepped back with a smile. "Very good. Come on in."

She entered the apartment, looking around. Did he have someone here? Was that the reason for the odd expression?

"I'm sorry to bother you. Again, I would have called, but . . ." She turned around in the center of the room as he closed the door.

"No problem. I was just . . . ah . . . putting away some groceries." He gestured vaguely with one hand to the side and that odd expression came back to his face.

"Please, don't let me interrupt," she said coolly, wishing she could tell if he was happy to see her or not. "Where's Folly?"

"She's in the bedroom. I didn't want her to bother . . ." His voice trailed off and he looked around the room as if a bunch of people had just inexplicably disappeared. "Anyone."

Marcy opened her mouth to reply but he continued quickly.

"That is, I didn't want her getting into the food. The groceries."

She studied him warily. "Well, don't let me stop you from putting them away."

"No, it's all right, I think all the frozen stuff's been unloaded and anything else can wait. Folly's okay in the bedroom for now." He moved toward her and touched her arm, motioning her to sit in the armchair. Marcy's breath caught at the contact but she disguised it by nearly tripping over herself to sit in the chair.

Truman sat on the couch. "I'm glad you came. Really glad."

Marcy inhaled slowly to get her pulse back to normal and was about to speak when she noticed the scent of perfume in the air. It seemed to be coming from the chair.

She looked down at it suspiciously. He'd just had a woman here. That's why he looked so odd. She felt herself flush furiously. Truman's expression looked guilty. Mercy felt whatever hope she might have had that he'd have a good reason for not calling her shrink to a hard kernel of anger.

"Can I get you something to drink? I'm pretty sure I probably have something this time," he said, rubbing his hands together in front of him.

She studied him just a second too long, in an attempt to make him squirm and keep talking, possibly revealing that he had, in fact, had a woman here. But he clammed up. None of her cheap prosecutorial tricks ever worked on him.

"Sure, something to drink would be fine." She sat

forward to loosen the way her skirt had caught under her—showing entirely too much leg—but he misinterpreted her movement.

"No, no! Don't get up." He practically leaped to his feet. "I'll get it. Let me just, uh, see what I have. Hang tight there for a minute."

He held a palm out to her—a *stay* command—and walked across the room. Marcy watched him with narrowed eyes. After a second's consideration, she rose and followed him into the kitchen.

There, in that tiny room, Truman stood lost amidst a sea of grocery bags. They covered the counters, the floor, and two more sat in the sink. Even the little spider plant on the windowsill was crowded by what looked like an ice cream bag.

"What did you do? Rob a bank?" she asked, staring incredulously at the abundance.

He whirled, a definite blush staining his cheeks. "Unfortunately, these bags are not filled with money."

"The grocery store, then?" She put her hands on her hips. Not that it was any of her business, but this was just weird.

"My, uh . . ." He held a hand out in the direction of the street and paused.

Marcy wondered if he'd been planning to say his girlfriend just dropped it all off. Then she remembered the limo. Good God, did he have a *prostitute* here?

Revulsion swept her.

But no. She frowned. Not only did Truman not seem like the hooker type, he certainly had the looks to be able to find free sex whenever he wanted it. She was living proof of that. In any case, the food still didn't make any sense. Hookers didn't generally deliver. And the way she understood it, you didn't have to go out of your way to impress a prostitute before . . . well, whatever.

"Your . . . ?" she prompted.

"My, uh, delivery service," he said, turning away from her to look in one of the bags in the sink.

"You have a *delivery service*?" She looked around the kitchen. "Truman, you barely have any furniture. What are you doing with a delivery service?"

"My . . . truck's not running?" He looked at her hopefully.

"I just parked right across the street from it. What, do you need it towed?"

He shook his head, eyeing her oddly. "No, I can fix it. I just haven't had a chance."

"How will you get to work in the morning?"

"Oh, I'll fix it before work." He nodded confidently.

"So, you can fix the car in a jiffy before work tomorrow, but you needed this"—she spread her arms wide to encompass the gargantuan horn of plenty before them—"tonight, and so badly that you called a delivery service?"

He studied her a second, then donned an irked expression. "Hey, what's with the third degree? Maybe you should have taken off your lawyer suit before going visiting."

She crossed her arms over her chest. "I only have lawyer suits."

He laughed once. "Don't I know it." He surveyed the kitchen again, then poked a hand in a bag on the floor. A second later he emerged triumphant with a six-pack of root beer. "Ha! She always knows what I like." He grinned, then squelched it when he caught the look on Marcy's face.

"She does?" *Good lord, does he have a—what would you call it?—a sugar mama?* "And how often do you use this delivery service?" Her voice dripped sarcasm.

He peeled two cans from their plastic rings and handed one to Marcy, pointedly not answering her question.

"I don't think she brought any ice," he said, popping the top on his. "Uptown Girl's gonna have to drink her soda warm."

"Listen, Fleming, before you exhaust any more brain cells coming up with lame excuses for why women are bringing you food, one reason I came by tonight is to tell you not to expect a repeat of the other night anytime soon. I think we both know it was a mistake, an impulse, so let's just get past it right now. We have work to do."

Truman just stared at her, seemingly frozen. "An impulse," he repeated.

She nodded once. "That's right. We were both . . . curious about each other. But that's all, right?"

Truman looked down at the soda in his hand and chuckled dryly. "Yeah, right. I'd never done it with a lawyer before."

Marcy swallowed hard, surprised by the depth of hurt his words caused.

Truman looked up at her and his expression softened. "Hey, I'm sorry. I didn't mean that. Listen, if you're upset because I didn't call, I can explain."

"I don't want you to explain, Truman," she said too quickly, thinking, *What are you saying? Of course you do!* "The other night can't be repeated for a whole bunch of reasons, not the least of which is that you're a witness for my case now."

Truman took one step toward her and touched her arm. "What if I wasn't?"

She stepped back but wouldn't look at him. She took a deep breath, wondering the same thing. What if he wasn't her witness? Did she want a relationship with this man?

"But you are," she said firmly. "Besides, there's another reason I stopped by." She turned away. "Let's go sit in the living room."

"I came by because I have some, well, news, I guess you could call it."

Truman walked behind her into the living room and couldn't help noticing the impeccable tailoring of her skirt. She had great hips and a tight little behind, but both of those paled in comparison to her perfectly shaped legs. It was a shame he knew just how perfect the rest of that body was, he thought, now that she'd decided to deny the turn their relationship had taken.

It didn't surprise him, and he knew she was bluffing but it disappointed him just the same.

"News?" he repeated.

She sat, then he sat. He wondered what would have happened if she'd arrived five minutes earlier, when she would have run into an obviously wealthy matron and her uniformed chauffeur in his apartment. If she had discovered the woman was his mother would she still be so determined to keep things platonic? Or would he have suddenly looked less like a witness and more like a prospect?

Marcy took a sip of her soda, then rested it on the arm of the chair. She looked at the can. "Yes. I got a visit tonight from Guido, do you remember him?"

He frowned, then realized who she meant. "Arthur? The guy from the coffee shop?"

She nodded and looked up at him, her eyes concerned. "He's still calling himself Guido."

Tru sat forward. "What did he say?"

"It was strange. He said he was just checking up on me, making sure I wasn't getting into any trouble. I assume he meant messing with Planners again, but he made no outright statements or threats to that effect."

"Did he make threats to *any* effect?" Truman's ire rose.

Arthur Crumpton was a wimp of the first order. The only people he could scare were the ones who didn't know him at all and could be intimidated by his size. His gangster style of dress didn't hurt any, either. Speak to him for ten minutes, however, or call his bluff, and it was immediately obvious he had nothing to back up his appearance.

Marcy's brows knit. "That's hard to say. The whole visit seemed kind of like a threat to me. I mean, why would he come at all if not to scare me? He showed up at my door without checking in with the doorman, then bulldozed his way right into the apartment."

"He forced his way in?" Truman was so incensed it was all he could do not to jump to his feet and go have a word with "Guido" right now.

"Not exactly. But I definitely had the feeling he would, if I'd tried to keep him out."

"What did he do once he was in? He didn't *touch* you,

did he?" Truman eyed her intently, looking for the slightest twitch, the tell that would give away any fudging of details. Women like Marcy didn't like men thinking they'd found themselves in a situation they couldn't handle.

Not that she couldn't handle Arthur. She just didn't know it.

"No, no. Nothing like that. He just . . . he came in and said he was checking up. Oh! Then he asked if I had a boyfriend."

"What did you say?"

"I said yes, of course." She flashed a quick smile.

Truman's heart sank. "You do? I mean, you did? You told him that?"

"What else was I going to say?" she asked. Truman's heart rose. "I also said he was on his way over, after which Guido—uh, Arthur—said he had to go."

"So he didn't threaten you, didn't ask you specifically about Planners or your interest in it, didn't ask for anything, just said he was checking up, asked if you had a boyfriend, and left?"

She nodded. "You've got it. That's about it. What do you think?"

Truman shrugged, thinking Planners had hired an imbecile. If they truly wanted to scare Marcy off the case, Arthur Crumpton ultimately wasn't going to be able to do it. Marcy was nervous now, but she wouldn't be after another encounter or two.

"I mean," she continued, leaning forward and peering into his face, "do you think he's dangerous? Could he, do you think he'd actually *do* anything?"

Truman started to scoff when a little devil on his

shoulder stopped him. "Is that why you came over here? Because you were scared?" The idea touched him.

She straightened up, her expression considering. "Yes, but, well, no. I mean, that *is* why I came here. Because you seemed to know something about Arthur. But I wasn't exactly scared. I guess I just need to know if I should be."

This was a tricky line to walk, Truman thought. He didn't want her to be afraid, didn't want to engrave his reservation in hell by lying just to scare her, but then again, he liked that she came to him for help. Really liked it. It was as if her mind was telling her one thing about him, but her heart was saying something else entirely. Maybe Truman just needed to wait until her mind realized her heart was right.

He rubbed a hand along his jaw, the scratch of stubble satisfying. He loved not shaving every day.

"I could see him becoming a nuisance," he started.

"A nuisance, but not a danger?"

He glanced over at her. She wasn't scared. Not plucky Marcy P. Not the girl who'd taken on Chuck Lang over a puppy. Would it be so bad to fabricate a little something, just a tiny hint of barely possible danger, so that she might think rejecting Truman wasn't such a good idea? Or would that be too devious?

"Well, that's hard to say. I don't know what he was hired to do, exactly." That much was true, at least. "He probably knows you live alone. He probably knows where you work. He definitely knows your car from that day with the camera."

Her hands twined together. The idea of a stalker was not sitting well with her.

"So what's he going to do with all that information?" he asked rhetorically. "Hard to say."

"I thought he might be a good way for me to gauge the effect my case is having on Planners. The more often I see Guido, the closer I am to damaging them."

Truman frowned. "I hope that won't be true. I mean, because your case is pretty strong. I'd hate to think that on the cusp of victory Guido suddenly gets the order to do something drastic."

Marcy's expression went perplexed.

"What?" Truman asked.

"'On the cusp of victory'?" she repeated. "How can you talk like an ignorant redneck sometimes, then turn around at others and say something that could come from the mouth of a tenured historian?"

Truman's cheeks heated. She was too quick and he was a lousy liar. But it was important, now more than ever, to keep up the charade. Because despite all she'd said and done, he still held onto the hope that Marcy might be the woman to fall in love with him for *himself* and not his money.

"Listen, tell you what I'll do." He hated to use techniques learned from his father, but he knew that if you didn't want to answer a question you just pretended it had never been asked. "I'll talk to Arthur. I think I can find him and I think I can make him talk. Let me see what I can discover and let you know."

The look of relief on her face was more than gratifying. It was guilt-inducing. She couldn't look so relieved if she hadn't been afraid, could she? He was pure evil, he thought, allowing her to fear someone she needn't fear.

Still, he didn't tell her that.

"Thank you, Truman." She stood up and held out her hand to shake.

He took it with a wry smile. From her bed to a handshake in one short week. "You're welcome," he said, holding her hand just a second too long.

They left his apartment and strolled at a leisurely pace down the sidewalk to her car.

"I do appreciate your help," Marcy said, as they neared her car and slowed.

"No problem. How 'bout if we meet Thursday night, I'll let you know what I've found out."

"Thursday?" She reached for her purse, dug through it and pulled out a Daytimer. She flipped to Thursday and ran a neatly clipped fingernail down the entries.

Truman remembered the day he threw his Franklin Planner in the trash. It was the most liberated he'd felt in years.

"Friday's better," she said. "I've got a dinner meeting Thursday, and client cocktails Wednesday . . ." She looked up. "Well, you probably couldn't do tomorrow anyway, could you?"

"Depends on Guido. Let's do Friday."

"Friday it is." She pulled the pen from the leather sling and wrote it down.

They stood there awkwardly. Truman debated taking her by the arms and kissing her good-bye. Would she pull away? he wondered, but something else stopped him. Was he really the only person she could come to when she felt unsafe?

"Well, thank you again, Truman." She nodded, started to hold out her hand, then switched the gesture to pat him uneasily on the arm.

He smiled. "You're welcome. And Marcy?"

She had started to turn away but stopped. Truman stepped closer and gently took her by the shoulders. He bent and kissed her softly on the cheek, then said quietly, near her ear, "You can trust me."

She looked quickly up at him, then glanced away. "I know." She walked around to the driver's door and got in, starting the car and putting it into gear almost simultaneously.

He watched her go, then went slowly back into his apartment.

He had some groceries to put away.

Truman found Guido with considerably less effort than he'd thought he'd have to expend. Arthur Crumpton was listed in the phone book and lived just over the line in Maryland. When Truman dialed the number, Arthur's pugnacious voice answered on the first ring.

Truman hung up, of course. He just wanted to be sure he'd found the right Arthur Crumpton, not warn him he was coming.

Pulling up to the small postwar brick rambler with the tidy green lawn, Truman was surprised to find that Arthur appeared to be a homeowner. It was tough to picture the big man with a weed whacker.

He parked the truck on the street, walked across the springy front lawn to the door, and pushed the lighted doorbell. On the door was a welcome wreath complete with plastic birds and fake flowers. Truman was starting to think he must have the wrong house, when the door opened to reveal a small, rotund, white-haired woman.

"Hello," she said in a granny voice with a granny smile. She wore a checkered apron over a flowered housedress.

Truman glanced past her into the house, caught a glimpse of a sideboard covered with framed pictures and a wall with a crucifix on it. "Uh, hello. I'm looking for Arthur, is he home?"

Her face lit up. "Of course. Are you one of Arthur's friends?" She had something of a New Jersey accent, like Arthur's, but her little voice had none of the gangster in it.

"Yeah. Sort of." He pushed his hands into his pockets, feeling like Eddie Haskell. He'd come over here ready to break "Guido's" neck for threatening Marcy. Now he felt like the neighborhood bully picking on the Beav. "Are you Mrs. Crumpton?" he asked, still unreasonably hoping he had the wrong house, the wrong Arthur, the wrong granny.

"Yes, and what's your name, young man?" She smiled up at him as she held the door and he passed through it. She wore clip-on earrings shaped like daisies.

He scratched one side of his face. "Gui—uh, Arthur knows me as Harley from the job site."

"Well, let me get him for you, Harley. Arthur?" she wandered off down a hallway calling.

Truman exhaled and looked around the living room. Powder-blue carpet complemented a blue and rose couch covered with dainty throw pillows. Two matching wing chairs flanked it. Truman could hardly imagine Arthur sitting on the furniture, let alone living in the neat little house.

From the kitchen came the smell of browning onions. One of Truman's favorite smells.

A moment later Granny Crumpton came back down the hallway followed by Arthur, looking grotesquely large behind his diminutive mother. He wore black sweatpants stretched to capacity and a yellow T-shirt two sizes too small from King's Dominion theme park.

He spotted Truman and looked embarrassed. "Whadda you doin' here, Harley?"

Mrs. Crumpton smiled up at him. Truman looked at her uneasily.

"I just wanted to talk to you about something, Arthur. If you've got a minute."

Arthur tugged his T-shirt further down over his belly. "I dunno. I guess so."

They both looked expectantly at Mrs. Crumpton.

"Oh, don't you boys mind me. I can take a hint. I'll just leave you two alone," she said with a wave, and shuffled back toward the kitchen. Before she got there, though, she stopped and turned back with an impish smile. "How 'bout I bring you both some iced tea. Would you like that?"

"Not now, Mom," Arthur groaned.

Truman shook his head. "No, thank you, ma'am."

She tipped her head, still smiling. "All right, if you're sure."

"We're sure, Mom. Jeez." Arthur rolled his eyes. Once his mother had disappeared he gestured to Truman. "C'mon out here. Quick, before she invites you to dinner."

The way the house smelled, Truman wasn't so sure that would be a bad thing.

He followed Arthur through the living room to a sliding glass door at the back. As they passed through the room, Truman noted a corner cabinet filled with baby dolls and glass rabbits. Beside it sat a tall wooden basket filled with yarn.

Arthur stepped out onto a cement patio and Truman followed, sliding the glass door shut behind him. The choice of seating was a picnic table and a turquoise-and-white porch swing hanging from a rust-pocked chrome frame. Arthur sat down on the latter. Truman eyed the sagging frame as he did, expecting the top bar to snap at any moment. He sat on the bench of the picnic table, far enough away that he wouldn't be hit by any flying parts from the soon-to-be-decimated swing.

"So, whaddya want?" Arthur asked. One foot pushed against the ground so his huge bulk moved gently back and forth on the swing.

Truman frowned. It was hard to feel threatening with Arthur looking the way he did. Using a little imagination, Truman could picture him twenty years and three hundred pounds ago, a fat, dirty kid on a porch swing as his mother cooked dinner.

"I wanna talk to you about Marcy Paglinowski," Truman said, crossing his arms over his chest and trying to feel tough. "The lawyer."

Arthur reddened and looked at his own hand. One finger peeled a layer of paint off the arm of the swing. "Yeah? What about her?"

"I think you know, Arthur. How come you keep threatening her?"

Arthur looked up sharply. "That what she thought? I was threatenin' her?"

"Well, yeah." Truman looked at him, confused. "First

you go after her in the diner, then you show up at her apartment. What's she supposed to think?"

He shrugged. An obstinate child. "I dunno. Not that."

"Come on, Arthur. Get real here. We both know Lang's paying you to scare her."

He shrugged again. "No he ain't. Not exactly."

Truman leaned forward, elbows on his knees. "What does that mean, 'not exactly'? It's not Lang? Is it Planners?"

Arthur's flat little eyes met Truman's. "Planners got it in for Ms. Paggalousy, you got that right."

"Paglinowski," Truman corrected, irritated on her behalf. It wasn't *that* hard to say.

"Yeah, well, whatever. Your girlfriend."

Truman scoffed. "She's not . . . Never mind. So what does Planners have in mind to do to her?"

"They got connections. Plenty a connections, Lang says, and he would know, ya know? And they wanna make her look real bad."

"Make her look bad? To who?"

"Everyone." He said it as if Truman were an idiot. "If she sues Planners they gonna make sure the judge don't like it, her client don't like it, and most of all her bosses don't like it. They think they can get Miss Paggalinousy to lose her job over this one. So really, I'd be doin' a good thing, performing a service, ya know, if I got her to stop suing 'em."

Anger started a slow burn in Truman's gut. He'd known there were some OSHA violations at the site, but he'd assumed it had been Lang's fault, lazy son of a bitch that he was. Hearing it was company-endorsed infuriated him. "So you were sent to her apartment to scare her off the case?"

"Actually," Arthur said, holding one finger aloft, "it's a *condo*. A condominium. Miss Paggalin—Paglanin—Miss P's doin' real good 'cause she prob'ly owns it, see?"

Truman looked at him for one long fatigued minute before saying, "I know what a condominium is, Arthur."

"Well, then you know if she loses her job, then she loses her place, see? Then she's, like, ruined, ya know?"

"So you were sent there to threaten her with that?" Truman asked, wondering why Arthur didn't say anything like this to Marcy.

Arthur shrugged again and looked toward the house. Truman glanced toward the house, too, and saw Mrs. Crumpton inside the kitchen window. She waved an oven-mitted hand at them. Truman and Arthur waved back. He half expected her to poke her head out and call them both in to dinner.

"Arthur," Truman warned. "I need to know what you were doing there, at her apart—at her condo. And I need to know *now*." He donned what he thought might be a menacing expression.

Arthur looked back down at his hand and the paint scratching began anew. "I just, you know, I think she's cute."

Truman felt the wind in his self-righteous sails diminish. "You . . . what?"

Arthur looked narrowly up at him. "She ain't your girlfriend, really, is she? I mean, I know you hang out with her sometimes, but you an' she ain't really . . . you know." He made a semi-lewd gesture with one fist.

Truman's eyes flashed to the kitchen window. "Jesus, Arthur. Your mother's right there." He tipped his head toward the house.

Arthur ducked and looked back at the window, where his mother waved that oven-mitted hand at them again. Truman almost laughed.

Arthur turned back to Tru, expression belligerent. "Well, *are* you?"

"Am I what?"

Arthur made the gesture again, with wide sarcastic eyes. "With Miss P."

"No." Truman gave him a disgusted look. Not that he hadn't done just what Arthur implied, but he didn't like anyone gesturing like that about Marcy.

"Well, then, I just went over there 'cause I wanted to see her again. You know, maybe ask her out if the, uh, climate got right. If ya know what I mean." He grinned and Truman winced to think of him taking Marcy out.

"And did the 'climate' get right?" Truman was sure of the answer but an irrational pang of jealousy shot through him just the same.

Arthur scrunched his lips to one side. "Naw. She's too rich to look at someone like me."

Truman did laugh slightly then. So even Arthur Crumpton knew the perils of dating a rich girl.

"What's so funny?" Arthur asked defensively, sitting up straighter and puffing his chest out as if he could look more manly there on his turquoise-and-white porch swing with his mother inside cooking his dinner.

"Nothing." Tru shook his head. "Just, she's too rich for me, too."

Arthur nodded in commiseration.

"So, what, are you giving up now?" Truman asked. "She's made it clear she's not interested, right?"

Arthur looked so sad then that Truman actually felt sorry for him.

"I mean, she's made it clear to me, too," Tru said, deciding to take pity on the poor oaf, "so I'm just packin' it in, you know. Who needs to be rejected by some snobby lawyer time and again?"

Arthur looked at him hopefully. "You givin' up?"

Truman shrugged. "Yeah, sure. Why should I beat my head against a brick wall?"

Arthur smiled, a disconcerting sight. "Okay, well, I'm glad you told me that."

Truman stood up, feeling as if he'd given millions to a charity. "Just one more question, Arthur. I want to be sure I got my facts straight. It's Planners that's out to get Marcy? Not just Lang?"

Arthur stood up too. "Oh, it ain't just Lang. He's just the one givin' the orders, you know? He told me so himself. It's Planners. Them guys at the top. Or somewhere."

Truman nodded, dismayed and incensed. Little did Marcy know, but Arthur "Guido" Crumpton should be the least of her worries.

They stepped back inside the house and Mrs. Crumpton scurried out from the kitchen to meet them.

"My, isn't this good timing!" she exclaimed. "Dinner is just ready. You boys go wash up now and come sit down at the table. Harley, I've already set a place for you and I won't take no for an answer."

Truman glanced back at Arthur, who shrugged and started through the kitchen.

"Bathroom's this way," Arthur said.

Tru looked again at Mrs. Crumpton.

"It's fried chicken with mashed potatoes and onion gravy," she said.

Truman smiled at her. "All right, then," he said, and followed Arthur's path through the kitchen to wash up.

10

Friday, October 25

WORD-A-DAY!

NYCTALOPIA: n., blindness after dark; or perhaps the naïve belief that events transpiring late at night are not strictly considered to have occurred

Friday afternoon Marcy barely left her office. That morning she'd met briefly with Win to tell him about Donnie Molloy's testimony and subsequent case of his own, and he'd been very encouraging about the work she was doing on *Burton v. Planners Building & Design.* She might even have impressed him with the information about Donnie, and that had motivated her like nothing else.

So she'd been drafting documents and working on points to cover in discovery all afternoon.

Planners's attorneys had rejected her renewed overtures to talk about a settlement, which didn't surprise her, so it was full speed ahead with the suit. The case was already on the docket, with a trial date less than two months away.

That wasn't the only reason she stuck close to her

desk. Halfway through the day Marcy had realized she and Truman had never decided *where* they were going to meet, let alone when. So she stayed in her office—foregoing even her afternoon Diet Coke from the machine down the hall—hoping he'd call.

She felt like she was in high school.

At quarter to five the phone rang.

"I'm sure you don't normally leave as early as five like the rest of the world," his quiet voice said, "but I thought we could meet at five thirty."

Marcy willed her pulse to stay slow. "Five thirty's fine." She leaned back in her desk chair, taking her first full breath of the afternoon. "Where?"

"Pockets Pool Hall."

She could hear the smile in his voice.

"Pockets Pool Hall," she repeated, somewhat deflated. "Why there?"

"Because they've got a great happy hour buffet. Hottest chicken wings you've ever tasted. Plus I figure I can take you for a few bucks with a couple of games of eight ball."

She massaged the back of her neck with one hand. "Did you talk to Guido?"

"In fact, I did talk to Arthur. He was . . . well, let's just say he's not the toughest nut to crack."

She would've liked to have seen Truman grilling Arthur. Based on Arthur's reaction to him in the diner, Marcy was sure Tru was in total control of the interview. Still, she asked, "He have anything interesting to say?"

"Five thirty, Miss P. I'll tell you what I know."

She sighed. She was hoping they could meet somewhere over here, like Restaurant Nora or even Childe

Harold, near her apartment. Some quiet place where they could discuss things over a half-decent bottle of wine. The idea of shouting over the clatterings of a pool hall while wrestling with some orange chicken wings just tired her out.

"Listen, Truman, it's going to be hard to talk in a pool hall. If it's just the free food you're after why don't you come over here and I'll buy?"

Silence gripped the line.

"You know, in exchange for your coming all the way over to this part of town," she added quickly. "Not to mention tracking down Arthur for me."

"Tracking down Arthur was easy," he said.

She could picture the look on his face, that half-defensive, half-disappointed one she'd seen when she flippantly said she'd rather buy him a phone than not be able to get hold of him.

"All right." She laid her head in one hand, elbow on her desk. Was she ever this stubborn about letting someone do something for her? Probably. "Where is this Pockets?"

He gave her the address—an okay part of Southwest—and said, "Five thirty," hanging up like a spy whose communication device would self-destruct if he took any more time.

Marcy stood up, bending backwards to stretch her back. Though it was short, it had been a good day. The rest would have to wait until tomorrow, she thought, pushing papers back into the various legal accordion files.

Someone knocked on her door. She called for them to come in and one of the secretaries from down the hall entered.

"Oh, hi, Jan, what's up?" Marcy asked.

Jan's face was apologetic. "I took a message for you earlier today and then completely forgot. I'm so sorry." The girl looked tired and harried, pushing her brown bangs up off her face where they stayed in an asymmetrical salute. She read off the pink message slip in her hand. "It was your mother. She wanted to remind you about the party tomorrow. And to tell you *not* to forget a salad. She was quite insistent on that last part." Jan looked worried, and handed her the message. "I hope it wasn't urgent. She didn't say to call back or anything."

Marcy shook her head, knowing the salad was her mother's code for *date*. "It's no problem. She's just after me to go to a family picnic. I'd just as soon not talk to her about it again, to tell you the truth." She looked at Jan in concern. "Is everything all right? You look exhausted. Anything I can do?"

Jan exhaled heavily. "Not unless you know any good caterers with nothing to do a week from Tuesday. Fotherington Banquets, the ones who are supposed to be catering the firm's fall party? They canceled today and I've called *dozens* of others and nobody can put something together that quickly."

"They canceled *today*? My God, that's just criminal. What is it, ten days away?"

"Eleven. I've told every caterer it's just hors d'oeuves, finger food, sort of a little client-firm, post-dinner happy hour, but I've been turned down by so many people I'm really getting frantic. I'm starting to believe I'll be spending next weekend making pigs in blankets."

Marcy shook her head, thought about offering to help

her—she at least knew how to cook pigs in blankets—but with the cases on her desk right now there was no way she could spend a weekend making hors d'oeuves. "How many people are supposed to come?"

Jan sighed. "Around a hundred and fifty."

"Oh my God. That's a lot of pigs."

Jan laughed. "Yeah. Well, better get back on the horn. Have fun at your party tomorrow."

"Yeah, right." Marcy looked down at her desk, then was struck by an idea. "Hey, Jan? Wait."

Jan turned in the doorway.

"I think I might know someone . . ." Marcy's mind raced. He could probably use the kitchen at the shelter. She could front the money for the ingredients. She was sure the food would be fabulous.

Jan's brow furrowed. "What do you mean? A caterer?"

Marcy met her eyes. "Yes," she said, a smile breaking onto her face, "I do know a caterer. And I'm pretty sure he's free right now."

Jan's expression went from confused to amazed. "Really? Is he good?"

"Best you've ever tasted," she said, hearing herself echo Truman's words. "You ever eat at the Bella Luna? Italian place on Connecticut Avenue?"

"No, but I've *heard* of it." Jan looked at her excitedly.

"Well, I know the original owner, who was also the chef. Let me get in touch with him and let you know. You're not working tomorrow, are you?"

"No, but here, let me give you my home number. Marcy, if you do this for me I'm going to owe you, big time." She picked up a yellow pad of Post-Its and began writing. "Call me anytime, tonight if you have to. We've got a pretty generous budget for this. I'll write down the range and you see what you can get him for, though I'm sure you'll have to go the whole amount, since it's so last minute." She handed the top sheet to Marcy and winked.

"Good. I'll call you." Marcy took the paper, stuffed it in her briefcase, then swung her bag onto her shoulder.

This was going to be great. Catering was the perfect way for Calvin to get back on his feet.

Marcy pulled up in front of Pockets Pool Hall and looked in the window. Or rather *at* the window. Neon signs advertising everything from Budweiser to bratwurst littered the plate glass, making it impossible to see inside.

Three men in jeans and hooded sweatshirts entered, and a guy dressed completely in camouflage exited.

Marcy sighed and pulled the car back onto the street from the no-parking-yellow curb to drive another lap around the block. For some reason, parking was tough around here. She'd already been around twice. She hoped it wasn't because Pockets was some tristate happy hour Mecca. She was dismayed enough about having to shout to Truman over the pool table about some guy who may or may not be threatening her, without having to be jostled by an onslaught of suburban chicken-wing aficionados at the same time.

She finally found a spot four blocks away that she took despite misgivings about how far she protruded over an entrance to an alley.

She got out of the car and started down the sidewalk. The evening was warm—Indian summer—and just turning dark. The smell of fall was in the air. She loved this time of year, loved the smell of woodsmoke and the crunch of fallen leaves beneath her feet. Not that there was much of that right in the city, but still. She could smell it on the air, and she didn't have to drive far to find it.

She imagined taking a hike in the woods with Truman. *There's* a place they could talk. She should have suggested they meet at Sugarloaf Mountain tomorrow morning.

She smiled at the thought and looked over her head to see a nearly full moon. Good luck, she thought. Good things always happened when the moon was full. Though what would constitute good luck with Truman she wasn't sure. That he would try to repeat what happened last week? That wouldn't be good. That he'd given up? Somehow that wouldn't be good either.

When she got to the bar and pulled open the door, she was glad she'd taken the time to change her clothes. Arriving here in a lawyer suit would definitely have drawn attention. Her jeans and dark sweater were much more innocuous. Truman had a knack for finding places devoid of yuppies—no small feat in Washington, unless you were willing to risk your life.

Her eyes scanned the crowd until she spotted him, bent over a pool table, his eye trained down the length of a polished cue stick. She paused a moment to appreciate the sight.

"Ten dollar deposit for the balls." A guy with multiple face piercings intoned from behind a counter to her left. "Four and a quarter an hour for the table."

She turned, and counted eight silver rings in one eyebrow.

"No thanks." She smiled. "I'm meeting someone. In fact, he's already here."

"Good for you," the guy said, in what she thought was a needlessly sarcastic tone, and turned back to his Stephen King novel.

She wound through the crowd, keeping an eye on each table she passed so she didn't interrupt anyone's shot or line of vision, and stepped up to sit on one of the tall chairs against the wall near Truman's table.

Looping her handbag across the back she crossed her legs and said, "I bet you're aiming for the seven but the four's the one that's gonna drop. In the left pocket."

Truman straightened up, looked behind him, and saw her sitting against the wall. His mouth started a slow smile that sent waves of giddiness to her stomach.

She squelched it by motioning to the empty pitcher on the table beside her. "Been here long?"

His gray eyes glanced briefly at the pitcher but came right back to her face. The smile in them was irresistible. "Not mine, sorry. I was waiting for you, of course. Now what were you saying about my shot?"

"Nothing." She smiled. "Just go ahead."

He lifted a brow and turned back.

She watched him bend over the cue. God, but he had a nice butt, she thought. He cocked his arm, followed through with a smooth, practiced motion, and proceeded to bounce the seven off the right bumper and send the four into the left pocket.

"Ha!" she said, swinging her legs once or twice in the tall chair before letting her feet catch on the bottom bar.

He turned back. "I was *trying* to drop the four."

"Well, you sure picked a roundabout way of doing it." She leaned back and crossed her arms over her chest, looking around the crowded room. Every pool table was in use and the bar was full. A long banquet server was surrounded by a line of people, and the jukebox blared Aerosmith.

She looked back at Truman, who had watched her perusal of the room. "Cozy," she said.

"I like it. I come here after work sometimes." He started toward her, not stopping until he was nearly in her lap. He was so close she pushed back in the seat and looked up at him suspiciously. *What on earth was he doing?* He leaned closer, near enough for her to see the ring of black around his pale gray iris, and the smile still in his eyes, as he reached behind her, jerked briefly and backed up. With a provocative smile, he handed her a cue stick.

She exhaled, trying vainly to quell the surge of adrenaline his closeness provoked. For a moment she'd thought he was going to kiss her. For that same moment, she'd thought she would let him. Again.

From the look on his face, she could tell he knew that.

"Thank you," she said, taking the wooden stick into a suddenly damp palm. "But I prefer to pick my own."

She dropped down from the chair and turned to the wall behind her, where, yes, there was an entire rack of them. If she hadn't been so busy checking out Truman's body she might have noticed it before. She pulled them out one by one, assessing the length of each, testing their weight and balance, deliberately drawing the process out just to keep from looking at Truman.

What in the world was she doing here? she chastised herself. Did she have no spine? Could she not have told the man it was inappropriate to meet in a pool hall to discuss business? Could she not have *insisted* they meet someplace reasonably quiet?

And was she crazy to even *imagine* giving him permission to kiss her? She mentally scoffed. Like he would ask permission, or even have to. She'd have folded like a house of cards all on her own.

Would that really be so bad? a little voice in her head murmured. *He's single; you're single. You just happen to be working on this case together, but that won't last . . .*

Marcy turned slowly back to him. He was gorgeous. And he wanted her still, she could tell. What would happen if she let her guard down again?

She'd end up in a dead-end affair with a construction worker, she told herself. And her raging hormones will have screwed up the first case Win Downey entrusted to her. No, it was better to resist him.

If she could.

"Find the magic one?" Truman asked.

"Ah, that explains it," she said. "You were relying on magic."

"Very funny. You're quite the big talker there, aren't you? So, what's your game?" Truman leaned one hip against the table, both hands folded around the top of the cue. "Eight ball? Nine ball?"

"Straight pool," she said, chalking the tip of her cue. "And since you were so anxious to meet me *here* of all places, I think we should make it worth my while." She gave him a sly smile.

He returned one in kind. "Buck a ball?"

"I'm thinking twenty on the whole game."

He shrugged. "It's your dime. You'll be thanking me later on for bringing you to a place where the chicken wings are free."

"Lag for break?" she asked, and the confident look on his face dimmed briefly.

He tipped his head. "You first."

She won the break, called solids, and pocketed six balls handily. Between Marcy's second and third shots, a waitress had appeared, and Truman ordered a pitcher. Between her third and fourth he'd gotten a plate of chicken wings. By the time he'd returned with those, she was stepping up to miss her seventh.

Truman stood by the chair where she had sat looking decidedly uneasy. "You gonna want that twenty tonight or can I work it off, Miss Paglinowski?"

She laughed. "Hey, I just missed. It's your turn. Go ahead, clear the table."

Truman took his time ambling around the table. "So, Miss P., since you grilled me last time, I figure I've got a few questions you owe me answers to."

Marcy swallowed and looked at her hands. "Questions?" *Good Lord*, she thought, *was he going to ask her what she thought she was doing going to bed with him last week?*

"Yeah." He leaned over, made his shot. "Like, are you an only child?"

Marcy exhaled in relief. "No," she said with a smile. "Two brothers."

"One of them teach you how to pick a lock?"

"Actually, I taught them, though that turned out to be a mistake," she said. "I was something of a tomboy." She gave him a smile that was a half-grimace.

He looked at her a long moment, his eyes warm. "Well, that wore off nicely."

She hated herself for it, but she blushed. "Thank you."

He missed his next shot and turned to face her. "Who picked this place, anyway?"

"I believe that was you, cowboy." She watched him as she moved toward the cue ball and the easy shot that would put away her last solid. She wanted to make sure he wasn't one of those men who hated losing to a girl. From his relaxed expression she was glad to surmise he wasn't. Not that she'd have changed what she was doing if he were.

"Eight ball, side pocket," she said, indicating the pocket with her cue. She promptly sank it and turned to face him with a satisfied smile.

"Where'd a nice girl like you learn to play pool like that?" His gaze was deceptively lazy. "One of the brothers?"

She shook her head, then said, "Prep school," and rolled her eyes as she approached the plate of wings.

"Tough competition, those preppies." He smirked. "I bet Daddy had to buy you your own table so you could practice over the summers."

"Yeah, that's right. Actually, we had several tables, so my less fortunate friends could learn the game too. So sad, you know, people who can't afford pool tables."

"All right, princess, I think we should make this best two out of three."

She shook her head as she tossed the chicken bone on the pile and licked her fingers. *This is good,* she thought. *Maybe if I look like a complete pig he'll stop giving me those "come hither" looks.*

"Tell me about Guido," she said, reaching for another wing.

So Truman filled her in on Guido—everything except the part about him wanting to date Marcy, of course—and tried to keep his mind from wandering. It was all he could do not to picture himself taking her hand and licking the wing juice from each of her fingers himself. And he *definitely* couldn't start thinking about where he'd go from there . . .

"I don't know what they can do, short of actually paying off the judge," Truman said, "but I know Judge—"

He stopped himself short, nearly biting his tongue in the process.

"I know judges can't really be bought," he amended swiftly.

Marcy let loose a hearty scoff. "Yeah, right. Tell me you're not *that* naïve, Fleming."

He smiled. "Just trying to respect your profession. We all know judges are just lawyers in dark robes."

They finished the pitcher, along with three more games of pool, in which Marcy cleaned his clock. He had to admit, he was embarrassed the first game and wished he hadn't talked so arrogantly before they started. But he was impressed and would bet the way she played, she'd beat anyone in the place.

"How 'bout one more pitcher?" Tru asked, holding up the empty plastic jug. "One last game and—"

"No, no." Marcy waved a hand in front of her face. "No way. I've got to go. All I've had tonight are those damn wings and a pitcher of beer. I've got to get home and get some sleep."

"Good idea," Truman said. "I'll come with you."

He was glad to see she was relaxed enough to laugh at the joke.

He'd enjoyed watching her strut around the table after each shot, her fine black eyes studying the arrangement of balls like a general studying troop movements. She knew what she was doing, and she did it confidently. The best part was when she took her shot, however. Aside from the spectacular view of her backside this afforded, she would pull her thick hair around to one side and reveal a pale column of neck he happened to know was quite soft and fragrant.

Every finger remembered how she'd felt that night in her apartment. And every nerve in his body wanted to go back and do it again.

Unfortunately, common sense told him that not only would she reject it, but that trying it would ruin any small chance there was she might change her mind about him after all. And he really wanted her to change her mind about him. Try though he might, he couldn't rid himself of the feeling that Marcy was someone he should hold on to.

She was unlike anyone he'd ever met.

"All right, we'll go, then." He flagged down the waitress and got out his wallet.

Marcy reached for her purse.

"No, no," he said. "I owe you. I lost every damn game."

She smiled with such childish satisfaction he had to laugh.

They walked toward the door.

"Where'd you park?" he asked.

She stepped out the door and gestured to her left. "I'm this way. Blocking an alley on Sixth."

"Let's hope you're still blocking it. Come on, I'll walk you."

To his surprise, she didn't protest this. Then again, she was a smart woman, and most smart women in this town didn't turn down an escort after dark. It was just common sense.

They walked down city streets now quiet, and he heard Marcy inhale deeply of the fresh night air.

"Smells good, doesn't it?" he asked.

"I love it. It's my favorite time of year." She laughed softly, a sound that made him smile. "I had the thought on the way over here that I should have told you I'd meet you at Sugarloaf. We could've hiked through the woods and discussed Arthur and the case and everything there."

He smiled in the dark. "Well, the hike sounds good. We should do that sometime."

They walked a few yards in silence.

"You know," Truman mused, "I often think about moving to the country. Some small town somewhere. I'd like to live where you can get to know your neighbors. Where you greet the postman by name, run into friends in the grocery store. You know what I mean?"

Marcy was quiet so long he thought maybe she hadn't heard him, which was ridiculous. He looked down at her, saw the look of concentration on her face.

"I've never lived anywhere but a city," she said finally. "Or a suburb that was too much like the city. I wonder if a small town would feel claustrophobic."

Truman shook his head. "Not to me. It's the city

that's claustrophobic. All these millions of people, all trying so hard to ignore each other, or get ahead of each other in line, or shoot each other for having something the other doesn't have. No, I think a small town would just feel . . . manageable. Personal."

"Personal . . ." she repeated softly, then tripped on an uneven sidewalk square. He reached out to steady her and her hand clutched at his for a moment, then abruptly let go.

They reached her car and turned toward each other.

"This was fun, Truman," she said, looking up into his face with a contented expression. "Thank you for inviting me here. And thank you for talking to Guido."

"You're welcome." His hands itched to take her in his arms.

"You really think he'll leave me alone now?"

He nodded. "Yeah, he wasn't really up to much anyway, though I wouldn't completely let my guard down, if I were you."

She looked nervous, gazing down the street, her fingers pulling at a zipper tassel on her purse.

"He's harmless, Marcy," he said, touching her forearm.

She looked up at him again and he slid his hand to her wrist.

As if they'd agreed upon it earlier, they came together at the exact same moment. Truman's hand drew her close and her arm slid up and around his neck. His lips caught hers, and with a wave a pleasure he felt her body meet his.

Gentle and pliant, she melded into him, sweeping over him like a disorienting cloud, spiraling his senses and dizzying his self-control.

He ran one hand up her back to tangle in the length

of her hair. His other arm pulled at her lower back, fusing them closer at the hips. Together they moved so she was leaning against the car, his hips pressing into hers and hers pushing up to meet them.

His blood heated instantly to boiling as his hands felt the supple grace of her body through her clothes. He ran his palms up her sides, their mouths still searching, entangled, their breathing out of control.

Around them the block of rowhouses slumbered. A low breeze rustled through the crisp autumn leaves on the trees and ruffled their hair.

They broke apart suddenly, Marcy gasping for air. But Tru didn't want the moment to end. He trailed his lips down her neck, along the very place he'd been coveting all night. She tilted her head back.

He ran a hand around to her breast and she inhaled sharply. But the way her hands kneaded his back told him she didn't want him to stop.

He wanted to take her right here and now and could barely contain himself.

He trailed his tongue along a place just behind her right ear and she gasped softly. "Oh God. We can't do this again."

But she didn't push him away. His heart slammed against his ribcage. "Marcy, why don't you turn off that brain of yours and start listening to your heart for once. Don't you want . . . this?" He kissed her again below the ear and ran his hands down her sides.

He felt her pause, then nod.

"My place isn't far."

She nodded again. They parted, breathing as if they'd just run a race, and Marcy fumbled for her keys. Finally pulling them out of her purse, she hit the button, and the doorlocks released.

Truman opened the door but watched as Marcy walked around to her side. He prayed to God she wasn't changing her mind. But if her blood was racing anything like his, changing her mind was virtually impossible.

She got in the car and so did he. They closed the doors simultaneously and fell into another kiss.

Finally, Marcy pulled back and started the car. Then, with what seemed to Truman like excruciating slowness, she drove to his apartment.

11

Saturday, October 26

WORD-A-DAY!

EISEGESIS: n., interpretation of a text based on reading into it one's own predjudices: a technique that rarely yields accurate results

It was after midnight when they practically fell into Truman's apartment. Hands grabbed at clothing, their own and each other's, tearing it off and tossing it to the ground. Folly leapt around them like a whirling dervish until Truman closed the bedroom door on her, this time with the dog on the outside of the room.

He didn't turn on any lights, but once inside his bedroom, he lifted her into his arms and placed her gently on the bed.

"Truman," she whispered. "What are we—"

"Shhhh," he countered, lying beside her and pushing her hair from the side of her face. She was silky everywhere, a symphony of tactile pleasures. Velvety, satiny, luscious, and smooth, like a dessert so rich you want to take tiny bites, but you can't stop from taking mouthfuls.

"But we can't—"

He kissed her deeply, and her fingers plunged into

his hair, holding his head as her mouth explored his. He would have stopped, he honestly would have stopped, if he'd thought her words were anything other than an obligatory utterance. But every fiber of his being felt her reaching out for him, and he knew as surely as he knew it was nighttime that she wanted him.

He reached down with one hand and lifted her sweater. They parted long enough for him to pull it over her head. Moving his mouth down to her breasts, he snaked a hand around her back and released her bra, pulled the straps down her arms, then tossed it aside. His mouth took her nipple and she arched beneath him.

"*Oh,*" she breathed. "Truman. I've never—never felt . . ."

He reached for the button of her jeans, but she stopped him with a hand. He rose up on one elbow, flushed and unsure, willing himself to stop if she'd changed her mind, but she undid the button herself.

Relief coursed through him. He hadn't read her wrong. In fact, at this moment, he felt as if he *couldn't* read her wrong. They were too connected. This was too meant to be.

Truman knelt above her and undid his own jeans. They came together skin-to-skin at last with a fervor Truman had never experienced before. He felt an urgency, an insatiable hunger, that would not be denied.

His fingers moved down her stomach and into her most private place, searching. She was more than ready for him, but when he found that one area she seemed to heat up in his hands. With a low moan she guided him to the exact place, and after that whatever reservations she might have harbored obviously disappeared. She arched into his caress and called out his name. He could feel her trembling beneath his touch and a wave of emotion threatened to overwhelm him. She was his, he thought then, with as much clarity as if she'd said the words. And he was hers. This was no ordinary passion. This was fate.

Just when he thought he would burst, he rose over her. She reached down and enveloped his hardness. Stroking him upward, she bit lightly at his bottom lip, her breath coursing between them as she came down from her climax. Truman knew he couldn't last much longer.

"Let me inside you," he whispered, kissing her again.

She smiled against his mouth. "*Yes.*"

He slid effortlessly into her, his skin exploding with chills of pleasure as he did. Though he would not have believed it possible, this time was even more powerful than the last. She met him pump for pump, her hand working magic around his manhood at the same time, while the other clutched his shoulder as if for dear life.

Truman's blood pounded through his veins. He heard nothing but her breathing, her gasps of pleasure, her impassioned pleading with him to never stop, never let go, never leave her.

He took her roughly, deeply, and came with a visceral groan. He felt on fire, and yet sated on a level so deep he wondered briefly if he had died. When he rolled to one side, she curled into him, warming him again, in a way that their entire night of passion had not.

With a smile on his lips, Truman fell asleep.

This time, it was Marcy who left Truman before the sun had a chance to come up. But it wasn't because she needed to get away from him and it wasn't because she thought she'd made another mistake. Not necessarily. No, it was because she needed to get ahold of herself, needed to examine the powerful, intimidating feelings that arose every time she was with Truman.

She needed to figure out exactly how much trouble she was in, emotionally.

She drove slowly through the city streets, her thoughts swirling like the tornado in *The Wizard of Oz.* Only instead of pictures of Toto and the wicked witch on her bicycle appearing out of the torrent, it was Truman Fleming. Then Win Downey. Then herself, tearing her hair out in indecision.

What was she doing?

She parked her car and walked heavily up the steps to the homeless shelter. The doors weren't open, so she sat on the stoop, her head in her hands. Moments later she heard a voice.

"Marcy?"

She raised her head and turned to look behind her.

Calvin stood in the doorway of the shelter wearing a sweatshirt and pajama bottoms. His eyes squinted into the early morning sun. He bent to pick up the newspaper that was donated to the shelter by a retired journalist for the *Post*.

Marcy got slowly to her feet. "Hi, Calvin." She mustered a smile.

"Well, hello. What're you doing here at this hour?" He looked at his wrist, noticed he hadn't put on his watch yet, and chuckled. "It's early, I know that."

"Yeah. It's about six." She sighed. "That's why I was waiting out here. I didn't want to wake anyone."

That, and I was contemplating the demise of my career, my common sense, my spine . . .

"Well, come on in." He waved her forward with an arm that he put around her shoulders as she reached the top of the steps. "I'll make you a cup of coffee."

"Coffee?" she whimpered. "Oh, thank God."

Calvin laughed. "Now, call me crazy, but I get the feeling something is wrong."

Marcy looked at him, fatigue making every limb weigh a thousand pounds, and thought there was no way on God's green earth she would lay her problem at Calvin's feet. For God's sake, the man had buried his wife six months ago. He'd since lost his home and his business, and now was living in a homeless shelter.

All she'd done was sleep with the wrong guy at the wrong time. In the wrong place. For the wrong reasons. *Twice.*

"No, I'm just tired. But actually," she said, forcibly brightening, "something is *right*. Really right. I've got some news for you."

They walked down the shelter's hallway. Above them Marcy could hear a crying child, toilets flushing, what might be an argument, or at least a loud conversation, between two men.

"News? Don't tell me, you've finally found Mr. Right!"

She shot him a look and he grinned down at her. They got to the kitchen door and Calvin gestured for her to precede him. She walked in and dropped her purse on the stainless steel counter.

"Actually," she said, "I'm afraid to say anything about that just yet."

"Well! That sounds interesting."

Marcy sat down on a chrome stool. Her sweater smelled like smoke from the pool hall and her hair felt heavy on her head. She needed to take a shower. She needed a lobotomy.

"Interesting, maybe. Understandable, no. No, my news is about you, Mr. Deeds." She smiled at him, excitement about what she had to say penetrating her haze of confusion.

He looked at her with something less than enthusiasm. In fact, one could almost call the look wary.

"Okay," she grinned, changing tacks. "Clearly my spin isn't going to wash with you. The fact of the matter is the firm is kind of in a bind."

"The firm? Your law firm?" he asked, obviously at a loss as to what he could have to do with that.

"Yes. You see, we're having a pretty important party. A sort of attorney-client happy hour. It's a real goodwill thing; we do it every year. But the firm has some very important contacts it invites, so the food has got to be top notch." She took a deep breath. "Unfortunately, the caterer my assistant hired months ago canceled. Yesterday. And the party's only ten days away."

He looked at her skeptically. "And you want me . . ."

"You would be doing me a *huge* favor if you'd consider catering the bash for us. It's a hundred and fifty people, so cold-cut platters from the grocery store just won't do. Neither will the pigs in blankets Jan and I briefly considered cooking."

"Pigs in blankets," Calvin scoffed vaguely.

Marcy smiled inwardly. Junk food had always offended his culinary sensibilities.

"Besides, anything less than the best would make us look very bad." She looked at him pathetically.

"But Marcy . . ." He held a hand out helplessly, then let it fall to the counter in front of him. "I don't have the resources. I'd need to get food—"

"Oh, there's an enormous budget for the thing. You'd be well paid, especially since you'd be helping us out on such short notice."

He shook his head as he looked out the window onto a scene of Dumpsters in the alley. "But I'd need assistants—"

"What about the assistant chefs, or whatever you call them, from your restaurant? The budget would easily allow you to hire a few people."

"Servers—"

"Same budget. Calvin, it's short notice, but if you can find people available, the firm will pay. They simply *can't* go without food at this thing."

Calvin turned, folding his arms across his chest, his expression considering. "Well, if you really need someone . . ."

"Oh God, *need* isn't even the word. We're desperate. Jan, my assistant, called dozens of caterers yesterday and none of them would do it."

He nodded, his mind obviously calculating what such an event would take. "They like any sort of food in particular?"

"Hors d'oeuvres, finger food, shrimp, caviar, that sort of thing. How about I give you a card for the girl who's setting the thing up? She can give you all the details." Marcy fished her wallet out of her purse and grabbed one of her business cards. "It's the same as the firm number but here's her extension. Her name is Jan." She scribbled a number at the bottom of the card. "And here's what you'll be paid. Tell her that's what we agreed on."

She handed the card to Calvin, who looked at it carefully, seeming to study the dollar amount at the bottom, probably calculating food and service costs automatically.

"Is that enough, do you think? Can you do it for that?" Marcy asked anxiously. She had no idea what caterers generally got paid, but it wouldn't surprise her if Downey Fin was a lowballer.

He laughed incredulously. "Oh, it's enough." He looked up at her, his brows knitted. "But Marcy . . ."

"Don't worry," Marcy said, "that's what she's expecting. And delighted to get the chef from Bella Luna at such a bargain rate, too."

Calvin's eyes suddenly turned misty and he smiled wanly. "Marcy P. . . ." he said affectionately. "Thank you, gal." He reached over and ruffled her hair.

Marcy felt a lump grow in her throat, so she just smiled and looked down at the counter.

Marcy went home and showered, then dressed casually and went to the office. It was Saturday, so the people working were mostly associates—lawyers like herself who were only three or four years out of law school. Marcy was lucky, however. She'd been given the Burton case despite being fairly junior. It was a mark of Win's trust and faith in her.

Now she felt once again that she'd let him down.

What was it about Tru Fleming that made her throw caution to the wind? Last night she'd chosen to . . .

well, to *forget* all about her obligation to the case. Just as she had last week. From the time she'd entered the pool hall until the moment she'd woken up this morning, she'd felt as if she knew Truman for a different reason. Like they were . . . friends. Even in a relationship. Or something.

She rested her forehead in her hand, elbow on the desk, and looked askance at the phone. She'd been here for hours already and had set the phone to DND, do not disturb. If he'd tried to call, she wouldn't know it. Not unless he left a message and she decided to check.

But she didn't know what she'd say to him if he called. She'd crept out of there this morning at the crack of dawn, like a thief making off with the stereo. She'd gathered her clothes and dressed outside the bedroom in the kitchen, Folly wagging and circling around her. She'd paused to play briefly with the dog, scratching her belly and promising to find her a home, or even a way to take the pup herself, as soon as she could.

Then, closing the door carefully behind her, she'd stepped out of the apartment and into the crisp morning air. She hadn't felt bad then. Just confused. And maybe even a little bit excited. But as the day wore on she felt progressively worse.

Guilty. Unsure. *Afraid.*

Marcy lifted her head from her hand, suddenly remembering Truman had left his truck near the bar. She glanced again at the phone. The message light was flashing, but then it always flashed.

He'd probably found a way to get it by now, she told herself. But she wasn't convinced.

"Hey stranger," Trish said from the doorway.

Marcy jumped in her seat. "Oh, Trish. God, I don't know where my mind was."

Trish laughed. "Sorry to surprise you like that. Everything okay?"

Marcy exhaled heavily, wondering if she should confide the problem to Trish. She could really use some perspective right about now.

"Tell you the truth, I don't know."

Trish entered the office and closed the door behind her. "What's wrong? Something I can help with? I've got that damn brief to write, but hell, it can wait. It's been waiting a week already."

"It's . . . it's this Burton case," Marcy said hesitantly. She knew she could trust Trish not to say anything, but could she trust her not to gloat? Good-naturedly, of course, but Marcy never liked I-told-you-so's. Then again, who did?

Trish leaned forward. "Run into a snag?"

Marcy met her gaze frankly. "No. Ran into a construction worker."

It took Trish a minute, then she broke into a laugh. "No *way*!" She laid her hands on the sides of her head. "You . . . ? You . . . ? Oh my God, don't tell me you went out with him."

Marcy nodded, keeping her eyes on Trish. "But that's not the worst of it."

"No. Did you *sleep* with him?" she hissed in a dramatic whisper, eyes wide.

"Twice." Marcy closed her eyes. "I was afraid I'd regret telling you."

Trish chuckled one last time, then sobered. "I'm sorry. I'm just . . . Well gosh, I'm just really surprised. You were so adamant. You seemed so *sure* he wasn't for you. I guess you found some common ground, huh?"

"Too much." Marcy shook her head, thinking how long and hard she'd worked to get away from the world of half-smokes and pool halls.

"Well, is it that bad? Was he awful in bed or what?"

"No." Marcy laughed wryly. "Definitely *no*, unfortunately, or the problem would be solved." She thought of Truman's self-deprecating laughter when she beat him at pool the last time and thought, No, even if the sex was bad, she'd still be in trouble. There was just something about him . . . something that made her want to be near him.

Trish's brows lowered. "And what's the problem? Exactly?"

Marcy gaped at her. "He's a *witness*. For my case. For the most important case of my career so far. It's extremely unethical, don't you think, for me to be sleeping with one of my witnesses?"

Trish leaned back and crossed her legs. "I guess. So you guys agree to wait for the trial to be over and then jump each other. I mean, so what? It's not like he's the murderer in a criminal trial or anything. Though I could kind of see the excitement in that . . ." she added speculatively.

"Really?" Marcy couldn't see anything exciting about sleeping with a murderer. A construction worker, on the other hand . . .

Trish pushed her blond-highlighted locks away from her face. "Oh yeah. Danger's always exciting, don't you think? But we're talking about you now. Maybe it's the danger of getting caught that's attracting you. Him being off limits makes him something of the forbidden fruit, doesn't it?"

"Well, yeah, but that's not what I'm attracted to. Believe me, the idea of getting caught is not at all exciting to me." She paused thoughtfully. "It's just that he's so good-looking. And funny. And really easy to talk to . . ." She remembered him mentioning his desire to move to a small town. Did he think she was easy to talk to too?

"Sounds pretty good," Trish said. "Sounds to me like someone's seriously *smitten*."

Marcy put a hand over her eyes. "I'm not smitten, Trish, I'm insane. Well, okay, maybe I am smitten. But he's *so* not right for me."

"No?" Trish's brows rose.

Marcy looked at her. "No, and what's more, he's off limits. Ever since I met this guy I've been worried to death about what Win would think of my, uh, lustful thoughts." She laughed dryly.

"Forget Win. What do *you* think about them? If you really like this guy, just remember the trial's temporary. True love isn't."

Marcy scoffed. "True love."

Trish smiled knowingly.

Marcy paused. "So you don't think it's a huge deal that I slept with one of my witnesses?" She asked, coming back around to the real issue, like a child hoping to be told it's really okay, everyone does it.

"Well, it's not a great idea, but it's not the end of the world, either." Trish gave her a pitying smile. "Jeez, the way you look you'd think you'd just made some kind of career-ending mistake. So you slept with the guy once or twice. Big deal. Call the relationship off till the trial's over. Then you can date him and nobody can say anything."

But Marcy didn't feel better. Even after Trish left and

they'd agreed that she should go to his place this evening to tell him they'd have to cool it until the trial was over, she still felt the unsettling weight of dread in the pit of her stomach.

It was then she realized that it wasn't so much Truman's status as her witness that bothered her—though that *did* bother her to no small degree—it was more the fact that he was a *construction worker*. A poor, working-class guy who drank Budweiser and played pool in his time off, who couldn't afford a phone and ate Dinty Moore beef stew every night for dinner. A guy leading a duct-tape style of life with no apparent aspirations to change it.

In short, a guy who would end up inebriated on the couch for the rest of his life, just like her father.

It was shallow, it was superficial, it was pathetically psychological as well as snobby and selfish. But God, it was *scary*. *He* was scary. He came from, was thoroughly ensconced in, and would probably never get out of the world she'd worked her whole adult life to escape.

She may have gone to bed with Tru Fleming, but she'd woken up with Johnny Calabresi, the bad boy of Georges Heights who'd gotten her best friend pregnant.

Marcy pulled up in front of Tru's apartment and slowly put the car in park. Her hands were shaking, her pulse was racing, her breath was shallow, and her stomach behaved as if she'd eaten something very bad.

She still hadn't decided what to say to him, but was anxious to see him again just the same.

She sat for a moment, reliving the moment they had come together in that kiss by her car. She'd felt as if she were possessed, as if an unseen force had pushed her toward him, as if he'd become some essential substance that, once tasted, her body could no longer do without.

That feeling had carried her from the pool hall to the car to Tru's apartment and all the way through until the moment she woke up this morning. *That's* when it had hit her.

She was in deep—too deep—to treat this casually. Not only did she have to figure out what she wanted, and what to do about it, but she had to find out what Truman felt. Was this a game to him? Had she misinterpreted the look in his eyes last night? Read into it what she wanted to see instead of what was really there? Or did he feel about her as strongly as she did him?

The sun was low in the sky, casting long gray shadows across the hard-packed dirt of the front "yard." She gazed at the window to his living room. Was he there? Was he thinking of her?

Was he worried about what they were doing?

She frowned. She couldn't imagine Truman worried. But then it wasn't as if *his* career were hanging in the balance here.

She bit her lip and stared at his window. He hadn't called her today. She'd checked her messages and he hadn't left one, not even to say he'd left his truck at the bar. He hadn't called last time, either, so maybe it didn't mean anything.

Or maybe it did.

Opening the car door, Marcy glanced around for his truck but didn't see it. Maybe he wasn't home. Her hopes somehow rose and sank at the same time. Chances were the truck was still over by Pockets Pool Hall. She glanced at her watch. It was nearly six thirty in the evening. Surely he'd be here warming up his Dinty Moore.

She walked to the trunk and opened it, leaned in, and grabbed the bag of dog food she'd picked up. The good kind this time.

Like the condemned man walking the plank, Marcy moved slowly toward the apartment house door.

The first thing she noticed when she entered the hall was the smell of roasting meat. Her mouth watered. Usually the hall smelled of some odd kind of spice, something used in Mexican or Indian cooking, but this smell was pure steamship round.

She tried to calm her jumping nerves and knocked on Truman's door.

After several long seconds and no answer, Marcy leaned closer to the door. The smell, it seemed, was emanating from Tru's apartment. Must have been a roast in one of those grocery bags, she thought briefly, before knocking again.

There was noise upstairs, somebody's radio played loudly, and the sound of children laughing came from the apartment across the hall. If Truman was in the kitchen cooking, chances were he couldn't hear her knock.

After wiping her palm down the side of her pants, she reached for the doorknob. It turned easily in her hand. Was he crazy? This neighborhood was awful. Why wasn't his door locked? She pushed it open.

She could hear the clattering of pots and pans from the kitchen. She stepped into the living room, closing the door softly behind her.

Folly did not appear, so Marcy immediately glanced at the bedroom door. It was closed. She pressed her lips together. Did he keep her locked up all the time?

She shifted the dog food in her arms, then decided to set it down by the couch. A slight humming came from the kitchen.

Marcy hesitated. The sound was barely audible but the humming didn't sound like Truman. It didn't sound like any man, in fact.

She walked slowly back toward the kitchen. Rounding the corner to the doorway, Marcy stopped short at the sight before her. A thin, gorgeous blonde woman in tailored black pants and a white shirt leaned over the open door to the oven. On her wrist were several thick gold bracelets.

Marcy gasped and the girl jumped, dropping the baster she'd held into the oven.

"Sorry!" Marcy said automatically.

"It's all right," the girl said, but she was frantically trying to pluck the plastic baster out of the oven before it melted.

"I—I must have the wrong . . ." Marcy backed out of the kitchen.

"It's okay," she heard the girl say—then gasp and swear lightly as if she'd burned herself.

Marcy continued backing into the living room. And she thought she'd felt sick *before*.

Rather than risk having any sort of conversation with

this woman who could only be Truman's girlfriend—who else would feel comfortable enough to prepare such an elaborate meal in someone else's apartment, especially when that someone else wasn't even *home*?—she turned and ran for the door.

Slamming first out of the apartment, then out of the front hall, Marcy bee-lined for her car. She started it up, threw it into gear, floored it, and peeled down the street, one hand at her throat and her eyes wide with shock.

12

Saturday, October 26

WORD-A-DAY!

BONUS WORD

WRITHE: v., to coil or wrench as from agony or struggle; to be left twisting, as it were, in the wind

Truman trudged wearily up the sidewalk to his apartment. He'd just walked, jogged, and hitchhiked over to Southwest to get his truck—a journey that had seemed far shorter last night with an engine and a great deal of anticipation on his side.

Today, however, that anticipation had turned to dread.

Last night had been amazing. More than amazing, it had been earth moving. He'd thought it couldn't get any better after the first time, but Marcy—unpredictable as always—had surprised him. She proved once again that she was more passionate than he ever would have dreamed from seeing her in those lawyer suits of hers. And she'd brought out something in him that he didn't even recognize, a kind of protective craving—a desire both to have her and to guard her from the rest of the world.

Last night he'd felt that only *he* could see her clearly, could know her thoughts and feelings, could say the things that would make her smile. Only *he* should be the one to touch her, feel her strength and softness, counter her desires with his own.

Which was *disastrous*. Because today she'd left before he'd awakened. That was never a good sign.

He'd expected it, of course. He just hadn't expected to mind it so much.

He tried to tell himself it was a good thing. That he couldn't feel that way about a girl like her. But he didn't really buy it.

She was, after all, so different. She gave him hope that she wasn't the type to just play around with a blue-collar guy but was perhaps willing to accept him just as he was right now. Because after all he'd done to get here, to give up luxury and affluence and the hypocrisy and superficiality that went with it, the last thing Truman needed was to go back to that mindset through a woman.

Even if the woman was beautiful, and smart, and witty, and a damn good lawyer, from what he could see.

Truman was lost in his thoughts until he reached his apartment door, which was standing slightly ajar. From inside he thought he heard movement.

He paused, listening. There was nothing to steal, nothing even remotely tempting.

He pushed the door open with one finger and peered in. Folly was nowhere to be seen, and she normally rushed the door and pounced on him the moment he walked in. From the kitchen came the noise, along with the amazing scent of real food being prepared.

His first thought was Marcy. Or rather: *Marcy!* He

couldn't help the way his insides gave a little leap of hope that she'd come back.

He suddenly wished he had some flowers to sweep out from behind his back as he surprised her in the kitchen. An apology for underestimating her. Maybe waking up in a nearly vacant apartment in Southeast with a recently unemployed construction worker hadn't scared her permanently back to her condo in Dupont Circle.

Maybe she wasn't as mercenary as he feared she might be.

He stole quietly across the living room, rounded the corner into the kitchen and stopped dead. At the same time a woman with long blonde hair and a knockout body turned from the oven with a steaming juicy roast in a deep roasting pan in her oven-mitted hands.

Who in God's name was *she*?

That wasn't his pan either, or his roast.

Quickly he glanced back down the hall to the living room. Yep, same sheet-covered, duct-taped sofa, same sagging armchair, bag of Eukanuba dog food by the couch. It was his apartment all right.

He looked back into the kitchen and said, "I'm sorry . . ." with a helpless expression.

She gave him a shy glance and said, "Hi," in a high, soft voice.

"Do I know you?" He glanced at all the ingredients littering the counters. Spices and herbs, vegetables and broths, a long loaf of French bread and an open bottle of wine.

"My name's Heather. I'm a surprise, from your mother."

He cleared his throat. "Excuse me?"

She laughed softly and her cheeks flushed just the palest shade of pink. "And you're Truman, right? Truman Fleming?"

Words rushed his brain but he couldn't pick the right ones out fast enough. "You're from—you're a—my *mother* sent you?"

"Yes, you see I work at Le Gaulois, in Alexandria? I met your mother last week, when she came in for lunch with a group of her friends." She paused and smiled with entirely too much warmth. "What a *lovely* woman, your mother. Just a lovely, lovely woman."

Truman, who'd been nodding at her though still not getting why she was here, said, "Yeah, lovely. And she asked you to . . . ah, surprise me?"

"Well, the way it happened was"—she brushed her ample hair behind one shoulder with a hand and a model-style shake of her head—"during lunch she asked how the veal was prepared. So I told her about the braising and the sherry-morel sauce and just the barest *kiss* of raspberry the chef likes to include." She made a little flicking motion with her thumb and forefinger on the word *kiss*. "He's quite creative, our chef, and I went into quite some detail, actually . . ."

Truman could imagine.

"So she asked me if I knew how to cook. Since, I suppose, I seemed to be talking so knowledgeably about the process." She looked bashfully at the floor. "At that point I had to confess that I don't normally waitress. I was just helping out that day because one of the girls called in sick. I usually work in the kitchen. You see, I'm hoping to become a chef one day. I spent a year in Paris at L'École—"

"So she asked you to come cook dinner for me?" Truman interrupted, cutting to the chase.

He was starting to get an idea of what his mother had in mind. A very clear idea. His eyes swept the girl's figure again and noted the fancy jewelry, the makeup, and the silk shirt she wore despite being here as a cook.

"Yes, she said you were living here, undercover." She said the last word in a whisper, with a covert look around, as if someone nearby might be spying on them. "And that you weren't eating properly at all. She's very worried about you, you know."

"Yeah, I've heard." Truman ran a hand through his hair and leaned heavily against the wall. Worried he wouldn't find a nice debutante with whom to insipidly spend the rest of his days.

"She strikes me as quite a devoted mother," the girl continued.

"Hah!" he said mildly. *Devoted, domineering . . . same thing.*

"She said that even though you were here, undercover"—again with the whispering—"that you needed to eat well and that a good, home-cooked meal once or twice a week would do you nothing but good. So she hired me!" She finished with a perky smile and her arms outstretched as if to show him the product.

Not that he thought she was selling herself. No, no, it was nothing so crass as that. She was *marketing* herself. As suitable wife material to Truman Foster Fleming, son of Senator Baxter Fleming and his wife, who was one of the affluent Maryland Trumans.

Marcy, at least, privileged girl that *she* was, had no idea he wasn't Tru Fleming, impoverished laborer.

Truman looked down the hall toward the living room. He didn't want to think about Marcy. And he didn't want to think about his *disappointment* that this girl hadn't been Marcy futzing around in his kitchen. And he *really* didn't want to think about the fact that his mother was hiring polished young women to come tempt him back to the fold.

He sighed. "Listen, uh . . ." He looked at her, unable to remember her name.

"Heather," she supplied, with a coy tilt of her head.

"Yeah, Heather. Listen, I appreciate what you're trying to do here—"

"Oh, it's all your mother's doing. She planned everything, even the menu."

"Then, okay, I guess I appreciate what she was trying to do." He shook his head. Nothing could have been further from the truth. "But the fact is, you can't stay here. I don't need this . . ." He swept a hand out to encompass the abundance around them.

His stomach growled, calling him a liar.

She smiled, her blue eyes actually seeming to twinkle. "Everyone needs this." She took off her oven mitts and reached back toward the stove for the carving knife.

"Heather, no. Wait."

He stopped her by touching her arm and she looked up at him through her lashes.

"The fact of the matter is . . ." He thought quickly, then lowered his voice. "You could be in danger here."

Her blue eyes widened almost comically.

He nodded soberly. "Yes. You see, I couldn't let on to my mother the extent of the . . . ah . . . *operation* here. But I'm involved in some very hazardous activities. And this is my home base. By coming here, being seen here even for a moment, you could put us both in the way of some real peril."

"You mean I've blown your cover?" she asked, her voice nearly a whisper.

"Exactly. So why don't we gather your things up here and I'll walk you to your car."

"But—" She stopped, looking at him helplessly. For a second he thought she might cry. "Your mother's driver dropped me off. He's not coming back until nine o'clock."

Of course, Tru thought, rolling his eyes. He briefly considered asking A.M. or P.M.? But this girl didn't deserve that.

"That's all right. I'll drive you home."

She started toward him, then looked back at the kitchen. "But the pots and pans, even the knives, they all belong to your mother. Though I do have my own set of knives, you know, all good chefs do, that I usually—"

"Don't worry about it." Truman grinned grimly. "I'll give it all to the driver when he comes back."

Heather stooped briefly by the kitchen door and picked up her purse. Coach leather, Tru noted. His mother sure had an eye.

"What should I tell her?" Heather stopped close before him, looking up at him with concern etched on her features. "Your mother. I can't tell her you're in danger, can I? She'll be so worried."

"*I'll* talk to my mother. Don't concern yourself with that." He guided her by the elbow toward the front door.

They passed the bag of dog food and Truman gave it a double take. This bag was unopened. The last bag he bought for Folly was almost half empty.

His mother even sent food *for the dog?* Jesus, she *was* trying hard, he thought, and followed Heather the Cook out the door.

Marcy stood by the Jell-O mold, miserably chewing on a celery stalk smeared with cream cheese. This had been the longest day of her life. It seemed like several years had passed since she'd woken up this morning beside Truman, and now here she was wishing she could melt along with the orange block of Velveeta at her Aunt Phyllis's birthday party.

It was a gorgeous day, warm and sunny as Washington's Indian summer days tended to be. But it didn't help.

She'd forgotten a salad. And a date, of course. Marcy thought she'd never have another date in her life—a sentiment that seemed to echo widely amongst her relatives as she'd walked onto the back patio alone.

"*There's* Marcy," her aunt Phyl had squawkcd as she'd stepped out the patio door. "And where's *your* young man, eh, missy? Your mother said you might be bringing someone and we've all been anxious to meet him. It's been so long since you brought anyone here. How long's it been, Joanie?"

Aunt Phyl turned to Marcy's mother. They were all perched around where Phyl lay corpulently on a chaise longue, like worshippers around a bad-tempered Buddha. They were all afraid of Aunt Phyl, who ruled every party like an evil dictator.

"Well, now, I don't know. Maybe it hasn't been that

long." Marcy's mother looked up at Marcy beseechingly, as if she could manufacture a memory for them all of some recent time she'd shown up at a family gathering with a date.

"It was Christmas Eve two years ago, I think," Aunt Phyl said, holding one hammy finger aloft and wagging it. "That fellow with the fancy shoes, remember?"

"They were loafers," Marcy protested.

"Oh yes. I remember, but they were some special *kind*," Aunt Verna contributed. "I remember he was quite proud of them. Told us all they were practically custom made."

Actually they *had* been custom made, Marcy thought. And he *had* been quite proud of them.

"I thought he was handsome as could be." Verna smiled and nodded in her direction. "And he was very taken with you, Marcy, if I recall."

Marcy smiled at her. Verna was a peach. One of the few people who weren't *completely* run over by Aunt Phyl. "Oh, I don't know . . ."

"*I* remember we all thought he was so *stiff*, remember?" Aunt Phyllis said, her frown like a black cloud over the entire patio. "He just stood there in the corner looking like he smelled something bad."

He was stiff all right, Marcy thought. He'd been mortified. Jonathan Brooks. A lawyer from the firm of Robinson, Rock & Knoll. Rock 'n' Roll, as it was known around town.

He'd *hated* her family. Had been aghast that she was related to such loud, tactless people. She didn't realize the depth of his horror until she'd gone to his family's house the next day and met his "refined" clan, the largest group of repressed stuffed shirts she'd ever seen in one place. No wonder he'd been appalled.

She'd never appreciated her own family so much. *They may be loud and tactless,* she'd thought, *but you don't have to live in fear of saying something they don't approve of.* Mostly because they rarely approved of anything, but that was beside the point. Jonathan's family all talked in whispers, as if in fear of being overheard and misunderstood. And God help you if you smiled. If you did, you were labeled frivolous and no one would have anything to do with you.

Not that that was such a hardship.

She and Jonathan had broken up by New Year's, after only three months of dating.

"He wasn't stiff," Uncle Roy objected. He was holding a Budweiser, and it was a pretty sure thing it wasn't his first. He never contradicted anyone until he was drunk; then he contradicted everyone. "He was a perfectly nice guy with some really nice shoes. I thought you shoulda married him, Marcy. How come you didn't marry him?"

She sighed. "He didn't ask, for one thing." Which was when she'd sidled over to the plastic-covered picnic table and begun eating.

Uncle Bruce was grilling burgers and hot dogs in the corner, trying not to converse with his wife. The smell reminded Marcy of summers long past, when the only grief she got from this crew was when she got grass stains on her little anklet socks or dress. Even then it was just a rueful shake of the head and a "kids will be kids" comment. Girls were really only free as children, she thought.

Her cousin Celia—the one who'd come out as a lesbian at one of the summer cookouts—was standing next to Uncle Bruce, looking malevolently at the clutch of people around her mother. She was the smart one. Nobody wanted to hear about her dating experiences.

Her other cousin, Byron, was so enormously fat everyone assumed he'd never get a date, so he was never harassed either. That, and no one wanted to initiate a conversation with him for fear of having to listen to an unending discourse on the life span of flies or the real reason light bulbs weren't sold in wattages between sixty and seventy-five.

Neither of Marcy's brothers was here, but that wasn't surprising. Neither was her father, who was apparently still at the track. They felt no familial obligation whatsoever. Marcy wondered how she'd ended up with any.

She bit into another celery stalk and watched Uncle Les, Phyl's brother, push himself off of his folding chair and come toward her. Les was a lean little man with a potbelly and some of the worst body odor Marcy had ever encountered. She stepped far left to make room for him to get at the Jell-O.

"So," he said, not quite looking at her. He was an awkward man who seemed shy but always managed to say things that were incredibly rude. "Not dating anyone still, huh?"

"That's right."

She briefly considered pulling him aside and telling him she was a call girl, but requesting that he not tell anyone. Then she'd get to watch him squirm with the news the rest of the evening. By morning it would be all over the family and the dating questions would be over.

Then the disease questions would start, she thought. And the morality speeches. And finally the prurient interest in how much money a call girl made these days.

More trouble than it was worth, she concluded.

"I'm surprised," Uncle Les continued, spooning a great glob of Jell-O onto his paper plate. "You're such a looker. You know, good legs, nice ass."

Marcy looked at him in apprehension. Good Lord, where was *this* going?

"Don't them other lawyers you work with got eyes?" he continued. "Maybe you oughta start wearing shorter skirts or something. Like that gal on TV. Ally something."

"MacDeal," Uncle Roy offered from across the patio.

"McBeal, you idiots," Aunt Phyl corrected.

"Yeah, her." Les flipped a slab of Velveeta onto his plate. "She's always got men wanting to date her, and she's a lawyer."

"She's a *TV* lawyer, Uncle Les," Marcy said. "They're different."

"But she ain't nothing but skin and bones and she still gets the boys. She just dresses in them little tiny skirts. Maybe you just ain't dressing to catch the guys' eyes, ya know? Get some of them little tiny skirts. I'll tell you what guys like—"

"Okay. Yeah, thanks, Uncle Les. I'll think about it." She stepped away from him, down the table, and got a plate. She filled it with celery. It was the healthiest thing on the table, despite being covered with cheese.

"I think Marcy dresses great," Uncle Bruce said from the grill.

She glanced over at him and he winked. She smiled warmly back at him. Uncle Bruce was her favorite, a big warm bear of a man. She often thought it was a shame he was so dominated by Aunt Phyl.

"It's a real shame you're still not dating anyone," Aunt Verna said, coming over to the table and getting a paper plate. Her green and orange polyester top seemed intentionally loud, as if she feared her birdlike body would otherwise disappear next to the enormous Aunt Phyl and cousin Byron. "Don't you want kids, honey?"

Marcy watched as Verna stacked her plate with potato chips, onion dip, saltines, and sagging Velveeta cheese slices. The woman must have a metabolism like a hummingbird's.

"I don't know, Aunt Verna. I'm kind of busy now with work. I've got my own case, a pretty big one, that'll probably be going to trial soon."

Aunt Verna shook her head. "You *modern* girls. So busy with your work, you're gonna miss out on the joys of motherhood, you know."

All of Verna's kids were in college now. Marcy remembered something about a big party being thrown when the third and last one left the house.

"Besides, you gotta start looking now, honey," Verna continued. "You don't wanna just up and have babies the minute you meet someone, do you? Gotta get to know the man. Gotta give yourself some time."

"Time? What time? The girl's already almost thirty," Aunt Phyl bellowed from her chair. "You're wasting your best years, girl. You better start looking or you'll find yourself with nothing, you hear me? No man's gonna want you once your ovaries have gone and shriveled up."

Marcy glanced at her mother, who nodded in agreement with Aunt Phyl. "That's just what I been telling her."

"Of course you have." Phyl patted her knee with a heavy hand. "You want grandkids, just like I do. But I ain't never gonna get 'em, not with *her* being the way she is." She jerked a thumb over her shoulder toward Celia. "You ain't one a *them*, are you, Marcy? One a them *lesbians*?" She glared at Marcy shrewdly.

Marcy met her shrewd gaze, considering.

"She might be, you never know," Uncle Roy volunteered. "Wouldn't surprise me. Nothin' surprises me! Betcha it was that jerk with the shoes what turned her."

Marcy glanced at him, then back to Aunt Phyl and said, "Actually yes. Yes, I *am* a lesbian. I've been afraid to tell you, but yes. That's why I don't date." She nodded definitively.

They all looked at her, mouths agape. Roy belched and started laughing.

Marcy smiled.

"Oh, I'm sure she's kidding," her mother said, low, to Aunt Phyl.

Aunt Verna looked at her askance. "You shouldn't joke about such things, dear," she said quietly. "People might take you seriously." She crept away from the table and sat down again, as did Uncle Les.

Uncle Bruce gave her a quick glance, then, with a chuckle, turned back to his hot dogs. They all went back to their conversations, leaving Marcy by the food feeling absurdly pleased with herself.

After a minute she noticed Celia coming her way. *Oh no,* she thought. *Please God, don't let her try to fix me up with someone.*

Celia took a plate and moved close to Marcy, spooning a tiny bit of potato salad onto her plate. Her wild curls were held back by a rubber band and she wore no makeup, but she still looked pretty. Celia was the prettiest girl in the family by far, Marcy had always thought. She'd been shocked when she heard about her announcement last summer.

"So, are you one, really?" Celia asked under her breath.

Marcy turned to look at her. The question was asked so strangely Marcy was sure Celia knew she wasn't. *They must know somehow,* she thought. *Maybe that gay-dar thing isn't just a joke.*

She turned her back on the crowd and rested her butt lightly on the edge of the picnic table.

"No," she admitted. "I'm just sick to death of them pestering me about dating."

Celia stifled a laugh, then turned her back to the patio, too. "Me neither," she said out the side of her mouth.

Marcy turned to her fully. "*Really?*"

Celia nodded. "Really. I couldn't take the pressure anymore either."

They both burst out laughing. It was the closest moment Marcy had ever had with her cousin.

"Oh, and now the lesbians have found each other," Aunt Phyl called from behind them. "Over there yucking it up while we sit here without any grandkids. Well, I got news for you, girls. It's still wrong to date your own cousin, even if you *are* a homosexual."

"She's *not* a homosexual," Marcy heard her mother protest.

And she and Celia burst into another fit of laughter.

Hard to believe, Marcy thought, but Aunt Phyl's party had ended up being the highlight of her day. The moment she left the gathering she felt the weight of all her problems descend on her again.

Not that they'd ever really left her.

Truman, she thought almost wistfully. He hadn't been out of her thoughts all day, though she'd kept pushing him away. While everyone grilled her about being dateless, she'd imagined how it would have felt to arrive at the party with him. How *impressed* they all would have been. So tall and handsome. So funny and charming. Her mother would adore him. Uncle Bruce would love him too. Even her father would respect him, if he ever turned up.

What would that feel like? she'd wondered.

Then she remembered what a lying snake he was. How could he take her to bed—*twice!*—when he had a girlfriend who came and made him steamship round for dinner? A girlfriend with gorgeous blonde hair and a body that wouldn't quit. For some reason, Marcy couldn't get the sight of those three gold bracelets the girl wore from her mind. They looked so . . . so *rich.* Marcy didn't know much about jewelry, but those bracelets had been twenty-four carat, without a doubt. She had such a moneyed look about her, she had to have been the one with the limousine that night.

Where in the world had he met a girl like that?

But what did it matter? Maybe it was a good thing, she thought, pulling into her building's parking garage.

Now she knew he was a lying, two-timing jerk, and that was a lot more motivation to stay away from him than the fact that he was her witness.

She shifted the car into park and swallowed over a lump of self-pity in her throat. He was inappropriate for her, she'd known that before she got involved with him at all. He was just like all those charming losers from her old neighborhood.

But still, she'd thought they might be building toward something really special. Even if it was wrong.

By the time she got to the lobby she felt as if she'd been put through the wringer. The events of the day had sustained her, kept her from thinking too much, but now that she was home, alone, she couldn't stop thinking about last night, and then the girl with the steamship round.

She was shuffling through the lobby, feeling like an old lady in need of a walker, when Javier called to her.

"Miss P! Miss P!" He came out from behind his desk and hurried toward her. "A man, he came here looking for you but I tole him you gone out. So he wait, right there." He pointed to the couch over which the ficus hung. "For like a *hour*. He only just left little bit ago."

"Who was he?" she asked, her heart leaping despite her mind's injunction not to. But Truman wouldn't check with Javier, she knew that. She just hoped it wasn't Guido. "Did he leave a name?"

"Yes, ma'am, he did. His name Truman Fleming." He drew the words out slowly, as if he'd been instructed to make sure to get it right. "Yes, that's it. Troo-man Flem-ming."

13

Sunday, October 27

WORD-A-DAY!

JETTISON: v., to rid oneself of encumbering cargo: as in dumping a companion whose value one might have overestimated

Marcy sat at her dining-room table and unfolded the yellow legal-sized piece of paper that she had found folded between doorknob and frame last night. In pencil, in a masculine hand, were the words, *Woke up and you were gone. Thought it must have been a dream.* Followed by a dashing letter *T* with a period beside it.

She flattened the paper out in front of her with her hands and studied his writing as if it could tell her more than the words themselves. Slanted and sure, the script was distinctive. Strong, honest. Too bad the man wasn't.

So maybe the blonde didn't tell him she'd come by. Maybe she believed Marcy's lame I-must-have-the-wrong-apartment excuse. Maybe she was not just a bimbo but a bitch and took credit for the dog food, too.

Which was unfair—that woman was as much a victim of Tru Fleming as Marcy was—but Marcy didn't care. Even if the blonde had told, it wasn't as if Truman would ever admit he was a philandering jerk. He'd just come up with some charming lie that Marcy would be all too tempted to believe.

No, it was better if he didn't know that she knew. Then she could just call the whole thing off because of the case and be done with it. She wouldn't appear jealous and he wouldn't believe he stood a chance with her. He was off limits to her for more reasons than fidelity, anyway.

So she had to talk to him, but not now, she thought. Besides, she couldn't call him and she wasn't *ever* going to drop by his apartment again. She'd just wait until he popped up in her world, as he always did eventually, then lay it all on the line.

Now she was going to go to work. It was Sunday, sure, but she had a *lot* to do. It was *not* because she felt like being childish and avoiding Truman. Honest.

But Truman didn't try again. He'd left her the note on an impulse. An impulse driven by the fact that Heather the Cook lived just a couple of blocks away and he'd felt obliged to drop her off. Okay, maybe more than a couple, but in the same neighborhood, anyway. The same general area. So he'd been drawn to Marcy's door like a moth to a flame. With similar results likely, he'd thought morosely.

Then, when she wasn't home, he'd waited. For what? he'd asked himself time and again. He wasn't sure. He'd just wanted to see her again. Because when he was with her, he thought things like *this could work* and *she's not like anyone I've ever known before.*

Now he wasn't sure what he should do next.

Because she left so quickly this morning, the enduring question remained. Did she regret sleeping with him because of the case, or did she regret compromising her standards?

It seemed he would never know. It was now nearly one week later—one *week*!—and she hadn't gotten back to him. Even after that nice note he'd left her.

To his mortification, it appeared she was dumping him.

This was not hard to understand. She was an expensive girl, and for all she knew he was broke. Naturally she'd be as practical as every other woman with an expensive wardrobe and a penchant for nice cars, and she'd decide he wasn't her type.

His disappointment in her was profound.

Which was why it surprised even him that when he saw her on Friday during his lunch hour—and hers, apparently—walking down K Street toward Vie de France for lunch, he rushed to catch up to her.

"Call me crazy, but I didn't think you were the love-'em-and-leave-'em type, Miss P," he said, drawing next to her and matching her stride for stride.

She looked up at him, startled, and stopped in her tracks. People behind them on the crowded sidewalk stopped short, looked annoyed, and edged around them.

"What do you mean?" she asked, giving him one of her direct looks.

"I mean, I thought I'd hear from you after last week. Did you get my note?" he asked, suddenly realizing it could well have fallen off the door. That would explain everything.

But she smiled politely and said, "Yes, I did. Thanks. And Javier told me you waited for me. I'm sorry. I had plans that night."

He crossed his arms over his chest. The girl was emotionless. What was the matter with her?

"And you didn't think some kind of . . . I don't know . . . *response* to all that was appropriate?"

She shrugged. He couldn't believe his eyes.

He was being blown off! He'd let his guard down and now he was paying for it. She was every bit as pretentious as he'd feared. More so, even.

"I've been really busy, Truman." She moved toward the plate-glass window they stood in front of to get out of the way of pedestrians.

Truman stepped next to her, feeling more foolish with every passing minute. "It's been almost a week. You didn't have a moment in all that time?"

"A moment?" she asked, eyebrows raised. "To do what? Call you up?"

"Well, hey, I'm sorry I don't have a phone, but—"

"But nothing, Truman. Don't go climbing up on that high horse again. Besides, I remember your going a week without talking to me quite comfortably the last time we, uh, got together like that. What's the problem now?"

"The problem is—" he began, but she cut him off.

"You know what? Never mind. Because the fact is this isn't going to work out between us and we both know it. Why drag it out? Why say a whole bunch of stuff we don't mean?"

He looked at her, stunned. Not that he hadn't expected it, but he hadn't expected her to be so . . . so heartless about it.

"Listen," she said, her expression all business. "*Burton v. Planners* is heating up, so it's probably a good thing we ran into each other. We're going to have to get together soon to prep you for depositions."

"I can't believe you're so . . . you're acting so . . ."

"What?" She cocked her head and looked at him knowingly.

And was that a trace of amusement he saw in her eyes? He hoped not. He really, really hoped not.

"Last Friday, I thought . . . Jesus. I thought you were different. How can you be so . . . ?"

"So practical?" she asked.

Aha! So there it was.

He scoffed elaborately. "Girls like you, you're always *practical* when it comes to guys like me, aren't you?"

"I've already explained to you, Truman. You're my witness. It's *extremely* unethical for me to be involved with one of my witnesses."

"It's not *that* unethical," he said dismissively. "I'm a fact witness, not your client."

She stood there shaking her head until he looked at her again. "Like you have any idea what's unethical and what isn't."

He paused, wondering if she meant that in the legal sense, or as broadly as it sounded. "I know more than you think I do. I've got a pretty sure feeling you're blowing me off because of something other than the case. And I think we both know what that is."

She looked at him stonily.

"All right." He threw up his hands. "Fine. You win. You know where to find me." He turned and started walking away, fury bubbling from every pore. He thought she would have at least couched it all in some sweet talk about how it just wasn't right, how her feelings were true but she just couldn't justify . . . *something* so it wasn't just wham-bam-thank-you-sir.

Truman couldn't believe how incensed he felt. She was shallow, that was what got him. He'd been telling himself for weeks now she was probably shallow, but he'd never believed it until this minute.

This minute, when she'd thrown him out like last week's news.

The following Tuesday, Marcy knew just what she had to wear for the firm's party. Her best suit, cream-colored merino wool, with ivory pumps and a tortoiseshell barrette holding her hair in a short, neat ponytail. She put on her best understated gold jewelry from Tiffany's, her Gucci watch, and a gold pearl ring she'd bought at an estate sale two years before to celebrate her first raise.

She had to look successful, she thought with a slow exhale, examining the ensemble. Not to impress the clients so much as her boss.

Dress for success, she'd heard him say on more than one occasion when complimented on a tie or pair of cufflinks. God knew Win Downey spared no expense on his wardrobe.

She took one last look at her makeup in her rearview mirror, then got out of the car and locked it. Her heels echoed in the parking garage as she walked to the elevator.

She was nervous—not so much for herself, as for Calvin. He'd been cool as a cucumber when she'd visited him last night. The food was ready, they'd rented a truck to get it to the party. And he'd hired enough servers and assistants to make the whole evening run smoothly. He was definitely a professional, Marcy thought. She didn't know what she was worried about.

Walking into the party, she wished Trish had been able to ride with her. Trish had brought a date—the infamous Palmer Roe, forgiven, apparently, for the tube-top incident—so Marcy was left to go solo. Despite the fact that she knew most of the people who worked at the firm, she always hated walking into a party alone. Especially one like this, where everyone noticed what you wore and with whom you arrived.

She really should have gotten a date. Her mind flicked briefly to Truman, then shuddered away. That was all she needed, a crush on a man with no ambition and even less character.

She made her way over to the punch table, waving to the guy from the copy room and eyeing the efficient collection of white-coated servers working the room. Calvin really did have it under control, she thought with a smile.

"Hey," a soft voice said as its owner goosed her from behind. "Lookin' good," Trish said, grinning, as Marcy turned, taking a glass of punch from the server at the same time.

Marcy smiled at her friend, who looked like a million bucks in a classic gray Armani suit. In one hand she held a glass of champagne, looking so natural and at ease Marcy thought she was probably born with a glass of Cristal in her hand.

"Lookin' good yourself," she said, glancing behind Trish for a glimpse of the infamous Mr. Roe. "Where's your date? Don't tell me he stood you up." She grinned. No guy in his right mind would stand up Trish Hamilton.

Trish gave a wry look. "Don't I wish. It would save me from myself. But no, he's here. He just went to the men's room."

"Be sure to introduce me. I'm dying of curiosity."

"Sure, that'll be a treat. I haven't been able to introduce him to anyone all night. Turns out Palmer knows more people here than I do. The man's a tireless socializer."

"He's probably trying to impress you," Marcy said, wondering what that would be like.

"He's exhausting me. Oh God, look at what Kendall's wearing."

Kendall Scott was a new associate just out of school, famous in the firm for wearing sexy little dresses to work that were more suited to evening wear.

Marcy had more than once thought about gently saying something to her—nearly every lawyer in the place made fun of her—but the girl always acted so snotty and superior she had finally given up.

"It looks like a spiderweb." Marcy squinted across the room. "Oh my God. Is it . . . ? Tell me it's not see-through."

They giggled softly together and continued to look around the room, exchanging little bits of gossip and commenting on who was with whom. Marcy and Trish each plucked a snow pea–wrapped shrimp off a server's passing plate, then a bit of sate, a crab puff, and stuffed mushrooms.

"The food is fantastic," Trish said through a mouthful of mushroom. "This is your friend who made this?"

Marcy nodded. "Calvin Deeds. Used to own Bella Luna."

"Sweet Lord in heaven," Trish said, snaring another crab puff from a passing waiter. "This is *so* much better than last year's."

Marcy smiled. This party could really make Calvin. "Listen, do me a favor, Trish. If anyone comments on the food to you, be sure to mention Calvin's name. This could be a great first step to his getting back on his feet."

"Absolutely," Trish said. "I guess I'd better find Palmer, make sure he hasn't gotten lost." She laughed cynically. "As if he'd *ever* be lost at a party."

"Let me know when you find him. Remember I want to meet him," Marcy said.

"You will," Trish promised.

The two parted and Marcy made a point of mingling with people, mentioning the food, and dropping Calvin's name whenever anyone complimented it.

As the party wound down, Marcy was a little bothered that she hadn't had a chance to talk to Win at all. She'd seen him here and there, but he was always with a group of people. She hadn't gotten a chance to speak to him alone for the better part of a week, which always made her nervous—as if she were afraid he would forget about her and her career would go down the tubes.

She was just putting down her glass and thinking she should go when she saw Calvin, dapper in a black tuxedo she'd rented for him, talking to a beautiful, well-dressed older woman by the windows. Deciding to tell him what rave reviews his food was getting, Marcy headed in their direction.

He and the woman were talking animatedly when Marcy approached.

"Marcy!" Calvin greeted, with the most unfettered smile she'd seen on his face in months. "Come and meet this charming lady. Marcy, this is Sheila."

"Hello," Marcy smiled.

The silver-haired woman smiled back warmly. She smelled like Joy and looked so elegant she could have been hosting this party in the ballroom of a grand English country house, instead of being just a guest in the offices of a K Street law firm.

"How do you do, dear? Aren't you looking smart?" She held out her right hand and Marcy took it, noting as she did that on the woman's finger was the biggest diamond Marcy had ever seen. "I love your suit. Is that Versace?"

"Thank you. Yes, it is." Marcy looked down at her suit self-consciously, surprised by the compliment. "You really know your designers." She blushed and amended, "Obviously," with a vague motion toward the woman's perfectly tailored dress. "I mean, not that I know what you're—but you look so nice too, you obviously know good clothes."

Shut up, Marcy! Just shut up! she thought, hoping the woman was nobody important, because she sure was making an ass of herself.

She turned quickly to Calvin. "Calvin, I came over to tell you what *raves* the foo—"

"Did I mention," Calvin interrupted so abruptly that Marcy blushed further. Had she said something wrong again? "That Sheila is planning a trip to Italy this month?"

"Oh." Marcy glanced back at the woman named Sheila, who was still looking pleasant despite Marcy's social clumsiness. "Well, Calvin knows Italy well."

The least she could do was try to make Calvin look good. Why did this woman make her so nervous?

"Well, not *planning*, really," Sheila said. "Just toying with the idea. For Thanksgiving, you know. Do something different. I've always loved Tuscany, and if you're going to spend a holiday eating, there is no better place to do it than Italy."

As the older woman described her house in Tuscany, Marcy spotted Win standing alone by the buffet table.

"I'm so sorry, Calvin, Sheila, would you excuse me, please?" she asked during a lull in the conversation.

"Of course," they both said at once, then looked at each other and laughed.

Marcy walked away, intent on Win Downey.

"I'm sorry," Calvin said to Sheila as Marcy disappeared. "I didn't introduce you properly but I'm afraid I didn't catch your last name."

Sheila laughed, touching him briefly on the sleeve as she did so. "It's Fleming, dear, Sheila Fleming. You're such a gentleman, Calvin. Wherever did you come from? Why haven't I met you before?"

Marcy rode down the elevator trying to suppress the grin she wanted so badly to let bound onto her face like an exuberant puppy. But she was surrounded by people, most notably Trish and her date, Palmer Roe.

When she'd finally gotten to talk to Win Downey, he'd gone on and on about how proud he was of the job she was doing on the Burton case. The way she'd presented it in the Monday meeting, he'd said, he could've closed his eyes and believed she was a senior associate.

Or better, he'd said with a wink, which Marcy took to mean "partner track."

Granted, he was talking so expansively he'd obviously nipped a little at the champagne, but still. He hadn't had to say the things he had.

Then there was Calvin, who was apparently romantically interested in that diamond woman. Even better, *she* had appeared quite interested in *him*.

And his food! It couldn't have been any better received. From everyone she talked to, she believed it had gotten universal acclaim.

The whole evening could not have gone any better.

Against her will the image of Truman flitted through her mind once again. Okay, she let herself think. It might have gone better had Truman been a completely different person and come with her as her date. Then, yes, the evening could have been better.

She looked over at Palmer Roe, who was good-looking, charming, and rich, as they rode down the elevator together. *Trish has all the luck,* she thought. *She finds interesting men and they're perfect. I find an interesting man and he's broke, lies effortlessly, and juggles women like a street performer with bowling pins.*

She sighed as the elevator doors opened and the three of them exited into the garage. The smell of motor oil and exhaust was practically a relief after an evening spent clouded in every expensive cologne on the market.

"Where are you parked, Marcy?" Trish asked.

She pointed down the aisle in front of them. "I'm just down here. Next to that black BMW, I think."

"Let us walk you to your car," Palmer said, tucking

Trish's hand in his arm. "No woman should be alone in a parking garage at night."

Trish beamed up at him as if he'd just offered to send Marcy to college. "That's *so* nice. Isn't that *nice*, Marcy?"

Trish might have had a little too much champagne too.

Marcy laughed. "Yes, it is. Thank you, but I'm sure I'll be perfectly safe."

Palmer shook his head. "Nope. I won't hear of it. We're only an aisle away anyway, so it's not even out of our way."

The three walked to Marcy's car, laughing about modern-day chivalry, but as they rounded the black BMW they abruptly stopped laughing.

All four of Marcy's tires were flat.

Palmer dropped Trish's hand gently and moved toward the car. Getting down on one knee he fingered the tread of the closest one.

He looked back up at Marcy, his face full of concern. "They've been slashed."

Marcy was shaken badly, but there was no way she was going to accept Trish's offer to stay with her. For one thing, Marcy lived in a secure building. Supposedly. But for another, things were obviously going very well with Trish and Palmer, and Marcy didn't want to mess things up for her friend just because someone was trying to spook her.

"Really, you guys, thank you for your concern," she said to Palmer and Trish as they dropped her in front of her building. The night was cold and she clutched her coat around her as she bent to look in Trish's window. "But if someone was really going to attack me, would they give me such an obvious warning sign first? No, they're just trying to scare me."

"Well, they've scared *me*," Trish said. "Are you sure you don't want to stay with me? I know I'd feel better."

"Really, Marcy. Why take the chance?" Palmer said, leaning across Trish to look at Marcy out the window. One arm was stretched across the back of Trish's seat.

Marcy smiled. "Because I don't think there is a chance, for one thing. Besides, this is a very secure building."

She pictured Truman as he'd looked that first day he'd gotten around the doorman and startled her at her front door.

"If you're sure," Trish said, shaking her head.

"I am. And thanks for the ride."

"Want me to pick you up for work tomorrow?" Trish asked.

"I'll just take a cab, thanks. I might have to get in early. Prepping for depositions, you know."

They both made a face, then laughed, and Marcy let them go.

She watched them drive off, wishing she had a Palmer Roe to go home with. She didn't know why Trish complained about him so much. He seemed like a really decent guy. Not like *some* she could name.

With a sigh, she went up to her apartment. She was a bit nervous entering the darkened living room, but as she walked about, turning on every light in the place, it became clear no one was there and nothing had been disturbed.

While she couldn't say she slept particularly well, she did sleep and get up early the next morning. The first thing she did upon arriving at the office was write a note to Truman asking him to meet her at The Guards, a bar in Georgetown, at five thirty that evening. She had something *important* to talk about. Then she called a messenger service to courier it over to his apartment.

She shouldn't have been surprised, but she was when she had trouble getting someone to take the letter into that part of town. Finally, however, she tracked down a service that would do it and instructed them to slide the envelope under the door when they got there. In that neighborhood there was no way any sort of envelope would go untouched in the hallway.

Five fifteen saw her in the bar of The Guards. She hadn't heard from Truman, though she'd thought he might call and try to talk her into a different place, so there was a chance he wouldn't show. In any case, though, Marcy hadn't gone straight home, so if anyone was banking on her sticking to her routine they were thwarted. At least temporarily.

She'd had her car towed in the morning and had picked it up on the way here. Four new tires richer and six hundred dollars poorer, she sat nursing a vodka collins in the dark, polished bar. Around her, men in power suits chatted and drank while eyeing women in business dress and post-work, reapplied makeup. Large palmlike trees graced every corner, casting shadows on select private tables in the dim light. She'd thought about grabbing one of those, but she didn't want Truman getting the wrong idea.

"Hi, you're looking lonely over here all by yourself. Are you alone or waiting for someone?"

Marcy looked up to see a nice-looking guy in a blue pinstriped suit gazing down at her. Red tie, white shirt, he had to be a lawyer, she thought. In his hand he held a martini.

She smiled. He looked exactly like the kind of guy she always imagined herself with—well dressed, well groomed, well spoken—so she wondered why she felt disappointed it wasn't Truman.

"Waiting for someone," she said.

He gave her a rueful look and shook his head. "Just my luck," he said, and went back to his buddy at the bar.

She looked down at her drink. Maybe Truman would stand her up, she thought. She had been pretty cold to him the other day, and he had no idea why. But that was stupid, she told herself. Whether he knew she knew about the other woman or not, *he* certainly knew he was jerking her around. He deserved whatever he got.

At five forty-five, Marcy was wondering how long she should wait. She was feeling a little foolish, since the guy in the pinstriped suit was still glancing her way every now and then. If she nursed this drink much longer she'd either look like a liar or a loser. She should have brought some work.

She glanced at her watch again. Nearly six. The waiter appeared at her table.

"Anything else?" he asked, clearly wanting the table for more profitable patrons.

"No, I . . ." Just then she saw someone skulking in the front door. He was dressed in jeans and leather bomber jacket, along with dark sunglasses. He was even looking toward the wall as if he were afraid the masses would recognize him and come begging for his autograph. She started to laugh.

"Actually, I'll have another," she said, looking up at the waiter.

He walked off without replying and she was sure she saw him rolling his eyes.

Truman spotted her—she wasn't sure how, since he barely looked around the room and probably couldn't see a thing in those dark glasses—and headed straight for her table. Once there, he sat in the chair facing the wall and let his hair fall forward over his face.

"What was all that about? Is something wrong?" she asked, leaning slightly toward him, still trying to contain her smile.

"No," he said curtly.

She paused, then said, "Then why are you acting so . . ."

"So what? You summoned, I came. Was there something else you wanted? Flowers, maybe?"

She frowned and exhaled in exasperation. "Truman, I'm sorry if I sounded high-handed in my note, but you're so hard to get hold of you don't give me much choice."

He gave her a hard look through his hair. Or what she thought was a hard look—it was difficult to tell what with the Tom Cruise shades and all. It was all she could do not to reach over and brush the heavy locks from his face.

She glanced at the guy in the blue suit. He'd turned fully away now, no longer intrigued by her since her "date" had arrived.

Oh, the hell with him, she thought. *Stuck-up asshole.* She didn't want to date another lawyer anyway.

"You didn't call me here to talk about the phone situation again, did you?" he asked. His words dripped disdain.

"No." She looked at him a long moment, wondering

if coming to him had been such a wise idea. "Last night someone slashed my tires."

For a second Truman froze. Then he pulled the glasses from his face and flipped the hair out of his eyes with a quick motion of his head.

"What?" He gave her a look so penetrating her knees felt weak.

"I was at a party. At work. When I got back to my car all four tires had been slashed."

"Where was the car?"

"In the garage at my office. The Finkletter Building on K."

"Were you alone?" His eyes were pinned on her like an interrogator's. She felt her cheeks heat.

"No, I was with friends. They gave me a ride home."

"Did you see anyone suspicious? Hear anything? See someone walking away in a hurry, either there or at your apartment? In the lobby, maybe?"

She shook her head. "No, the garage was empty. My apartment was untouched. Truman, do you think Guido did this?"

He was silent a minute. "I don't think so."

"Why not? He was the first person I thought of. Maybe Planners knows I've talked to Donnie Molloy."

Truman pushed his glasses into the pocket of his coat and ran a hand through his hair. It was getting quite long, but Marcy was starting to like it.

"I'll ask Donnie tomorrow if anyone has contacted him," he said. "Or if anything weird has happened. Seems to me if something had, though, he'd have said something today. You might have noticed he's not exactly the quiet type."

The waiter stopped by at that moment and Truman ordered a beer. A Budweiser. Marcy sighed, picturing her father on the couch with a Bud in his hand.

"But who else would it be," she continued once the waiter had left, "if not Guido? They don't have another, what would you call him, a hit man? Do they?"

Truman looked at her closely and was sure he detected some real apprehension in her eyes. Of *course*. What a fool he'd been, thinking just because Guido was inept that Planners wouldn't hire someone else. But he really hadn't thought Planners was behind it all.

The whole thing had Lang written all over it, despite what Arthur had said. Lang was the one whose butt would be in a sling if Marcy won this lawsuit. Or rather, the one whose butt would be on the street, looking for a new job. And Lang was the one nasty, and stupid, enough to try to frighten someone off with dirty tricks. Planners would know they'd just find themselves in criminal court as well as civil.

"Marcy, I wasn't completely honest with you about Guido, uh, Arthur the other day." He thought with shame about his motivation for not telling her about Arthur's crush. He'd wanted her scared, just a little bit, just enough to keep him around.

Clearly that strategy had failed.

Her midnight eyes studied him. "What do you mean?"

"For reasons I don't want to get into, I didn't tell you all of what Arthur said and I'm sorry. The real reason he came to your apartment that night was because, well, he's got a little crush on you."

Marcy looked startled. "A crush?"

Truman nodded and she started to laugh.

"I'm serious. He said he went by your place to see if you'd go out with him." He smiled a little ruefully. "I guess you didn't make him feel very welcome."

She laughed again and Truman felt a pang of pity for the big oaf. "I guess not. Lucky me. I seem to attract all the—" She stopped, cast him a mortified look, and continued, "I just, I've had some bad luck with guys the last year or so."

He kept his eyes on her face. "And you think I'm bad luck too."

She started to say something—though it wasn't clear she was protesting—but Truman stopped her.

"It's okay, I know all about girls like you and how you don't want to be seen with guys like me."

She cocked her head and scrutinized him with narrowed eyes. "And by *guys like you* you mean guys who are . . . ?"

"BMW-free." He leaned back in his chair. "Don't worry, sugar, I understand completely. Guys like me are really only good for one thing."

He let that hang in the air a minute while her face grew red. Only she didn't look embarrassed or chagrined. She looked furious.

"Listen, Mr. Holier Than Thou," she said lowly, but she was interrupted by the waiter dropping off Truman's beer.

"You were saying?" he asked once the guy left.

"I think I explained my reasons for not continuing our . . . whatever you want to call it, our *affair*, the other day."

"The case."

She nodded. "The case."

"What a crock of—"

"Look, this should be good news for you. One less *chick* to juggle. Surely that's a relief." Her words came out incensed. "By the way, I'm finding a home for Folly this week. I think she needs to be somewhere she's not locked up in a bedroom all the time."

He leaned forward, his arms on the table in front of him. "What are you talking about? First of all, Folly's *fine* where she is. In fact, she's *so* not cooped up I had to tape the pieces of your letter together tonight to find out what it said. Anything that comes in under the door is a chew toy to her. And second of all, I'm not juggling anything, least of all chicks."

"Uh-huh. So that girl there the other night was just your chef, right? Or wait—maybe she's part of the delivery service you employ on your extravagant salary? Which is it, Truman? Girlfriend? Chef? Delivery service?"

He sat stunned. She knew about Heather. How did she know about Heather?

"Can't decide?" she continued. "Well, I'll tell you something, Truman. Don't bother, because I wouldn't believe what you told me anyway."

She stood up.

"Marcy, wait," he said, reaching out as if to take her by the hand.

But she whirled, grabbed her coat and purse off the back of the chair, and marched for the door.

Truman stood and started to follow but was caught by a hand on his arm.

"You're not going anywhere, buddy," the waiter told him. "Not until I get eighteen dollars and seventy-two cents. *Plus* tip."

14

Wednesday, November 6

WORD-A-DAY!

JACTITATION: n., a restless tossing to and fro: as when one reverses one's decision, yet again, about associating with a companion just recently jettisoned

Truman yanked his wallet out of his back pocket and shoved a twenty at the waiter. Another twenty out the window before it had a chance to cool off from the ATM.

"Hey," the waiter called as Truman bolted around tables and through the crowd at the door. "What kind of a tip is that?"

He caught Marcy halfway down the block, her high-heeled strides fast and purposeful, carrying her away from him as quickly as they could without running.

Panting, he got close and grabbed her arm, pulling her aside and out of the stream of people on the sidewalk. "Marcy, wait."

She turned and glared up at him. "I'm so sorry, Truman. I haven't been very professional. I forgot to mention that depositions are two weeks from today. The twentieth. My office will be in touch with you to set up a time to prep for them."

She started to turn but he didn't let go of her arm. She stopped.

"She was a chef, all right?" he said, regaining his breath and dropping his hand from her arm. "I know it's ridiculous and you probably won't believe me, but my mother, whom I definitely do not wish to talk about, thinks I'm not taking care of myself, so she hired Heather to come cook for me."

His heart was hammering in his chest. He didn't want to tell her about his mother, he didn't want to reveal any more about himself or his circumstances, but there was no story believable enough that it wouldn't sound like a lie.

"Heather?" Marcy asked, her voice strained and light. "So you have a chef named Heather now?"

He shook his head, frustrated by her stubbornness. Why did she want so badly to believe he was a jerk?

Because she'd slept with him and then found another woman in his apartment. It made perfect sense.

Because it meant—*possibly*—that she hadn't blown him off the other day because of his lack of money, and that elated him.

"I didn't even know she was coming. She showed up while I was getting my truck from over near the pool hall." Just the mention of that night roused his senses. She'd been so . . . so funny and open and incredible. Looking at her now, poised like a cobra ready to strike at any false word, he could hardly believe he'd ever held her as she quivered beneath his touch. "Marcy, I was as surprised to see her as you were. Probably more so."

Marcy narrowed her eyes. "Most mothers just bring

over a bunch of casseroles in Tupperware. *Your* mother sends a chef? And a steamship round?"

"Yeah, I know." He tried to laugh and leaned against a nearby parking meter. "Who expects a chef? *I* certainly didn't. It's just my mother. She's not the kind of person I can explain. We're . . . I guess you could say we're estranged."

She put one hand on her hip and regarded him skeptically. "*She* doesn't seem to be estranged. She sent you a chef named Heather."

He stuffed his hands in his pockets as a chill wind ruffled his hair. Looking down the street in consternation, he continued. "Listen, I told her not to come back. The chef, that is. I wish I had a better explanation, but I don't." He shifted his gaze to her, feeling honesty trapped in his chest along with his racing heart. "I'm not lying to you, Marcy. Heather is nobody. Nobody to me, anyway."

Marcy opened her mouth to protest but he held up a hand to silence her.

"Listen, I know you think you and I are wrong for each other, and maybe you're right. Trust me, I've had some of the same thoughts. But I wouldn't—really, you have to believe me—I wouldn't juggle women, as you put it. And I most definitely wouldn't juggle you."

She was silent a long time. Then, "Why wouldn't you juggle me, Truman?" she asked quietly.

A cold sweat broke out across his forehead, despite the chilling breeze. He could not wrest his gaze from hers. "Because . . ." He stopped, the words lodged in his throat.

Her brows rose, but she looked uncertain.

"Because I respect you, Marcy."

She laughed, but her eyes were still unsure. "Oldest line in the book, Fleming. Though I guess I'm lucky to get it *after* the nights of passion, instead of before."

He pressed his lips together and looked at the ground. God, she was a tough nut to crack.

"If things were different, if you and I came from different places . . ." He shook his head, a small smile on his lips as he studied her face. She was so feminine and strong and smart. And so damned determined to keep him at bay.

She looked away and he thought he could see her blushing under his gaze. His eyes dropped to her throat as she swallowed.

"Okay, Truman." She turned back. Her dark eyes glittered in the lights of the city street. "Let's say I believe you."

"But you don't?"

She pulled her coat closer around her. The breeze blew strands of her hair across her face. She tucked them behind her ear with her fingers and looked down the street again.

"I don't know. But it doesn't matter, because we aren't going to work. We've both said it. We both know it." Her voice was tired, defeated.

He wondered if she felt as sad about that fact as she looked.

"Listen," he said, glancing at the restaurant behind him. "Let's pop in here for an Irish coffee, get warmed up, figure out what we're going to do about Guido, and get past all this."

If he could just get her to loosen up a little, maybe she'd see that what was important was right here in front of her. Strip away the power suits and the tool belts, the career considerations and the minimum wage issues, and what you had were two people who were dangerously attracted to one another. Two people who wanted each other so badly they threw all caution to the wind. And that was a hell of a lot of caution.

She continued to look down the street and he wished he could see her face.

"Deal?" he asked, bending his knees and tipping his head to catch her eye.

She met his gaze, her own dark and inscrutable. After a second, she smiled slightly. "All right. But only because I'm freezing."

He smiled and she looked at the ground again.

"How about this place right here?" He swept his hand behind them. "Look, you can see their fine, shiny bar right through the window. I believe I can even see the Jameson's."

The wind picked up again and Marcy said, "Brrrr," and walked past him to the door. "I'm going in. You can stand out here and wax poetic about it if you want."

Marcy couldn't believe it. She was sitting across from Truman, they were talking about a subject near and dear to her heart, namely her own safety; she was trying to believe, God help her, that stupid story about his mother hiring a blonde bombshell named Heather as his cook; and all she could do was watch Truman's lips as he spoke and imagine them nibbling at her ear, leaving a line of kisses down her neck . . .

"I'm telling you," his lips were saying, "after I talked to him I was sure Arthur was going to back off. This . . ."

He turned his hands palm up on the bar. "This could well be the work of someone else, someone more . . . threatening. Truthfully? I'm worried, Marcy."

She nodded soberly and looked at his hands. She remembered those fingers touching her, exploring her body in exquisite ways, ways most men didn't know how to explore.

"Is there someone you can stay with for a while?" he continued. "Just until the case is over? I don't like the idea of them knowing where you live, and that you live alone."

She picked up her Irish coffee, pictured Truman's bedroom, and sucked the last of the whipped cream from the bottom with her straw. "I guess I could stay with my friend Trish. But I really don't want to do that. She's just starting to see this new guy . . ."

"Marcy . . ." He touched her hand, then quickly crossed his arms over his chest. "I can't believe she'd mind. I mean, I don't know her, but if she's a true friend she'd want to be sure you were safe."

Marcy nodded and glanced out the window to the street. It was cold out there, and so warm and cozy in here. She never wanted to leave. Never wanted to step back into the world where she was a lawyer and Truman was an aimless laborer, and life's shoulds and shouldn'ts got so confusing.

"I know, I know," she said. "Trish already offered to let me stay. But I think she has real feelings for Palmer and I'd hate to be there, cramping her style, when I'd probably be perfectly safe in my own apartment."

"Palmer?" Truman asked, in a strange voice.

Marcy glanced at his face. "Yeah, Palmer Roe. He's a really nice guy, and seems to be interested in her too. But you know how it is at the beginnings of a rela—"

She bit off the word and glanced at him through her lashes. Perhaps he thought *they* were in the beginning of a relationship. No, no of course he wouldn't, because they weren't; they'd just decided that. But they were in the beginning of *something*. Oh God, it was all too confusing. Her feelings about him bounced so wildly back and forth, pro and con, yes and no, they were giving her emotional whiplash. And now here she was stuck in the middle of this sentence with nowhere to go.

But Truman didn't appear to be noticing. He was lost in some kind of reverie of his own.

"Okay, maybe Trish's place isn't the answer," he said. "But you at least shouldn't be going out alone. You don't have any more parties to go to, have you? I mean, not alone, I hope."

She looked at him, considering. "Actually, I do have a function. A formal party. A week from Friday."

"You're going alone?"

She felt her cheeks warm. *Alone? Again?* What a loser he must think she is, always without a date. But before she could answer, he continued.

"Because what I'm thinking is, maybe what you should do is go with a bodyguard."

She laughed. "A bodyguard!"

"I'm serious. No one would have to know but you that's what he was, but you'd be safer. If someone wanted to get to you—even just to scare you or intimidate you—finding you alone in a frilly dress wearing high heels would be a perfect time to do it. You wouldn't exactly be mobile, or ready to fight back in that situation."

Marcy felt her pulse accelerate. "I don't wear frilly dresses. Besides, I wouldn't even know where to find a bodyguard."

"Well . . ." Truman drummed his fingers on the bar. "Maybe just a big friend. Big *male* friend, that is." He sat up straight and sent her a sidelong glance. "Someone to make whoever might be watching you think twice."

Watching you . . . The words sent a shiver down Marcy's spine. She hated the idea of someone, particularly Truman, thinking she couldn't take care of herself, but what was the harm in being cautious? After all, she had plenty of evidence someone was trying to intimidate her. Getting some protection, even just another pair of eyes on the lookout, would simply be smart.

Besides, maybe Truman would like the idea of becoming a bodyguard and possibly consider that line of work. It would have to have a better future than drifting from construction job to construction job.

"Well," she said, going for as matter-of-fact a tone as possible, "you'd really be the best one because you know many of the Planners employees. Like you knew Arthur. That was a big help."

He nodded. "That's true. I did know Arthur."

"And it's not like it would be a date."

He shook his head. "Definitely not."

"Because you'd just be there to keep an eye out for . . . for another Planners . . . infraction, so to speak."

He nodded again. "Absolutely."

"So really, *you're* the perfect person. You ever give any

thought to being a bodyguard? Could be an interesting career. Probably better money than construction."

One side of his mouth kicked up. "Trying to better me again, sugar?"

She sighed. "God forbid."

"So when's this party?"

"A week from Friday. But I don't know, Truman. It's black tie. Would you be comfortable at a function like that?"

"What's that supposed to mean?" he asked.

"It means it's formal. You'll have to get a tux."

He looked at her, exasperated. "I *know* what black tie means. I meant . . . oh, the hell with it. I'll be fine." He paused, then added, "In fact, I used to work at The Four Seasons. So I may even know some people there."

She raised a brow. "You? You used to willingly hob-nob with the well-to-do?"

"I wouldn't call it hobnobbing. I only worked there." He gave her a sideways glance. "But don't worry. I'm not gonna go out of my way to talk to anyone. I'll sink into the background like I'm not even there, so don't be concerned I'll embarrass you around your friends."

She smiled wryly. "They're not my friends. It's another firm's party. I was only invited because I worked with them on a case earlier in the year."

He looked at her in a way she thought looked almost stricken. "Another law firm?"

"Yeah. Rock 'n' Roll—uh—Robinson, Rock and Knoll. They're on Connecticut and L. But the party's at the Hilton, I think."

"Jesus," he muttered, and pushed a hand through his hair.

"What?" She leaned forward.

He straightened. "Nothing."

"No, what is it?"

"It's nothing. I just, I think I know someone who worked there. But probably not. Not anymore."

Marcy felt a cloud of something like jealousy form in her chest. It was a woman, it had to be. Guys didn't get that look when they talked about other guys they didn't want to see. He probably dated some woman who worked at the firm. Good God, for all she knew he was *still* dating someone who worked at that firm. Maybe he had some sort of weird *thing* for lawyers.

"Look, if it's some girl you don't want to see," she said in a voice that was too hard to seem unconcerned, "then I'll find myself another bodyguard. I have no intention of being the victim of a jealous ex-lover in addition to whoever Planners has got after me." She paused, noticing the expression on his face. "*What?*"

Truman was smirking at her. "It's not some girl I don't want to see. Thank you for sounding jealous, though. Does the old ego good."

She forced a laugh and took a sip from her empty glass, trying to regain her composure. "Like your ego needs any help. Besides, I'm not jealous. Just not in the mood to meet up with any more *chefs*." Now she *was* sounding jealous, she thought, even to herself.

"Actually *I* was hoping to," he said, grinning. "What other reason is there to go to one of these things if not for the food?"

They arranged a time to meet—Truman would come to her apartment and they'd take her car—and they left the bar, Marcy reiterating that this was not a date and she would expect to pay him for being her bodyguard.

Truman just smiled and told her he'd see her next Friday.

Marcy drove off with the image of that smile in her head all the way home.

He must have been out of his mind to agree to go to this damn party, Truman thought, pulling his truck noisily up in front of the wrought-iron gate at the house on California Street Thursday night. The muffler was barely hanging on to the exhaust pipe, making him something less than inconspicuous.

Trouble was, he'd already made a big deal about going before she mentioned the damn party was at Rock 'n' Roll. By then she'd been suspicious he was worried about running into another woman, so he couldn't back out.

Or at least he didn't think so at the time. Now he thought he should have done whatever he could to get out of it and convince her she was wrong about him later.

He pulled the truck close to the entry panel and punched in the code. With a well-oiled hum the gates drew open and Truman drove through. He hoped his mother wasn't home but if she was, she would know he was here from the subtle beep the alarm system gave off at the opening of the gate. Either that or the thunderous noise his truck made every time he pushed on the accelerator.

He parked in the circular drive and sure enough, as

Reginald opened the front door, his mother was descending the stairs.

Truman greeted Reginald, inquired about his children, then turned to his mother.

She was dressed to the nines and wore a shocked look on her face. "Truman! What are *you* doing here?"

Reginald discreetly disappeared into the back hallway.

"You say that like you're not happy to see me," he said. He'd anticipated having to ward off her happy assumptions that he was back for good. Not that he'd lived here for many years, but back in the fold, as it were.

"Don't be silly, I'm always happy to see you." She waved the question off with a gold-ringed hand and continued to look at him in concern. "But what are you doing here?"

"I've just come by to pick something up. Is everything all right?"

"Pick something up?" she asked, her voice a tad higher than normal. "What is it? Do you know just where it is or shall I help you look for it?"

He studied her. She was acting oddly. "What is it, Mother? I'm sorry I didn't call, but I didn't think it was necessary. Are you expecting someone?"

She laughed and patted her hair, descending the rest of the stairs, not looking at him. "Expecting someone? Me? Who would I be expecting?"

He shrugged and started for the stairs, entering her cloud of perfume as she reached the foyer. "I don't know. You're just acting . . . strangely."

She looked miffed. "*I'm* acting strangely? You're living in a slum and *I'm* acting strangely?"

"I didn't mean it that way." He stopped next to her

and kissed her on the cheek. "What's gotten into you? You seem nervous."

"I'm not nervous." She made a visible effort to calm down. He saw her take a deep breath, then look him up and down with a deep exhale. "I'm so tired of seeing you in those ratty old jeans, Truman. Don't construction workers ever wear anything nicer?"

"Not often," he said, mounting the steps. "Not this one."

She followed him. "Will it take long to find what you're looking for?"

He paused on the middle landing and turned to give her a bemused look. She stopped several steps below.

"I'm not sure, but I'm starting to think maybe it will. I'm starting to think I might be here until . . . oh, I don't know . . . until the doorbell rings?"

"Oh, all right," she said, kneading her bejeweled hands together. "Very well, I *am* expecting someone."

Truman's brows rose and he couldn't stop the grin that broke onto his face. "A *male* someone? As in a *date* someone?"

"If you must know, yes." She ascended the last few steps to meet him. "And if you don't mind I'd rather him not see my son looking like he was just pulled from a trash heap. He's a gentleman with class."

Truman eyed his mother with a smile on his face as they walked toward his old bedroom. "What's his name? Where'd you meet him? Have you gone out with him before? I think maybe I should stay and make sure his intentions are honorable."

She opened the door to his bedroom and went in. "Don't be impertinent. If things work out you'll meet him eventually. He's only coming for dinner."

He cast a playful glance down at her dress. "I don't know, Mom, you're looking pretty spiffy. He may want to stay for dessert too."

"Truman!" she scolded but he saw the blush hit her cheeks. "Calvin is not that kind of man."

"Believe me, Mother, they're *all* that kind of man."

"Calvin is a *gentleman*, and I'd appreciate it if you didn't bring your gutter mentality into my house."

"Actually it's your gutter mentality, Mother. I meant dessert as in pie, not—"

"That'll be enough of that." She held up a hand. "Now, what is it you're looking for?"

Truman moved to the closet and rummaged through his old suits, slacks, dress shirts, and polos. He'd moved them here after giving up his own house to live in Southeast. He reached the back of the closet and pulled out a garment bag.

"Just this," he said.

This time it was his mother's turn to look intrigued. "Your tuxedo? What on earth do you need that for in that tenement you call home?"

"I'm going to a dog and pony show," he said, thinking sourly of the pretentious posturing he was sure would be going on at Rock 'n' Roll.

"A dog and— Have you still got that wretched dog? I thought you said you were only keeping it temporarily."

He shrugged, unzipping the bag and inspecting the contents to make sure everything was there. "I thought so too, but now I've changed my mind. It looks like Folly's here to stay." *In so many ways,* he thought.

He hadn't wanted to resort to his old wardrobe, but

the idea of wearing, and paying for, a rented tux seemed not just unappealing but wasteful. For one thing, he needed to conserve his meager cash. For another, he had no desire to wear a polyester tux left over from the Carter administration, which is what he thought most of those rentals looked like.

"I know you're not going to wear that Armani tuxedo for a *dog*, Truman Fleming. Now tell me what you're doing. Have *you* got a date?" She gave him a sly smile. Much like the one he'd given her, he was sure.

"It's not a date. It's a job. I'm doing some security work." It wasn't a lie.

"In a tuxedo?"

"It's an undercover job," he said pointedly.

"Ah." She nodded sagely. "This must be the *dangerous* undercover work you sent poor sweet Heather away from."

He glanced at her, saw the knowing look in her eyes and couldn't stop a low laugh. "Really, Mother, did you honestly think that would work? How desperate do you think I am?"

"Pretty desperate," she said, "judging by the looks of your apartment. Are you at least playing security for a woman?"

He gazed at her, gave her the smallest smile and nodded once. "Yes, it's a woman. And that's all I'm going to tell you."

He zipped the garment bag back up and headed for the stairs.

"Is it a woman you're interested in?" she asked, following him back down the hall.

"I told you, I'm not going to tell you any more."

"Is it the woman Heather saw in your apartment?"

He stopped on his way down the stairs and looked back up at her. "*Now* I see what you liked so much about Heather. She's a blabbermouth."

"Well, she was blonde. And I know how much you like blondes. You haven't answered my question."

He started back down the stairs and stopped by the door. "What question?"

"Is the woman you're working security for the same woman who went to your apartment that night?"

"Don't you have a date coming?" he asked, opening the door and glancing down the driveway toward the street.

She leaned forward and looked around him. The street was empty. She gave him an irked look. "That wasn't nice. Now answer my question and I'll let you get out of here."

He grinned. "I hate to break it to you, Mother, but you're not actually stopping me."

"Truman . . ."

"All right, yes. It's the same woman."

His mother's brows rose and she nodded. "Aha. Very interesting."

"Not really." He stepped onto the porch and swung the garment bag over his shoulder.

"I have a feeling about this," she sang.

He trotted down the front stoop and opened the door to his truck. "How can you have a feeling about it? You don't know anything about her. She could be a hundred years old and ugly."

"Not according to Heather."

Truman shook his head and laughed. "Well, I'm glad

Heather found her attractive. I'll pass it along if it seems appropriate."

"Truman!" she scolded, but her eyes were laughing.

"Have fun on your date tonight, Mother."

"And you on yours," she countered.

"It's not a date," he said out the window.

"Whatever you say, dear." She smiled.

Truman started the truck, the noise making any further conversation impossible. He waved, she blew him a kiss and he pulled out of the driveway, pausing to let the gates open.

He wondered if Marcy would resist him if she knew he came from all this. Something inside him thought he knew the answer, but it wasn't the one he wanted to believe. So he put the car in gear and drove decisively away.

If he was going to get her, he thought, he was going to get her without the trappings of his family's wealth. Otherwise he'd never believe she wanted him, and him alone.

15

Friday, November 15

WORD-A-DAY!

ALIEN: n., foreign, extrinsic to a thing's fundamental nature; extrapolated, one who could not possibly understand or become an essential part of one's life

Marcy was nervous. Truman was picking her up in fifteen minutes and her stomach kept crawling into her throat.

Did she believe his story about Heather? Was she a fool to think he could be trusted? Was she judging him with her head or her hormones?

She paced in front of the mirror, paused long enough to look at herself in her red velvet gown, then continued on past toward the dressing table. She was dressed appropriately for a fancy party, she thought. She was ready to rub elbows with others in her field.

Where she was getting confused, though, was whether she was dressed appropriately to be going out with Truman.

But even that was not completely right. While she wished she could wear something like she'd worn to the benefit ball—that killer black dress that had prompted such gratifying appreciation in Truman—she knew for a party amongst colleagues she had to be more conservative.

So, she told herself, she was fine. It didn't matter that her dress was conservative.

What she really ought to be worried about was Truman's attire. He said he knew what black tie meant, and she had mentioned the fact that a tuxedo was required. Should she have been more specific? All she could do now was pray to God he didn't show up in a powder-blue high-school-prom-style tux.

She stopped again in front of the mirror. She looked all right, she thought. The dress was from Neiman Marcus and plenty expensive enough to impress those who cared about such things. And there'd be plenty of people there who cared about such things, she knew. So what was she so wrought up about?

Truman, she thought, forcing a deep breath into her lungs. She was in a knot because of Truman. Because this felt like a date, not an arrangement with a bodyguard.

She sat down on the bed and put her head in her hands.

She *wanted* it to be a date. She wanted Truman's jaw to drop and his eyes to pop out of his head when he saw her. She wanted romance with a capital 'R' with him but she couldn't let herself even hope for it.

His life was too different from hers. They were on opposite trajectories. What she kept falling back on, however, was that they didn't *need* to be. Truman could be so much more. He could find a better job, ensure a better future, and she had to believe he'd be happier doing it. He just had too much to offer to live in a rat's nest and work as a laborer for no money.

He should network tonight, she thought, standing up and moving to the dressing table. There'd be plenty of people there who could help him find a job. Maybe something in sales, or marketing. In a tuxedo, he'd look as suitable for certain positions as anyone else in the room. She'd try to steer him to some of the right people, she thought. He had to want something more for himself. Everyone did, didn't they?

A knock sounded on the door and Marcy jumped so drastically she dropped the bottle of perfume she'd just picked up. Fortunately it was a spray bottle so it didn't end up all over her bedroom floor.

She picked the bottle up and set it on the table. Then she took a slow, deliberate breath—deep in and long out—and walked down the hall.

She unlocked the bolt, slid the chain from its track, and opened the door.

The sight of him nearly knocked the breath clean out of her.

He wore a black tux, classically tailored, that looked like it was made for him. His hair, while still long, was neatly combed, and he had obviously shaved that evening. He stood with his hands folded in front of him and a wide stance as if he were on the deck of a ship.

He looked incredible. Like a model. Like an ad for Mercedes. Like the Aramis Man.

Marcy was speechless.

He gave her a short bow, his striking gray eyes smiling as he passed her to enter the apartment.

"One bodyguard, at your service," he said, his gaze streaking down her body in the red velvet dress.

Marcy pushed herself to respond. "Is that a *rental*?" She reached one hand out to finger the material of his tux.

"What kind of question is that? I could ask you the same thing, you know."

Marcy blushed. "It's just . . ." She held a hand, palm up, toward him. But the question was rude and she didn't feel like having her manners corrected by Truman Fleming. "You look great," she finished lamely, if sincerely.

"So do you, Miss Paglinowski."

She suddenly wished she had some wine or something to drink to ease her tension a little. But she hadn't wanted to do anything that would make this look like she thought it was a date.

They stood in awkward silence a minute before Tru said, "Shall we go?"

"Sure. Yeah, we should go." She glanced around for her purse, realized it was in the bedroom—blushed at the mere thought of her bedroom—and excused herself to go get it.

Once there, she sat down on the bed a second. Her heart was beating a mile a minute and her mouth was dry. Her skin felt electrified, as if her nerves were reaching out to be touched by him, and she wondered if testosterone had some sort of magnetic quality that could pull her to him even against her will.

She was as nervous as she'd ever been with a guy. And she was usually only nervous when she was interested in someone. Very interested. In fact, the last time she remembered feeling this way was on her first date with Stephen Howe, her junior year in college. She'd been in love with Stephen Howe since she'd been a freshman and they'd ended up dating for two years.

So the fact that she was nearly incapacitated with nerves for Truman Fleming was nothing if not portentous.

What, exactly, did she feel for him?

Or rather, what did she want from him?

She closed her eyes and couldn't answer, not in words, not even in her head. But her racing heart told the whole story.

Marcy picked up her purse and joined him in the living room. He turned when he heard her heels on the hallway floor and smiled as she entered the room.

A rush of longing rose within her. He could be her dream man, standing there in a tux in the middle of her living room. Of course, he could have been her dream man standing naked in the middle of her living room too.

"Let's go," she said brusquely, grabbing her coat from the hall closet.

They left her apartment and rode down the elevator in silence. As they made their way to the parking garage, Marcy fished her keys out of her purse and handed them to him.

"Would you mind driving?" she asked. "I hate driving in these heels." She swept her skirt up a few inches to show him the spike heels.

She didn't want him to think she wanted him driving because this was a date. No, it had nothing to do with the image in her head of how he would look pulling up to this party behind the wheel of her car instead of his rattletrap truck.

"Trusting me with the Lexus," he mused. "My, we have made great strides, haven't we?"

"If you're going to get all sentimental about it, give them back." She held her hand out for the keys.

"No, no. I'm all right. I just like to acknowledge these little landmarks as a sign of ongoing progress."

"Progress?" she repeated. They stepped into the garage and their words began to echo.

"Yes. Progress toward you trusting me."

"And you being trustworthy?"

"I've always been trustworthy," he said.

She looked up at him and he smiled down at her.

Her heart lurched.

She'd parked in the corner, near the stairwell, so the area was dimmer than the rest of the garage. But as they approached she was sure she saw someone duck behind a nearby van.

She froze in her tracks and looked up at Truman. He'd stopped too and his eyes were riveted to the van.

"You saw him too?" she whispered.

He glanced down at her and nodded. Then he put one hand on her arm, warming her even through the coat, and said, "Why don't you go back to the lobby? I'll pull the car around and pick you up at the front door."

She glanced nervously between him and the van. Nobody was getting into the other vehicle and there were no sounds of footsteps or movement of any sort. Whoever was there was hiding. No doubt about it.

Fear slunk into her chest and coiled like a snake in the center.

"I should stay," she whispered back. "What if something happens to you?"

His lips quirked and his eyes smiled down at her. Chills ran up her spine.

"Don't worry, doll. I know how to take care of myself."

She gave him an irked look. Serve him right if he did get beaten up. "Fine. I'll wait upstairs." She stalked off back toward the door to the lobby.

Truman walked slowly but surely toward the van, stopping when he got to within a couple yards. He pushed his hands into his pockets.

"You can come out now, Arthur," he said. "She's gone back into the building."

Some shufflings and a little sniff came from the other side of the van.

"I know it's you, Arthur. I saw you."

A second later Arthur, all dressed up and smelling of cologne, emerged from around a concrete pillar.

"What're *you* doing here?" Arthur asked, his face a mask of belligerence.

"I'll tell you what I'm not doing. I'm not hiding in a parking garage, lurking near the car of a woman I admire who happens to live in this building. What are *you* doing here, Arthur?"

Arthur crossed his arms over his chest, his feet splayed wide, and continued to give him a hostile glare. "I thought you said you wasn't goin' out with her. I thought you said you was givin' up."

Truman frowned. "I was. In fact I did give up. But she, ah, she needed me. For something. But this wasn't part of our deal, Arthur. Remember the deal we made at your house? How is your mother, by the way?"

Arthur looked at the ground and scuffed one shoe against an oil stain on the cement floor. "She's awright."

"That sure was a good dinner we had that night. And I thought we had a good talk. How come you lied to me, Arthur?"

Arthur looked up, angry again. "I didn't lie. *You* did. And I don't remember no deal. You told me you was givin' up on her, givin' me a clear shot. That's why I wanted to be sure she wasn't your girlfriend or nothin'. I didn't wanna be steppin' on any toes. But now here you are, *with her*. I think you're steppin' on my toes now, Harley."

Truman looked around the garage, then back at Arthur in his black, three-piece suit. "We were both supposed to give up. That was the deal, Arthur."

"If that was the deal, then you broke it too." He jabbed a fat finger through the air toward Truman, the kind of motion that usually poked one in the chest but Arthur was too timid for that, Tru knew. "'Cause here *you* are. But I still don't remember no deal. I remember you givin' up and tellin' me I had a clear shot. That's what I remember. This ain't fair." He looked at Truman's tuxedo. "That's a nice suit," he said finally.

Truman tilted his head. "Thank you. But I'm pretty sure I didn't say anything about giving you a clear shot. I think I would have remembered saying that." He studied Arthur's face, noting the mottled red color on his cheeks and what there was of his neck. "Arthur, were you by any chance in the parking garage at Marcy's office about a week ago?"

The red in his face got deeper and his head sunk lower. His chin was resting on his chest as he worked his shoe around the oil blotch again.

"What were you thinking?" Truman asked, though not in a rough tone of voice. "Did you knife her tires to scare her?"

"*No,*" Arthur protested, like a kid who's been accused of doing exactly what he did. "I just wanted to give her a ride home. Get a little alone time with her, ya know."

"And you thought that by slashing her tires . . . what? She'd realize your affection for her?"

"No. If her tires all gone flat then she'd *need* a ride home, wouldn't she, smart ass?" he asked, looking at him as if he were an idiot.

Truman's brows lowered. "Art, didn't you think she'd be suspicious? I mean, she comes out, her tires have been flattened, and there you are ready to give her a ride home. She's pretty smart. Don't you think she'd put two and two together?"

Arthur hung his head again. "I know. I suddenly thought a that when she came out the door. I was tryin' to come up with something to tell her what happened, you know, so she wouldn't think it was me, but I didn't get no chance. She was with some other people and they give her the ride home *I* wanted to give her." He poked one of those fat fingers at his own chest with the words.

"Arthur, she thought you were threatening her before," Truman said reasonably. "Remember, I told you that? I don't think she's ready to trust you for a ride home, even if you could have somehow convinced her you didn't slash her tires."

Arthur was silent a long minute, then looked up at Tru. "So you dating her now? She called you, so I guess that means she wants you, huh?"

Truman thought for a moment, then figured what the hell. Put the poor guy out of his misery. "That's right. We're dating now, Arthur. Sorry, but I guess I got the girl this time."

Arthur's arms dropped to his side and he looked at the ground. "Would you do me a favor, then?"

"Sure, if I can."

"Would you tell me if it don't work out with you two? Maybe I'd have a shot then, ya know?"

Truman pressed his lips together. "Sure thing, Art."

Arthur nodded. "Thank you."

Truman slipped the keys from his pocket and flipped them into his palm. "Well, gotta go now, Arthur." He glanced at the tires. They seemed to still be inflated. "You better go home now, too. This is a pretty fancy place. They don't like loiterers. They might call the cops on you."

Arthur looked irate anew. "I ain't thrown any trash! This place was a mess way before I got here. Besides, who calls the cops on people for that?"

"*Loitering*, Arthur, not littering," Truman said, but Arthur's expression was still confused. "Okay, I gotta go. I'll see you around. Say hi to your mom for me."

"Yeah, okay."

Truman got into Marcy's car, but watched Arthur walk down the aisle toward the exit before starting it up and pulling around to the front.

Truman was an idiot to be doing this. He was bound to know people there and they were bound to say something incriminating. His best bet was to try to be invisible, which was, naturally, a challenge. Or to stay away from Marcy unless they were alone, just in case someone did ask where he'd been.

He pulled up in front of the building and Marcy, looking as polished and graceful as a dark-haired Grace Kelly, swept out the revolving door to the car. The night was foggy and a mist swirled around her dress as she strode across the sidewalk.

Looking at her, it was hard to remember that this elegant creature was perfectly capable of picking a lock and stealing a dog.

Marcy didn't give him a chance to come around and open the door for her. The moment he stopped the car she took the door handle, opened it up and slid into the passenger seat.

"So," she began without preamble, "you told Arthur you were backing off and giving him some working room, huh? Nice of you guys to work that all out for me."

He glanced over at her and her dark eyes held his. "You listened in."

"Sure I did. I wanted to make sure you weren't getting stabbed or shot or robbed or anything. But when I heard you'd made some kind of *deal* with regard to me, I confess, I had to stay and hear it all."

Truman put the car into gear and pulled out toward the street. "Then you heard me say I didn't remember telling Arthur anything of the sort."

"I also heard you tell him that we're dating now, so forgive me if I don't take as gospel everything you said down there."

"You're prickly tonight," he said, smiling.

"I'm always prickly after I've been bartered like a leg of lamb."

Tru laughed and turned onto Massachusetts Avenue. The street lamps glowed in the fog as if misty globes had been placed around them. "I wouldn't put it that way."

"Of course you wouldn't. But that's how it felt. Do you know where you're going?"

He paused, lifting his foot automatically off the accelerator. "Uh, the Washington Hilton, right? Isn't that what you told me?"

He glanced over and saw her frown.

"I didn't think I had told you."

He kept going. "Listen, Marcy, I only told Arthur whatever it was I told him so he'd leave you alone. I don't want you thinking I've got any . . . ideas, or anything."

He thought he heard her sigh. "I know."

He drove the car three-quarters of the way around Dupont Circle, appreciating its smooth acceleration and cornering, then headed up Connecticut Avenue. After months in his truck, he'd forgotten how good a nice car could feel.

"So this means Planners wasn't behind the tire slashing, either, doesn't it?" Marcy said finally. "It's all been Arthur."

Truman paused. If she figured out it was all Arthur then there'd be no need for her to have him, Truman, around. But if he tried to perpetuate the Planners-is-out-to-get-you idea he'd feel like the worst kind of scum there was.

"Isn't that what it means?" she asked. "Or am I missing something?"

"I guess that's what it means," he said finally.

She didn't say anything. Was she relieved? Should he excuse himself for the evening?

They rode in silence up Connecticut Avenue.

Marcy eyed Truman as they walked through the lobby of the Washington Hilton. He looked as if he owned the place, from his gorgeous tux to the confident way he walked. She couldn't help thinking he seemed like someone completely different than the guy who lived in the slum in Southeast.

Looking at him, there was only one reason Marcy could come up with for his lack of achievement. He must not want to do the work.

It was criminal, she thought, the way he was squandering himself.

They made it to the ballroom and entered. The room was large and filled with people dressed in their best, which in this crowd was saying something. Women wore floor-length, mostly black dresses that showed an enormous amount of shoulder, back, and breast. So much for dressing conservatively, she thought. Jewels glittered from every ear, neck, and wrist like icicles on a snowy night. The men looked like immaculately bred clones in their black and white, the shapes of their bodies the only immediately discernible difference between them.

"I'll go check our coats," Truman said.

"Good idea." Marcy took hers off and handed it to him. "I'll meet you right over—"

"Marcy!" April Smith approached her, dragging a man behind her who looked distinctly uncomfortable in his tuxedo. April was an associate at Downey, Finley

& Salem with Marcy. "I'm so glad you're here. I don't know a soul. I only worked with one guy on that case—Joe Simons—and he's not even here."

Marcy felt rather than saw Truman moving away with their coats. "He's not? That's too bad, I would've liked to have seen him."

"Marcy, this is my husband, Bart."

Introductions were made, as were speculations about the food they were likely to eat and the people they were likely to know, then the conversation inevitably turned to work.

Just as Marcy was wondering where Truman had gotten to, she spotted Jonathan Brooks—he of the custom-made loafers that had so impressed her family—in a knot of people not too far away. He seemed to be threading through the crowd in her general direction. *Perfect time to go find Truman,* she thought, excusing herself and moving in the opposite direction.

As she looked for him she spotted a headhunter to whom she wanted to introduce Truman. As well spoken and nice looking as Truman was, maybe he could do something in sales without needing a whole lot of education.

She found him re-entering the ballroom.

"There you are. I just saw someone I'd like to introduce you to—"

"Not yet. I'd like to find the bar," Truman said, touching her elbow. "Would you like anything?"

"God yes, I'd love a vodka collins."

He smiled and her stomach flipped over. "Coming right up."

"Wait—" she started, wanting to go with him, but someone called her name from her other side.

It was Dennis Fairlaine, an associate from Rock 'n' Roll with whom she'd worked on that joint case earlier in the year.

"So glad you could make it. You look fantastic."

"Thanks, you too. My date's just getting me a drink, but when he comes back I'd like to introduce you," she said quickly. When they'd been working together, Dennis had made several clumsy passes at her that she'd successfully ignored. She didn't want to spend tonight pretending to be oblivious as well.

While they made small talk, Marcy glanced around for Truman's return, but he was a long time in coming. She finally excused herself from Dennis and went looking for him.

She found him next to the bar, standing perilously close to a fake palm tree. He looked as if he was trying to hide behind it. Some of its fake leaves were sticking into his hair.

"Truman." She came toward him, ducking as a leaf threatened to poke her in the eye. "What are you doing? I thought you were bringing me a drink."

"Yes, I got you one." He reached down into the pot of the plant and pulled out a sweating, full cocktail glass. "I couldn't find you again, though, so I thought you'd know to look for me here. Let's move over."

He edged away from the bar.

"I was right there where you left me," she said, stretching an arm out to indicate where she'd been, barely twenty yards away.

He shook his head and smiled wryly. "I've always had a bad sense of direction."

She raised her brows and glanced toward the brightly

lit entrance to the hallway. "Truman, we had just walked into the ballroom. Are you telling me you couldn't find the door?"

"Hey, why don't we dance?"

Marcy glanced from him to the empty dance floor. So far the band was playing soft torch songs while people chatted and drank.

"People probably won't be dancing until after dinner." She looked back at him, then moved closer and put a hand on his arm. "You don't have to be so nervous. People here aren't going to bite you. Just make small talk. Be yourself. You'll do great."

Truman inhaled deeply. "I'm not nervous. I just, well, I don't really like big gatherings. But you, honey, you look like a million bucks. Shouldn't you be out there schmoozing and networking and all that, sugar?"

Marcy shook her head but a smile played on her lips. "You know, you may be able to *look* the part, but those *honeys* and *sugars* are going to give you away, big time."

He shrugged. "What can you do? You gotta be who you are, dontcha think?"

She narrowed her eyes as she looked at him. "And who are you, Truman?"

He looked startled, then laughed uncomfortably. "Hell, I don't know. Does anybody really know who they are?"

"I do." Then she smiled. "Come on, let me introduce you to some people."

Truman downed the rest of his drink. "Fine, but wait. Let me use the men's room first."

He took off in the direction of the lobby.

Marcy frowned as she watched him go. He was uncomfortable. Dreadfully uncomfortable. It was almost painful to watch. How could she even consider being with someone who was so blatantly wrong for her way of life?

Not that this way of life had come easily to her, either. It had taken her a long time to feel comfortable in an environment like this, but she'd done it. She'd had to. This kind of thing was vital to upward mobility in her career. That didn't mean she wouldn't prefer hanging out at home with a video on most occasions, but still. At least she knew how to get herself out to do some mingling.

Marcy got swept up in several conversations while Truman was gone, and before she knew it an hour had passed and dinner was being served. She wandered toward the lobby to look for him. Maybe he'd made some contacts on his own, she thought. Wouldn't it be great to find him deep in conversation with the headhunter?

She found him deep in slumber on a couch in the lobby, one hand over his face as his elbow rested on the arm.

She sank down next to him on the cushions.

He roused as she gently shook his arm.

"Marcy." He blinked rapidly several times. "Sorry, I . . ." He yawned. "I got up really early this morning. I'm sorry."

"They're serving dinner."

He pushed up to sit straighter on the couch. "Really? So soon? Okay."

But she didn't move. "You hate this, don't you? You'd rather be anywhere but here."

Her eyes were steady on his and he held her gaze.

"Let me ask you something. Do *you* like it here, Marcy?"

She felt as if he'd read her earlier thoughts. As if he saw that she too had to force herself to do this sort of thing and was now in a perfect position to call her a hypocrite.

"Yes," she said, but her voice lacked conviction. She cleared her throat and tried again. "Yes."

He smiled sadly. "Are you that convincing when you tell yourself you like it?"

"Listen, this is what I do, Truman. This is part of my life," she said, feeling unaccountably defensive. "I do this so I can make something of myself. Be a success. Just like *you* could be. There are people in there you should talk to. I just saw a headhunter who's a really decent guy. If you'd just talk to him I bet he could find you something in sales or marketing, even. You could make some really good money—"

"Save it," Truman said, abruptly standing up. The expression on his face and the tone of his voice seemed the same as if she'd just proposed he sell heroin for a living. "Just save your breath, sweetheart."

She stood too. "Why? What's the matter with you? All I said—"

"I heard perfectly well what you said. The words *and* the subtext."

She glanced around to be sure no one was noticing their sudden altercation. "I don't know what you're talking about. There was no subtext."

He turned on her, his eyes fierce. "Wasn't there? Then why won't you answer my question? *Honestly*."

She felt confused, spun around and directionless. "What question?"

"Do *you* like it here?"

He *was* trying to call her a hypocrite. Anger welled

up inside her. "That isn't the point. The point is I *do* this sort of thing so that I can achieve something in my life. Maybe you're not familiar with the concept, Truman, but most people work to improve their lot in life. Not just to buy the next can of stew."

His eyes blazed as if she'd just poured a can of gasoline on his fire.

"*Most* people?" he asked. "*Most people?* What do you know about most people, Miss Paglinowski? Miss Dupont Circle Lexus Saks Fifth Avenue Paglinowski? I've got news for you, princess, most people *are* working for that next can of stew, and a lot of them aren't getting it."

"Don't you preach to me, Truman Fleming. I know a lot more about—"

"You don't know anything about how real people live. You—" He cut himself off, looking away from her and shaking his head. His color was high and his breathing was fast.

Marcy looked at him, half outraged, half afraid. Where had this come from?

"I should go," he said finally. "You're not in any danger. Not from Planners, anyway, and I . . . I just really need to go."

He started to walk down the wide carpeted hallway toward the front lobby. Marcy glanced behind her, imagined going back into that ballroom and trying to make small talk with a bunch of people she barely knew, and strode after Truman.

"I don't know who you think *you* are, judging me," she said in a low voice when she caught up to him. Her eyes skittered around the hotel to make sure no one noticed her leaving so early with an irate date.

"I was wrong about you," he said, shaking his head and not losing a step.

"What do you mean?"

"I mean, I thought maybe there was more to you than the typical upper-crust champagne-and-caviar belle. But now I see I was wrong."

"You *are* wrong, there's no doubt about that," she said, thinking that if he could've been at Aunt Phyllis's cookout he'd have a lot less to say on this subject. "You don't know a *thing* about me."

He stopped in his tracks so suddenly Marcy had to backtrack a step to look him in the eye. "Listen, sugar . . ." he began, leaning close and keeping his voice low.

They stood in the middle of the front lobby now. The revolving front door was on a constant sweep, bringing people into and carrying them out of the opulent place.

"I know you think I'm not good enough for you, but I'm good enough for me, so stop trying to fix me. Stop trying to put me in the way of job offers and headhunters. Stop trying to dress me up and turn me into the same kind of status-seeking, money-conscious, career-driven . . . *person* you've turned yourself into."

Marcy had trouble catching her breath, stunned by the intensity of his attack. She stood stock-still in front of him, looking beyond Truman but seeing nothing. *That's* how he saw her? That's who he thought she was? So stupid, so blind, so *shallow*?

After a second Truman said with a sigh, "Marcy, look, I'm sorry. You don't . . . I don't mean to insult you. I suppose . . . I suppose you can't help the way you see the world."

Her eyes refocused on him, a flame of fury reigniting in her chest. "I can't help the way I see the world?" she repeated.

He shrugged and looked at the door, longing to go through it, Marcy was sure.

"I don't know why I thought you were different. Different than you are, that is," he amended, obviously having to work not to blatantly offend her with his feelings about her.

But Marcy knew what he was saying. "Listen to me, Truman. I'll make no apologies for who I am and what I'm doing. I'm working for *security*. I went a long time without it and I'm never going back to that again. Don't you want security, Truman?"

He gave a hollow laugh. "What *is* security? How much does security cost? Are you going to know when you have it, Marcy? Are you going to know when to stop?"

"Oh, I'll know it," she said through clenched teeth. An image of her mother's pale, pinched face as she opened the electric bill one winter when Marcy was a child sprang into her mind.

Truman swept her with a hard look. "Then what about the expensive clothes, and the car, and the condo . . . that's not enough security for you? Don't you ever wish for something *simpler*? Some quiet way of life that doesn't involve dressing the right way and driving the right car and having the right job? Don't you want to *live honestly?*"

"The only way to live a quiet, *honest* life is to have money, Truman. Take it from me. Money's the only protection you have in this world and that's the God's honest truth."

"Money," he said.

"That's right."

He laughed again, without humor. "Well, that's your version."

She crossed her arms over her chest and glared at him. "Jesus, you are *so* condescending. I know a hell of a lot more about this than you think. You can believe I was trying to better you for my own ends if you want to, but all I ever wanted for you was for you to live up to your potential. You're an intelligent, industrious man. Why are you working construction? Why are you living where you are? You could do so much *more*."

"You mean I could *be* so much *better*."

"Of course! Truman, you—" She shook her head and looked away, so frustrated she could barely find the words. "Right now you have no future. You don't even seem to *want* a future. Is it *okay* with you to be living in a slum? Is it okay with you to be living hand to mouth? Do you really want to be sitting on a duct-taped couch ten years from now? Twenty? Thirty?"

"Maybe," he said, facing her with his own intensity and frustration. "Maybe that slum in Southeast is exactly where I want to be."

She felt as if her throat were closing up. As if he were standing there telling her he wanted exactly the opposite of what she wanted because he didn't want *her*.

"It's not where *I* want to be," she said in a voice quavering with emotion. "And you can bet twenty years from now *I* won't be sitting on any duct-taped couch."

"Well, guess what, sugar, I didn't ask you to be." He glared at her a long moment, then looked away.

She felt as if she'd been slapped. "Then what is this all

about? Why are you so angry with me? Why have I disappointed you so much? What in the world have we been doing these last few weeks—"

She broke off, unable to continue. Why was she doing this? What would arguing with him accomplish? They were two different people. *Too* different people.

"I've got to go," she said, turning away toward the ballroom. She needed to get her coat, she thought. She needed to get her coat, find her keys, and get out of here, back to her apartment. Back to her empty, white apartment. Where she couldn't even have a dog.

She turned back, hoping against hope, against her own reason even, that he would smile at her and make some joke that would enable them to get past this, if only for the moment. "If you want, I'll give you a ride."

He looked at her. His eyes appeared almost confused, tormented. "No. I'll get a cab."

She swallowed over the lump in her throat. "Fine," she said, and walked away from him down the hall.

Fine, she thought. *I was fine without you before, and I'll be fine without you now. I'll figure out a way to take Folly, or I'll find a friend who will take her. I won't need you for anything.*

But when she got to the coat check she turned to look back at him.

He was gone.

The lobby might as well have been empty.

16

Sunday, November 17
WORD-A-DAY!

HYPOBULIA: n., the decreased ability to reach a decision; or a state of mind that makes for wild vascillations about people and whether or not they are appropriate to date

Despite misgivings about contacting him, Marcy messengered Truman a note on Saturday asking if he could meet her on Sunday to prep for his deposition, which was to be held the following Wednesday. Regardless of how she felt about him, she had to do what was right for the case. There was no avoiding Truman this time.

She asked the messenger to wait for a reply if Truman was there, but he wasn't. Instead, Sunday afternoon she picked up a message he'd left early that morning on her voice mail at work saying he didn't need to prepare. He was going to tell the truth and that was all the preparation he needed.

He ended the message by saying, "And don't worry, I'll show. I'm not going to blow the case for you."

She hung up the phone—saving the message—and again felt as if he'd been reading her mind. And not the charitable part of it. Since their altercation Friday night she'd worried that he was so disgusted with her he'd go out of his way to make sure she lost the case—a sentiment she knew gave him no credit.

Someone knocked on her office door and she called for them to enter.

Trish cracked the door open and peeked inside. Even in jeans and a long-sleeved cotton T-shirt—standard attire for Sunday work—Trish managed to exude elegance.

"Hi," Trish said. "Got a minute?"

Marcy sat up straight in her chair and stretched. "Sure, I'd love the break."

"I was just wondering how the party went Friday night. April said she saw you there but didn't see your date." Trish's eyes practically glowed with curiosity.

"Oh no." Marcy put her palms on the sides of her head. "Please tell me you didn't tell April Smith who I was there with."

Trish waved the question off. "Don't be silly. I just told her you had a hot date and I wanted to know what he looked like. So? How'd it go?"

She dropped her hands and to her own mortification felt the sudden urge to cry. "It was awful. Trish, it was the biggest mistake of my life."

"Why? What happened?" Trish looked stricken. "Oh Marcy, I'm sorry. I wouldn't have asked if I'd known it didn't go well. Do you want to talk about it?"

Marcy paused. "I'm not sure."

She'd never told Trish about the circumstances of her childhood. Not that they were anything to be ashamed of, but just as she hadn't let Truman know she wasn't a trust-fund baby, she'd never contradicted Trish's assumption that she'd grown up with money either. Why, she wasn't sure. And she certainly didn't want to analyze it now.

"Well, I'll be working all day if you want to talk," Trish said. "You know where to find me. God knows I'll be wanting a diversion." She started to get up.

"No, wait." Marcy leaned her elbows on the desk. "I guess I do want to talk about it a little. See, I'm not exactly sure what happened myself."

She told Trish the gist of the argument, as she remembered it. But even as she recounted what she thought they'd both said, she couldn't remember how it had gotten so heated.

"I guess he just hit a nerve in me. And I hit a nerve in him. But, damn it, what am I supposed to do? Go crawling back to him and apologize for who I am? For all I've accomplished?"

"Of *course* not. He's being totally unreasonable. It sounds like he's one of those men who are so insecure they can't stand it when their woman makes more money than they do."

Marcy shook her head. "I really didn't think he was like that. Plus, I don't think he thinks of me as his woman. But maybe you're right. Although . . . he only really got mad when I suggested *he* could do better. He seems determined to live hand to mouth. He has no desire to get a better job, make more money, move to a nicer place. He has no future! What if he broke his back and couldn't work anymore? What if his wife ended up having to support him? How would they ever have kids? And what kind of role model would he be?" Marcy exhaled, feeling hopeless. "How could any woman in her right mind contemplate having a relationship with someone like that? And for *him* to judge *me*, well, that just really burned me up."

Marcy paused. She felt like her insides had been bruised by an enormous bowling ball since their fight.

Trish was quiet, so Marcy went on.

"Still, I think I was most hurt by his disapproval. And the fact that he seemed to have no idea at all of who I really am. All this time I've been so attracted to him, I felt as if he knew me, really *knew* me. As if he could look into my eyes and see who I am without me having to say anything." She laughed once and shook her head. "Apparently, I was dead wrong. Either that or I really *am* the money-grubbing prima donna he seems to think."

Which was a thought that gave her dreadful pause.

She glanced up at Trish, who was looking at her gravely.

"Want to know what I think?" Trish asked.

"Of course."

Trish took a deep breath. "What I'm hearing is, and correct me if I'm wrong, that you're upset because he misjudged you. Or rather the fact that he judged you at all, and then misjudged you on top of it." She flashed a small smile. "He doesn't understand what you're working for, why you work so hard, that money and status are not your priorities."

"Right," Marcy said, planting a light fist on her desk. "Exactly."

"But Marcy, I'm also hearing that he's upset about the same thing. That you've judged him to be without ambition, without a future. In short, maybe he's upset because you don't seem to understand him, either."

Marcy bristled at the thought. She wasn't judging him, she was only trying to help him.

"If that were the case," Marcy objected, feeling inexplicably defensive, "why wouldn't he contradict me? Why wouldn't he tell me that he *does* have ambition? Or he does have plans, or *something*. Why wouldn't he correct me? Make me see?"

Trish shook her head. "I don't know." She paused, then said cautiously, "Did you correct him?"

Marcy busied herself the rest of that weekend and in the two days before the deposition getting ready for the case. She was lucky, she thought time and again, that she had something pressing to throw herself into, so she didn't sit around thinking about what a mess her feelings were.

If she hadn't had so much work to do she'd no doubt have devoted days to the question Trish had asked her. Why *hadn't* she corrected him? Why hadn't she told him that the reason she worked so hard was to make sure she never, ever went back to the way of life in which she'd grown up?

Because she couldn't, was all she could think. Because bringing all that up, explaining it all, telling him she was so much less than what he believed her to be . . .

She stopped. She wasn't so much *less*. She knew that. She was just different than he thought. And yet . . . and yet less was how she felt. She was ashamed, she realized. She was ashamed of her roots.

What's more, she thought, feeling truly unbalanced, she was ashamed of her shame.

It was a revelation she had no idea what to do with. She

needed a shrink, she thought. Or a guru. Maybe a psychic.

In any case, she was smack dab in the middle of a case and couldn't afford to indulge in psychological analyses of herself. She needed to work.

So work she did.

The day of the deposition she was a nervous wreck. She waited for Truman in the lobby of the opposing counsel's building with her hands, heart, and stomach all in a knot.

What would he say to her? What would she say to him?

As far as she was concerned, she thought as she stood there in her power suit, he owed her an apology.

She was working herself up into another self-righteous lather thinking about all he'd said to her at the party when she saw him enter the building. She glanced at her watch. Great, they had five minutes to spare. Five whole minutes for her to prepare him for what could be a nasty barrage of questions lasting hours.

He was briefly silhouetted against the light from the front doors but she could see he wore torn jeans and a denim jacket. In fact, she saw when he got further into the building, he looked quite a bit more shabby than he ever had before in her presence.

She pressed her lips together. He was doing this just to piss her off, she thought. To prove he didn't give a damn about what she or anybody else thought of him.

His hair had gotten so long he'd pulled it back in a ponytail, and he wore those dark glasses he'd had on the night he'd met her in Georgetown. It was a look she was sure would be welcomed by the opposing counsel.

As far as her case was concerned, at best he didn't look credible. At worst he looked like a desperation witness dragged off the street to give the only favorable testimony they could dig up.

Thank God there was no judge at a deposition.

"Hello, Marcy," he said solemnly when he got close. He nodded to her once, all business.

"Truman," she returned stiffly. "I see you got out your Sunday best for the occasion."

"I came from work. The truck broke down so I didn't have time to go home and change." He gazed at her with those blank, sunglassed eyes. "Not that it should matter. Showing up and telling the truth is what matters, not how someone looks while they're doing it."

She shook her head. "You don't understand. *Perceptions* are as important in this game as words. Maybe not so much now, for the deposition, but definitely at the trial."

"That's your problem, you see it as a game. I see it as justice."

She laughed cynically, feeling stung to the core. "The day you see justice given without prejudice, preconception, or bias being taken into account, you let me know."

She started walking briskly toward the elevators. Truman lagged behind but she could see him from the corner of her eye.

"I'm going to get you a suit for the trial. I know that offends the hell out of you but you need to—"

"I'll get my own suit."

She shot him an openly skeptical look. "I'm serious, Truman, you need to—"

"I said I'd get one." He said it sharply, but when she looked at him he didn't appear angry so much as frustrated. Perhaps he knew she was right and that was what bothered him.

For a second her heart lifted in hope. If he could just understand why she did what she did . . .

They stopped in front of the elevators. "Listen, I need to tell you a few things, to prepare you for what you're about to do. I'd have rather had time to practice this with you—it can be pretty intimidating—but there's no sense lamenting that now."

"Thank you for not bringing it up, then," he said, watching the lighted numbers over the elevator.

She gave him an exasperated look, despite the fact that he wasn't looking at her. The doors opened and they stepped into the elevator. Thankfully they were the only ones in it.

"First," she said, "tell the truth."

He started to speak but she held up her hand.

"I know that's been your intention all along, but when they ask you how you were prepared, I want you to be able to say the first thing I told you was to tell the truth."

She thought she saw a slight smile on his lips.

"Second," she continued, "*pause* before answering each question. Make sure you understand what they're asking. This gives me time to object if I have to, and it also gives you time to think through your entire answer before you begin. I want you to know exactly what your last word will be before you start speaking."

"Got it," he said, arms folded over his chest.

She nodded once. "Good. Remember, the transcript won't reflect how much time you take to formulate your answer, so don't worry about that."

"I won't."

"Now, we can't consult while a question is pending, but if you're unsure of anything or you have a question for me, just ask to take a break. It's a courtesy; they don't have to let us; but as long as it's not just after they've asked a question, most of the time it's not a problem."

"I don't expect I'll be needing any advice." He stared at the elevator doors.

"All right." She took a deep breath and exhaled heavily. "Third, be brief. Don't volunteer any information. This is *very* important. Witnesses get hung by their own words all the time. Do you understand?"

He glanced down at her. "Sure, don't volunteer information."

"I mean it. Nothing extra. Do you know what time it is?"

He shifted his arms and looked at his watch. He opened his mouth to tell her, then paused, and smiled wryly. "Yes."

She grinned. "Excellent. Perfect."

The doors opened into a small area just across from a set of glass doors. Truman pulled his sunglasses from the top of his head down over his eyes.

She stopped at the glass doors. "You don't plan on wearing those glasses during the deposition, do you?"

He looked down at her, his expression flat and unreadable thanks to the glasses. "Don't worry about me, sugar. I'll get the job done. No matter what I look like."

A week later Marcy still couldn't believe it. The afternoon of the deposition had been surreal. Truman had answered the questions like a pro, starting with her test in the elevator. Most people, when asked that question, answered by saying what time it was, but that was, technically, elaboration. If a yes-or-no question was asked, then a yes-or-no answer was all that was required.

Truman had been brief, truthful, confident, and compelling, despite the fact that Planners had *four* attorneys sitting in, no doubt hoping to intimidate the witness—not to mention increase their billing to Planners, which made Marcy happy.

Truman had worn the damn glasses throughout, but rather than make the other attorneys feel superior, it had instead seemed to rattle them. Here was a witness who was unshakeable, despite their using every trick to make him nervous: staring at him after a short answer, hoping he'd keep talking; leaning forward into their questions; being alternately confrontational then friendly. None of it had fazed him at all.

After each answer he even sat back in his chair, signifying he was finished and no amount of staring by the opposing attorney would compel him to elaborate. That was a technique Marcy usually went over in preparation, but she'd forgotten it in their hasty ride up the elevator.

It had been exhilarating, watching him. He seemed to be a natural at handling contentious lawyers, but she didn't allow herself to think about what this could mean for his future. Apparently he had the job he wanted. And so did she.

As a result of Truman's performance, her case was even more rock solid than before. Planners's attorneys were fools if they didn't see it. Still, they didn't want to settle and that was fine with her.

Though she'd been nervous about seeing Truman again after their fight on Friday, she was profoundly disappointed when, after the deposition, there was no chance to speak with him. Immediately after Truman's testimony, Marty Strape, the defendant's lead counsel, had asked if she could stay and clarify something she'd sent over in some discovery materials.

As soon as she'd paused to answer Marty, Truman had left without her, without even a good-bye.

Seeing him again had shaken her more than she wanted to admit. She kept remembering what Trish had said, that maybe she had misunderstood Truman as completely as he'd misunderstood her. For some reason this theory alarmed her. If it was true, she was every bit as at fault for their confrontation as Truman was. Which meant there was a good chance she was just as stupid and blind as he'd accused her of being.

But if what Trish said wasn't true, and she was right about Truman? Then it meant there wasn't any way things could ever work out between them. The lesser of the two evils was hard to determine.

The day after the deposition she'd spent a morose Thanksgiving with her family. The aunts, uncles, and cousins were all at her mother's house this year, so Marcy had gone early and stayed late to help. For the most part they'd laid off their dating questions, though she wasn't sure whether or not that was because they now believed she was a lesbian. In any case, she was profoundly glad not to have to answer any questions about the men in her life because she was doing all she humanly could to keep from thinking about Truman.

Not that it was doing any good.

Now, a week after Thanksgiving, she'd pondered the intricacies of their argument so many times and in so many variations she could barely remember what had actually happened. She'd also shuffled together their circumstances, their occupations, their personalities, and their mutual desires so much that she'd only come up with more confusion.

For the last week she'd both hoped and feared he would pop up again either at her door or on the street so she'd have a chance to talk to him. About what, or why he would seek her out, she wasn't sure. She just didn't want to believe that their confrontation at the Rock 'n' Roll holiday party two weeks ago had been the end of it all.

But he hadn't popped up. She'd kept an eye out for him on her lunch hours, answered every call in her office, and kept up with her messages both at work and at home, but she hadn't heard from him. She'd even hit *69 on her phone to see if he'd called without leaving a message. But no dice. He hadn't called, and he was not coming back.

She could, of course, go to see him—and Folly, whom she missed terribly—but the thought of returning to that apartment and possibly finding him with the lovely blonde Heather was so intimidating she wouldn't consider it.

She comforted herself with the knowledge that she'd see him at the trial in two weeks. Maybe by then she'd have figured out what was going on, and what she could say. Or maybe not.

Marcy pulled up in front of the homeless shelter that Friday night and put the car into park.

The last time she'd spoken to Calvin he'd gotten several calls about catering jobs. It helped that they were well into the start of the holiday season. Everyone, it seemed, was having a party, and Calvin's confidence had been so boosted by the Downey, Finley & Salem affair that he was ready to take them all on.

She walked into the kitchen of the shelter having followed an aromatic trail of garlic.

"Marcy P.!" Calvin boomed upon seeing her.

She smiled and marveled again at how much more alive he looked now than even just a few weeks ago. While she could flatter herself that finding him work had given him back his spark, she suspected that the largest part of his renewal came from the lovely Sheila, with whom he'd had several dates since the party. She'd even postponed her Thanksgiving trip to Tuscany just, Marcy was sure, to spend more time with Calvin.

"Not to rain on your sunshiny face, Mr. Deeds," Marcy said, once she'd scrubbed up and donned an apron to begin slicing mushrooms, "but have you told Sheila the truth about yourself yet?"

Calvin turned away to the sink to wash a knife that was barely dirty and said, "Well, now, the timing hasn't really been right . . ."

"Calvin," she scolded, "the woman is a *dear.* She's not going to think any less of you because you fell on some hard times. Give her a chance."

Calvin shook his head and got out his cleaver. He was chopping up chicken a local grocery store had donated that day to make chicken tetrazzini for the residents of the shelter.

"Yes, she is a dear. But there are some extenuating circumstances. I really don't think she'd approve of me living . . . well, where I live." He gestured vaguely around himself with the knife.

"What circumstances?" Marcy asked.

"Well now, I don't know all the details, but she's alluded to something that makes me think she wouldn't like someone who has to live as poorly as I do. You heard her, Marcy, she's got a house in Tuscany, for goodness' sake. She wouldn't understand having to live someplace like this."

"You never know. I think she might. But Calvin, if she's that pompous about it, would you really want her?"

He shook his head. "It's not that she's pompous. Not in the least. She gives lots of money to charity. She seems to care a great deal about the underprivileged. But I'm pretty sure she wouldn't want to be courted by one of them. She's just so extremely wealthy, you see. A very classy lady. She deserves to be with . . . I don't know . . . with *royalty*."

Marcy thought about this a second. "But that could be all the better. She's probably secure enough to feel she doesn't need a man who can support her."

Calvin shook his head again.

"What?" she said, throwing up her hands. "Why are you so negative about this?"

He sighed. "Because she's got this son," he said. "She loves him dearly but she's angry with him too. She said he left home and is now living in . . . well, in severely reduced circumstances."

"You mean he's a runaway?"

"No. He's a grown son, an adult, who apparently had a very bright future. But he decided to give it all up and live with the poor."

He paused.

"What, like the Peace Corps?" Marcy asked.

"I don't think so."

"Is he a drug addict or something? Did he mess up his life and she can't help him?"

"No, no. I'm sorry. I'm not explaining this very well." He cleared his throat. "As I said, I don't know all the details, but I definitely got the impression this was some sort of choice he made. Like an experiment. He chose to give up his privileged life to see if he could make it as a . . . a common person. Or something. Whatever it is, she's horrified by it. She says he's living like a *vagrant* and she can't even stand to think about him." He gave her a tortured look. "Marcy, who could be living more like a vagrant than myself? How can I tell her about this place"—he gestured around himself with the cleaver—"knowing how she feels about it? I can't tell her the truth, I just can't."

Marcy was silent a long moment. "Calvin, your circumstances are totally different. No one could fault you for doing all you've done. It was for Pen! Surely any woman would be impressed by that, not horrified."

Calvin was shaking his head again.

"Then think of it this way," Marcy continued. "What the son is doing sounds *admirable*. If she's as rich as you say, he's obviously given up the easy life for a taste of what the rest of the world experiences. What an intelligent, compassionate mother she must have been to have raised a son like that."

Calvin's eyes brightened with her words. "Yes!" he exclaimed, putting the knife down on the counter and

turning to face her. "Marcy, that's it exactly! She's been thinking of herself as having failed him somehow, when really it's just the opposite. She's been berating herself for nothing, the dear lady."

Marcy smiled. "And that same dear lady, that intelligent, compassionate woman, will understand when you tell her what you went through too, Calvin. Don't underestimate her. It'll only hurt both of you."

Calvin was shaking his head again, but this time it was different. This time he looked as if he was thinking he'd have never believed he could feel better about the situation.

"Marcy, girl, I don't know how to thank you," he said, taking up his cleaver again. "I'm to see Sheila again tomorrow. I'll try talking to her some more about this. She's so worried about the boy. I don't think she's looking at it as the noble venture it really is."

"Of course it's noble," Marcy said, feeling it.

Who but someone noble would give up all that security? Not that he'd really given it up, of course. Having a wealthy mother to turn to was a far different thing than leading a purely hardscrabble life, but still. How many people would even *think* to give up wealth in order to walk a mile in a poor person's shoes?

"I think the son must have a great deal of character to do something like that," she continued. "And besides, she hasn't disowned him or anything, has she?"

"No, no, of course not. She's just worried sick about him. And afraid she did something to drive him away."

"Well, there you go," Marcy said. "There's not a doubt in my mind that this woman has her head on her shoulders. She's not the kind of woman who's so shallow that a man's circumstances are going to stand in the way of a relationship that's meant to be."

Calvin smiled and gleefully chopped the leg off a chicken.

But Marcy stood frozen, hand raised and ready to slice another mushroom, her heart in her throat.

Sheila may not be shallow, she thought suddenly, her cheeks burning despite the fact that no one else could hear her thoughts. But *she* was.

She, Marcy Paglinowski, was so shallow and money conscious that she had let a man's circumstances stand in the way of a relationship that was . . . was it meant to be?

Or was it meant to be over?

She swallowed hard and laid her palms flat on the cutting board. Should she have let Truman get away?

Or could it be that he was the best thing that had ever happened to her?

17

Saturday, December 7
WORD-A-DAY!

VACUITIES: n., empty spaces; and perhaps, as a result of confusion, empty heads, hearts, habitations...

Marcy popped the cork on the bottle of wine that Trish had brought—their second—and poured some into each of their glasses.

"I wish I had some tarot cards. You don't have any tarot cards, do you?" Trish asked as Marcy brought the new bottle and full glasses back into the living room.

They were drinking red wine on Marcy's white couch and she didn't give a damn. In fact, she didn't care about the carpet either. Or the throw pillows or that stupid, ugly painting hanging over the couch that she'd only bought because it was supposed to be a good investment and the colors went so perfectly with her furniture.

"Do you know?" Marcy said, making an effort not to slur her words. She wasn't exactly drunk—they'd eaten a prodigious amount of penne pasta with sausage from the Italian place down the street in addition to that first bottle of wine—but she wasn't exactly sober, either. "That I bought that painting because I thought it would make me look sophisticated?"

"What painting? Where?" Trish bent her head back and tried to look at the wall behind her, upside-down.

Marcy giggled. Apparently she wasn't the only one feeling the effects of that first bottle.

"That one," she said, pointing. "That hideously ugly thing that cost me a friggin' *fortune*."

Trish swiveled on her butt and looked at the canvas. "Ew, God, that *is* ugly. I've got one almost just like it." She bent close to the corner and squinted her eyes at the signature. "Only I think mine's by somebody different. Rowsher, or something. They're good investments."

"I *know*!" Marcy raised her glass to her friend. "Thank you. So it's not just me living with ugly art for the sake of the future."

"Oh no. I don't know anyone who likes stuff like this." She flung a hand back toward the painting. "I've got a Powell in my bedroom, though, that I *adore*. It's a huge, flowery thing that you can practically *smell*, it's so vibrant."

"A Powell, huh? I should look for one of those next. Maybe trade that thing in." Marcy sipped her wine. "I should get rid of this furniture, too."

"Really?" Trish asked, leaning toward the last sliver of tiramisu residing in its open plastic box. "Why?"

Marcy regarded the furniture resentfully. "I hate it. Really, it was all that interior designer's idea. I can't even have a dog here."

Trish made a face. "A dog? What would you want with a dog?"

Marcy allowed herself to drift into a little reverie about Folly. "Dogs are great. Really. You'd love Folly. She's so funny. Always smiling."

"Hm," Trish said skeptically.

Marcy sighed and brought her focus back to the furniture. "I hate all this white. The whole room is sterile. My whole life is sterile."

"Oh now . . ." Trish leaned back and popped a bite of tiramasu into her mouth, then licked her fingers. "You had sex just, what, a month ago?"

Marcy scoffed. "Try a month and a half." She brooded for a second on how much had happened since then. How much misunderstanding and argument and, finally, how much *nothing* had happened since then.

She hadn't seen Truman since the deposition. Hadn't even *heard* from him. He'd given up on her. And she . . . well, she couldn't give up on him. No matter how much she tried. And she was trying.

The fact was, she *missed* him.

"Has it been that long?" Trish asked. "God, it seems like only yesterday."

"No, yesterday was when *you* had sex," Marcy said, grimacing. "Bitch."

They both laughed.

"Oh yeah," Trish said, with a satisfied smile. "That was me."

"So you think I should contact him? Really?" Marcy asked, going back to a conversation they'd had earlier, over the pasta, when Marcy was still restrained enough to put a strong face on the emotional bewilderment Truman's absence had produced in her.

"Of course. Look at you, you're miserable. And *listen* to you, you keep coming back to this like you're trying to convince yourself it's all right. That's why we should have some tarot cards. I'm sure there's even a special card for someone like him . . . in some blue-collar deck in which the King of Wands wears a tool belt."

Marcy laughed. "I'm sorry. Do I go on about him? I just . . . I guess I just . . . well, I miss him."

Trish smiled. "There, now. Was that so hard? To admit that you like a man who doesn't have a 401k?"

"Hey, I was only trying to follow your advice, Miss Three *P*s."

Trish held her hands up in surrender. "Okay, okay, but you should have known that I'm a money-grubbing status seeker, or whatever it was he called you. Just look at who I'm dating. The friggin' *poster* boy of status seeking."

"Oh yeah. You're such a fool, dating a great-looking, fabulously wealthy, nice guy like Palmer Roe."

Trish frowned for a second. "Hey, what's your guy's name, anyway? I keep forgetting to ask. I was trying to tell Palmer about him the other day and realized I've been calling him 'the construction worker' since all this began."

"What were you telling Palmer?" Marcy asked, alarmed for no reason she could articulate. "That I've been dumped by a guy in a hardhat?"

"Just that you liked a guy with kind of a chip on his shoulder about wealth, or lawyers, or imported cars, or something."

Marcy sighed. "His name's Truman," she said, feeling the word on her tongue like forbidden fruit. "Truman Fleming."

"Truman Fleming . . ." Trish mused. "That sounds familiar. You must have told me before."

Marcy shrugged. "I don't know. Believe it or not, I've been trying not to talk about him. Not much, anyway. I've been trying to forget him, since he's obviously forgotten me."

Trish snorted. "I doubt that. I bet he's pining away for you, too. He'd be a fool not to be. You just need to tell him how you feel. Tell him you're sorry if you misjudged him, but he misjudged you, too. I'm telling you. You should do this now because years from now, if you don't, you'll always wonder about him. That's why I gave Palmer a chance, despite his womanizing past."

Marcy looked at her hopefully. "And you don't regret that, do you? I mean, you guys are doing great, right?"

Trish laughed and obviously tried to look cynical but couldn't pull it off. "Yeah, we're doing great. He's . . . he's amazing."

Marcy felt a lump in her throat. She'd have felt the same way about Truman, except that she'd been so wrapped up in convincing herself how wrong he was for her. Why had she spent so much time worried about the future, as if he'd asked her to spend the next forty years supporting him instead of simply asking her back to his apartment? Or hers. Or out for half-smokes, or to a pool hall . . . He'd even said he'd like to hike Sugarloaf with her . . .

So many things had gotten in the way of her realizing how she felt about him, things that now felt so insignificant. The ache she felt without him was intolerable.

"But if he thinks I misjudged him—or rather judged him to be inadequate . . ." She suddenly remembered him saying *I know you think I'm not good enough for you* and blushed with shame. Why hadn't she said right then, the minute he'd said it, that it wasn't true? That she'd never thought he wasn't *good enough*, she'd just feared for his future. For *their* future.

Which was stupid, because she had no desire to give up her career and she made enough for the both of them. So what if he turned out like her father and spent his days on the couch? As long as he was himself, the Truman she had come to—to love?

How could she have been so stupid? She didn't want to be without the guy.

"Earth to Marcy," Trish said, then giggled and took the last sip of wine from her glass. "You were saying?" She leaned forward for the bottle again but missed and sent it skittering across the glass-topped coffee table.

For one heartbeat the bottle teetered on the edge of the table while Marcy and Trish sat rooted in frozen anticipation. Finally it tipped over the edge, spraying red wine across the cushion and down the front of the couch, then into a puddle on the white carpeting.

Marcy stared at the growing stain, inert.

Trish leapt across her and grabbed the bottle, righting it as quickly as she could and setting it on the table. She grabbed the roll of paper towels nearby and started blotting at the floor.

"Oh my God, Marcy, I am *so* sorry," she said, frantically trying to sop up wine that had instantly soaked into the white couch. "I'll have it cleaned, recovered, whatever. I'll buy you a new couch, a new carpet. I'm so sorry."

Marcy felt laughter tickling at her breastbone, then the back of her throat. She let it out, laughing softly at first, then more loudly. Finally she couldn't stop, and when she saw the confused expression on Trish's face she laughed even harder. Tears streamed from her eyes and she doubled forward.

"Oh God, Trish," she said when she could catch her breath. "You've done me a favor! I feel positively liberated!"

"Marcy, honey, we've had an awful lot to drink," she said carefully.

"I'm serious. I'm not drunk." Another shot of laughter burst forth. "Okay, I'm a little drunk. But trust me, I'm not upset. I've lived in fear of this for three years, that something would happen to these damn couches, and now it has. Thank God! I'm so glad. And on the very day I realized I hated them."

Trish began to look hopeful. "You're sure you hate them? I'm still going to clean them for you, but I'll feel better if you really and truly dislike them."

"Trish, I *loathe* them. Don't you see? This is a sign. The hell with tarot cards." She laughed again. "This is the assassination of my former life. I'm going to start to 'live honestly,' as Truman put it. I'm going to stop buying ugly things for my portfolio and living with things that seem appropriate but that I really hate . . ." She shook her head in wonder at how free she suddenly felt.

"And you're going to go find your construction worker?" Trish braved with a smile.

"Yes!" Marcy stood up. "I'm going to go to Tru Fleming's apartment and tell him I'm sorry. I'm sorry for being a selfish, superficial idiot and I'm going to ask him to forgive me for judging him. I want him just the way he is. Unpretentious, down-to-earth, funny, handsome, articulate . . ."

Trish smiled and squeezed Marcy's arm. "You're getting that dreamy look on your face, Marcy. I'm not sure about you, but I *know* this is love. Whether you like it or not."

In the end, they decided it would be best if Marcy waited until she sobered up. At the same time, Trish said, if she then felt upset about the wine stains, she was to call Trish immediately so she could apologize profusely again.

Sunday evening Marcy dressed and redressed, then redressed again, scattering her bed, chairs, and the floor of her bedroom with clothes. What did one wear to eat crow?

Not that she didn't think Truman owed her an apology too, but the more she thought about their conversations the more she realized how constantly she'd brought up jobs, or clothes, or things he didn't have that most people did. Like the phone. She cringed to remember how many times she'd inadvertently complained about him not having a phone.

She also cringed to remember her offering to treat on more than one occasion. His pride had to have been stung by that.

How many times had she discounted his life by pasting her own interpretation onto it? Not to mention coloring it with her fears and anticipations, her mother's expectations, her father's mistakes . . .

He'd been hard on her the night of the holiday party, but she could see now he'd been hurt. Dreadfully hurt. That's why he'd spoken so harshly.

She could also see now what he'd seen: that she was not living honestly. She dressed to suit whomever she was to be with. She drove a Lexus because Win drove a Lexus. She *liked* the car—she wasn't sycophantic—but she'd made her choice based on what would appear correct.

Everything she did was based on what would appear correct for a given situation. She'd thought she was being smart. She hadn't realized she was being someone else.

She even lived in Dupont Circle because Trish lived there. Going purely on her own desires she'd have moved to Adams Morgan, the eclectic neighborhood just east of Connecticut Avenue she'd always loved.

Now it was time to live according to her own tastes, she thought. Leaving out everyone else's decisions, opinions, and mistakes. This was *her* life.

Once she'd settled on an outfit—jeans and a sweatshirt, because that's how she was most comfortable—she got in the car and drove to Southeast.

Her heart was in her throat the whole way, and several times she was tempted to pull over, just to reevaluate what she was doing, but she didn't.

What if he wasn't happy to see her?

What if Heather was there?

What if some other, unknown woman was there?

What if he wasn't home?

Doubts rolled through her mind like steamrollers over fresh asphalt, quashing her determination to talk to Truman again and again. Still, she drove on, propelled by a force she'd never felt before.

She pulled up in front of his apartment and her stomach sank. His living-room window was dark. He could be in the bedroom, but as it was only seven o'clock, that was doubtful. Maybe he'd gotten some curtains, she thought hopefully, but she knew that was grasping at straws.

She got out of the car and went up the walk. With every step, she remembered the times she'd done this very thing, knowing that Truman was there. Knowing that he wanted her. What a fool she'd been to resist him for so long. And now . . . had she missed her chance?

She opened the door to the hallway and went to his apartment. She lifted a hand to knock, but noticed the door was ajar.

She pushed it open.

The room was dark, but she could tell it was empty just the same. Not just empty of Truman, empty of everything.

"Truman?" She said his name hesitantly, half-heartedly. She knew he wasn't here.

Barely breathing, she slid her hand along the wall just inside the door. Her fingers found the lightswitch, pushed it up and the overhead light sprang to life, revealing the empty space with a suddenness that felt like *gotcha!*

Marcy brought both hands to her mouth. Her eyes trailed slowly around the room. Nothing but dust bunnies. She glanced back at the door to be sure she was in the right place.

She was.

She walked back toward the bedroom, footfalls echoey in the vacant space.

She felt sick. Pausing at the door to the tiny kitchen, she flicked on the light and saw that even the little spider plant was gone.

She turned and moved to the bedroom. The door was closed and, God help her, she still found an iota of hope in her heart that Truman had been robbed, or decided he hated his furniture too, and was in there sleeping on his mattress on the floor.

She turned the knob, felt for the lightswitch and pushed it up.

She screamed. Then jumped back.

There in the corner, like something cobwebbed and forgotten in an attic, sat a street person. He was dressed in layer upon ratty layer of clothing, had a beard that had obviously developed into the tangled nest it was over the course of years, and he looked at her through wild, red-rimmed eyes.

"I thought nobody lived here. I thought it was empty," he said, staring at her like an untamed animal about to be caught and caged. "Empty. Empty. Empty, I tell you!"

She held her hands out to him, palms out, so that he wouldn't move, would not get up. "It is, it is. I'm sorry to have disturbed you," she said, backing away from the door. "It's all right. You stay there. I'm going."

She leaned forward to close the door and he shrank back against the wall. Marcy closed the bedroom door and rushed to the front door. She paused, cast one last look around the barren space, then turned out the light and left.

Empty. Empty. Empty.

Her eyes streamed tears as she drove slowly home.

"That all looks real good then," Donnie Molloy said, rising from the chair opposite Marcy's desk. "Thank you,

Ms. P. I'll be happy when Burton's case is over and we know just where we stand."

Marcy stood too. "Well, regardless of the outcome of Mr. Burton's case, we'll go forward with yours. While I believe *Burton versus Planners* will be successful, even if it's not, that doesn't mean yours won't be."

Donnie shook his head admiringly. "I wish I could do what you do, Ms. P. Helping people like me and Bob Burton."

She smiled wryly. "Well, I'm not doing it for free."

He shrugged, grinning. "Yeah, but you ain't taking any money 'less we get some. That's the same as free to me. Least for now."

"I'm glad. In any case, I've got good reason to believe we'll be successful."

Donnie laughed and slapped his palms together. "If old Bob Burton walks away with a great big check, then you can be sure the first thing I'll be doing is making my reservations at Avenel."

"Avenel?"

"Only the best golf course in the Washington, D.C., area. That's what I hear, anyway. I got a connection can get me in, but I ain't never had the money to try it before."

"Well, you don't have it yet," Marcy cautioned. "You never know what a judge will do. And I mean *never*. Let's not count our chickens—"

"Or birdies!" Donnie cackled.

She laughed. "Right. That's very good. But you know what I'm saying, don't you, Donnie?"

"Oh sure. I know most people don't get the kinda

money you hear about in them big cases. Like what was that one? The McDonald's one?"

Marcy sighed. Everyone brought up the McDonald's case. The one where a woman won a huge settlement for spilling hot coffee on herself. There was so much people didn't know about that case, though. Circumstances and injuries that went far beyond a mere spilling of a hot cup of coffee.

"Yes, well, that was a jury trial, for one thing, and juries are even more unpredictable than judges. But I'm glad you know most cases don't end up like that."

"Yeah, yeah, I know. But I can dream, can't I? Thanks again, Ms. P. I know you're doing what you can."

"You're certainly welcome. I'll do my best. But, uh, Donnie?" she said hesitantly as he began to turn away. She looked at the desk, at her fingers tented on its surface. "There is one thing you could do for me, if you wouldn't mind. Just a small favor."

His brow beetled. "Sure. You name it."

She opened the long desk drawer in front of her and took out an envelope. "Would you mind, and please tell me if this makes you uncomfortable in any way, would you mind giving this to Truman Fleming when you see him at work?"

Donnie looked solemnly at the envelope she held without making a move to take it. Dread moved into her stomach.

"Well, I *wouldn't* mind," he said, "not if it ain't a death threat or nothing . . ." He chuckled and she smiled uncertainly. "But, thing is, he quit, Truman did. Up and quit, oh, 'bout a week and a half ago."

Marcy was stunned. "He *quit*?"

Donnie nodded. "Sure did. Said he was starting fresh, or something like that. Promised to keep in touch, though, 'cause we got to be friends, Tru 'n' me. Hope he does."

Marcy felt as if she'd been punched. Truman was gone. *Really* gone. He'd disappeared.

She'd lost him for good.

"Did he mention anything about the case?" she asked, the uncertainty finally hitting her that if he were well and truly gone he might not be planning to testify.

Donnie thought for a second. "No, don't think he did. Wished me luck on mine, but I don't recall him saying anything else."

She nodded slowly, working to keep her composure.

"If you want," he offered, his expression worried as he looked at her, "I'll take the envelope and give it to him if I see him. I invited him to stop by the house for dinner any time he got the urge. That boy ate the worst kind of junk food I ever seen."

Marcy swallowed hard and forced a smile. "That would be great, Donnie. Thank you."

She held the envelope out to him and he took it. He was her last, best hope, unless Truman showed up for the trial on Thursday. In which case she would talk to him herself.

If he didn't show up, though . . .

Well, it just didn't bear thinking about.

She wondered, though, how she'd manage to think about anything else.

18

Thursday, December 12
WORD-A-DAY!

JEOFAIL: n., a mistake or oversight during a legal proceeding; quite simply, something a lawyer did not plan or want to have happen in a court of law

Marcy was a mess. It was seven A.M. the day of the trial, she'd been up since four, and she was sitting at her desk at work, sure she was going to throw up at any moment. She'd already rushed to the bathroom twice and felt better once she got there. Which was only one reason she wished to God she could spend the entire day, if not the rest of her life, there.

It had started with waking up. Waking up with the instant knowledge that Truman was gone, untraceable. She'd asked her assistant to try and track down the landlord to see if he knew where Truman had moved—he was, after all, a missing key witness—but to no avail.

"The landlord, one Mr. . . ." Jan had paused and flipped back a sheet on her steno pad the previous day. ". . . Calhoun, said he had no idea where Mr. Fleming was. Said people come and go all the time and there's no way he can keep track of them all. Actually, he said it a lot more colorfully than that but that's the gist of it."

Marcy felt tears pushing at her eyes. Again. It seemed they did that every time she thought of Truman.

"He didn't have anything else to say? The landlord?" she'd asked.

"Yes, he said Mr. Fleming was at least paid up on his rent, which was more than he could say for most people who disappeared. So I asked him *how* Mr. Fleming paid his rent, if he used a check, and if he did, did Mr. Calhoun remember which bank he used?"

"Oh, good thinking." Marcy had felt a smidgen of hope blossom in her breast at that.

But Jan had shaken her head. "He said that was one memorable thing about Mr. Fleming, he always hand-delivered his rent in cash."

In cash. Marcy had been surprised at that. And disturbed. Who paid for things like rent in cash but drug dealers and members of the mob?

But none of that mattered now. All that mattered was that he was one of her key witnesses, one she planned to call today, and he was nowhere to be found.

Okay, she let her head sink into her hands, fingers in her hair. That wasn't *all* that mattered now, but that was all she would allow herself to think about. She could tell herself she only sought him because he was an important witness but the anxious murmurings of her heart were difficult to ignore.

She let her eyes drift up to the calendar on her desk—her Word-a-Day! calendar—and felt nauseous all over again. How in the world had that hideous word—*jeofail,* of all the godforsaken words they could've chosen—managed to show up today? Was it a sign from God? An omen to persuade her to give up the case? Had Planners made this calendar?

She couldn't do it, of course, and there was no reason she should drop the case even if Truman didn't show. The evidence was strongly in her favor even without his testimony. But she was so tired from lack of sleep, so anxious about Truman, so conscious of the broken state of her heart, that chances were she wouldn't have any trouble using that word in a sentence by the end of the day.

She was more than distracted enough to make a mistake.

Three hours later, Marcy had pulled herself together enough to make her opening statement and question Mr. Burton on direct examination without mishap. In fact, she'd felt stronger as soon as the trial had started. The familiar rush of adrenaline had kicked in and her confidence that she had a strong case returned. She'd have felt better if she'd seen Truman in the lobby beforehand. There was no denying her case for willful negligence would be much stronger with his testimony, stating that he heard Lang refuse to install the required guardrails. But, all things considered, she was doing all right.

She was just taking a deep breath after Marty Strape cross-examined Donnie Molloy in a relatively mild way when Win Downey leaned over the bar behind her and whispered, "Why didn't you tell me Tru Fleming was one of your witnesses?"

Marcy sat bolt upright and swiveled in her seat. What difference did it make to Win that Tru Fleming was her fact witness?

"I, I . . . didn't I? Is he here?" she asked.

Win nodded, still smiling at her.

"Nice going," he mouthed, giving her a thumbs up as he sat back down.

Marcy's eyes scanned the courtroom, but of course he wouldn't be there even if he'd arrived. Defense had requested that all witnesses be kept out of the courtroom, a common request, to lessen the chance that they'd influence each other's testimonies. She wished she could ask if Win had actually *seen* him, or if he'd just seen the witness list.

"Miss Paglinowski?" Judge Bailey asked. "Your next witness?"

She'd never argued before Judge Bailey, but Marcy had heard she was a fair, if tough, judge. A gray-haired woman with a strong-jawed face, she surveyed her courtroom with sharp eyes and a no-nonsense demeanor.

Marcy stood, praying to God that Win was right and Truman was here. "Yes, your honor. Plaintiff calls Truman Fleming."

Marcy turned to watch the bailiff open the courtroom doors. Truman Fleming took two steps into the room and the breath left Marcy's body.

He looked—incredible. Not because she hadn't seen him in over three weeks but because he was dressed like he'd just stepped out of *GQ Magazine*. He wore a perfectly tailored charcoal-gray suit, had cut his hair, and was cleanly shaven. He looked as if he'd just come from a boardroom.

She gave Truman a tentative smile, and suddenly Strape jumped up and said, "Defense objects to this witness, your honor."

Truman stopped.

Judge Bailey cast Strape a steely glare. "On what grounds, counselor?"

Strape sent a nasty look Marcy's way. "On the grounds that defense has evidence that the witness and my esteemed colleague, Ms. Paglinowski, are engaged in a personal, and I can say with some authority, *intimate* relationship. Defense contends that because of this relationship this witness will say anything she tells him to regardless of the truth, making his testimony unreliable, or at the very least suspect."

Marcy's stomach hit the floor and for one perilous second she honestly thought she would pass out. Her head swam as the blood drained from it.

"That—that's . . ." She turned to the judge. "Your honor, that accusation is *at best* irrelevant. It's also erroneous. The witness and I are not engaged in a relationship of any sort."

She cast a glance toward Truman whose expression gave little away, though she saw a tightening around his mouth and his eyes narrowed dangerously at Strape.

"I beg to contradict my esteemed colleague," Strape said, pulling a manila folder from his briefcase from which Marcy saw with horror he tipped out several photographs. "If you'll just take a look at these . . ."

Marcy placed a hand over her mouth, then quickly dropped it and said, "*Your honor—*"

Judge Bailey interrupted. "Mr. Strape, I will not have this courtroom turned into a peep show because of photographs you managed to dig up that are not directly relevant to the case at hand."

Strape raised his voice. "They are relevant because—"

"I was not finished!" Judge Bailey boomed imperiously.

Strape bowed his head and put the photos on the table in front of him. Marcy noticed he pushed them toward the bench, obviously hoping the judge would catch a glimpse of something lewd.

What could be in them? she thought frantically. She closed her eyes briefly. Making out on a public street near the pool hall, she thought, for one thing . . .

Marcy's heart hammered in her chest and she wasn't sure she would be able to speak without losing her composure. She didn't dare look back at Win Downey, whose eyes she could feel on the back of her head like a branding iron.

Consorting with a witness . . .

"I will consider," Judge Bailey continued, "allowing you to address this issue on cross, Mr. Strape, if it seems relevant at that time. But I want it to be known that I do not like, nor do I condone, such tactics as these"—she gestured disgustedly toward the pictures—"in my courtroom."

"I understand. Thank you for your consideration, your honor," Strape said, sitting. He left the pictures where they were.

"The witness may continue," the judge said, waving Truman forward.

Marcy watched him come down the aisle. Had he gone on a shopping spree at Brooks Brothers? Even his shoes were polished and looked like something straight out of a Johnston and Murphy store.

As he passed through the gate at the bar and walked confidently toward the witness stand he cast her a glance that she thought contained some sympathy—

she even thought she detected a tiny, compassionate smile—but it was over so quickly she couldn't be sure.

With a deep breath for fortitude, she rose from her chair and started asking the questions she'd prepared. Without looking at him any more than she had to, for fear of giving the judge the impression that Strape's allegation had merit, she guided Truman through the beginning part of his testimony, allowing him to explain when he began working for Planners, what the conditions were, and whether or not he had known her client, Bob Burton.

But Marcy was so rattled by Strape's accusation she couldn't tell at all how it was going. She could barely tell if she was asking the questions in order or coherently, so distracted was she by the pile of photographs fanned across the opposing counsel's table. She had notes on how to proceed, thank God, but she couldn't for the life of her say if she was sticking to them logically or not.

At one point she glanced over and saw a thunderous expression on Win Downey's face. He was looking slowly around the courtroom and when his eyes met hers her knees nearly folded beneath her. She remained standing only by placing a hand on the table and turning back to Truman.

"Mr. Fleming," she said. Her voice was at least emerging normally, if not exactly powerfully. "What happened on the morning of February the ninth?"

Truman's eyes were on her. Where they trying to convey commiseration or was that just wishful thinking? She let her gaze skitter away, feeling a blush burn her cheeks. She hoped to God the judge didn't notice.

"February the ninth I arrived a couple of minutes late to work and ran across Chuck Lang, the site superintendent, and Larry Standish, foreman for the subcontractor's crew, arguing in the parking lot."

That same parking lot where she and Truman had met. Where she'd found Folly . . . Good Lord, could Strape have pictures of them stealing the dog?

Marcy kept her eyes on her notes. Where were they? What had Truman just said? "Was Bob Burton part of Larry Standish's crew?"

Tru nodded. "Yes. That's right."

She imagined a photo of herself locked in Truman's embrace by her car that night near the pool hall. The way she'd pressed herself against his body it would be a wonder if either one of them was recognizable in a photograph.

Yes. That's right. That's what Truman had just said, wasn't it?

She cleared her throat, kept her eyes on her notes. If she looked at his face she would imagine them in bed. Jesus, did his bedroom have curtains? Could someone have gotten a picture of *that*?

Intimate, Strape had said.

"And what were Mr. Lang and Mr. Standish arguing about?" she asked, feeling sweat break out on her forehead.

"*Objection*, your honor!" Strape's voice was so loud Marcy jumped and dropped her notes. The index cards fluttered across the floor in three different directions.

Judge Bailey looked at Strape. Marcy ducked to pick up the index card closest to her.

"This witness's testimony is *hearsay*," Strape declared in an incensed tone. "What he heard or didn't hear is as inadmissible as whatever pillow talk these two engaged in to come up with this pathetic—"

"Mr. Strape!" Judge Bailey boomed.

Marcy froze where she crouched on the floor, her fingers on the edge of an index card. She could barely believe what he'd just said.

"Your honor—" she began, rising.

But Truman's voice was louder, and far angrier. "It's allowed as an admission of the defendant, you arrogant twit," he said, glaring at Strape. "Because as superintendent, Chuck Lang is an agent of the corporation, making anything he says the same as a statement issued by Planners Building and Design. I would think even a sleazy, two-bit lawyer like yourself should know that."

Strape colored deeply. "And just where, exactly, did *you* go to law school, Mr. Fleming?" he sneered. "Hm?"

Marcy opened her mouth to intervene, but Truman, who looked ready to kill, spoke first.

"Harvard," he said firmly. "Class of 1994."

Marcy's jaw dropped.

He'd just perjured himself. He'd been trying to put Strape in his place and he'd perjured himself. His entire testimony would be thrown out.

She glanced over at Win Downey who was—*smiling*?

Strape, who'd just been purple, now grinned with malicious glee. "May I remind you, Mr. Fleming, that *you*, sir, are under oath?"

Truman's face was composed. "I am aware of that, Mr. Strape."

Strape looked desperately to the judge. Marcy followed suit.

Judge Bailey suddenly seemed to be enjoying herself. "I am," she said slowly, "familiar with Mr. Fleming's status as a member of this bar. And I will take his word for his credentials."

Marcy's breath left her as if she been sucker-punched in the gut.

Strape sat down in his chair, missed the seat, and clattered to the floor. While he struggled to rise, Marcy turned her gaze slowly to Truman.

He sat still in the witness box, his gaze on her. This time, however, she was sure the look in his eyes was a bit less certain than before.

"In addition, Mr. Fleming is correct," Judge Bailey continued, once Strape had found his seat again. "Defendant's objection is overruled." She turned to Truman. "In the future, Mr. Fleming, while I'm aware of your status as a member of the bar, you should allow your attorney to speak to the admissibility of her line of questioning."

Truman nodded. "Sorry, your honor."

"You may continue, Ms. Paglinowski." The judge inclined her head toward Marcy.

But Marcy's mind was blank. The only words in her head were *living honestly*. Living. Honestly. Words that had resounded within her for weeks now.

Don't you want to live honestly? Truman had demanded that night they had argued. *Honestly?* she thought again now with growing outrage. He was a lawyer, living in a slum and working construction, giving her shit for not living honestly when he did the *exact same thing?*

"Ms. Paglinowski?" the judge prompted.

Marcy looked up at her and swallowed. "I'm sorry," she said vaguely, then cleared her throat and spoke firmly. "I was just taken by surprise by Mr. Fleming's . . . credentials."

She was amazed she could even get the mild words out. Fury grew within her at a frightening speed. Who the *hell* did he think he was?

"Do you require a break?" the judge asked, her expression clearly saying she shouldn't need one.

Marcy shook her head slowly. "No, your honor. It's not important. I'll continue." She looked back at Truman, whose eyes were still watching her, caution in every line of his body.

He should *be cautious,* she thought, glaring at him. Every superior word he'd uttered about her not knowing how real people lived, every guilt trip he'd sent her on for offering to pay or for lamenting his lack of a phone, every feeling she'd had that she'd been unfair to him because of his disadvantaged situation in life now snapped back upon her as clear as the crack of a whip.

"Now, Mr. Fleming," she said as composedly as she could, "please tell the court what Mr. Lang and Mr. Standish were arguing about."

"I heard Standish tell Lang that guardrails on open-sided floors were required by OSHA, and that if Lang didn't put some up he'd be in direct violation of OSHA regulations."

She strode toward the witness box, her eyes boring into his. "And what did Mr. Lang say to that?"

He met her gaze. "He told Standish that the job could be finished by the time he'd complied with all of OSHA's requirements. Then he said something like, 'OSHA, my ass,' and flatly refused to install any guardrails."

Marcy hesitated one deliberate moment, her eyes on Truman's, then said, "Thank you," in a tone just short of derisive. She turned to Judge Bailey. "No further questions, your honor."

She turned on her heel and sat down at her table without looking at Truman again.

Truman could read anger on Marcy's face. But it was anger that had been there since Strape had objected to his testimony, so he wasn't sure what to think. Clearly she'd been shocked by his revelation, but if he'd been looking for relief, renewed interest, or anything to suggest his new status had affected her, he hadn't seen it.

"Your witness, Mr. Strape," Judge Bailey said.

Truman looked to Strape, wishing that for one brief moment he could have been imbued with the power to burn a hole in the man's forehead with his eyes. He'd never met Strape before the deposition, and had heard nothing about him—surprising considering the cheap tactics he'd used today. Usually lawyers like him were known by reputation in a relatively short amount of time, making it easier for attorneys arguing against them to be prepared for something underhanded.

Obviously Marcy had heard nothing about him either.

Truman had felt such anger on her behalf and had wanted so badly to jump out of the witness box and strangle the wretched Strape for causing that devastated look on Marcy's face that it was all he could do to keep seated. Never in his life had he seen such profound shock on anyone's face, and he hoped never to see it again. Especially not on Marcy's.

Strape rose to his feet and took a couple steps in Tru's direction. He, too, looked nonplussed, however. The day's proceedings had taken their toll on everyone. With the possible exception of Judge Bailey, who seemed abnormally pleased with the strafing of Strape. Apparently *she'd* seen his tactics before.

"Mr. Fleming," Strape said, "what is the nature of your relationship with Ms. Paglinowski?" He tried to give Truman a penetrating glare but couldn't sustain it. He let his eyes drop to a point on Truman's tie.

"I wouldn't say we have a relationship," Truman said. He glanced at Marcy, who sat stiff-backed at her table, her eyes on a yellow legal pad in front of her on which she wrote rapidly.

"You wouldn't say you *have* a relationship?" Strape repeated. "Surely you're mistaken, Mr. Fleming. At the very least she is your attorney in this matter."

"She is Bob Burton's attorney. I am a fact witness for this case. That's all."

Strape narrowed his eyes at Truman. "Are you saying you have no *personal* relationship with Ms. Paglinowski?"

"Objection, your honor," Marcy called, looking up from her paper at the judge. "Asked and answered."

Good girl, Truman thought.

Judge Bailey nodded. "Sustained. Move on, Mr. Strape."

Strape issued a hearty, long-suffering sigh. "Have you *ever* had a relationship with Ms. Paglinowski?"

"Objection," Marcy said again. Her tone was calm. "Even if a current relationship could be construed as relevant because of its effect on this trial, surely any relationship terminated prior to the trial is not."

"Sustained," Judge Bailey said.

"But your honor," Strape protested, "you said you would allow—"

"I said I would *consider* allowing questions and determine relevancy at that time. I have now allowed questions on the subject and have determined further exploration of this issue is irrelevant."

Truman could barely contain a smile.

The rest of Strape's questions were routine, spineless examinations of his answers on direct examination. He tried to keep Truman on the stand as long as he could, nitpicking every angle in hope of finding one that might discredit him, but Truman's answers were so brief and unhelpful that Strape eventually gave up and excused him.

Truman rose from his seat in the witness box and moved across the well between the judge's bench and attorneys' tables. His eyes were on Marcy, hoping for a sign of what she was thinking, but she did not look up from her paper.

With an inward sigh, he moved past her, through the gate at the bar, and down the aisle to the courthouse lobby.

Once there, he stood, paralyzed with indecision. Should he leave? Or should he wait for Marcy? Tell her to her face that he knew they were finished, that he could never know now whether she wanted him for himself or his position.

He didn't want to hurt her, though God knew he was hurting from the angry end to their relationship. He just knew, if they got together now, he'd always wonder if she was just another social-climbing woman. If she had her eye on the prize, more than the person.

He shook his head and turned back toward the closed courtroom doors. That wasn't Marcy, he thought. That wasn't the Marcy who'd bantered with him over half-smokes, the Marcy who'd stepped so passionately into his arms in his dingy little apartment.

Perhaps he should stay, he thought, indulging his deepest desire for just a moment. Maybe he should wait for her to emerge from the courtroom and confront her, have her tell him he was wrong, that she had *always* cared about him, and hadn't cared at all that he was penniless.

But he knew that wasn't true, either. She'd been honest enough to admit as much. She wanted someone with a career, with *money*—she'd said the very word herself. What else did he need? A stick to beat himself with?

No, he'd had his answer. She didn't want him if he didn't have money to provide that secure position for which she strived. *Security,* he thought with a pain in his chest. What an artful euphemism for wealth.

He turned back around and headed for the exit.

Marcy Paglinowski had made it clear what she wanted, he thought, walking with growing purpose across the marbled floor. And it wasn't the Tru Fleming from Southeast.

But Tru Fleming had standards too, he thought,

opening the courthouse doors and exiting into the frigid December sunshine. And they included a woman who would love him no matter what.

A woman who loved the man, not the money.

19

Thursday, December 12
WORD-A-DAY!

BONUS WORD
SOCKDOLOGER: n., a decisive declaration or knock-out blow that finishes the argument; quite often this blow is of an unexpected and startling nature

As the judge left the courtroom, Marcy stood and gathered her papers. They had one more day of the trial to go, but she had little fear that they would lose now. She'd seen the defense's list of witnesses and knew they didn't have much to refute what hers had proven today.

But she couldn't feel good. In fact, she was so far from feeling good that all she wanted to do was go home and spend the next six months in bed.

She'd been lied to by Truman, betrayed in such an expansive, unexpected way she was still reeling from the shock. What had he been thinking? Had he *wanted* to hurt her, showing up in court this way and making his admission so public? Had surprising her in the middle of a trial been his way of avoiding a scene?

Or had he thought perhaps the truth would not have come out? Strape's accusation was hardly predictable, and Marcy was pretty sure it was anger over that accusation that had triggered Truman's experienced response to Strape's hearsay objection.

It didn't matter, though. Whether or not Truman had planned to reveal himself at the trial was beside the point.

The point was he'd lied to her. Not just one little white lie or a fib that could be excused or explained away. He'd lied about *everything*.

Every nerve quivered with outrage.

Then there was the way she'd been made a fool in front of Win Downey. The look on his face when she'd turned around after Strape's accusation could have melted polar icecaps. She was afraid to think of all the things he had to say to her now.

As the courtroom emptied and she stuffed her pad, pens, index cards and notes back into her briefcase, she felt Win come to stand beside her table.

"Ms. Paglinowski," his deep voice, the one that resounded so authoritatively in courtrooms and intimidated too many judges and jurors to count, said.

She looked up, steeling herself for the reprimand she knew was coming. Despite having triumphed on the ruling, she was sure it was obvious to everyone that there *had* been some sort of personal relationship between herself and Truman. She'd been unable to catch a glimpse of Strape's pictures, but she'd sooner poke out her own eyes than admit to any interest in photographs of that sort.

"Win, hello," she said. Straightening and pressing her palms down the sides of her skirt. "I wanted to tell you I'm sor—"

"I just wanted to congratulate you," he said with a beaming smile.

He held his hand out to her and, dazed, she put hers into it.

"You were brilliant today, Marcy. Just brilliant," he continued. "By God, when that contemptible . . ." He cast his eyes towards Strape's table and shook his head, pressing his lips together. "You know I don't like to speak ill of other attorneys, but when he pulled that stunt with the pictures I was ready to leap over the bar and have at him myself."

Marcy could only gape at him, her hand still being shaken by his. So he wasn't angry with *her* when all that had come out, he was upset with Strape. Relief coursed through her.

Win contemplated the contemptible Strape's table a moment longer, then turned a brighter expression to Marcy. "But you recovered, Marcy, and you let him have it. I tell you, I couldn't have been more proud. You've lived up to every ounce of expectation I've had of you since you wrote me that first letter from college."

She swallowed. "Win, thank you. That means so much. I . . . I don't know what to say."

He beamed again and clapped her on the shoulder. "That's all right. You had enough to say when it was important. And getting Tru Fleming as a witness! My word, what a stroke of luck it was that *he* was at the site, though I have to say I'm a bit perplexed by that. Maybe it was some sort of research for a case, as unorthodox as that would be. I suffered one of my most devastating losses at his hands, did I ever tell you that story?"

"No, I don't think so." She was pretty damn sure. If she'd ever heard Truman Fleming's name before that day at the construction site, it could have saved her weeks of torment.

"*Sullivan versus the D.C. Board of Education,*" Win said. "Remind me to tell you about it someday."

"I will. Yes, that would be very interesting."

He let go of her hand and twisted his watch around his wrist to see the face. "Gotta run. I didn't mean to stay the whole day but you were doing so well and that—that—well, let's just call him *opposing counsel,* shall we?" He grinned and winked at her. "He stirred things up so much I decided I had to stay in case he tried anything else."

"I do appreciate your being here, Win. I was really quite nervous."

"Didn't show a bit, Marcy. But now I'm behind, so I'd better run. More tomorrow, eh? Well, you shouldn't have any trouble taking care of that. Come to my office once things finish up, all right?"

"Of course," Marcy said. "And thank you again for being here."

Win laughed, the sound echoing around the now empty courtroom. "Thank *you* for making it too interesting to leave."

Marcy watched him go, then finished gathering her things. As she headed for the doors she turned and looked at the witness stand. The last place the Truman Fleming she had known had been, and the first place from which the *real* Truman Fleming had emerged.

She turned, glanced at her watch, and walked up the aisle to the doors.

She was meeting Calvin and Sheila for dinner in an hour, giving her just enough time to stop by the office, then go home, change her clothes, and drive to Kalorama to look for Sheila's house.

Apparently Calvin had told Sheila the truth and she'd taken it every bit as well as Marcy had thought she would. Now, tonight, they were having a small dinner in celebration and Calvin said it would mean the world if she could be there. After all, he and Sheila would never have met if it hadn't been for Marcy.

He also wouldn't be on his way out of the shelter, he'd added on the phone last night, if not for her making it possible for him to begin catering. He was so excited about it all there was no way she could turn him down even though she knew she would be exhausted.

Little did she know she'd also be shell-shocked. The day had taken everything she had out of her, and more.

Truman watched his mother flutter around Calvin Deeds like a wildly hospitable butterfly. She was crazy about the man. And Truman had to admit he liked him too. Calvin Deeds was a gentleman of the old school, with quiet manners and an aura of dignity. From the moment he'd entered the house, handing Reginald his hat and overcoat with a gracious little bow and a "Thank you, sir," Truman knew he would like the man.

"You sure I can't freshen your drink?" Tru's mother asked Calvin again.

"You can freshen mine," Truman said, holding up his tumbler, now empty of scotch and soda.

"Oh, you can freshen your own," his mother said, with a wave of her hand.

He chuckled and went to the bar as the two of them talked.

He didn't normally drink hard liquor, but the day had been extraordinarily draining. Not just the trial, but the agonizing period afterward when he second-guessed every decision he'd made in the last two weeks. Though he'd left his failed secret life without a clue to Marcy where to find him, he still struggled with what he'd done, from disappearing to revealing himself to her.

Not that he'd planned on the latter, necessarily. He'd actually planned to show up, testify, and leave. He and Marcy had said everything to each other they'd needed to say that night at the Rock 'n' Roll holiday party. They'd each stated their beliefs and they were mutually exclusive. What good would revealing himself do?

Then the moment in court had arrived and Strape had pissed him off so badly that without giving it additional thought, Truman had done what he could to push the man off balance.

Ultimately it didn't matter, however, he told himself. Even if he hadn't said who he was, Win Downey, whom he hadn't realized was involved enough in the case to actually be there, would have told her just who he was and would probably even tell her where to find him now, if she really wanted to know.

And if she sought him out now, he'd know it was because he'd been transformed from the pauper into the prince.

His only real problem was that he couldn't let the damn thing lie. He kept asking himself if ending things with her was the only answer. Would he really never know if she cared for him? What if they tried a relationship with everything out in the open? Would he not be able to tell how she felt about him? Surely the worst that would happen was he'd discover in her what he'd discovered in other women—that they liked the socialite life-style more than he could tolerate.

But it was no use. His own wariness, he knew, more than anything else, would make a relationship impossible.

Besides, he thought, he'd made his decision about the life-style too. Instead of trying—unsuccessfully, he'd finally determined—to make it in a blue-collar world, he was instead going to put his education and training to work in the small town of Windslip, North Carolina. He was going to open his own firm and hopefully get a chance to help people who couldn't ordinarily afford to hire an attorney.

The doorbell rang and Truman saw Reginald cross the hallway outside the parlor and head toward the door.

"That must be Calvin's friend," Tru's mother said. "I do hope she's not too tired from her busy day."

Truman experienced a sinking feeling in his gut. He hadn't known Calvin's "friend," also invited to dinner, was a woman. Were the lovebirds setting him up with someone? He closed his eyes in dread.

"She's a lawyer, too, Truman." His mother gave him an encouraging smile. "She was in court today, so Calvin was afraid she wouldn't be able to make it."

They *were* trying to set him up. Truman wondered how he could excuse himself early, like before the appetizer. He was through with women, he thought resolutely, at least for a while.

Calvin stood as the noises of entry sounded in the hall, soft talk, the exchange of coat for drink order, then the footsteps toward the parlor.

Calvin approached the archway to the hall. Truman just caught a glimpse of dark hair on a small, slender woman before Calvin hugged her and Marcy's face appeared over his shoulder.

Truman's breath stopped. How—when—did his mother *know* about Marcy?

But it was Calvin who was hugging her.

A second later Calvin turned her loose and, with a smile, she moved toward his mother with her hand out. As her gaze scanned the room, however, it landed on him and she froze, hand still outstretched toward his mother.

Okay, Truman thought, so she hadn't known he would be here.

But how—if she knew his mother, surely she must have thought there was a chance . . .

"Truman," she said. "What on earth . . . ?" She glanced back at Calvin.

Calvin gave a chagrined jump and came forward. "I'm sorry. Where are my manners? Marcy, this is Sheila's son, the one I was telling you about."

Marcy's stunned gaze was still on her friend. "The one you were telling me about?" She looked confused, then aware. "The *Peace Corps* one?"

"The Peace Corps?" Truman echoed.

"Well, not really, but yes, that's the one. You remember, don't you, Marcy?" Calvin asked.

Marcy turned slowly back to Truman. "*You're* Sheila's son? You're the one who . . . ?" She stopped talking and looked into his face, into his eyes, with such a penetrating look of astonishment he didn't know what to say.

"Yes. I am Sheila's son," he said finally. "How do you know my mother?"

"You two know each other? How wonderful!" His mother clapped her hands together once. "Although I guess it's not really surprising, since you're both lawyers."

"There are thousands upon thousands of lawyers in D.C., Mother. I didn't meet Marcy until . . ."

He looked at her, unable to continue. He pictured her that night they'd stolen the dog. So beautiful and so capable. She was always so sure of herself. Even today in the courtroom she'd handled things better than he ever would have expected in the face of what had happened.

Marcy turned suddenly toward his mother. "Sheila, I'm so sorry. How rude of me. I haven't even said hello. It's nice to see you again."

"You too, dear," his mother said, taking Marcy's hand in both of hers.

"I had no idea you were Truman's mother. He was an important witness in my case today. That's how we know each other. I guess I never got your last name when we met at the Downey Fin party. And Calvin always refers to you as 'Sheila,' or 'dear lady.' " She sent her friend an affectionate smile.

Truman thought she'd never looked more beautiful. Or more untouchable.

His mother smiled, gratified. "Isn't that sweet?" She turned to Truman. "I didn't know you were a witness in a case."

Truman raised a brow. "No?"

Frowning at him his mother turned her attention back to Marcy. "Well, I'm so glad you could make it."

"Yes . . . I . . ." Marcy glanced at Truman. "I'm so sorry, as it turns out I can't stay long, only a minute after all."

"Oh, no," his mother said, looking truly crestfallen.

"Didn't things go well today?" Calvin asked, worry mottling his brow.

"Actually," Marcy glanced fleetingly at Truman again and he noticed the pink tingeing her cheeks. "Yes, things went very well. But there's still one more day, and I really need to prepare. The opposing counsel in this case is apparently adept at coming up with unexpected, and disturbingly unorthodox, ways to seek the advantage."

"Surely you can stay for dinner, though," Tru's mother said. "We'll eat right away. You have to eat sometime, don't you, dear?"

He'd known his mother would like her. He just hadn't known she'd meet her unless he'd orchestrated it.

"Yes," Truman said, feeling suddenly afraid that if she walked out that door now he'd never see her again. He didn't think about the fact that never seeing her again was precisely what he'd planned just hours ago. "Do stay. For dinner. It's all ready." He swept a hand out toward the dining room.

She was here, after all, he told himself. And like his mother said, she *did* have to eat sometime. Surely one dinner together wouldn't hurt. And he'd have a chance to tell her why things wouldn't work out between them, despite their being more alike than she'd previously known. She probably thought she should leave because he was still angry with her after their argument.

"No," she said flatly, looking him straight in the eye. She turned to her friend. "Calvin, I'm really sorry. We'll have to do this some other time. But I did want to stop by and say how happy I am for . . ." She glanced between Calvin and Tru's mother. "Well, just for seeing you two together."

"We *will* do it again. Soon. When you're free," Truman's mother said.

"Thank you for stopping by anyway," Calvin said, kissing her on the cheek as she turned to leave.

"I'll walk you out," Truman said suddenly, surprising himself.

"That's really not necessary," Marcy replied.

"I think it is."

They all looked at him. Marcy just shrugged and turned to the door.

As they walked to the hallway Truman berated himself with everything he had in him. What on earth was he walking her out for? He had no idea what she could be thinking, but he was pretty sure she was miffed at him for not telling her he was actually a lawyer not a construction worker. But was that something he should apologize for? If not, why did he want so badly to see her alone?

He mentally cringed. What a godawful mess.

Reginald met them by the door and handed Marcy her coat and purse. The same camelhair coat, Truman noted, that she'd worn the day she'd first confronted Chuck Lang.

They stepped out onto the front porch. Truman shivered in his long-sleeved polo shirt.

"Where's Folly?" she asked the moment the door closed behind them.

"She's out back." The hard tone of her voice took him by surprise. "There's a yard—"

"I'll be coming to get her. I'm moving out of my apartment and I'll be able to take her." She glared up at him. "I know you never wanted her. Not really."

"Not in the beginning," he admitted, still at a loss to decipher her mood. He didn't want to lose the dog, too. But how stupidly sentimental would it be to hang on to her? "But now, I . . ."

"You know, Truman," she said, the words bursting from her as if they could not be contained any longer. "You really have some nerve. You had me questioning my *entire life*, everything I thought and did, and wore and bought for that matter, all for your stupid, pretentious experiment. Living honestly, you called it. Give me a *break*. Every person I know is living more honestly than you are, Truman Fleming, and that includes that snake Marty Strape from court today. While you were out there playing poor, and preaching to me about the real world, how real people live, did it ever occur to you to ask yourself how *real* you were, Truman?"

She stopped for one quick breath and continued, "Of course it didn't. Because you know everything. You're superior to everyone. You can sit there in your hovel with the comforting knowledge that the family bucks will bail you out of any *real* trouble. And you sneered at my desire for security. Now you'll be able to sit in your luxurious home or your posh office assuaging your affluent guilt with the knowledge that hey, you gave it a shot, you lived like a poor person once for a few months. You know how the other half lives. Well, guess what, Truman, you'll *never* know how the other half lives. Only a person who's had money his entire life could think that playing poor could possibly be the same as *being* poor. You're an affront to all working people, you know that? And you ought to be ashamed of yourself."

She exhaled once, in finality, spun on her heel and strode down the steps toward her car. Truman stood paralyzed on the top step.

As she opened the Lexus's door, however, she turned. "By the way, where's the truck, Truman? Didn't it go with the outfit?" she asked, sweeping one last disparaging glance over him before getting in the car and slamming the door.

She peeled out of the driveway, barely stopping in time to let the gates open before speeding down California Street toward home.

Truman stood in the frigid air, no longer feeling it, staring at the red vapor trail left in his eyes by her taillights.

She didn't want him.

She *really* didn't want him.

The money had made a difference all right, but not the one he'd expected.

She thought he was a hypocrite.

He exhaled slowly, his own perceptions of himself crumbling within him.

Maybe he *was* a hypocrite.

He turned numbly to the house and opened the door.

"Truman, we've decided to eat now anyway," his mother called as he walked in a daze across the hall. "Come to the dining room."

Truman did as he was told, unsure of himself in a way he'd never felt before, though he'd certainly come close in the months he'd spent in Southeast, an outsider there, too. What did one do when one wasn't comfortable in one's own life? Was it really so wrong to seek another?

No, he thought, *just to preach about it.*

"She's such a lovely girl," Calvin was saying as Truman entered the dining room and sat down. "When you get to know her, Sheila, I know you'll love her, as I do. She's made of strong stuff, that one is."

"Yes, she must be," his mother concurred, spreading a napkin across her lap. "Didn't you say she grew up in a bad neighborhood?"

Calvin nodded. "Georges Heights, in P.G. County. Her brothers were a rough crowd too. One of them just got out of prison, I believe. I'll tell you, not many people make it out of that neighborhood, and certainly not with a law degree from Columbia."

Truman's eyes were riveted to Calvin's face. Marcy grew up in *Georges Heights*? Land of the midnight murder and drug emporium neighborhood of the year? Jesus, no wonder she didn't seem all that worried about driving in Southeast.

"And bright," Calvin continued. "Well, you must have seen how bright she was, Truman. In court today?"

Truman nodded, his mind spinning. "She was excellent."

Calvin looked as proud as any father might. "Got

herself into college when everyone around her was either working at the Gas 'N Go or landing in jail."

"Her parents," Truman asked, "didn't they help her at all?"

Calvin came as close to a scoff as someone of his dignified nature could. "Her mother would have, if she could've. But she was working two, three jobs, trying to raise those children. From what I gather, her father was never around, and when he was he wasn't good for much. Spent a lot of time on the couch with a beer in his hand, is how Marcy characterized it."

Truman lay his head back and sighed. *Ah, God, it explained so much, so much about her.*

He tipped his head back up and asked, "How do you know Marcy?"

"We volunteer at the same homeless shelter." Calvin cast a meaningful glance at Tru's mother that Truman couldn't interpret. "For years, even after she went away to school, she'd come help on holidays when she was home. Then after law school she got this job and things dropped off quite a bit. I guess like all young lawyers she was working long hours. Still, she managed to get by every now and again and keep up with her old friends." Calvin smiled, then turned a tender look on Truman's mother. "And thank God she did, eh?" He reached out to take her hand and squeeze it. "Thank God she did."

One week later in Marcy's office, she reached across her desk and handed Donnie Molloy a check.

"This is great, this is just great. Planners caved pretty quick after losing to you last week, huh?" Donnie said with a laugh. "Bet old Bob's already pickin' out his boat."

Marcy smiled. "They were anxious to make a settlement with you, that's true. They may still appeal the Burton verdict, but settling with you shows some realism on their part. They know they were at fault."

"Well, this is great, this is just great," Donnie said again, shaking his head and looking at the check.

"Now you can go play that golf course," Marcy said. "Which one was it?"

"Avenel!" Donnie said with a grin. "Teein' off eight A.M. Saturday morning."

"*This* weekend? Good heavens, won't you be cold?"

Donnie shook his head. "Naw. Long as it ain't below freezing outside I love to get out and play. Besides, getting into Avenel'd be impossible for me in the really nice weather. So I been at the putting green every day this week after work. Want to look respectable out there."

"Well, good luck. Let me know how it goes," she said.

"I sure will!" He left, waving the check at her as he disappeared out the door.

At least she could make some people happy, she thought, if not herself. She'd been in a quandary about Truman ever since last Thursday. She'd lit into him at the time, but the more she thought about it the more complex it seemed. As she strived to reconcile the working-class Truman Fleming she'd fallen for with the "son of Sheila" she'd admired for daring to see how "the other half" lived, the more she thought she might have been unfair.

She just wasn't sure what to do about it.

He'd already made it clear he wanted nothing more to do with her. He'd moved out of his apartment and quit his job without a word to her about where he was going or what he was doing. So she couldn't tell him she forgave him for lying to her, only to hear him say he couldn't forgive her for being a materialistic snob, could she?

Marcy sighed and sat back at her desk. There was nothing she could do. She just had to hope that he was doing the kind of thinking she was and realizing that she wasn't just looking for a guy with money. She was looking for him.

Reginald opened the door to the study and said, "Palmer Roe is here to see you, sir."

Truman looked up from the ledger at which he'd been staring sightlessly. "Palmer? Great, send him in."

By all means, he thought, *send anyone in*. All he was doing was sitting behind the desk brooding, as he had been since last Thursday. Thinking about Marcy was about to drive him crazy. He went back and forth and round and round, trying to figure out exactly what it all meant and what to do about it.

If he tried to explain it to her, would she understand what he'd been trying to do? If he apologized for sermonizing about being poor, or knowing how the real world lived, would she believe that he really did understand how misguided his "experiment" had been? Would she ever believe that his heart had been in the right place?

And if she did, could he ever accept that she did so because she wanted him in spite of, and not because of, the fact that he had money?

Maybe he should be accepting the fact that she'd told

him off and probably never wanted to see him again, he thought. She was, after all, not the pampered rich girl he'd always assumed. Maybe she'd never been all that interested in him. Maybe she'd just been doing a little experimenting herself.

He didn't know. He just didn't know.

Palmer entered the room with a hand outstretched. "There he is, the intrepid traveler. Boldly going where no Harvard graduate has gone before. How are you, Truman?"

Truman took his hand and smiled. "I'm all right. How are you, Palmer? Still hitting the links?" He motioned for Palmer to sit.

Palmer laughed and took the red leather chair across from Truman. "Like a champ. Just parred Avenel this weekend, first time."

"No kidding. You *know* you're addicted when you play golf in December. Addicted or insane."

Palmer shrugged. "Hey, it hit fifty. It was a nice day."

"Sounds like you've really gotten good."

"It helps if you can spend seven days a week at it. My golf game improves in direct proportion to my portfolio." He grinned.

"Don't tell me you slow down when the market falls." Truman gave him a mock look of skepticism.

"Oh hell no. I just don't *feel* as confident. Anyway, I didn't come here to regale you with tales of my golf or investment prowess, though golf does enter into my tale."

Truman raised a brow. "You've got a tale? Does this have anything to do with the fair Trish Hamilton?" Truman was amazed to find even mentioning Marcy's *friend* caused him some pain.

Palmer didn't look surprised that Truman knew about Trish. "In a way, in fact, it does. Or rather, with your mutual friend."

Truman stopped breathing momentarily. "Marcy."

"The very one. You see, I was playing golf this weekend with a gentleman named Donnie Molloy."

"Donnie Molloy? *You* played golf with Donnie Molloy? Where on earth were you playing?"

"Avenel, believe it or not. Seems Donnie just got a handsome settlement from Planners Building and Design, thanks to one Marcy . . . something I can't pronounce."

"Paglinowski."

Palmer grinned. "I had a feeling you'd know. In any case, Donnie also had another fellow to thank, the guy who'd put him in touch with Miss . . . ah . . ."

"Paglinowski," Truman said again, wishing Palmer would get to the point.

"Thank you. But it seemed the guy had recently disappeared. One thing led to another in this conversation, and before long your name came up. 'Well, I just happen to know that fellow,' I told Mr. Molloy." He paused to display an incredulous look that Truman didn't share. "Why, the poor man was positively overjoyed. Turns out he also had something he wanted to *give* you, in addition to his thanks. And so . . ." With a small flourish, Palmer reached into his inside breast pocket and pulled out an envelope.

Truman leaned forward. "What is it?"

Palmer flipped it over and back, looking at it. "I believe it's a letter. One he's had in his possession for a couple of weeks now."

Truman frowned and held his hand out impatiently.

"A letter," Palmer added, "from Marcy . . . uh . . ."

"*Paglinowski*," Truman finished, leaning forward and snatching the envelope from him.

Palmer leaned back in his chair and rubbed his hands together. "Yes," he murmured as Truman ripped the envelope open. "I thought you might be interested."

Truman looked up before pulling the single sheet from the envelope. "You didn't read it, did you?"

Palmer looked insulted. "Of course not." He paused, then smiled slyly. "But I do happen to know what it says. Trish, you know. She encouraged me to give it to you. And if you want my opinion—"

"I don't, really." He unfolded the paper and saw neat, feminine handwriting. *Dear Truman . . .*

"I believe I may give it to you anyway," he mused. "You'd be a fool not to find her, Fleming. Marcy, that is. She's a great girl, much better than you deserve."

Truman looked back up at him. "I think you're probably right about that."

"Of course I am. It's a gift I have, knowing women. Good luck, Tru," Palmer added seriously, rising from his seat. "I'll leave you to it. Give me a call sometime."

"I will."

"Oh, and I gave Donnie Molloy your phone number. He's going to call and invite you for dinner. Steak, he says, because you should have a stake in his winnings from Planners."

Truman laughed. "Sounds good. I'll call you soon, Palmer."

Truman waited until Palmer had closed the door behind him before unfolding Marcy's letter once again. *Dear Truman*, it began. And it was dated December 9, *days* before she found out the truth about him.

I almost don't know where to begin, we've been at such cross purposes for so long. So perhaps I should begin with my apology. I believe, now that I am thinking clearly, that trusting you with my most sincere and abject regret for being a selfish, self-righteous, materialistic snob could not be a mistake. You are, I have come to learn over the last couple of months, a man of the most admirable character and integrity.

Please believe me when I tell you that I realize now I could not have been more wrong about you. Though it may have sounded like it the other night at the party, I do not believe that everyone should be chasing the almighty dollar, as I seem to do. If I had properly explained to you the reasons I do this then I am sure that you, as a compassionate person, would have understood. But I did not explain them properly and for that I am sorry, too.

But my biggest regret is that I made you feel as if you weren't good enough for me. Truman, that is as far from the truth as could be. If anything, you are too good for me. Too honest. Too courageous. Too true to yourself. I am ashamed of how I have acted around you.

If you find that you can accept my apology, Truman, do you think you could also find it in your heart to give me another chance? While my apology is sincere, whether or not you find yourself still interested in me, my feelings for you, so clear and acute these last weeks, demand that I ask. Is there any hope that we might renew our friendship?

But here I find that friendship is not the right word. Because the truth is I have fallen in love with you. And I hope with all my heart that you can forgive me, and perhaps find a place for me in your life.

Regretfully and affectionately yours,

Marcy

20

Tuesday, December 24
WORD-A-DAY!

THEURGY: n., the art of compelling fate to perform a miracle; as when something is so right and two people want it so badly that the universe can say nothing but yes

It was Christmas Eve when Marcy cast a final critical glance around the empty living room of her former apartment.

Good-bye, white carpet, she thought. *And good riddance.*

Good-bye, white walls and chrome fixtures. Good-bye, high rent and low security. Good-bye, impersonal neighbors and incompetent elevators.

Good-bye, too, she thought with a rueful smile, *to the stuck-up Marcy P. who used to live here. I won't miss you.*

She turned and walked down the silent hallway to the elevator. Trish was waiting in the lobby for her, having spent the day helping her clean the apartment. She'd taken the box of cleaning supplies out to the car while Marcy took a final look around.

The day before, a moving company had taken the rest

of her things to a storage facility. She'd be staying with Trish until she found a house for herself somewhere.

She wanted a place she could have a dog, though she'd decided not to take Folly from Truman unless he really didn't want her. Which she knew he did. He loved that dog, and because of that she would never take her from him.

The day before, when the movers were taking her furniture, she'd actually smiled when she was told the freight elevator was broken, so she'd have to use one of the regular ones and go through the lobby. She was remembering Truman and the night they'd gone out for half-smokes. She half hoped she'd see the man they'd encountered in the elevator that night. He'd gotten so upset about seeing Truman in the lobby elevator, she'd have loved to hear what he had to say about six sweaty moving men and an eight-foot sofabed.

She was also thinking about leaving Downey, Finley & Salem. She'd learned a lot there, and since the *Burton v. Planners* trial it seemed opportunity at the firm was hers for the taking. But she'd found herself thinking more and more about what Truman had said about small towns. Maybe she'd look for a house in a little town that needed a lawyer. A place where she could do some good and yet lead a simpler, saner life. A place where maybe she wouldn't worry so much about what people thought of her, and whether she drove the right car and wore the right clothes.

As she descended in the elevator, Christmas music tinkling through the round speaker in the ceiling, she thought with trepidation about what she was about to do next. Not the moving. No, that decision, while swift and spontaneous, was so right she didn't feel a moment's hesitation.

No, what she was unsure of was her plan to go to Truman's mother's house and, hopefully, speak to Truman. She wanted to tell him why she was the way she was. That she wasn't really snobby and materialistic, that she wasn't even the spoiled trust-fund kid he seemed to think she was. As clichéd as it seemed, she was just a twenty-eight-year-old woman still reacting to the deprivations of her childhood.

Not that she wanted to go into much detail. She wasn't interested in handing him a sob story about her upbringing. Apart from it being humiliating, she would feel like she was making excuses.

No, what she needed to do was go to him with her heart in her hands and hope for the best.

So that was her plan.

The elevator doors opened and she found Trish sitting on a sofa in the lobby.

"Ready?" Trish asked, looking up from the *Town & Country* magazine the building subscribed to.

"All set," she said, taking a deep breath and expelling it.

They had both parked on the street because Marcy had turned in her passkey to the garage. They walked out into the cold December air in front of her building.

Traffic was light, so the sound of an extremely loud motorcycle or a car that had lost its muffler was especially obtrusive on the otherwise calm city street. Marcy winced against the volume and looked down the street.

"Jeez, buddy, get a muffler!" Trish complained over the sound.

But Marcy was nailed to the spot. A truck, the exact

kind, color, and decibel level as Truman's old one, pulled into the loading zone in front of them. Out the passenger side window was the head of a black dog with a happily grinning face.

"Oh my," she heard Trish say beside her. "He's nice-looking, isn't he?"

"It's Truman," Marcy said through bloodless lips.

"*That's* Truman?" Trish said. "Lord, girl, you know how to pick 'em."

"Trish, what am I going to say to him? I—what if—but—"

Trish laid a hand on her arm. "Tell him just what you were planning to say to him at his mother's."

"But I thought I'd have the ride over there to plan!"

"You'll do fine," Trish said. "I'm going to go. I'll leave the door open, but I won't be worried if you don't show up." She grinned wickedly as Marcy, in a panic, watched her go.

Truman got out the driver's side door and came around the hood. He smiled quickly at Marcy but looked away to open the passenger door, clip a leash on Folly, and let her jump out of the truck.

Marcy squatted as the dog raced over to her, grabbing Folly's body as she leapt into her arms. Folly's tail whipped back and forth so fast it took her whole body with it, and her tongue lapped at Marcy's chin and cheeks.

Marcy felt a lump grow in her throat. She stood and faced Truman.

"You don't have to give her to me," she said, preemptively. "I know you want to keep her."

"But she really belongs to you," he said, his voice low and delicious against her eardrums. "We both know *I'd* have never gotten her out of that kennel Lang locked her in."

Marcy shook her head. "But she's spent more time with you. You're her home, Truman, I think you should have her."

Folly still wound around Marcy's legs, pressing her face against her thigh as Marcy looked down at her.

"Look at her," Truman said, slight smile on his face. "Looks to me like she's made her decision."

Marcy paused and looked him in the eye. "I couldn't, Truman. She'd be this happy to see anyone who'd pet her and you know it."

They stood looking at each other for a long moment. "Maybe . . ." Truman began, then stopped, his face troubled.

"Maybe what?" she asked, heart pounding hard in anticipation.

"Maybe we could both keep her?" He shoved his hands into the pockets of his bomber jacket.

"Both of us?" she repeated. "You mean like . . . like shared custody?"

One side of his mouth rose in a smile. "Well, maybe not something with so much paperwork involved."

"But . . . you'd have to see me then," Marcy said. "You know, when we swapped her off."

"And you'd have to see me," he said quietly.

She took a deep breath. "Truman, I *want* to see you."

For a second she thought he'd misunderstood her. His expression became so open, so hopeful, that she wondered if he understood what she meant. That she wanted to *see* him, date him. Love him, if he'd let her.

"I want to see you, too, Marcy."

She wasn't sure what to say, how to elaborate, tell him what she meant.

He looked behind her at the door to her former building. "Do you think we could go inside and talk about this?"

Marcy glanced back at the door behind her, then, with a small laugh, she looked at Truman and said, "We can't. I've moved out. I was just here today to clean up."

He looked concerned. "Moved out? I thought you owned it. Where did you go?"

She lifted one shoulder and let it drop. "I was just renting. I'm at Trish's, for now. My lease was up at the end of the month and I realized I didn't want to sign up for another year of . . . this." She gestured toward the building, then looked back at him. "I guess . . . I realized I wasn't living the life I wanted. I was making too many decisions based on things that shouldn't matter."

"Marcy, I—"

"No, wait." She held up a hand. Now that she'd gotten started she didn't want to stop. "I want to tell you this. In fact, I was just on my way to your mother's house to talk to you."

He looked amazed. "You were?"

She nodded. "I wanted to tell you how wrong I was, and how right you were. I know you were—"

"Marcy, wait. Stop right there. I came here to apologize to *you*. First of all, I didn't tell you the truth about myself, I let you believe I was this blue-collar guy who knew all about life on the seedy side." He chuckled once, ruefully. "But you set me straight on that. And you were absolutely right."

"I was an absolute bitch."

"No." He shook his head. "No, you were right. Second of all, I wrote you off as spoiled and money-driven and all those awful things I said that night when I didn't know you well enough to make those assumptions. I had no right to criticize you, Marcy. And regardless of whether or not I had the right, I didn't even have the facts."

She felt a smile pressing to come forth. "But I could say the exact same thing to you, Tru. In fact, I *planned* on saying the exact same thing to you."

He smiled and his eyes were so warm on her face she felt emotion well up in her breast.

"Then maybe we should start fresh," he said, taking her hand.

She gripped it tightly, letting the smile burst onto her face. "Yes. Start over, without any preconceptions. No fears, and no doubts."

"Well, I do have one preconception," he said, looking down at their locked hands. "If you'll allow me to keep it, I'd appreciate it."

She took one step toward him, took his hand in both of hers. Folly stepped between them, licking alternately at Marcy's shoes, then Truman's.

"Of course," she said. "Anything. What is it?"

"It's that I love you, Marcy. And I know I'm not wrong about that."

He stepped forward, placed his other hand against the side of her face, his thumb caressing her cheekbone. Marcy felt the rough leather of the leash in his palm against her skin and smiled.

"I love you, too," she said, the words husky with emotion. "So much more than you can know."

He pulled her close, his arms encircling her. Marcy could feel the beating of his heart against hers as he bent to kiss her, and she put her arms around his neck, holding him close, thinking she'd never let go again.

After a moment he drew back. "I have another proposition for you, Paglinowski," he said, gazing intently at her. "I'm thinking about opening up a private practice in a town called Windslip, North Carolina. It's a small, seafaring town on the coast that needs a competent lawyer or two."

She drew back a fraction, hands clutching his shoulders, and looked at him in fear. "You're going away?"

He shook his head. "Not without you. Would you consider coming with me? Don't answer me now. Just think about it."

She tilted her head, and smiled, relief making her feel giddy. "I don't need to think about it, Truman. I'd love to be your partner."

He grinned. "Do you mean that?"

She nodded.

"Then perhaps you'd consider another partnership proposition," he said, stepping away from her and bending down on one knee.

Marcy looked at him in shock, her heart in her throat.

Folly leapt on him, licking him in the face, on the ear, along the neck. He gently pushed her away.

"Marcy Paglinowski," he said, reaching into his pocket and pulling out a small, velvet box. "Will you marry me?"

Marcy put her hands to her mouth, incapable of speech. Her heart thundered and her breath caught in her chest, but she could nod. And nod she did, tears streaming from her eyes, until Truman stood up and took her in his arms again, kissing her soundly until the tears nearly dried on her cheeks.

Coming in August
Two very special Avon romances!

An Affair to Remember by Karen Hawkins
An Avon Romantic Treasure

"Karen Hawkins is destined for superstardom!"
New York Times bestselling author Julia Quinn

An arrogant earl is seeking the perfect wife. A strong-minded governess is determined to transform him into a perfect man. Who will win—the Earl of Greyley or Miss Anna Thraxton?

When Night Falls by Cait London
An Avon Contemporary Romance

"An exciting, distinctive voice."
New York Times bestselling author Jayne Ann Krentz

Uma Thornton has always kept the secrets of her small town safe, until Mitchell Warren returns . . . Soon, Uma's quiet safety is shattered by a shadowy murderer, and she feels Mitchell knows more than he lets on.

Also available in August, two classic Julia Quinn stories, beautifully repackaged . . .

To Catch an Heiress
and
Dancing at Midnight

REL 0702